Coven of Dolls

By
Jeremy Varner

Coven of Dolls
Book 3 of the Agent of Argyre series

Paperback Edition

www.jeremyvarner.com

To those who've stuck with me and those who left a positive mark even when they had to leave.

Table of Contents

Prologue

Everything went dark after a flash of light and pain. Rough, thick skin rubbed my cheek raw as a heavy fist did its best to rearrange the bones in my face. My visor shattered into a dozen little pieces and scattered through the room as I spun on my heels. Wobbling, distorted masses of color danced around me as the darkness passed. When my vision cleared, I made eye contact with "Marionette", the side of my face seized with pain.

Being punched by Commissioner Alston was like being hit with a brick.

The sympathy across Marionette's face felt disingenuous. If she felt anything at all in that moment I would have been surprised. For all I knew she'd caused all of this and I was acting as a pawn in her little game. And right behind me was a rook ready to bring his stone-faced wrath down on top of me.

He was on me again before I could have a chance to recover. Powerful arms wrapped around me and started to squeeze for all they were worth. It was the worst hug I'd had in my life and soon I was helpless to do anything about it as he lifted me effortlessly off the floor. Kicking and struggling against his hold, I managed to plant a foot against a table and pushed at it to no avail, sliding it away from us as Alston's footing didn't change in the slightest. All the while, Marionette just watched on.

I couldn't help thinking of the first time this happened.

Back then, there were a lot more blurred faces, partially hidden behind bright lights and a chain-link fence. It was almost impossible to focus on them, what with the man across from me pounding my face repeatedly with jabs I could hardly see. The speed of his punches and the weight behind them felt unreal. Dazed and confused, I regretted all of my life decisions for a solid five minutes as that man handed me my first real beating in a mixed martial arts match. There weren't a lot of life decisions to regret at 20, but there were enough to fill those five minutes since I kept losing my place whenever he made contact again.

I couldn't have been happier to hear the bell ring and end the round. My body practically moved on its own to get the hell away and shamble to the safety of my corner. Though, what was left of my coherent mind was trying to tell my feet to find the exit instead. The corner men guided me to my seat before that part of my brain could win the debate. Waiting for me, a warm voice welcomed me to that place, even if it wasn't saying anything helpful.

"Oh my god," the sweet voice strained over the noise, "You look horrible!"

I turned enough to see the small, delicate old woman trying her best to get close enough for me to hear her. She was wearing one of my team shirts and one of the jackets we made when I started to book semi-professional fights. Silver hair was pulled back into a tight ponytail, a stray lock still falling over her cloudy aquamarine eyes as she tried to hold back tears over my condition.

I smiled weakly and tried to ignore the pain as the side of my face gradually swelled. "Thanks Gram," I said sarcastically, trying to sound nonchalant, "that makes me feel *way* better."

"I'm not trying to make you feel better," she snapped, jabbing a finger through a gap in the cage. "This is why boys your age are usually in college instead of being punched in the face for a living!"

Trying not to wince as my guys did their best to piece me together, I drank some water and looked at my grandmother, unsure how to respond to her. My opponent was dominating me and it was hard to argue with her logic at the time. My trainer buzzed in my ear, becoming background noise as he tried to tell me how to get hit less in the next round. I was drifting into a world of my own.

Then, floating through the crowd and hovering a couple rows behind my grandmother, another woman caught my eye. Brilliant green eyes caught my attention even as my vision blurred. It was the woman I would eventually know as Marionette.

Even then, that familiar feeling gripped me. In fact, back then I'd say it was stronger than when I met her again years later. She had that same concerned look on her face, that false face I realized I couldn't trust now. And that feeling like I knew her, like I was supposed to know her, seemed to make everything else fade for what was apparently too long.

"Leone!" My trainer cried out in a harsh, gravelly voice, grabbing my chin and turning me to look him in the eye. "Get your shit together, kid. You don't got that long before this guy destroys you."

I took a deep breath and glanced past my trainer at my opponent, Aaron "The Boulder" O'Brien. He was untouched, pristine. His alabaster complexion and bright red hair looked almost ethereal against the sea faces around us. Feeling the ache of his assault settling into my bones, I knew how grim my situation was.

"O'Brien's an Alter," I muttered, "I can feel it."

Without missing a beat, my trainer, in his gruff, sharp voice of experience, snapped at me, "No shit, kid. Even the Irish aren't that pale."

I shook my head and tried to ignore his tone. Maybe I was the last one to catch on but the rest of them didn't have to be punched in the face by the pale slab of meat across from us. I averted my eyes and gazed out over the crowd again, watching the mysterious woman that was drifting ever closer to the ring. My trainer's voice continued on, trying to tell me how I could manage to break stone with my fists as it tried to break me. But it was moot; I had given up and was doing my best to distract myself with the mystery girl locking eyes with me.

Gesturing with a nod out to the girl, I asked, "Is it just me or is she familiar?"

My grandmother glanced over her shoulder into the crowd, shook her head and gazed back at me, gripping at the cage and giving me the most steadfast tone I'd ever heard from her. Her voice reached through the haze and grabbed my attention as she scolded me, "You don't have time to worry about her. You have more important things to worry about right now. That boy over there is going to hurt you if you don't stop him."

Pulled back into the moment by the power in her normally faint voice, I frowned and replied, "I can't win against this guy, he doesn't have any weaknesses. He shouldn't even be in my weight class!"

Calmly and with one of the most confident voices I've heard in my life, my grandmother said, "Sweetheart, everyone has a soft spot somewhere. You just have to find it and abuse it until he begs you to stop."

Memories of that gentle voice followed me through the years, reaching me as I struggled in the arms of Omero Alston as he brought the full strength of a Golem down on me. Even if he was hard as a rock, there was a soft spot somewhere. Catching sight of our reflection out of the corner of my eye, I realized how near to his face I was and threw my head back into his nose as hard as I could.

A pained groan and a powerful crack escaped the both of us as our heads came together. But for as hard as he was, I knew it did him more harm than me. So, I did it again.

Repeatedly, I threw my head back against his, making louder cracks in his nose with every swing until the massive arms released me. In a moment of adrenaline, I managed to drop to my feet and not collapse to the floor, spinning to face him and throwing a fist into his face as hard as I could manage, dedicating my whole body to the motion and putting my weight behind that one strike.

His head turned, blood splattered from his nose, and the towering man began to teeter as I stumbled into him and nearly fell over myself. To my shock, as I collided with his chest, I felt no resistance as he fell away from me, collapsing to the floor with a heavy clap. Staring down at him, watching his massive chest rise and fall, I was both relieved to see he was okay and disappointed I couldn't join him on that floor.

Turning to her again, I met with Marionette's bloodshot eyes. I walked away from Alston as steadily as I could manage, churning the situation through my head and coming to a simple understanding:

Grams was right about everything.

Chapter 1
Perfect Trance

The beginning of a case is usually in some cold, dark corner. Normally you receive the call and go to find something has gone wrong in a place where few wish to tread. Every once in a while, though, you find the darkness seeping out of those corners into the rest of the world. Every once in a while, you find yourself standing at the scene in what was once a warm and safe place before.

On a warm Friday evening, I was where I usually was before the beginning of a shift, sitting in the comforting embrace of the Ahab's coffee shop, nursing a cup of coffee so black it could drive mere mortals insane. The usual Alter jazz played in the background and the news of the day scrolled by on a tablet I only recently purchased so I could stop browsing the news off of my phone or my neighbor's tablet. It was comfortable and familiar, a place to collect my thoughts.

It was a good place to relax and try to catch up with the world in a little peace and quiet. Idly swiping through news stories, I lazily watched for any strange sightings or incidents out in the woods. Part of me was always ready to see mention of a giant homunculus lurking in the mountains or prowling the streets. But the more time passed the more I started to consider that maybe that particular homunculus just wanted to be left alone. It was strangely comforting that the only mention of hulking creatures in the Pacific Northwest had to do with the local Sasquatch commune trying to open a co-op. It gave me that all clear to just settle in, sip my coffee, and try to forget I had to get to work soon.

And then a small voice pierced the room and startled everyone out of their stupor, crying out, "Uncle Nate!"

A short figure bounded through the shop doors and darted between the tables. Elven ears perked and bright eyes sparkled as Amelia practically lunged at me, smiling ear-to-ear with a sheet of paper gripped in both hands. Presenting a test to me with a great big "A" scrawled across it, Amelia cheerfully announced, "I got an A! She has to take me with her to Argyre now, right?"

I smiled and nodded. "That's how I remember it."

Amelia beamed and shot a look back at the door, waving the paper over her head back at the slender Elf entering the room. Dulaf Nénharma, Amelia's guardian, walked through with a small eye-roll and a grin. She was dressed more conservatively than usual, almost dressing her age, if that was even possible for her anymore. Given the outfit and Amelia's frantic waving of a test, I figured the two of them had to have come straight from Amelia's school.

The kid and I had formed some camaraderie. She'd seen some shit and was still rolling with the punches. Orphaned at a young age and dealing with trauma that would probably mean therapy for years to come, it was kind of amazing how cheerful she was. And, much as it surprised me, that seemed to have a lot to do with the other Elf in the room.

"Okay, fine," Dulaf said with a hint of mischief, "I'll be taking you to the science conference with me."

The little girl's ears folded back like a cat as her nose wrinkled. "I don't want to go to the science conference," she muttered, glaring.

"Yeah, I think it has more to do with visiting Peaches and something in the submerged sectors," I mused, sipping at my coffee and returning to my news feeds. "What was it again, manatees?"

Glancing over, I saw the little girl give me the same look of death she'd been giving Dulaf. I knew exactly why the kid wanted to go to Argyre. But it was still entertaining to watch the little spitfire react as we shined her on.

"Mermaids!" She cried out, slapping a hand onto the table in front of me to try to command some respect. "I want to see the Mermaids!"

Dulaf walked over and sat across from me, shaking her head as she commented, "She insisted we come down here so you could be her witness."

Chuckling, I sat back and looked between the two of them. It'd been a while now since Dulaf had taken the little girl in, rescuing her from what we found to be the nest of a quarter-ton fruit bat now living as "Peaches" in Argyre's special holding. The longer I saw them together the more natural it started to feel. The little girl was enough like her new mentor that it was sometimes easy to forget they weren't blood relatives.

It was still surreal to see Dulaf responsible for someone else. Watching her torment Amelia with good-natured ribbing, it even seemed to echo some of Dulaf's attitude towards me. She didn't quite take it as hard on the kid, not quite reaching the level of "hazing", but it had that same energy behind it. Though, the implication she put me in the same category as an elementary schoolgirl was irritating in itself.

"You did tell her you'd think about it," I said. "You wouldn't want to go back on your word, would you? You also promised her you'd never leave her with someone else."

Dulaf shot me a dark look and said dryly, "I was planning on leaving her with *you*. Then again, I don't know if I want to expose the kid to whatever's in your fridge."

"Hey, I cleaned that fridge," I said, doing my best to ignore her attempted jab, nodding and grinning at Amelia. "Besides, if she was with me, we'd just order out a lot."

Amelia giggled and pulled a chair from another table to sit with us. Climbing up on it, she chimed in cheerfully, "But the last time I looked in the fridge it was like Xander's lab experiments."

Leaning over and lowering my head to look the runt in the eye, I murmured to her, "You know you're not supposed to cap on the guy that just backed you up."

Her cute little smile somehow managed to grow broader as she reached up and poked at my nose. "I already got what I wanted," she said whimsically. "But Xander's experiments are pretty sometimes, so it's okay!"

Faking a sigh, being melodramatic for the child's sake, I sat back and accepted defeat. It was a little surreal to be sitting around and having such a laid-back conversation before a shift. Normally I'd be too stressed or sleep deprived to be able to fake a smile, let alone tease a kid. But it was getting to that time of year where my shift rolled back just enough for me to catch up on sleep and have two cups of coffee before I'd start. The coming summer months were bringing longer days, making the ACTF's busy shifts shorter with every passing day.

While that meant that people on the day shift like Dulaf were free to go to conferences in Argyre, guys like me were left to stare into space until sunset. When at least half of your jurisdiction is confined indoors while the sun is out, you start to have a lot of time to catch up on your reading in the summer months. Really, it was kind of nice being able to sit back, relax, and enjoy the company of my Elven tormentors.

None of us expected the crack of a gunshot blasting through the neighborhood like a thunderclap.

Everyone around us moved on instinct, bolting away from the doors and the windows. Trey, my friend behind the counter, yelled to the crowd to stay calm as I bolted to my feet and everyone else dropped to the floor. Out of the corner of my eye I saw Dulaf's figure lunge over Amelia and pull her in as close as possible, taking the little girl beneath the table before I could circle to the exit.

My hand was already on the grip of the Helios pistol at my side, ready to draw in case the shooter was just outside. It didn't seem far from the shop, echoing off the nearby buildings as people scattered in a panic. But as I reached the door, the front of the shop was clear. Wherever the shot came from, it was further down the street than the echo made it seem.

I looked down at Dulaf and nodded. "Keep her down, I'm going to check it out."

She met my gaze and nodded back, holding Amelia as close as she could and shielding the child from the window behind her. Putting on my visor, I saw the flashes of colors around them as Dulaf's strength seemed to radiate into the little girl and calm her. I wasn't sure if it was training or if she'd just had a lot of experience ducking under tables over the years. But, whatever it was, I didn't have the luxury of ducking with them.

When I made my way outside it was easy to see just where the sound came from. People were practically stampeding away from the corner down the block. Normally, under daylight, the street is fairly easy to walk. There isn't a thick crowd at that time of day in Fangtown. But with all of them pushing at each other to get away from the gun, I was faced with a wall of people moving like a shockwave.

Pushing through, I found a break in the crowd and ran down the block as fast as I could. Expecting whoever pulled the trigger was going to be in a fight or flight state, I drew my gun and ensured it was in crowd control mode. But the scene I found wasn't quite what I expected. Standing in morbid curiosity, a small group gathered around the scene of a man on the ground and a woman standing over him with a gun.

The shooter was seemingly a young woman, looking no older than her 20s and dressed like she'd just come from the office in a buttoned-up blouse and a grey skirt now stained red. She was lean, short and unassuming. A simple glance would have looked like she was anyone else in the world. It was only through the auras of my visor that I could see this girl was an Alter hiding in plain sight.

Her victim, an older man in a suit, sprawled across a pool of his own blood, face down as the shot had hit him in the back of the head. Normally when I saw someone like this, I would have had to scour the city to figure out who would have taken the shot. Firing into the back of someone's head was rarely the sort of thing you did impulsively. He didn't see it coming at all; he had no reason to be facing her as she pulled the trigger.

So why wasn't she running?

There were a lot of people around us, murmuring and whispering among themselves as they assessed the situation too. Gawkers had crept closer for every second she wasn't shooting up the rest of the neighborhood, likely as confused as I was in this eerie calm that shouldn't be happening. Unfortunately, none of them seemed to know anything of value as I edged past and heard them whispering questions and comparing notes.

I wished they weren't there. It was easy for the tension to break violently with this crowd of people surrounding us. Normally, I would just aim my weapon at her and try to take control of the situation. But I couldn't risk her opening fire at me and hitting one of the others around us. Luckily, she hadn't noticed the uniform hovering behind the group.

In fact, looking at her face, I wasn't sure she was aware of anyone. Her eyes were practically glazed over as she stared down at him. Her hand was as steady as I'd ever seen after a shooting. In fact, her aura was reading like nothing I'd ever seen at a crime scene before. They taught us what sociopaths would look like through the visor - in case we ever encountered someone the system couldn't read. I just never expected it to look like a 5'2" brunette straight from accounting.

She was so entranced by what she'd done that it was easy for me to circle around behind her. I gestured to the onlookers not to make any sudden noises and slipped between the people as quietly as I could. Raising the Helios, I inched in before leveling it to her back.

"Put the gun down, kick it away and put your hands on top of your head," I commanded, startling her out of her trance.

Her aura shifted dramatically and a rush of color radiated up through her like a flame being lit. It was almost like watching her soul reignite as she recoiled at her situation. For a brief moment my finger tensed on the trigger, worried this was the start of one of those incidents where the gunman opened fire on everyone in sight. But when those colors stabilized and her shoulders relaxed again, I watched her head tilt down to the weapon in her hand and the body at her feet.

Her scream pierced the uneasy silence that had covered the block as she jumped away from the pool of blood and whipped her arm up towards the crowd. Her sudden movement scared everyone around us, scattering them like roaches as they did their best to dive into the nearest building they could find. When I was younger, I probably would have fired right then and there. But I could see what was happening as her finger released the trigger before she flung it into the air.

She wasn't trying to fire; she was throwing it away in a blind panic.

That was what washed across her body as the aura was growing stronger. She was terrified, utterly terrified and there was no mistaking it in the visor readings or in her posture. I grabbed for her and turned her to face me, holstering the gun as I realized this woman wasn't looking for a fight. Locking eyes with my visor, she stared in shock and trembled. The light splash of blood across her cheek was starting to streak as tears streamed down her face.

"How did I get here?" She asked timidly. "What happened?"

I couldn't figure out what to say to her. The scene was pretty clear to me and without the visor I would have thought she was faking it on the hopes of an insanity plea. But it was there, the readings confirmed her actions were legit and her actions were telling me that she had no clue what the hell was going on.

Finally, I gathered myself enough to reply, "We're in Fangtown, just a couple blocks from the Forum." I hesitated for a moment, studying her expression and realizing she needed to know, "I think you just shot someone."

She grew pale, her breath quickened. I watched the aura flutter on the display again, her vitals shifting rapidly. Before I could say anything or try to calm her down, her eyes rolled back and she collapsed. It was like someone flipped a switch in her brain and shut it all down. Catching her, I cushioned her head with my hand before it could bounce off the pavement.

The moments of silence following her scream were surreal. Kneeling on the pavement, I could feel the eyes of the entire neighborhood leveled on us and peering from every corner and shadow. They were watching for some sign that she'd rise again and begin to take her wrath out on the rest of us. But the fact was we weren't in that sort of situation. Unfortunately, that situation would have been easier to understand.

This was something different, something I'd never seen before. For as much time as I'd been on the force, I'd never seen someone lose their shit so completely and so randomly after committing a crime that appeared to have been premeditated. After all, who takes a gun to work?

Looking down the block, I saw Dulaf's head peek out of the Ahabs down the street and watched a smaller figure poke out behind her hip, their blade-like ears flicking together as they seemed to listen for something like a pair of curious cats watching from the brush. Tapping my badge, I opened a channel to the station and sent in the request.

"This is Leone, home in on my beacon," I said loud enough for the two of them to hear, "I just witnessed a shooting and the assailant has fainted, send an investigation team, medical crew and the coroner."

Dulaf's posture relaxed and she stepped out from the cafe's doorway, tugging along Amelia in her wake and keeping the little one behind her protectively as she nodded my way.

The response teams only took a couple minutes to arrive with us being so close to the headquarters. I had just enough time to section off the scene and place the woman in my car, handcuffing her and restraining her in the passenger seat. I didn't quite close the "coffin" around her like normal. Considering she just fainted, the reaction she may have had when she woke up probably wasn't going to be good for anyone.

The onlookers were hovering again by the time the team arrived, curiously drawn to the body lying in the middle of the crosswalk as they murmured once again, safe in the knowledge the shooter was locked away. Though my car was only just down the block, they didn't seem to have much interest in the woman herself. Even the gun, which had landed on the sidewalk and skidded up against a wall, was of little interest to any of them. The morbid curiosity was in the dead man on the pavement, who he was and how he ended up in this situation.

To be honest, I would have liked to know myself. Unfortunately, it wasn't exactly something I could have pulled from the aether and I was sure that I didn't have time to get it from his pockets.

Whoever he was, his death was far from a random act. Even if her trance was entirely genuine, she was carrying that gun and fired on that man for a reason. I couldn't read any signs of drugs on her once her trance broke, her pupils were normal and her biometrics were reading clean. Whatever had put her in that state wasn't directly chemical but it wasn't natural. There weren't a lot of explanations for something like that and none of them would have made this anything other than premeditated murder.

The investigation team hovered the scene and did what they could to catalogue it as quickly as possible. Outdoor crime scenes are horrible for trying to collect information, especially those that are in public or are exposed to the elements. But I couldn't bring myself to join them as they gathered evidence, I'd been there to see who was holding the gun and knew that the true mystery wasn't on the pavement, it was in her head. Watching the medics with the suspect, waiting for a sign she may stir again, I wondered how long I would have to wait to hear the truth from her.

"That was definitely not the surprise I promised Amelia," Dulaf said, bemused, strolling up to join me by the car. "You need to move to a better neighborhood."

I glanced her way, searching her voice for sarcasm before I replied, "I live a couple blocks from headquarters, what neighborhood could possibly be safer than that?"

"Well, I think that's the fault of the local patrolman then," she said, jabbing at me with her elbow. "Why didn't you have her locked down in the coffin?"

I looked back at the woman strapped into my passenger seat and said solemnly, "You didn't see her when I ran up, it was like she was almost completely blank."

Knife-like ears perked at what I said, Dulaf's eyes darting over to the woman in the passenger seat and quickly studying her. "She was blank?" Dulaf asked with an edge to her voice, "Like she was in a trance?"

I nodded, seeing a mixed look of surprise and concern crossing her face. "I've heard of two other cases during the day shift like this in the last month," she murmured uneasily. "They thought it was just strange coincidence, but..."

"Three times is a pattern," I interjected, frowning.

Dulaf nodded and looked back over her shoulder at Amelia sitting in another car parked by the Ahab's. Reaching out, she swatted my shoulder and said, "I have to get her home, but get to the bottom of this, okay? That was too close for my tastes."

She walked back to the car and got in, flashing a strained smile at Amelia before starting the car and driving away. I watched them go down the street towards the headquarters and disappear around the corner. Despite her jabs, since Amelia and Dulaf lived in the sanctuary under the headquarters, this was their neighborhood too.

It was easy to get used to dealing with crimes in Seattle, even Fangtown as a whole. But for the first time the crime was right on our doorstep. Well, it was the first time if you didn't count when a monster literally kicked in my door. But this, this was the first time since I moved in that someone had broken the little shred of peace we had without aiming for me.

I felt a little violated by that idea.

Walking over to the car, I watched as the EMT packed up and stepped away from her.

"Do we need to transport her to the hospital?" I asked.

He shook his head. “Her vitals are clean, no sign of injuries, we could take her for observation but the ACTF medical bay is more than equipped for her.”

I nodded, closing the door and watching her through the window. “Pulse her?”

“Yeah, one of us could do that,” he said, patting a hand over his bag. “I think she was just shocked.”

“Okay, thanks,” I said, walking around to the driver’s side, “I’ll do it at the headquarters if she doesn’t wake up by the time we get there.”

We exchanged waves and I got into the car, thinking about that proximity again. I watched the crime scene investigators for a moment before starting the car and heading back for the headquarters myself. The drive was short, but I knew it was going to take me a bit longer than Dulaf to get inside. The shooter, who I still hadn't gotten the name for, was still out cold. But I couldn't just sit there watching them work through the scene right then, I needed to get her into the station and get her awake so I could try to get to the bottom of this.

The sun was setting as I approached the station, the scarlet-colored sky reflecting off the black, mirrored surface of the oddly shaped building. The increased traffic in and out of the garage below was a changing of the guard without any of the typical ceremony behind such a thing. The day shift was moving out as the night shift moved in. The thought crossed my mind as I entered the underground structure that the day shift's case files were going to be important to figuring out what just happened. The other cases like this were probably in broad daylight too. So, which one of these cars passing me by was going to be the Agent with some answers?

I parked closer to the elevator than usual and took a moment to take the woman's purse out of storage. Opening it, I decided it would probably be a good idea to get her identity before I tried to book her or check her into the medical bay. The purse wasn't anything out of the ordinary, practically invisible in the chaos as she waved a gun. The contents inside were what you'd expect from just about anyone that age: gum, receipts, cosmetics and a card for the bus. Finding her wallet, I opened that and finally got at least one part of the puzzle.

Her name was Kathryn Blake.

Her Alter Registration ID shed some light on what I was dealing with as the holographic photo cycled through various faces she'd had over the years. She was a registered Witch, clocking in at about three times the age she appeared to be and clearly having used her abilities frequently. After a while of living across from an elderly Witch that hadn't used her powers in years, I'd forgotten how easily my landlady could have reversed her age like the woman sitting next to me.

Putting her wallet away and closing her purse, I kept the ID on hand and slipped it into a pocket as I climbed out of the car. Going around to the passenger seat, I fished through a pouch on my belt and pulled a kit from it. I reached towards the side of her head and held a small device the width of a pen by her ear, pressing a button and setting off a tone to stir her awake. It was a little odd in some lines of work to be carrying around the modern equivalent of smelling salts, but in mine it was actually somewhat required.

She startled and jerked, nearly jumping from the seat before the restraints caught her. Her eyes were wild for a moment, darting about as a look of panic crossed her face again. Taking in the scene around us, realizing where she was, she calmed considerably but still looked at me with unease.

"I'm sorry, Kate," I said, resting a hand on her shoulder, "but I'm afraid you're under arrest."

Chapter 2
Random Acts

As Kate was being processed, I went to one of the free desks to get a look at the other cases. Whatever had happened in the day shift wasn't just a random coincidence anymore. If what happened to Kate was any indication, I was almost sure someone or something was controlling her, pulling her strings like a puppet. The look in her eyes, the shock of what had happened, even the way her aura appeared were screaming of something other than her at the wheel. Maybe it was just a mental break, but I'd rarely seen someone snap back from one of those so quickly.

The other two didn't really have a whole lot in common with her, either. They weren't working or living in the same areas of the city. They weren't the same age, gender or race. Only one of them was an Alter, an Elf man who had been working as a door-to-door salesman and eventually shot the resident of a house he visited. The other, a human woman in her 40s, worked as a waitress until she opened fire on a man dining in her restaurant. None of them remembered a thing when they came to and all of them did it with guns that had the numbers filed off.

The thing that was disturbing most to me was how blatantly open these incidents were. I'd seen contract killing before and those had happened almost exclusively behind closed doors, from far off perches, or with a clear escape route. This was broad daylight, out in public, and with lots of witnesses. Even if one of these people had been faking it to try to get out of being convicted, the idea that more would think that was a good idea was ludicrous. Even the really unhinged people I've encountered understand you can't go shooting someone on the street without being arrested.

Not to mention, I don't think someone in that altered state would have been as calm as I saw Kate on that street.

The victims didn't seem to have a whole lot in common either. The first victim, the man in the restaurant, was an accountant of all things. The second was a real estate agent. I didn't have any idea who Kate's victim was at that moment, but I doubted it was something that could string together the other two neatly. Something felt familiar about the situation, old memories of my rookie years nipping at the back of my mind, but nothing that made sense of it all. I needed to talk to her and I needed to do it quickly.

Getting up, I waved my hand over the glass top of the desk and shut down the projected display. I walked out of the bullpen as quickly as I could without looking panicked in front of the dozen or so agents in the room with me. I couldn't quite explain why there was a nagging feeling about this, but it was the sort of paranoid feeling I had whenever other cases turned out bigger than I'd expected. Though, honestly, how often can you uncover a monster lurking in the shadowy depths?

"Practically every day," I muttered, scolding myself for not thinking that one through.

Walking through the underground levels and into the sanctuary, I crossed the idyllic fields towards the much more intimidating entrance to the lower depths. It was always a little surreal to walk through an actual sanctuary to reach a prison. It wasn't ideal, but limited space meant we had to make the most of everything we had. It's not like we had the luxury of a visitor's center and at the very least the prisoners didn't get transported through here. But a quick glance showed me Amelia and the other children of the sanctuary running around and playing in the flowers, their parents watching on, somehow unfazed by this notion. I didn't see Dulaf with them for once, so I had to assume she was yelling at the minions in the lab and telling them to get their asses in gear.

Crossing the heavy gates, past the heavily armed guards, I entered "Limbo". Past the sanitarium and through the processing center, it wasn't too much further to the holding cells. It was times like these I was reminded why we put the holding cells next to the mental hospital. People like Kate weren't always crystal clear on which direction they needed to go. However, with luck, I'd find Kate lucid and ready to talk to me. Not that it would matter since my gut told me that she wasn't going to know a lot herself.

The holding cells were strangely bare that day, though that wasn't completely surprising. It'd been quiet with the longer summer days. Though the nights were still fairly busy, it was enough to stifle a great deal of Alter activity on the surface. Quite a few things still happened down in the depths and in the dark corners. But rarely did you get called to address anything that happened in those places until days after the fact. No, these were the arrests made with the people who actually reared their head into the more public spaces and decided to do something stupid.

As a result, for the moment, lithe framed Kate was probably the one in here for the most violent offense. That wasn't exactly something you'd expect. It was almost a novelty. That novelty even drew some onlookers as I found Lancer Nguyen and Devotee Ramirez standing outside the processing center, watching Kate being escorted to holding. Their expressions were a blend of morbid curiosity and confusion at the idea this unassuming figure could shoot someone in broad daylight. You couldn't blame them after looking at her - she was a mess, makeup streaking down her face under bloodshot eyes. Her body shook, shoulders slumped, as she tried to keep herself steady.

"Doesn't look like the type," Ramirez muttered, glancing my way.

I shook my head, leaning against the wall by the window and peering through the glass. "She was in a complete trance," I said quietly, "like she was under hypnosis."

Nguyen nodded and solemnly commented, "We brought in one of the earlier cases like this. I had a feeling it wasn't going to go away."

I perked up at the mention. The agents I'd hoped to speak to were standing right in front of me. Nguyen and Ramirez were among the few Agents to transfer over from traditional law enforcement. Normally I should have noticed their involvement - they were among the few friends I could say I had. But, somehow, I hadn't even realized they'd changed shifts while I wasn't looking.

"When'd you go day shift?" I asked, surprised and a little ashamed I hadn't caught their names on the report.

Nguyen subtly smirked and gestured at Ramirez with a slight sideways bob of her head. "The rookie couldn't handle the graveyard," she said, gently ribbing.

I understood the feeling all too well, though I also understood Nguyen teasing Ramirez. Early on he was doing pretty well, having experience in a fairly high stress job, but I could see in his eyes that it was starting to wear. As a former member of the red-and-blues, Ramirez's prior experience was a bit of a mixed bag. He got to use any of his previous training and applicable classes as credits for the academy, speeding up his time there. On top of that, he got to skip the cleric stage where you share a sweaty van with a half dozen people for a year. But he also got extra scrutiny, a doubled length stint as a devotee, and tossed into whatever shift his lancer happens to choose. Technically she was showing him mercy.

I chuckled knowingly and nodded. "Too much weird shit?"

Ramirez rolled his eyes and shook his head. "It's just harder to adjust to things in the middle of the night, that's all."

We fell silent at the sound of doors closing on the other side of the glass. Kate's processing was done and she was taking the long walk to the holding cells where she could be staying a long time. I could imagine what was going through her head at a time like this.

"Taking point on this one?" Nguyen asked.

"Yeah," I said, hesitantly, "I brought her in."

Donning the visor, I went through the side door to follow them to the holding zone, catching sight of the guards and waving for the interrogation room. It was a quick flick of the wrist, nothing too dramatic. The general vibe around Kate was that she could crack again soon. I didn't want to put any new stress on her until we were nice and secure in the room. She was a Witch, despite her appearances, and that wasn't something you wanted to provoke.

The curates made a minor detour and took her to the interrogation room not far from where she would have been left in the first place. In a place where one of your prisoners could easily hurl you down a hallway, it was best to keep transit times down to a minimum, after all.

They sat her down and secured her to the floor restraints usually reserved for the dangerous or powerful Alters. Glancing through the window in the door, I couldn't help feeling like this broken person wasn't either one of those. She was, for all intents and purposes, looking more like another victim than the actual offender. I couldn't trust that feeling, though. I'd been played before. I just hoped, if she was legit, that she'd be able to keep her wits about her long enough to put me on the trail of an actual answer.

Entering silently as the guards left, I considered how to approach someone in this situation. I needed to treat her like a potential suspect, despite everything. It was a hard balancing act to achieve when she literally had her emotions on her face. Worse was, as a Witch, those emotions could be used to attack me. A bit of a pickle, I had to admit.

"Hello Kate," I said calmly, trying not to sound harsh but still not wavering. "I'm Agent Nathaniel Leone of the ACTF, the one that brought you in."

She nodded, shaking lightly and fidgeting in her seat, trying to get into a position where the chains to the floor didn't rattle or make themselves known to her. Quietly, she stammered, "I, I don't know what's happening, but I didn't want to hurt anyone."

Sitting across from her, I took out my link and pulled at the frame, expanding the unit to show her a larger screen projected across a thin sheet between the halves. Displaying a picture of the victim, his profile running down the right side, I glanced back up to her and asked solemnly, "This was Kenneth Moore, did you know him?"

She stared at the screen for an uncomfortable amount of time, paling as she took in the grisly details of the shot I'd taken of his corpse. I could sense her locking up on me again and could see her anxiety rising on the visor's readings. Swiping my finger across the screen, I removed the image taken from the pavement and expanded his profile, showing the friendlier face the Oracle snatched off the network.

Settling in her seat once again, trying to compose herself, Kate replied, "He was my boss." Frantically, her voice rose as the concept started to overwhelm her again, "I swear I don't know what happened and I didn't kill him! I didn't have any reason to!"

"You were holding the gun," I said firmly. "Your clothes were spattered in his blood and the gun you had is being analyzed right now to confirm it's a match. I have no doubt you pulled the trigger. I'm just trying to figure out why."

"I didn't!" She yelled, pulling at the restraints again as she tried to move from her seat, momentarily forgetting they were there like so many prisoners before her. "He was a wonderful boss and we were great friends! We had lunch together all the time, every Friday like clockwork! It's even scheduled for tomorrow on my phone!"

Listening to her, a new wrinkle appeared in that innocent little admission. Unless she was a very good actress, I was sitting across from a woman who had completely lost a day. I saw no deception in her aura, heard nothing in her voice and knew that the other cases gave some credibility to the idea she wasn't in complete control. It was just a matter of confirming it now.

"So what happened then?" I asked. "Did you go today?"

"No, I'm telling you, we go on Fridays," she protested, shaking her head with an exasperated expression.

Despite her reaction, I wasn't crazy or ignoring her. I couldn't have been paying attention to her any closer at that moment. I studied her face, her aura, the tone of her voice for anything that might have suggested for a moment she didn't believe what she just said. Most people aren't good enough to make such an obvious lie so convincingly. It was Friday evening and she was claiming that was supposed to be "tomorrow". What day and time did she think it was?

"Okay then," I replied in a casual tone, "could you tell me how you ended up there with the gun then? Do you remember why you two were standing there?"

She stared where my eyes would be beyond the visor, a distressed, confused expression passing momentarily as she seemed to be grasping for an answer. Stammering, she said, "I, I wasn't there, I'd just left the club and then I was standing out there. It..."

She sank in her seat, shoulders slumping and lip quivering for a moment, eyes beginning to tear up again as she continued, "Oh god, it was dark, why was it light out? That doesn't make any sense!"

Matter-of-factly, I interjected, "It's 6:30 Friday evening."

Her eyes darted up again and everything tensed like a flinch. Frantically she raised her voice, nearly shouting at me, "That can't be! It was Thursday night and I was just leaving the club with my date!"

"And who was your date, Kate?" I asked, pulling a stylus from my belt to jot down the note on my hand-link. "Where was it?"

She watched the stylus in my hand, almost reassured that I was getting ready to take notes. Maybe for a brief moment in that small motion I'd given her the hope that I was going to be looking somewhere else – at *someone* else.

Quietly, haltingly, she answered, "His name was Mark Robinson, we met at the Moirae Club in Fangtown a little after sunset and left about eleven. I had work in the morning."

I jotted down the name and ran a check on it, looking for any active Alters in the city with the name. Glancing back up, I asked, "Any idea if Mark was an Alter too?"

She shook her head, beginning to chew on the inside of her lip and ducking for a moment to get low enough to wipe away a tear. I felt a pang of sympathy for her at first, seeing someone in my age range sitting in front of me. But I needed to remember her age was deceptive and, despite all of my gut instincts, it wouldn't have been the first time I'd been fooled by a really skilled liar.

Focusing back on the screen, a set of photos appeared, active Alters from the registry side-by-side with the mug-shots of a few humans who happened to have the same name. Turning it towards her again and sliding it halfway across the table, I tapped the stylus against the screen. "Is one of these the Mark you were with?"

Bloodshot, watering eyes drifted across the collection of photos. Nodding and gesturing with her finger, unable to actually reach over and point, she said hesitantly, "The third from the left on the second row – that was him."

I tapped the profile and opened it up, closing the hand-link back into the more portable mode and picking it up again. “Mark Robinson” was a human with a record for conning women out of money, which wasn't exactly the best thing to find out about a date. I doubted that the charges had anything to do with the events right now, one of the three shooters was male, after all, and it didn’t seem that Mark would have swayed him in the same fashion.

But it was worth looking into. Nodding to the curates, I stood and pocketed the hand-link. Waving to them, I gestured for the curates to take Kate away again.

"Since we caught you in the act of doing this, you might be here for a while," I said to her, "but I'm going to ask them not to put you into general holding."

"What does that mean?" She asked, eyes locked on me as they released the chains and helped her to her feet.

I stepped away from the door and let them pass by, nodding to her and saying in a reassuring tone, "It means I'm making sure they keep you in a private cell until I know for sure what's going on here or your attorney can get you out."

She watched me as they turned the corner, making a quick, unsure nod as she tried her best to look strong despite a quivering lip. As they turned the corner to the holding cells, I walked into the hallway and pulled the link from the pouch again, studying Mark's profile.

Whoever this guy was, even if he didn't have anything to do with the event, I knew he was going to be able to at least tell me what happened for part of that missing day. Hell, if I was lucky, there was even a chance the guy saw something. Fortunately, having a record meant he was likely to come out with just about anything useful as quickly as possible.

Anything to keep me from cracking him like a coconut.

Chapter 3
Effectively Gone

Mark lived in a rather upscale apartment building downtown near some of the usual tourist traps. The sun had set by the time I arrived and the whole place was under the neon glow of the Space Needle cutting across the horizon. Vague childhood memories told me that it used to have only simple neon lights before being covered in Fangtown's favorite paint. It was a given that the most famous landmark would be covered by those murals once the paint was available. Besides the fact it was cheaper to run since they required no electricity, they also provided some novelty in the dead of the night while disappearing in the daylight for the average tourist. Regardless, Mark's home was awash in that faux electric glow as I strolled through the doors.

His apartment was a few stories up, not quite near the top but high enough that it still cost a small fortune. It was hard to ignore the fact that a guy with a record of con jobs managed to afford the place. The building's interior had a particular smell, like refinement and money made manifest in the air. The hallway floors were tiled and the edges of several doorways were gilded like an upscale hotel. There was even a doorman who watched me cautiously as I entered. As much as I hated to admit it, I kind of wanted Mark to be responsible so I could throw his ass into a plain, uncomfortable box instead.

Knocking at his door, I prepared my serious lawman face to try putting the fear of God, or at least the fear of me, into his soul. I heard a shuffle behind the door, the sound of fumbling and furniture being bumped into as a muffled voice called out. He opened the door, hardly awake, eyes bloodshot with dark circles under them. His robe, the only thing he had on, was wide open and left little to the imagination. Swaying slightly, he squinted and strained against the light of the hallway from the darkness of his apartment.

This wasn't how I figured I'd find him right after sunset.

Shifting position, I slipped a foot just inside the doorframe and asked, “Mark Robinson?”

He stood straighter as his eyes caught sight of the badge, clutching at the belt around his robe and tying it closed as quickly as he could. Rasping and wheezing, he tried to speak unsuccessfully before clearing his throat and straining for a moment as he swallowed. Finally mustering the strength, he replied, "Yeah, what the hell do you want?"

I knew they were called confidence men, but that was more confidence than I was expecting.

A little old-school posturing was expected in some environments. Rarely do you see it when you're armed and the other guy is wearing a bath robe and looks like he's hung-over. Then again, the hangover was probably driving some of the attitude. I knew the feeling of being so zombified that you didn't care about the risk of someone trying to beat you down.

Putting some bass into my voice, I replied, "I'm Agent Leone and I'm here about a murder investigation."

What little color was left quickly drained from his face. Eyes darting about, I could see he was desperately trying to piece together what he'd done the night before. Though, by the looks of him, it might have been the morning.

"I didn't do anything!" He cried out, gripping at the door like he was getting ready for me to drag him out of the apartment.

"Actually," I corrected, "I'm here about Kathryn Blake. But that's good to know."

"I definitely didn't do anything to Kathryn," he snapped back, a strange emphasis in his voice.

"What exactly is that supposed to mean, Mark?" I asked suspiciously, stepping closer.

He backed away and got the look on his face like he just realized I knew his record. Stammering, he protested, "Look, you can't just storm in here asking me questions, I haven't seen her since last night when she went nuts on me and stormed off."

"Went nuts?" I echoed.

"Yeah, we were leaving the Moirae when she started giving me the cold shoulder like I wasn't even worth her time," he said, irritated. "By the time we were out the door she just started walking the other direction, ignored me the whole damn time. I paid for the dinner and everything and she just treats me like shit!"

Watching him as he squirmed and continued to back away, I followed him in and pressed, "So you're saying you have no idea why she was acting that way?"

"Hell no," he snapped, "I spent the whole night trying to charm her and then she just brushes me off like I was nothing. I almost want to press charges for the wasted money!"

The man was as charming as a rat, no doubt, but he was telling the truth as far as the visor was concerned. Small bursts of red flickered through a cool blue aura, like a flame reflected off water. I briefly wondered if an average human could learn to fake out the Oracle. Still, for whatever reservations I had, the system thought he was being sincere. Despite that, his face and an apartment in shambles told me his night didn't end there.

"Who else was here with you, then?"

Blearily, he looked around the room. With little more than an ambient glow coming through the windows and the lights outside his door, what was visible to him seemed to be as odd to him as it was to me. Furniture was knocked over, cushions and pillows lying around the floor, a wine bottle no more than a couple feet from him. He staggered over to a lamp and fumbled around for the switch, turning it on and looking back across the wreckage that was his apartment.

Slowly scanning the apartment, he distantly replied, "I don't know."

"How much did you have to drink last night?" I asked, walking over to the bottle and fetching it from the floor. It was empty, and a cursory glance to the nearby recycling bin showed it had a lot more friends over there.

Looking at the bottle in my hands, he muttered, "I couldn't drink all of that."

A sinking feeling set in. Walking over to the bin, I dropped the new bottle in with the others and kicked it lightly so he'd hear the sound. "How many people did you have over here?"

"Honestly," he started, his voice becoming meek, "I don't remember anything after Kate left me last night."

"You mean to tell me you remember her walking off," I asked skeptically, "but then you completely blacked out *after* leaving the Moirae?"

He shook his head and sat in the nearest chair that was still upright. Resting it in his hands, he rubbed his face and ran his hands up across his forehead, stroking his fingers back through greasy hair. I searched the room for clues to who or what he was with at the time this all happened, finding stray clothes from several people of varying sizes and gender. A pair of pink underwear lying next to pants that were far too large for Mark made me think he had more than a few people help him through those bottles.

"What did you do at the Moirae?" I asked. "Did you meet with anyone that was out of the ordinary?"

"It was the Moirae," he groaned, "everyone there is 'out of the ordinary'."

He had a point; I did get back to the place fairly often. The busiest place in the strangest corner of the city was bound to have a few rough spots form. Still, I'd yet to see one of their patrons black out so thoroughly. At least, I'd yet to see one black out and still reach home.

"You need to get serious about this," I said, frowning. "Kate was involved in a shooting incident this afternoon, she claims to have blacked out too. And I'm standing in a room with a man who has a record suggesting he wouldn't be entirely beyond slipping her something."

He sat upright and yelled, "Hold on! Nothing out there would have made someone black out ***and*** go get into some shit."

"So you know the drugs, huh?" I shot back, cutting across the room and crowding him. "Did you give her anything?"

He leaned back in the seat and stared up at me, eyes wide and face pale like he was watching a ghost. "Look, I've done some shady things," he said timidly, "but I've never drugged anyone and I don't remember anything from last night either. I'm telling you I didn't do anything."

I studied him for a moment before easing back from him, crossing my arms. "What do you know about Kathryn, then?"

Composing himself, he adjusted his position in his seat and made sure his robe was secured, clearing his throat again before replying in a slightly firmer tone, "She was a Witch, literally – a lot older than she looked."

"She bring that up over dinner?" I asked, once again scouring the room.

Shaking his head, he replied with a smirk, "No, I have a bit of a thing for Alter girls and I'm especially into the ones who still look mostly human. You get all the danger without horns, hooves, or fangs."

The visor could barely contain my rolling eyes. "Did you run into anyone else while you were there? Did someone stop to talk to either of you?"

"No one except the waitress," he said, sitting back a bit more casually with a growing smugness. "Really I would have probably hit on her instead, Kate wasn't exactly what I expected out of a Witch."

"And what exactly were you expecting?" I asked, pulling my hand-link and snapping photos of the room around us, cataloguing the aftermath in case it was important again.

"Well, she didn't exactly have that intuition you'd expect," he replied. "I've dated a lot of Succubi and they really know what you're into. I've heard Witches can do the same but either she couldn't or wouldn't."

"Witches aren't always on," I explained, edging around the room to get every possible angle on the mess. "She probably didn't think she'd have to perform tricks for her date like a sideshow."

"Hey, all I did was ask her to show me something during small talk and she said she couldn't," he protested. "She used that lame excuse all the old hacks used about 'not being focused'."

"Could you tell why she wasn't feeling focused?" I asked, pocketing the link and drifting back his way

Getting up, probably trying to get some distance from me again, he went into the kitchen space and right to the mini-bar he had across the back wall. There wasn't a lot left there, clearly the bin was full of most of his collection, but that didn't stop him from grabbing a bottle of brandy and filling a glass. Looking at me, he shrugged and replied before taking a long drink, "I just figured it was the same old bullshit the cold readers said back in the day."

Eyeing the glass, I couldn't imagine that was going to help him any in the condition he was in. Withholding my contempt, I just continued on, "Well I can confirm she's a Witch, so was there anything that could have been distracting her?"

He nursed the drink for a moment and hovered behind a counter. Watching him stagger about, nothing about the guy really felt "dangerous". If anything, I couldn't help feeling like he was almost as pathetic as his record made me believe. But there was still an itch in the back of my head that something was off. Maybe it was that feeling like you never let someone get behind a counter with drawers like that. Watching his hands, I realized his grip on the glass was really the only thing steady about him.

Finally, he lowered the glass and placed it on the counter, nodding with some confidence as he said, "They had a new singer there, background for the live band that they had playing up in the third floor. She was pretty hot but every time I focused on her voice it felt like I was getting drunk off of it."

A Siren? It wasn't out of the question – a lot of them did make a living doing live performances at local venues. There were probably a dozen of them working the city that I could name off the top of my head. Still, even a Siren would have struggled to accomplish what he was describing.

"That would have to have been some song," I said, "especially to make you guys black out immediately after."

That damn smirk crossed his face again, the smug tone rising in his voice as he reminisced over the show. "She was definitely good, had that primal thing about her where she just lured you in when you looked at her. I mean, if I wasn't sitting with the girl I was with, I would have tried to get her number as soon as she was done."

That should have been confirmation of my theory, but it didn't exactly seem that far outside of Mark's normal behavior. Shaking my head, I stepped up to the counter and rapped a knuckle against it to draw his attention again, "Focus!"

His posture stiffened and he watched me carefully as I continued in a calmer voice, "Was that woman still singing when you left last night?"

He contemplated for a moment, then nodded along and answered, "Yeah, pretty sure she was still working while we were leaving. She was on her third set by the time we left that night. Probably a good thing we left. I can't remember the last time I spent so much there at once..."

He trailed off, taking another long drink from his brandy and staring out the window on the far side. Watching him, I couldn't help feeling annoyed at how casual he was about the situation. Maybe he really was just so blitzed earlier that he couldn't remember a thing. But even then, his attitude was irritating.

Begrudgingly, all I could do was say, "Thank you for your assistance, Mr. Robinson. If I need anything else I'll be in touch with you."

Snottily, he snapped back as I neared the door, "Yeah, well next time you should wait until I'm out of bed!"

Suppressing my cringe to the best of my ability, I turned to face him again at the open door and replied, "the sun just set, jackass," before slamming it behind me.

I'm man enough to admit, it wasn't exactly the professional way to leave.

On the way out, I browsed the photos I'd taken and tried to find any sign he might have been making it up. Maybe there was something that showed Kate was there, or that he'd been completely coherent of the night before despite his insistence. But all I could find were signs the guy had a lot of uninhibited friends that weren't against wildly partying through the night. At best, all it would provide were witnesses to Mark's behavior and that felt like a pointless venture.

Both of them shared a detail though, their last memories were at the Moirae. I knew Anubis' business practices and I knew he wouldn't hire anyone that didn't pass every background check imaginable. He didn't leave something like that to chance. However, it was completely legal to use a Siren to lower inhibitions and that sounded exactly like the sort of thing they'd do at the busiest nightclub in Fangtown.

Against the warnings of ancient lore, I set off towards the Siren's song.

Chapter 4
Lyrical Hypnosis

The club was swarming. As the center of the nightlife in Fangtown, the Moirae was always busy on a Friday, but not quite like this. There were three clean-shaven Werewolves acting as bouncers at the door, more than the usual, and a line half-way down the block. The place was clearly near capacity and no one in that line was willing to accept the notion of fire codes. One particularly brave jackass, face-to-face with a man contemplating how chewy he might be, was getting pretty close for someone who had to look up to make eye contact. And, from the thousand-yard stare on the bouncer's face, he wasn't the first for the night.

The parking lot wasn't any better as cars filled every space and then flooded out to the rest of the block. It was one of those scenes that almost made me support "personal transports": those tiny one seat vehicles that could stack like shopping carts. Club guests, dressed to the nines to get past the small wolfpack at the door, were walking from all the way around the corner to get into line. Luckily for me, I managed to find a spot down the block. Yet, despite that distance, I could still hear the music when I exited the car.

There was definitely a unique quality to the music this time. Though the layered nature of Alter music was a staple, there was something different. The usual club beats pulsing from the basement floor were still there, radiating to the surface and echoing down the florescent street. But the normally muted sound of the top floor, typically soundproofed with active noise cancelling and cut off from the thumping below, was strangely joining the mix.

It was an ethereal sound, an unusual feeling, that floated through the neighborhood at a barely audible level. Like a whisper on the wind, it was surrounding me, enveloping me with a feeling like I needed to go to the source. Warm and comforting, the sound became stronger the closer I came to the entrance.

Anubis had hired one hell of a Siren.

Bypassing the crowd was harder than usual. More than a few unhappy customers glared as I walked by them before they saw the silver badge against the black coat. But not everyone noticed y passing. The humans seemed particularly enthralled by the new sound coming from the top floor, watching the building more than the rest of the line as it slowly marched forward. The most disturbing thing about it was that they didn't seem at all aware of why they were so drawn to it, like they could feel the music rather than hear it. Realizing I wasn't doing much better, I put in my Banshee filter earplugs and hoped the frequencies were similar enough to work.

Luckily for me, they were. The slightly drunk feeling faded, the warmth leaving my body as I saw the entranced crowd in a new light. It was an interesting marketing tactic, practically an outright coercion of the masses. But it was also perfectly legal within certain regulations.

I got past the bouncers with my usual ease. They never put up much resistance to the guys in uniform and I'd been around enough to have gained some rapport with the wolfpack within. The ground-floor bar, sandwiched between the thumping beats of the techno basement and the singing of the Siren above, was busy even for a Friday. This was normally the day when people bled into the two other parts of the Moirae where they could get in touch with something a bit more primal or sophisticated. But on this night, in these new conditions, all three floors had gained new life.

Anubis himself towered over the rest, smiling to his guests as they filled every seat in the relatively normal bar. He weaved through the sea of people, passing with ease despite his size. With a quick glance he shot a look my way, acknowledging I was there, before returning to the broad smiles he had for his customers.

He pushed through the crowd as gently as he could and made his way to me at the door, the smile fading from his face once none of the customers could see his expression. With his deep, powerful voice, he strained to whisper low enough not to be heard even in the raucous environment as he asked, "What'd we do now?"

I looked around the room and made a quick gesture towards his office in the back. "I need to talk to you about some customers," I said, "There was an incident and I need to know what they were doing before they left."

Staring me down, he loomed over me for a moment before shrugging and turning to the office, waving for me to follow. I couldn't hear the music anymore, the earplugs thankfully filtered the frequencies that could hit me while letting me hear something like Anubis' baritone, but I could feel it moving through me as I followed him. Making an effort to follow exactly in his steps, it almost felt like following a man through a minefield of the drunk and disorderly. The crowd was a little rowdier too, people from dance club below now floating up to a higher floor, mixing in a strange way with the more reserved, slightly older regulars of the ground floor bar.

"That Siren does wonders, doesn't she?" I asked with a chuckle.

Anubis peered over his shoulder and nodded with a knowing grin. "Best hire I've made in years," he said, "tripled revenue for the center floor almost overnight."

Glancing up, I gave him a quick nod and a point to the ceiling while asking, "And what about business up there?"

It was incredibly rare to see Anubis genuinely smile in our meetings. It was a broad, toothy grin stretching almost ear to ear. It felt less like the Werewolf I knew him to be and more like the Cheshire Cat as his smile dominated the scene under the moody lighting of the first-floor bar. Hell, it was so infectious I had to remind myself I was there on business.

Nearly laughing, hardly restraining his joy, he responded with only one word: "Obscene."

Surreal as it was to see Anubis so happy, it actually felt pretty good to hear that the business was doing well. Though we'd butted heads in the past, Anubis has always been one of the more trusted faces in the Alter community and a pillar of Fangtown. Though he'd never been exactly struggling for money, a small part of me felt like we could all share in his victory. It was a different feeling than it was back in the days when I came to his doorstep armed and ready for a fight.

He opened the door to his office and slipped inside, holding it for me as I followed through. With a raised finger he gestured at my ear and laughed. "You put in the earplugs?"

"Of course," I said, "I don't make enough for your front-woman to brainwash me."

The interior of his office was surprisingly quiet even with the door open and cozier than the last time I came through. Anubis' personal table was now pushed to a corner with a floral arrangement acting as a centerpiece. A luxurious couch sat to the side next to a private liquor cabinet. Plush chairs sat in the center of the room, facing a wood desk with the tell-tale signs of hand crafting in the grooves and the facade along the surfaces. Behind that desk sat Marionette, working on a computer built into the desktop, momentarily in a world of her own.

She looked up at us with her brilliant green eyes and sat a little straighter as though she were taken off guard by us being there. The visor caught a flicker of her aura as we came inside, showing briefly before it died down to a dark blue like her whole body was on a dimmer switch.

"It's not brainwashing," she protested, picking up a tablet and getting ready to clear Anubis' seat. "It's subtle suggestion to drink more in a bar. People have done that sort of thing for centuries."

Rising from the chair, she stepped around the desk with her tablet tucked under her arm, swiping a stray hand across the desktop to shut down the programs she'd been running in tandem. With a second motion she rested her hand atop the desk's screen and pressed down, folding the screen closed, concealing it perfectly with the hard wood surface. It wasn't a major gesture, hardly worth noting, but I couldn't get past the idea that she was hiding the screen, her work and her aura all at the same time. That was the kind of thing that bugged me about her, even when it wasn't anything more sinister than doing her job.

"Hello Agent Leone," she said coldly, averting eye contact while she migrated to the couch.

Pushing the suspicion aside, I waved and replied half-heartedly. "Hey."

Taking his seat now that she'd cleared the way, Anubis added, "She's right though, the Sirens are legit. I checked the regulations three times and we're good on all of them. So long as we make sure people can opt out with earplugs like yours, keep the messaging tight, and cut people off when they've had too much, we're gold."

Sitting back and making himself comfortable, the toothy grin reappeared as he said, "It's all perfectly legal so long as no one gets hurt."

I grimaced at the words. It wasn't a dramatic expression, I did my best to suppress it, but it was enough for him to see. A borderline scowl crossed his face before it too melted away and his head dropped ever so slightly in defeat.

"Shit."

Realizing I couldn't soften the blow of this, I crossed my arms and nodded, replying solemnly, "Had an incident today with a woman claiming she'd blacked out right up until the moment she shot her boss in broad daylight."

Marionette, now sitting on the edge of the couch behind me, interjected with an actual surprised tone, "And she said she was here last?"

Looking over my shoulder, my visor caught extra colors in Marionette's aura again. They weren't profound, just slight shifts into more violet tones that suggested something agitated her about the statement. In anyone else, it wouldn't have meant much, but I'd never known Marionette's aura to crack.

Warily, I answered, "Yeah, and her date confirmed it and mentioned you guys had a Siren."

Anubis spoke up again and drew my attention away from his subtly flustered assistant. "Wasn't this one," he said. "We hired an agency, Cascadia Sirens, they send us their best on the weekends and whoever's available the rest of the week."

"So, you didn't vet the singer yourselves?" I asked.

Quickly, he sat forward, tapping a finger on his desk with authority, and added, "We vetted the ***company***. They were clean when we looked, no incidents on record."

"Alright," I said, trying not to focus on the idea those records could have been faked, "do you have a name for the girl at least?"

"Angelique," he said, hesitating for a moment before continuing, his brow furrowed, "she seemed okay."

Watching him, I could see the tension in the way he sat while he said those words. I assumed it wasn't sitting right with him to have one of his employees, even a temp, tied up in something sinister. Intimidating as a Werewolf could be, they all tend to worry about their people.

Knowing this, I tried to console him. "It's better we catch her now than let her get in tight with the group and cause real harm."

He took a deep, cleansing breath and sat back again, looking to be deep in thought for a moment before he said, "Yeah, you're right. Anything we can do to help that along? The sooner she's caught or cleared, the better."

I checked between him and Marionette, taking in their auras again. His emotions were all close to the surface, reds and oranges like a fire dancing across him. Hers, yet again, were back to those cold and distant hues I'd come to be accustomed to. Neither of them were getting highlighted for deception – hard as it was to tell with her. I nodded back to Anubis and answered, "It'd be nice to see if she slipped any messages into her songs last night. I don't know if it would pick up on a microphone but it's still worth a look."

Glancing past me to Marionette, he ordered, "Have security pull up the recordings of Angelique's set and get them to the ACTF."

Marionette nodded along and stood, acknowledging the both of us silently before turning and leaving the office. Watching her, I looked for signs of that crack in her façade, briefly seeing violet hues dancing up her back through a near indigo space. It was a faint ripple across a still pond, a hint of something deep beneath the surface. On anyone else it would have meant nothing, but on Marionette it was practically screaming.

I should have stopped her right then and there. For reasons I couldn't understand at the time, I didn't even consider it until I was half way to the agency.

Chapter 5
Astonishing Gifts

I'm not sure what I expected when I entered the Cascadia Sirens office. The very idea of a Siren staffing agency felt like a trap in the making. Sure, the stories of running ships aground were all from a group of well documented pirates, but no one really ever looked into what the rest of them were doing. Really, most of them were flying under the radar until a couple of Nix – their male counterparts – got big in the 20th and unleashed swarms of obsessed fans. You should've seen my grandmother's reaction when she found out Elvis was alive and well in Argyre.

So, I guess I was a little more surprised than I should have been that it seemed like your run-of-the-mill talent agency when I first stepped in. The chairs in the lobby were posh, semi-comfortable pieces that seemed to be chosen more for their appearance than their actual comfort. The colors were all somewhat subdued like they were meant to avoid drawing too much attention away from the people walking through. The lights in the ceiling were strategically placed to avoid casting any hard shadows. But the thing that drew my attention almost immediately were the seemingly decorative pieces that my visor told me were gently vibrating. Pulling one of my earplugs out for a moment, I could feel the subtle push for me to relax in the room – a feeling that faded quickly once I put it back.

Sitting behind a desk, eyes practically shining under feathered locks of auburn hair, the receptionist was clearly a Siren herself. Though hard to tell generally, the way her hair feathered and her aura radiated faint silver tones in sync with the speaker vibrations was a dead giveaway. She smiled and greeted me with a voice practically tailored for customer service. In fact, that's probably exactly what it was.

"Why hello," she said warmly, "what can we do for our boys in black today?"

Even with the Oracle's help, reading the colors of the visor can be a bit of an artform. Though many colors on the spectrum have a meaning, the fact is they tend to blend. Primary colors are an easy read, secondary colors a little less so, and often times a person would have more than one depending on where you were looking. On top of that, every person can have a different baseline. You need experience and care to read them out. But the woman in front of me, surrounded in silver and a mix of pastels as gentle, friendly and inviting as they could possibly be, was reading like an open book.

She was trying to play me.

Staying as unmoved as I possibly could, I replied sternly, "I'm here looking for a specific Siren, an Angelique that performed at the Moirae last night. She's needed for questioning."

Caught off guard by the tone, her pastels darkened momentarily before she grinned mischievously. "Felt like you needed earplugs? I guess Angelique is in some trouble."

"Just need to ask her a couple questions," I remarked with a casual tone, trying my best to avoid showing my cards. "There was an incident and she might be a witness."

Browsing her computer, the receptionist's aura continued to move between unnaturally light shades in a very controlled manner. Despite looking unfazed by my presence, she was maintaining a disciplined focus while searching for Angelique. This calm tension radiated from her for at least a minute before it broke and her colors returned to a much less taxing scale. It was like watching the weight literally lifted from her shoulders.

"She's not in tonight," she remarked, finally looking up from her screen.

"Where can I find her, then?" I asked. "Another job?"

Shaking her head, she turned and started to rummage through a drawer in her desk. "We staff for everything from musical theater to call centers," she explained. "But sometime the girls will have independent projects of their own that they feel will help their profiles."

Pulling a binder from her desk, she began to thumb through professional headshots of their employees. Though most of them were conventionally attractive, it didn't really make much sense to me why they would require it. After all, if they were skilled at what Sirens or Nix do, it wouldn't matter what they looked like. Regardless, I was fortunate their industry kept working the same as the rest of ours as she plucked a picture of Angelique from the binder and quickly wrote an address on the back.

"Angelique is currently doing some community theater," the receptionist said brightly, "an independent musical production *completely* unaffiliated with *any* staffing decisions made by Cascadia Sirens."

It all clicked at that moment, her attempts to manipulate me, the tension while looking up the profile – it all made sense in that last sentence. Amused, I took the picture and replied, "And, of course, I'll do my best to avoid making a scene so long as she doesn't give me any problems."

She nodded with the shittiest grin on her face, that old worry I would be ruining their reputation washed away by plausible deniability. I returned the nod and walked out with the photo, scanning a copy of it into our system with my hand-link on the way to the car. Fortunately, despite the deception inside and a well-produced headshot, Angelique's picture managed to sync up quickly with a much less flattering ID picture. Her profile populated my link and the displays in my car as I climbed in, a surprisingly uneventful read that barely warranted the space. She was 24, a couple years out of some school for the performing arts, and there was more information on her resume than her criminal record.

It certainly didn't read like a woman who'd push someone into murder.

The address on the back of the photo sent me sent me on the surreal trip south of Fangtown and through the International District. While Fangtown had been carved out of part of the International District and Pioneer Square back when I was a kid, the two neighborhoods couldn't look any more different in the evening hours. Fangtown, though still holding many of its roots and preserving historic sites, always puts a strange nighttime spin on everything within. There were always murals, glow in the dark paints, and strange window shades to remind you of where you were. But the deeper into the proper International District you go, the more those things bleed away. In other directions, to other places, you might have crossed the harsh boundaries of New Skids. But on this route, all I had to tell me I was headed in the right direction was a growing lack of neon Zombie signs.

The theater itself was situated not far off of one of the far edges of New Skids. It was a small venue, part of one of the many failed efforts to keep the Skids from growing. Ostensibly a place to see Alter culture without having to step into the neighborhood, all it seemed to do was chase out people who actually wanted to stay according to the Oracle's records. The result was a monument to irony: an attempted tourist trap that had long ago become painfully niche and forgotten. Still, it was one of the only places in the city with acoustics tuned specifically to Siren songs. And, most importantly for a group of young performing arts graduates, it was dirt cheap to rent out for an independent show.

The theater house was relatively small, nestled between an art gallery and a glorified showroom calling itself a history museum. The buildings were constructed in a style I'd seen in photos of Argyre's surface levels – clean, sleek, but evoking elements that reminded of others from bygone eras. The theater itself felt like a modern take on the old baroque style, with tall, narrow columns made of a gleaming white material that caught the glow of recessed lights hidden from direct view. It wasn't quite tall enough to be real baroque, but it did its best to fake it. Still, despite their inspiration from Argyre, the three structures were quiet, simple, and lacking the gaudy glowing murals of Fangtown. They seemed classier, trying to put their best foot forward. It was almost downright deceptive.

Walking into the lobby, that same energy persisted. The room felt like it was trying to be grand despite its relatively small dimensions The furniture, meanwhile, seemed much more fitting of what it actually was. Likely changed over several times in the years since the building was constructed, what was there now were old second-hand pieces that felt like they'd been purchased from the personal collection of some little old lady. It was a more humble, homey sort of feel – almost lived in despite being a theater.

Taking this in, I didn't quite notice the usher hurrying along my way. A kid even by my standards, the old hand-me-down uniform he wore barely fit and made it look like he was just doing his part to help a high school production. He nervously fidgeted for a moment out of the corner of my eye, his red coat alerting me even before clearing his throat to catch my attention.

"Can I help you, sir?"

Despite the nervous energy, the aura was reading human, yet he had all the mannerisms of someone afraid to look into the shades. Hoping to settle the nerves a little, I took them off and tried to look him in the eye while I answered with the canned officer tone reserved for the nervous, "Yes, I'm Agent Nathaniel Leone with the ACTF. I'm looking for one of the performers, a Siren woman by the name Angelique. Is she here?"

He calmed slightly but still seemed a bit twitchy as he replied, "I don't know all of the performers yet, sir, but I'd be happy to help you after the show's done."

"I'm afraid this can't really wait," I said, "she's a person of interest in an ongoing investigation."

The kid stammered and stumbled over fragments of words as he tried to think of what he should do in a situation that probably didn't come up very often. He looked around frantically for a moment before making a brief wave to someone at the far end of the room. Emerging from around a corner and hurrying our way, an older man with a severe face approached in a uniform that actually fit. Even without the shades, I felt the power trip in the way the man walked, almost like he got off on hushing people and escorting them out of a theater. I'd seen the personality before in security guards and cops, but I'd never quite experienced it with someone who literally showed people to their seats.

"What's the problem, Jake?" The surprisingly vintage usher asked in a strangely annoyed tone.

The kid, Jake apparently, finally stopped stammering long enough to reply, "This officer- *agent*, needs to question one of the performers about something."

The older usher, for reasons I couldn't quite gather, stepped closer to me than most would be comfortable with. I didn't think he was a threat, just tripping on some strange authority granted to him by this hand-me-down from a failed PR stunt, but my muscle memory didn't know it. Though I doubt he understood the weight of it, my foot slid back and I took a defensive posture that'd been hammered into me by a couple years of training and a memorable groin shot from Dulaf a few years back. Mistaking it for a win, the usher's face took a subtly smug expression that was soon reflected back at him in an iridescent mirrored visor as I put it back on.

"I'm *terribly* sorry, sir," he started obnoxiously, "but no one is allowed in after the show has begun until intermission."

I'd felt bad for the kid, but his supervisor was quickly erasing any sympathy I had for their position. It wasn't just the tone, or the posture, but the flickers of emotion on the aura which told me he was pretty psyched to be getting the opportunity. I admit, watching those flickers of color against the otherwise blue hues of a human read, I got a touch petty.

"Look," I replied coolly, "I'm here on a murder investigation and you're keeping me away from a material witness. Either you're going to escort me backstage where we're going to make some understudy's day or you're going for a ride in my trunk.

Because I've only got one box and I'm not calling in reinforcements for a dude dressed like a nutcracker."

The subtle shift in his expression and aura suggested he couldn't tell how serious I was being. Truthfully, the trunk was loaded with gear and, if I had to, he would just ride in the uncomfortable bucket seat in the back. But the fact we put people in boxes probably helped the lie.

Taking a step back, he nodded and gestured to a side hallway. "Backstage should be possible, sir."

He walked with a bit of urgency as I followed, glancing back every few steps to make sure I was behind him, picking up speed when I was too close. A hint of the music echoed through the halls as we approached the back end of the theater, washing over us as the door opened and a powerful voice came through. I still had my plugs in, filtering whatever inaudible tones might have been in the music, but I could still tell from the vibe and the sudden flashes of color across the usher's aura that it was one of the Sirens on stage.

The area backstage was buzzing with activity as people scrambled to prepare for the next scenes, with costumes changing and props being moved into place at a hurried pace. Despite their concerns, no one took time to notice the usher and I as we drifted through their chaos. Scanning the room, I could see a few Alters in the mix: a Siren, a Nix, and an Alkonost immediately visible as they readied themselves for their next scenes. Beyond them, I even laid eyes on an old familiar mess of colors I recognized as a possible Shapeshifter who seemed to have manipulated their body into the role. But none of them were Angelique, making me wonder if she might have been the one on stage.

The usher turned to me and said in a hushed voice, "I don't see her so I'm going to check with the others. Please wait here."

Hesitating for a moment, I nodded and waved for him to go ahead. Though he had an attitude, I didn't imagine he'd be stupid enough to interfere by tipping her off. Moreover, the voice carrying in from the stage had the quality and power I would expect from a Siren. Maybe Angelique wasn't backstage. Maybe she was out there serenading the audience in period clothing.

Letting the usher wander away a bit before I made my move, I sidled over to a space where I could see out onto the stage, lurking just off stage to avoid the audience seeing me. But the audience couldn't have cared less about my being there, enthralled by the Siren's voice. She stood there in the closest thing their budget could get to 19th century French fashion singing of broken dreams, abandonment, and disappointment. From the shadows, I watched the audience in the Oracle's vividly enhanced detail.

I'd seen Sirens manipulate people in a small setting before, but never quite like this. Waves of color rolled through the auras of the audience like ripples on the surface of a pond. With every rise and fall of her voice, the colors shifted as the music washed over them. I could see them all get swept up into the emotion of her song, and not entirely because of her unique talents. Even though it wasn't Angelique, I couldn't help but give the show my full attention for at least that moment myself.

I recognized the song from one of many stakeouts with my Vampire mentor, but I'd never actually stood by a live performance. It'd always struck something of a chord with me, the story of someone who'd been abandoned and forced to deal with the consequences alone. I couldn't say I understood the character's situation exactly, but I couldn't help feeling a connection in that moment despite the earplugs. And I could see, in the looks on their faces even under the dim light of the theater, that not everyone in the audience needed a little Siren boost to feel the same. Whoever she was, she was giving it her all.

Shrieking from all corners, an alarm shattered the moment and stopped the music dead in its tracks.

The colors of the audience came to an abrupt halt before turning to chaos as people snapped out of their pleasant trance. Echoing through the building, I took a moment to realize it was a fire alarm and immediately thought on the fact I sent a god damn usher to grab a Siren. Quietly cursing under the discord, I sprinted in the direction I last saw the bright red coat and down a long hallway running the full breadth of the building. At the far end I could see people gathering around an open door, a fire exit used in a hurry, and picked up speed.

"Who went out?" I yelled from down the hall, drawing the Helios from my side.

Dumbfounded and panicked, auras ranging from orange through pink, they all frantically shook their heads and scattered from my path. The exit went straight out to an alley behind the three buildings, a slightly wider space with loading access for the "museum" and art gallery. But, as I ran into the open air, I discovered that layout made it perfect for an escape. The alley connected to a square lot centered behind the three buildings, making two perfect corners to run around in short order. Worse, the sound of the alarm drowned out any chances of hearing someone's footsteps. Sprinting to the open space between those corners to get line of sight in both directions, there wasn't a trace to be found.

Whoever opened that door was a damn good runner.

Studying the area around me, I tried to think of which way I would go to lose a tail. The problem was, there were too damn many good choices. The alleys had access to other adjacent paths at the far end of the buildings, even a shot at getting to the street. The museum had an open loading bay to duck into. And, hell, if it wasn't actually a Siren but something that could fake it really well, it was entirely possible they could have mocked gravity and bounced up the buildings like a well-dressed pinball. A nagging feeling crept over me, an urge to keep looking, but I had to accept the fact they were gone.

Holstering the Helios, I started walking back to the fire exit. Waiting for me was a confused bunch of people in partial costumes staring with the hope I could provide answers. Beyond those vacant expressions was a face I wasn't quite expecting. Standing just over their shoulders was the older usher, now lacking that smugness he had before and instead looking deeply concerned. I considered for a moment he was worried I was going to drag him in for aiding and abetting. But, as I came closer, he started to jockey his way through the crowd to meet with me at the door. That was never a good sign.

Stammering like the kid now, the older usher said quietly, "Agent, sir, there's something you need to see."

Giving him a once over from behind the visor, his readings were all over the place. He was going through every emotion possible in a random panic. Whatever he needed me to see was really bad news for me one way or another. Warily, I gave him a nod and gestured for him to lead the way.

The way he walked had changed as he led me down the hall. It wasn't a huge difference, just a drag in his stride and the way his shoulders sagged, but it was noticeable after seeing his usual attitude. Whatever waited for us had completely drained that attitude from him. Through that long corridor and past an array of faces both confused and shocked, I realized at least some of them were looking the direction we were headed. Before long, the murmurs gave way to muffled sobbing in one of the dressing rooms that gave me a familiar sinking feeling. As the usher entered the room, I caught sight of partial footprints stepping out the door and starting down the hall. It was a woman's shoe, given the size and shape, but the visor was more concerned about the composition – bloody footprints confirming that sinking sensation.

Reaching for my hand-link, I muttered a couple quiet curses before looking up to the others and ordering, "Everyone clear this area, and I want the feed of any security cameras!"

Only a few reacted to my orders while the others stood motionless in their daze. The ones inside the room, a couple of actresses and the usher, were gathered around a body on the floor. One of them was on her knees in a growing pool of blood, cradling the head and sobbing. I could tell from the readings and the blood-soaked costume that the crying woman was the Siren from the stage. And as I approached, I quickly figured the connection. Angelique was now dead in the arms of her friends from the agency, at least one gunshot wound in the chest.

A gunshot no one seemed to hear.

Looking to the usher, I reached over and rested a hand on his shoulder, moving closer to calmly ask, "Is there security here?"

"We, uh," he said haltingly, "we kind of serve a dual function around here."

Nodding, I patted his shoulder and said, "Okay, I need you to get these two somewhere out of the way and then if you have any security cameras, I need the feeds."

He looked them over, nodded, and walked to the closest of the two, murmuring for her to follow him. The actress, visibly shaken, nodded along and started to back away. The other, still cradling Angelique, was in a world of her own. Exchanging a look with the usher, I nodded and moved to deal with her. Hesitating a moment, I considered if she'd even noticed I was there. She was locked in on her friend and I hadn't made a lot of noise once I was in the room. Moving around to where she could see me, I crouched in roughly her line of sight – careful to avoid touching anything that could be evidence. Waiting silently, I gave her a minute to recognize I was there. Last thing any of us needed was to freak her out worse in the middle of a crime scene.

"Miss," I said with the most reassuring voice I could, "I'm Agent Leone with the ACTF. I understand what you're going through, but we need to clear the room."

Still sobbing, she choked out, "I don't understand, I just saw her, how could *no one* hear this?!"

"It's a good question," I answered. "But if I'm going to figure that out, I need to have control of the room."

Lip quivering, stage makeup streaming down her face, I saw a flicker of rage in her eyes as she locked them on me. Bitterly, she asked, "Who did this?"

Glancing past her behind my shades, not moving my head to make sure she couldn't tell what I was doing, I considered the same question. The footprint out of the room had to be someone who'd been in here after the blood started to pool, but had left the room before the usher arrived and was well on their way to the fire exit without him noticing. Given the layout of the rooms and the hallway itself, I had to wonder if it was possible for him to see someone who didn't belong here and not try to intercept. Could it have been someone else in the show?

Filing the thought away for later, I said, "I don't know yet, but I intend to find out."

The sobbing had stopped, though the tears kept rolling, her hatred for the shooter giving her something to hold onto. I adjusted my gloves and reached over carefully, cradling Angelique's head and nodding for her to let go. She slid back a bit, releasing the body and letting me lower Angelique carefully back to the floor, but sat motionless no more than a foot away. Seeing the other actress still hovering just outside the door, I gestured for her to come back in for her friend. She took the cue and moved in, helping her friend to her feet and escorting her out, both of them transfixed on the body the whole way.

As they left the room, I caught sight of the usher again. I thought he was just waiting for the other actress at first. But as they passed him by, he whispered to the two of them and gestured down the hall before stepping back in. He'd turned pale in the minute or two since I last saw him, looking worse than he did when he came to tell me about Angelique. The visor lit him up with a nervous energy and registered beads of sweat along his brow.

"What's wrong?" I asked.

Fidgeting again, he stammered, "I-I went down the hall to the security room and checked the cameras like you asked."

"Did you spot them?"

"Well, you see, somehow…" he said, hesitating for what felt like an eternity, "she walked right past me."

No wonder he was pale as a ghost when he walked in. I'm sure he thought I would place the blame on him, but a more troubling idea came to mind. Somehow, he'd managed to be completely oblivious in person but instantly recognized someone wasn't supposed to be there on camera. The possibilities ran through my head on how that could happen, and none of them felt all that pleasant. Quietly, I took a second to call the investigators and snap a few quick shots with my hand-link before leaving Angelique's side. My silence wasn't meant to unnerve the guy, I just wanted to be sure I wouldn't snap at him, but I could see his posture change as I stood up. Taking pity on him, I finally took the visor off as I carefully approached again.

"I have a team coming in, can this door lock?" I asked.

He glanced over his shoulder and nodded.

Nodding along with him, I continued, "Do you have the key?"

Again, he gave a quick, nervous nod.

"Then let's lock this room for now so no one else walks in," I said, "and then I want you to show me the security footage."

Up close, without the visor, I could see just how pale he actually was. Whatever he saw on that feed, it was putting him into a complete spiral. Turning him to the door, I patted his back lightly.

"Thanks for the help so far," I said reassuringly, "I know this isn't something you were prepared for."

Easing slightly as we walked, he nodded along but didn't reply. He pulled the keys from his uniform pocket and held the door for me as I stepped out, hands shaking as he locked the door from the outside. Taking a last look at Angelique before he closed the door, I saw his brow furrow and his lips purse like he was about to lose all composure.

Honestly, I was feeling pretty sorry for threatening to put him in the trunk by this point.

Escorting him down the hall, I started to run the possibilities through my head. Maybe the shooter was in disguise and he didn't see their face until it was on camera. Maybe the cameras showed her exiting and walking past him. Maybe he just wasn't paying attention thanks to me winding him up seconds prior. But none of my theories prepared me for what I saw on that screen.

The cameras were set in the hallway, one at each end and pointing down the length to get an angle on anyone no matter what direction they were facing. I saw the usher enter the frame first, going down the length to a man with a clipboard and exchanging words with him before being directed back towards the dressing room. As they spoke, that door opened and someone stepped out, too far from either camera to be clear at first but clearly out of place all the same.

She wasn't part of the cast or crew, wearing a pencil skirt and a blazer like she just stepped out of the office. Even as I watched the back of her head, I could feel that itching, nagging familiarity at the back of mine. She walked down that hallway with an urgent pace, holding a suppressed gun at her side like no one would notice. Somehow, she was right, as even when they were practically face-to-face the usher didn't seem to see it. In fact, he didn't seem to notice her at all as he walked like there no one in his path. He didn't slow, he didn't sidestep, he didn't even pivot as they approached each other. She just stepped around him as he continued on and didn't even bother to look her direction. Him and every other person in that hallway seemed oblivious as she passed on the way to the exit.

Then, walking into focus of the other camera, I saw a face I didn't expect out here. She wasn't confused like Kate or blank like the other shooters in the reports. She wasn't scared or traumatized by what just happened. No, the look on her face spoke more to determination than anything else as she maintained a steady gaze on that fire exit in the distance, gracefully weaving through the unsuspecting crew. The only time her eyes broke from that exit was when she caught sight of the camera and briefly looked into it. The camera was a bit older, a couple skipped frames here or there, but the image was crystal clear.

Marionette wasn't concerned with anyone seeing her face.

Chapter 6
Apartment Trouble

Something never quite felt right about Marionette. She'd always fade into the background as quickly as she could, rarely making herself known for longer than she had to. She presented like an Alter but her aura was always suppressed like she was actively hiding herself. When I first met her that bothered me to no end, but I grew to accept it over time as I realized some Alters just didn't like the idea of the visors peering into their proverbial souls. The thing that I could never accept, though, was that strange feeling of déjà vu I had every time I stood next to her. It was like she was a ghost and now I'd just watched a dozen people ignore her as she strolled by with a gun at her side.

Shit, maybe she was still out there when I was standing in the alley.

Running the image of her face through my hand-link, I asked the Oracle for her last known address and hurried out of the theater. I couldn't be sure of where she'd go next, but her home seemed like a good place to start. I hadn't seen her all that long ago and she was still in the clothes she had on in the Moirae. If she was there to eliminate Angelique before I could get to her, then it was entirely possible she had nothing but the clothes on her back. Maybe, if I was lucky, she'd head home to grab a few things before trying to skip town. After all, there no chance we wouldn't have identified her.

Despite never seeing her outside of Fangtown and never in direct sunlight, I found her address matched with an apartment building in the Pioneer Square district. Inside Fangtown was an easier place to live for most Alters. The windows were generally tinted, covered walkways were the norm, doors were modified for easy entry, and rarely would you see a hint of older ironwork that could make even the Faelish queasy. But this place, nestled between older brick buildings, stood with great big windows and small balconies that provided no shelter from the light. The front doors still had regular handles with visible locks. The neighborhood spoke of a time where nothing was particularly built with concern for electromagnetic fields or UV rays. Honestly, the longer I looked, the more it looked like the place you'd go to avoid Alter neighbors.

So why was she there?

Stepping through the doors, I was greeted with modern décor and a tenant looking at me like I just stepped off a UFO. She was younger, well-dressed, and showed no signs of being anything out of the ordinary. In fact, it looked like I was the most interesting thing to happen to her all day. She watched me stroll by, waited a few moments, then drifted along behind me. It was hard to tell what concerned her more: the fact that I was there or that I had a *reason* to be there. What was clear was that I had her full attention as she followed me all the way to Marionette's floor before stopping and peering down the hall as I walked on. Approaching Marionette's door, I finally heard her whisper "I *knew* it" before she disappeared around the corner.

Standing outside the door, I started to feel a strange unease again. There was nothing remarkable about it, nothing to separate it from the rest in the building beside a number, but it felt more imposing than it should. Something about it, something I couldn't see, felt toxic and maybe even dangerous. I scanned the threshold for any signs of what was making me feel that way and then took one last look through the hallway for something I might have missed on the way.

Though there were some chemical traces on the readings, nothing seemed too out of the ordinary in any direction. If anything, the whole area felt intentionally boring. Few things had made me feel quite like this in the past, and none of them were ever good when I finally figured it out. Was it something subliminal? Was it intuition?

Was it her?

Reaching up to knock on the door, I stopped as a flash of her silenced gun sprang to mind and I remembered that the normally quiet woman in the background was dangerous this time. I drew my Helios, made sure my visor was secured with my handy strap, and stepped aside so I could use the door frame as a bit of a shield. The uniform would stand up to most small caliber rounds, something I'd learned the hard way. But the lack of head protection and a blurry view of the gun made standing directly in front of that door when I announced myself a bad idea. Taking a couple calming breaths and making sure no one was in the hallway, I knocked as hard as I could without alerting the whole floor and called out, "Marionette Corbin! Agent Leone with the ACTF!"

After a moment of silence, I tried again, banging on the door hard enough this time to draw a couple neighbors to the hallway. Shaking my head quickly, I waved for them to get back inside. Though one listened, I noticed another raise her phone and start recording from down the hall. There was a twinge of frustration at that, I'll admit, since my biggest concern at the time was crossfire. But, frankly, I'd seen enough videos from that perspective to understand what they were thinking. Gesturing to them again, I waved my hand down and mouthed the words "get down" repeatedly. Raising an eyebrow, she hesitated for a moment before piecing it together and taking a knee by her doorframe. Giving her a brief thumbs up, I went back to banging on the door and waiting for anything resembling a response.

The dead silence coming out of the apartment suggested she wasn't home, but that video in the theater told me that didn't mean a damn thing. I ran the possible options through my head and considered as many outcomes as possible. If she was in there and I tried to pick the lock, she could pick me off through the door. Kicking doors wasn't as effective as movies had made it seem, and blowing the door open with a Wisp would probably get more than a few complaints filed against me. On the other hand, the door and the frame seemed to just be made of wood and the lock was an old brass knob.

Keeping the Helios ready, I reached to the set of rods at my side and pulled out a Banshee. I couldn't set it off full blast in a residential building, not in this situation. But the lowest setting would be enough to disorient anyone inside and give me a chance to end this without crossfire. Adjusting the settings and taking a moment to double check and make sure I wasn't about to blow all the windows on the floor, I shifted my stance again. My camerawoman also shifted and started to back away. Making a quick gesture with my finger to my ear, I tried to warn her about the noise. Watching her fumble with the phone for a second, I took a step back, set my shoulders and raised the Helios to the door.

Cranking up the power temporarily, I let off three shots in quick succession – two into the hinges and one through the lock. The fully powered Helios rounds vanished into the door, leaving red hot holes and faintly glowing blue mist in their wake. They didn't fully penetrate, dispersing their heat through everything they touched, but they turned the hardware into a weakened mess. Taking a few quick steps and putting some old Muay Thai training to use, I push-kicked that thing for all I was worth and saw the old brass and charred wood snap away like tinfoil and plywood.

That uneasy feeling surged as the door flew open. The dark spaces of the apartment seemed imposing despite nothing being there – like the shadows themselves might be alive. Every corner of the room beckoned for my attention like I'd kicked open a nest of hostile creatures. For a brief second, I even thought I saw a flicker of an aura reading under her furniture. Though that reading passed into thin air, the visor's night vision wasn't even enough to prove it wrong.

So, I chucked the Banshee under the couch just to be sure.

Even at the lowest setting, the Banshee's wail could be felt throughout my body. I hadn't taken out the earplugs since I first ran into a Siren, but there was never mistaking when one was active. My camerawoman visibly cringed out of the corner of my eye and nearly fell back into her apartment, fumbling with her phone and trying desperately not to drop it. I could only imagine how blurry and shaky that video was going to be. But, being a trooper, she soon recovered, one ear pressed to her shoulder while her free hand covered the other. I imagine the video quality was going to be ass regardless after all of that, but I had to credit her dedication. Eventually, the sound subsided and that strange vibration stopped giving me a full body massage.

Lingering at the door for a moment, I realized that there was still a possibility she was standing right in front of me. I hadn't checked what she was on the way in, possibly still foggy from her manipulations, but I knew whatever it was could be effectively invisible. So, reaching into another pouch on the belt, I pulled a Halo strip and quickly dropped it across the entrance, straightening it with my foot before it ignited. It wasn't the cleanest deployment, but I couldn't afford to lower my guard to do it right.

Crossing the threshold, passing through the curtain of light and chemical mist from the strip, I checked the corners quickly and watched for signs of any actual movement. The interior was amazingly quiet even considering the earplugs. A scent drifted on the air that nagged at the back of my mind as familiar but hard to place. It was an earthy smell like crushed leaves and flower petals blended with cut grass and wet soil, but with something in the blend my brain was telling me I should have known.

Similarly, though the flickering auras were gone, the feeling of being watched remained. It wasn't just paranoia about her being invisible. Despite the fact it was a rare ability, they did train us on how to watch for Alters you couldn't see so I wasn't completely blind. But this feeling was like something crawling across my skin, a strange sensation like the air itself was touching me.

I slowly swept the area as I moved from door to door, checking every room without going all the way inside. If she was there, she was waiting for me to clear her path. Instead, I closed every door after ensuring she wasn't standing inside and moved on to the next. If she was hiding, she would still have to open the doors. Theoretically, it would tell me if she moved. Still, that uneasy feeling grew into a pit in my stomach.

The apartment itself was fine, even cheerful in how it was decorated. Older furniture, reminiscent of my landlady Babs' plush couches and cloud-like cushions, stood in immaculate shape in every room. Even most of the appliances were somewhat out of date, from a flat screen almost as old as I was to a toaster similar to one I set on fire a couple years ago. The most modern conveniences were kept to a single room in the back.

One of the bedrooms had been converted into an office, a solid oak desk from a bygone era sat against the back wall with a newer computer atop it. That system was the newest thing in the whole place as far as I could tell. A panel was laid out like a mat on the desk acting as an adaptive control surface like the sort I'd normally see in an ACTF building. The screen was a flexible touch display curved to kind of surround her while she worked. She was up to date on data, if nothing else.

The main bedroom, meanwhile, seemed a polar opposite in every fashion. There were no signs of any modern conveniences in that room, with well-maintained wood furniture, an antique bedframe, and a lamp that looked to be well over a century old. Everything was meticulously cared for, even recently dusted as far as I could tell. Despite the still growing unease, there wasn't a single thing out of place in the entire apartment.

Of course, that only contributed to the sense something was way off.

A two-bedroom apartment for a single person who was almost constantly at the club should have had some sign of neglect. Maybe she wasn't there enough to mess the place up, but there should have been dust or signs she'd forgotten to take out the trash. Did she never drop a coat over the back of a chair or toss something onto the couch to pick up later? It was like the place had been scrubbed.

Having shut all the doors in the apartment but the last, I moved to check the rest of the bedroom for signs that she'd cut and run. Stepping in, I did a quick check of the corners and under the bed to ensure she wasn't actually there. Given the trick from before, I couldn't be sure she wasn't, but what else was I really supposed to do? I wasn't even sure how her trick worked yet. Regardless, I was satisfied there were no monsters under the bed.

As I was starting to check her closet, finding it mostly full, I finally registered just what that scent was. It'd drifted to me from across the hall of my own apartment, part of one of Babs' concoctions. She'd explained it to me once during small talk, a passing exchange of peculiarities that didn't stand out all that much for Barbara Zdunk, but here it set off alarms and made my whole body tense.

I abandoned the closet and hurried for the door as the whole room started to tilt under my feet and objects around me began to rattle. The door, relatively unmoved as far as I could tell, seemed to grow more distant as I moved towards it, like the apartment was stretching to prevent my escape. Closing my eyes, I fixed on its location and barreled ahead, crashing into the door with my shoulder and nearly falling through it. It hurt, but I was happy to find something to grab onto and swung myself around into the hallway while opening my eyes again. Hesitating, I stared ahead and found all of the doors had reopened while my back had turned.

Hearing the rattling grow and feeling the floor continue to shift under my feet, I holstered the Helios and went for a full out sprint through the apartment. Shadows danced around me, the flickering auras returning like rainbow-colored flames in the dark. The rattling grew, now joined by sudden bangs, until they became nearly deafening in an apartment that seemed to be tearing itself apart. As I reached the living room, within sight of the busted door, I could see the furniture around me actually shaking and bouncing. Pausing at the sight, I watched a lamp start to levitate above a corner table, light rapidly flashing on and off as it rose. Everything felt lighter as I stood transfixed, a force starting to lift me from the floor.

And then it launched my ass out that door like a three-hundred-pound bouncer tossing a drunk out of a bar.

The wind was knocked out of me as I hit the wall outside the apartment – horizontal and at least five feet in the air. I bounced off of it with a loud crack and braced myself as I went shoulder first into the floor with the most graceless of thuds. My head was pounding, my back and shoulder seized with pain, and my legs felt like jelly as I tried to get back to my feet. The camerawoman, letting out a short yelp as I hit, raced to my side and did her best to help me back up.

"Are you okay?" She asked, frantically.

Grunting an acknowledgment and trying to regain my bearings, I leaned against the wall and slid back down. Truthfully, I didn't know how to answer her. I was still dealing with the shock of hitting the wall. My mind was racing to try to figure out what the hell just happened. I couldn't exactly tell if I was severely hurt or not. What was it Babs told me that smell was? The name lingered at the tip of my tongue while I struggled to breathe through the stitch up my side.

Finally, that old conversation with Babs clicked. Breathlessly, I stammered, "Get clear, dragon's blood."

The look on her face would have been priceless any other time. A mix of confusion, concern, and disbelief someone could only get when talking to a man speaking gibberish. Sure, fairies were real, but dragons were a step too far.

"Seriously," I said steadier, "the apartment is booby trapped. Get inside."

She hesitated, a hint of understanding in her eyes but a sense she felt bad leaving me behind. I waved for her to go quickly, doing my best to look 'okay' as I did. She relented and stood again, backing up a few steps before turning on her heel and running like someone scrambling from a spider. Watching her, I was almost amused again despite the pain yet relieved she wouldn't be there for the next part.

It wasn't literally the blood of a dragon, of course. It was a succulent plant that was often used for incense. Babs had explained to me once that some of the old Wiccan practices of herbs and incense really were functional in the right hands, but not in the way other practitioners would expect. Witches like Babs could leave a mark on a place, a chemical and physical change like an actual spell. These changes could boost creativity, influence decisions, or make people see strange sights. Stronger apparitions or effects required a group effort. The incense, chosen with care, would be used to cover or neutralize some of the smells left behind. Dragon's blood was used for protective spells.

I'd just run into my first poltergeist.

Tapping my badge, I uttered a sentence few got to say on the job, "This is Agent Leone, I need an exorcism team at my location."

The beacon lit up to let me know the Oracle heard and I settled in for the wait. I couldn't really be sure what did and didn't happen in that place. I could have been hallucinating the whole thing. But, as I stared back into the room, I could see that lamp toppled over onto the floor and some of the furniture had moved. To say I had questions would be an understatement. Despite that, at least one question had finally been resolved.

Marionette was a Witch and she had a coven.

Chapter 7
Enigmatic Ejection

Even if they couldn't prove anything I saw was true, the exorcist team was nice enough to assure me I hadn't gone crazy. Decked out in ACTF designed hazmat suits, they scoured the apartment for every sign of the mark left behind. The face shields of the suits, like the helmets of the SOL teams, acted like giant visors and scanned for every chemical trace. The suits were shielded against EM fields, came with their own air supply, and were made of a Vesperadin weave to avoid any tears. They were perfectly comfy and secure in their spaceman suits so long as that lamp stayed down.

Officially, psychic powers didn't really exist. Argyre's scientists had long categorized them into what they called "para-psychic phenomenon": not quite psychic but damn close. Someone didn't actually read minds or see the future, they just responded to stimuli on a level so deep that they could extrapolate an accurate guess. It's something like how animals can feel natural disasters coming. The key difference is that if someone could actually read your thoughts you couldn't do much about it but a really nice hazmat suit could shield you from most mind tricks and reads.

Telekinesis, on the other hand, they had no clue about. Theories ranged from simple hallucinations and manipulations of magnetic fields to something about quantum mechanics and extra dimensions. Truthfully, the more extreme theories went right over my head at the academy. What I did know was I'd seen the mayor walk on water once and I was pretty sure hitting the wall as hard as I just did usually required help.

So, I couldn't be sure that a lamp really just kicked my ass, but I wasn't about to take my eyes off the bastard.

Once the apartment was clear, investigators moved in to see if there was any sign of her. Far as any of them could tell, there wasn't anything out of place. Nothing indicated she owned a gun. There was no sign of missing luggage or clothes. Her computer didn't even have a password on it. Seeing as it was going to take them time to get through that last one, everyone politely informed me I looked like shit and sent me on my way.

Though I left a literal impression in the wall, the sting of hitting it was starting to pass. My head had stopped spinning and my sides had stopped burning, despite a lingering daze. Muscles still ached like after a night of heavy lifting, but that was gradually fading. No, the only thing that really hurt in the moment was my shoulder. Unfortunately, it wasn't the shoulder I landed on.

Old wounds, long healed, beckoned for my attention. It was a strange pain that defied explanation. Every doctor and physical therapist said it shouldn't be there. Though it looked like some sort of arthritis for a while, it came and went with little rhyme or reason. An agency mandated therapist suggested some theories, but nothing I couldn't already guess.

Idly rubbing and rotating the arm to try to work out the kink, I made my way downstairs and out to the car. Where I'd go once I got there wasn't exactly clear. She hadn't come back to her apartment and the Oracle didn't have anywhere better to look. No car to her name, no use of a credit card, and she'd even managed to avoid all the local cameras. Once she left that theater, she might as well have been a ghost herself.

As the car hummed and the displays populated across the windshield, a vague tension in the arm told me what I had to do. I've never dealt well with being manipulated. When a Shapeshifter started to take the faces of people in the neighborhood, I practically melted down. I needed to touch base.

Turning the car around and heading back into Fangtown, I actually listened for once and drove back to the HQ. If the investigators found anything, they could reach me there. In the meantime, if I was lucky, Lucian would be available. As long as he'd been doing this, I'm sure he'd chased more than his fair share of Witches. The old order wasn't really into witch trials, but that didn't mean they hadn't put a couple through a traditional trial or two. He had to have caught one over the centuries.

I mean, it was either that or ask Babs if she could narc on a fellow Witch.

Despite the relative peace and quiet of the summer months, I found the headquarters in the midst of the post-sunset rush. After what was likely a nearly dead day shift, I could see people from all walks of the Alter spectrum and even a couple humans being escorted in. With a good part of our population cooped up through the daylight hours, they were clearly making up for the lost time. A small but unmistakable line was starting to form through the parking garage to get into processing.

Seasonal changes in activity aren't all that uncommon. In human populations the crime rates tend to go up during the summer months and heat waves and no one's perfectly sure why. Maybe there were more people out and about or maybe the heat was just making everyone cranky. But for Alters the changing behavior was easy to explain: there were only eight hours for some people to do ***anything*** and they were all stacking on top of each other. Not everyone needed to hide from the sun, of course, but old habits die hard.

Even as I approached the elevators, a lancer and his team of clerics were unloading even more people out of the back of a wagon. The suspects were a band of misfits from a wide range of backgrounds. Everything from an Ogre to a mean looking Brounie went marching by as I stepped aside for their drunk parade of shame. The Brounie, with the face of a toddler and the stature to match, glared up at me. His glassy eyes, bright red cheeks, and uneven walk said he was at least half way through a six pack. It was both adorable and incredibly unnerving, halting me in my tracks for a bit as I watched them get escorted into the prisoner transfer entrance.

Twenty years ago, that would have been a strange sight.

The employee entrance was a lot less busy as I walked the sterile hallway and passed through the multiple scans. With the first wave of pain passing and the stiff aftereffect slowly setting in, I wondered if the Oracle could see just how roughed up I actually was. Though I didn't say it out loud to anyone, I'd started to use the hallway as a bit of a DIY examination. After all, she was checking my bones to make sure I wasn't a Shifter. That should give her a decent enough look, shouldn't it?

Lifting my gaze to the corner of the elevator, I entered the silent one-sided standoff with the security camera and waited for someone to say something. I know that wasn't the purpose of the place, but it's always a little reassuring that alarms don't go off every time I walk through. At the very least, I knew nothing inside me was pulverized enough to not match the old scans. It wasn't much, but it was enough to step off the elevator and not hobble straight to the medical wing.

Despite the line in the garage, or possibly even because of it, the corridors and bullpen were amazingly quiet. As I stood in the bullpen itself, I could see a half dozen other agents working at the desks, leaving most of the desk space unused. The Oracle display above flashed some activity here or there but not quite as much as the crowd outside suggested. Despite how busy the building was at that moment, the general traffic was still down. The summer's strange punctuated equilibrium was at play: long stretches of nothing followed by short bursts of insanity.

I'd arrived just in time to miss the rush on desks for report filing – a chance to sit and stare frustrated at a screen until inspiration struck. The others around me weren't moving particularly fast themselves, one even seemed to be trying to get an old video game to run off the desktop. Everyone was just kind of enjoying the last moments before the big wave hit.

The lab division was the only place where the rush never mattered. They were always working to catch up during the winter months when activity stretched across the day. But the summer months meant they had twenty-four hours to work through the cases of eight. Dulaf's day shift position made it so she probably never even saw the rush. Though the passing thought made me wonder how Dulaf and Amelia were dealing with an oddly eventful day.

Pausing before I reached a desk, my eyes drifted towards the corridor leading to the Limbo housing block. I had to find Marionette, but I hadn't really checked in on them since the shooting. There weren't any real solid leads right now. Maybe there was enough time to check in on them and make sure the bright-eyed Elven child was okay and that her caretaker hadn't started assembling an armory in their apartment. As if she could somehow hear my thoughts, Dulaf stepped into the room and started to walk my way.

Of course, this meant she was probably about to hand me a copy of The Exorcist.

"Novel or movie?" I asked as she got into earshot.

Ears perked, eyebrow quirked, Dulaf echoed, "Novel or movie?"

To say I was surprised she didn't have a prank gift ready after literal air whipped my ass would be an understatement. "Didn't hear about my newest flight?"

"Oh," she said, voice rising as she started to catch up, "the poltergeist?"

"Yeah, the poltergeist," I said. "I think there'll be video online if you want."

I'd taken my visor off, but I didn't need it to see what her aura would have shown. Her brow was furrowed with concern, her ears were drooping ever slightly and nearly reared back. Elves were terrible at hiding their emotions in general, but Dulaf was usually better at it than this. And, the longer I looked at her face, the more I was starting to feel it too.

"Is Amelia okay?"

Quickly waving at me and shaking her head, Dulaf answered, "Oh, no, no. Amelia is perfectly fine. She's watching a movie with some of the other kids."

Her expression once again told me all I needed to know. The instant I brought up Amelia's name, even before she started to respond, I could see that it wasn't the kid she was worried about. It was a subtle but profound change in her face as some of the tension lifted and her ears relaxed.

But if it wasn't the kid, why was she acting so strange?

Giving me a once over, she said in a hushed tone, "I heard what happened with the poltergeist."

Starting to migrate to a chair, still very confused by this development, I mused aloud, "And yet you're not holding a copy of The Exorcist."

I caught sight of something out of the corner of my eye that damn near chilled my blood. Sure, she'd had a long day so maybe she didn't have time to mock me. Yes, there'd been a shooting near the kid, so maybe she had other concerns. But, as I said that line, I saw her literally stop in her tracks. Dulaf Nénharma, professional mischief maker and devout believer in hazing, was actually worried about me.

"Dulaf," I said, softening my tone and trying to be reassuring, "I'm okay. It was just a Witch trap."

Quietly, she replied, "Marionette Corbin."

"Does that mean something?" I asked, finally taking a seat.

The tension returned, something lingering on the tip of her tongue that she seemed to be holding back. We locked eyes as I tried to figure out what was going on and she looked back at me like she had terrible news. I had half a mind to reach for the visor and try to get a read on what was going on, but I knew it wouldn't tell me anything I couldn't already see. There was something heavy in the air, an elephant in the room that only she could see.

Suddenly standing behind me, Lucian's voice cut through the tension and snapped us out of our little staring contest. "You've been telling us about her for a couple of years now," he said firmly, "And it seems she has an entire coven at her side."

I turned to face him as he loomed over me. As lean as he was, as often as he managed to avoid attention, you could almost forget what he was. But right then, chin up and shoulders back, light gleaming off the gold bits on his uniform, I could almost see the ancient Vampire knight. His eyes were narrowed and focused into a piercing gaze and his face was the most serious I'd seen him in this building. I'd seen him angry, but this was something else. Lucian had the posture of a man on a mission.

This was how Leo knew him.

"What's up with you guys?" I asked, trying my best not to sound nervous.

A hint of a scowl crossed Lucian's face and he briefly glanced away before he answered, "We don't think you should be on this case."

The words left me spinning. Even as his devotee, Lucian had never pulled me from a case. As an agent, he even seemed to encourage me to be more proactive. But now, all of a sudden, he was trying to bench me? No, it wasn't just him. He said "we".

Looking between Lucian and Dulaf, I stood from the chair and stepped back so I didn't feel so cornered. Laughing it off, I waved and protested, "Good thing I'm not your devotee then, eh?"

Dulaf's ears folded back and a serious expression set in as she stepped closer to Lucian. "No, he's right, Nate. You have to step back from this."

I scoffed, "Her spectral watchdog tosses me into a wall and you think I'm letting that go? Have we met?"

Lucian looked to the floor for a moment before looking me in the eye again with that piercing gaze. "You've said for a while now that she gave you a strange feeling and you could never pin down what she was. It's clear she's been pushing you."

I echoed in disbelief, "Pushing?"

Dulaf nodded. "The strange feelings, the fact you never pushed any harder on it. We think she's been in your head."

Hearing it laid out, remembering the video from the theater, a part of me had to admit they were right. I'd always had a feeling like I'd seen her somewhere before but couldn't place it. Something about her was always off. Yet for all the times it had happened I never bothered to look closer or press for answers. It wasn't like with Trey and our game at the coffee shop. I always pushed the thought aside, ignoring her just like the usher as she walked by with a gun.

Defiantly, I snapped, "Then I sure as hell can't let her go!"

Lucian stepped closer and reached out, grabbing my shoulder with a firm grip. His expression softened, his eyes almost sad as he said, "You *have* to let this one go."

I nearly pushed the hand away but caught myself in time. I could understand the problem but I'd never been pulled from something like this before. It was a punch in the gut and even as I started to see their point it didn't feel any better.

"It's about more than her," I insisted, looking between the two of them for some sign they could hear me. "Nguyen and Ramirez were saying there were other cases. I saw a woman standing over her boss' body, holding the gun, with no idea what she did! It's not just about Marionette. There's something bigger going on."

Lucian peered over his shoulder at Dulaf and then back to me. He very lightly nodded and eased his grip on my shoulder.

"Fine," he said, stepping back, "if you leave Marionette to me, you can work the other angles of the case."

Part of me hated that idea. The rest of me realized it was my only chance. I swallowed that urge to fight back and nodded along. I didn't say anything, I knew I would get right back into the fight if I did, but the gesture seemed to be enough.

Lucian patted my shoulder and turned to walk away. As he passed Dulaf and made his way for the exit, I could see the tension lift from her as if he picked it up himself. For some reason she just felt safer about him dealing with this. For some reason both of them wanted me to back down. And, watching him march through the room with a clear purpose, adjusting his gloves like he was preparing for something, I could only focus on one thought.

There was something about this they weren't telling me.

Chapter 8
Vexing Associations

Sitting at a desk and staring at a screen was more frustrating than I thought it would be. I already knew it was going to be a lot of dead ends and missing pieces when I first walked in. But the notion that I was now forced to avoid the one solid lead I did have because other people were freaked out wasn't making it any easier. Worse, the things that I could go through were the things that had already been covered by people like Nguyen and Ramirez. If I was going to find anything, it was going to have to be something no one would bother to look at.

So there I sat, for longer than I would like to admit, scouring every inch of the victim profiles. Opening up the search to try to find similar cases from anywhere or any time, I was surprised to see some from outside Seattle happened within the last couple years. They were almost everywhere, scattered like buckshot, even one coming from as far away as New York. At first it seemed like there'd be some connection: I had an accountant, a real estate agent, and two lawyers – including Kate's boss Kenneth. But the further I got down the list the less they seemed to make sense. What would these high rollers have to do with a retired store owner from Pioneer Square and a tour guide for the Seattle Underground?

They all died in different locations, they all worked in different professions, and I could now see that all but 3 had left the city in the last few years. It was easy to see why no one made any connections. The only things they really had in common is that they all worked or lived in Seattle at one time and died under really freaky circumstances. Since then, none of them had any reason to even be standing on the same block in the last few years. Some weren't even in the same time zone anymore.

Were they even in the city at the same time?

Going back through their profiles one more time, I started to have the Oracle scour the system for overlaps in location and events. Maybe there was an unsolved case in an area they all had reason to pass through. Some of them could be witnesses, bystanders, accomplices. Even if none of them ever came forward, at least the old man would have been questioned if something went down near his store. Maybe his name would show up in a report from far enough back.

But, of course, that would have been too easy. The longer she processed the more I wondered if the Oracle ever got tired of looking through pointless shit too. Every single one of them had managed to avoid talking to someone for anything more than shoplifting or an armed robbery from back in the 20th century. And I should have known that, I should have known Nguyen would have checked something like that. Feeling stupid, I reached to close the window and end the search when a document caught my eye. I closed everything else and stared at the document with Ken's name on the paperwork from when the old man sold his store.

Stopping the search through criminal records, I sent the Oracle down a new wild goose chase. What if the great big connection wasn't criminal? I had her scour the real estate records and watched as several of the white-collar names appeared on deals made in and around the same part of the city. Not everyone lined up, I still didn't understand the tour guide, but enough dots started to connect that it felt like something for the first time since Marionette's imaginary friend used me as a frisbee. The white-collar guys all bought, sold, or brokered a deal in real estate in the same vicinity. More than that, they all did it around the same time – a time I was actually familiar with.

With an almost giddy awe I whispered to myself, "The war."

Practically jumping to my feet, I swiped to shut down the projection and walked out of the office with a new found purpose. Most people wouldn't have felt such an adrenaline rush from real estate deals, but this was like a dream come true. For years I'd had this theory that I couldn't prove. Now, someone had gotten sloppy enough to give me a lead.

Years ago, there'd been territory disputes between the big three Alter gangs. Two of those gangs, the Locusta and Jiangshi Tong, gained and lost territory in this almost perfect balance. Meanwhile, the Third Avenue Hunt basically got wiped off the map as their people scattered. The entire time I was convinced that the Locusta and Tong had to have something going on between them. Hell, I said so straight to the Locusta's boss once. But now I had something juicy: the real estate deals were all made in the Jiangshi Tong's old stomping grounds at the time they pulled out.

Dulaf caught sight of me on the way to the garage and hurried across the room to catch up. Walking alongside me, a hint of that same concerned tone in her voice, she asked, "Did you find something?"

I didn't worry about her tone this time – the rush of the lead was too good. Grinning, I answered, "The Tong sold a bunch of real estate a couple years ago. The guy Kate shot was involved."

"No," she said with a light gasp. "You don't mean…?"

"They closed the deals as everything was still going."

Dulaf's ears perked and her eyes darted about for a moment as the dots connected for her too. She bounced a few steps ahead to look me in the face and said with something akin to pride, "Oh my god, your stupid theory might be right."

Throwing my hands in the air, I refuted, "Clearly it wasn't that stupid!"

Mockingly, she took on an awful, whiny voice and leaned hard into a terrible impression. "Yoouu guuyyss, they're just ***pretending*** to try to kill each other with real bullets."

Finally stopping, I turned and pointed at her. "First," I said, doing my best to have a little bass in my voice, "I do not sound like that. Second, I might be about to prove they were cooperating."

Completely ignoring the finger, she pushed the hand aside and patted my cheek lightly as she said, "I know, and it's really great you finally hit puberty, but it was still a conspiracy theory."

I had to admit, annoying as it was, it was still good to see Dulaf back to normal. The tension and concern melted away long enough to torment me. It was a strange comfort, but it at least meant things were normal. Still, she could have let me have the win.

"But there might have been an actual conspiracy," I muttered.

Cooing like she was looking at a baby, she pinched my cheek and bounced back out of reach before I could react. She was definitely back to normal.

"So, are you going to try to push Rufus on it?" She asked, an ear and eyebrow raising together. "You know he'll probably deny everything."

It was true, Rufus Plagas would run me in circles if I tried to get anything out of him. But thankfully I didn't need to go to him for this. As much as everyone seemed to march to his beat, quite a few on the outside were more than ready to talk. Besides, if what was happening had to do with the Jiangshi Tong, might as well go to the source.

"Yeah, he wouldn't say anything," I said, idly rubbing my cheek. "I was figuring on hitting the Plaza."

She scratched her cheek and rocked on her heels for a moment before nodding along. "Yeah, okay, that makes sense."

I put on my visor and went on my way. She remained this time, lingering as I stepped into the elevator and turned to face her. Despite the different attitude, her aura still read like something was weighing on her mind. It wasn't strong, but there was a faint stain of color across those shimmering Elven hues. Still, there was a wry smile on her face. So I gave a quick wave and a bob of my head and tried to ignore that feeling again.

Cheerfully, she called out and waved back just as the elevator doors started to close, "Just don't let them stomp on you too much, okay?"

At least she was feeling well enough to get in one last jab.

Getting in the car, I took a minute to check if there'd been any progress on Lucian's hunt. I resisted the urge to actually open up Marionette's profile, but I checked his beacon to see if he was anywhere interesting. The locator had him in Marionette's apartment, likely scouring for evidence I was too tripped out to see. I wondered if the room shook for him the way it did for me. I figured he'd have experience, I was hoping he would, but I couldn't shake the idea I made a wrong move somewhere I wasn't seeing. Shaking it off, I started the car and drove out of the garage, making my way down into the International District and off to "Harmony Plaza".

The plaza started construction about the time Fangtown got its name. Ostensibly, it was another attempt to create a cultural exchange center like that little collection of buildings around the theater. However, unlike that center it had the idea to provide services beyond simply being a tourist trap. Constructed like a cross section of the Argyre arcology, it was practically a second International District inside a building with a distinctly Asian aesthetic. Inside you'd find everything from housing and stores to a garden that I imagined was a popular place to relax midday. At this time of night, long after the sun set, I could see the lights from a distance like welcoming rays of a sunrise on the horizon.

When the building first went up it was portrayed as an attempt to strengthen the ties between the local communities and prevent the spread of New Skids. The city council championed it as a place where all people could unite in harmony. It featured low-cost housing to help absorb the impact of a new population moving in. It gave space for new businesses to open and take advantage of the new 24-hour world. It held art festivals and holiday celebrations to show off the rich tapestry of international cultures.

And it was a massive front for the Jiangshi Tong.

The term "Tong" has been associated with a lot of organizations throughout history. They've been a source of support for Chinese communities from their very inception. So when the Jiangshi Tong quietly backed the Plaza's construction it was seen in the same light as those other societies. However, some of those societies once had ties to criminal enterprises in their earlier history, particularly the Triads. This wasn't really a problem for most Tongs in the modern day, but for the Jiangshi? Well let's just say the Immortal Triads and the Jiangshi Tong share some family ties. No one in the force was ever quite sure what to make of the Plaza. Maybe they really were considering going legit like their human colleagues. Then again, it was probably a bad sign they kept their names out of the construction as much as possible.

Luckily for me, as part of their community outreach, they provided space in the Plaza's basement levels for an ACTF substation. So it was incredibly unlikely they were going to start trouble on their doorstep. Unfortunately, they provided space in their basement for an ACTF substation – so they also understood the virtues of plausible deniability. Still, they weren't likely to start shooting.

That substation was eerily quiet as I drove up to their relatively modest parking garage. There were enough spaces for about a dozen vehicles and nothing else with a single space reserved for an extra patrol car in case someone like me came knocking. I could even see a living, breathing curate sitting behind a Vesperadin reinforced sheet of glass instead of the usual holographic receptionist or Oracle checkpoint. Slouched over, reading from a tablet, I could recognize the posture of a man who hadn't seen another soul in hours.

Walking up to introduce myself, looking for signs of a palm scanner to no avail, I greeted the curate, "Agent Leone from headquarters, here to ask the Tong a few questions."

An eyebrow rose and the curate quickly sat at attention. A raspy, gravelly voice came through speakers that seemed to surround me as he said, "I hope you're kidding."

"Why?"

He leaned forward towards the glass, as though it made a difference. "I know you're patrol, so you're used to going it alone," he whispered into the microphone, "but we aren't exactly staffed for a raid here. We're just here to provide security for the stores and apartments and hold people until someone else can take them off our hands."

I looked back at the relatively empty structure and the couple of vehicles parked inside. Turning back to him, I asked, "Exactly how many do you have here?"

Face faulting, he stopped whispering and said flatly, "Three."

Okay, so maybe they would start shooting on their doorstep.

Nodding along, I made sure to attach the strap to my shades and put them on, tightening it a bit to make sure the visor was secure. Running my finger across the wrist band of my glove, I activated the silver plates on my gear. The curate's aura turned anxious with flashes of red and orange as he sat back from me. Reassuringly, I smiled and said, "don't worry, not planning to start anything."

Turning to walk away, I waved over my shoulder. "Just be ready to call a SOL team if things get ugly."

I didn't get a response out of him, didn't look back to see if he acknowledged it, but I was genuine in what I said. I wasn't going in to start a fight but I wasn't about to walk in unprepared. The last time I walked into a front I ended up having a shootout in a lingerie shop. Going in without my gear ready was practically suicide. Still, I waited until I was in the elevator and long out of sight before I pulled the Helios and made sure it was on crowd control. I didn't want to give the poor guy a heart attack.

As the elevator rose through the building and entered a glass shaft, the garden at the heart of the plaza was revealed to me. Even at this hour, the flower blossoms closed for the night, I could see the beauty of it under the perpetual glow I'd come so accustomed to. It was serene and beautiful, the outlines of carefully crafted trees cutting through the soft lights and the faint lavender glow. With every floor I could see more of it unfold, like it'd been created specifically for that one elevator, a small show of peace.

Basically, it felt like a trap.

As the doors opened on the top floor, the hallway beyond was filled with similarly soothing music and exotic, inviting scents. The walls were covered in a variety of art from every corner of Asia that would have taken a human lifetime and a small fortune to collect. Old woodblock prints from Japan, intricate Chinese ink wash paintings, and dazzling tapestries from the Middle East all hung between a series of doors. The accompanying music was a calm tune blending classical styles from all across the world. Soft strings and woodwinds played in a pleasing pentatonic scale. Of course, knowing that Alter music could slip in subliminal cues, it reminded me to put my earplugs back in.

Entering the hallway, I watched a pair step into sight at the far end. On the left stood a petite Asian woman in a modest dress with a red tint to her hair and an aura suppressed much like Marionette's. She was hard to place, understandably, but I'd had a few theories in mind almost immediately. The vibe I was getting, now that I knew what Marionette was, said she was at least related to Witches. Meanwhile, I kept getting the distinct impression that her skirt, otherwise unassuming, was moving subtly as she stood there. I couldn't see it, but I had a hunch there was a fox tail gently swaying out of sight.

On the right, a behemoth of a man with bronze skin and a literal bird face towered over her. It would've seemed unreal, like a mask, but I could see the texture of his blazing red feathers and the unmistakable movement of the beak. If it hadn't been for those features, I might've just assumed a giant with his towering frame and a body that seemed carved from stone. While I had to guess at what she was, he was clearly a Garuda.

Garuda were a rare sight in this part of the world, but they left a great impression on Southeast Asia. Either named for or inspiring a legendary figure, depending on who you asked, stories of their strength mirrored the mythology itself. In Alter circles, they were the guardians of powerful figures, said to be able to face down almost anything else. Just watching him stand there evoked memories of Patch and the things he could do.

Big man was not to be fucked with.

Keeping watch on him through the visor, I slowed to a stop at what I hoped was out of arm's reach. The woman I suspected to be a Kitsune stepped forward and bowed lightly, keeping her eyes fixed on me as she did. The Garuda, still looming over the two of us, crossed his arms but otherwise remained perfectly unmoved - watching us with an intense glare as his associate approached me.

"We welcome you to Harmony Plaza," she said. "How is it we can help the ACTF tonight?"

Resisting the urge to bow back, I nodded instead and answered, "I'm Agent Leone, I have a few questions regarding some land deals a few years ago."

She stood straight again and I heard a light swish behind her. A faint frown crossed her lips that passed quickly into a broad smile. Brightly, she asked, "So the ACTF investigates real estate deals now?"

If she was a Kitsune, it was a bad idea to give her an in. They were tricksters, using parapsychic talents to push illusions and alter behaviors to the point most never even noticed the tail unless allowed. Normally I wouldn't have been as concerned about being manipulated, but I'd apparently been getting hit hard for a while. And, thinking back on the dragon's blood in Marionette's place, I had to wonder what the current scents might be covering for the fox. Given my night, I had to consider the big man wasn't really the muscle between them.

Cautiously, I said, "The properties in question showed up during an ongoing investigation."

"Given how extensive our holdings are, you would find such coincidences are quite common," she said tightly. "However, I'm afraid I wouldn't be able to give you any specifics. Perhaps you could make an appointment?"

Her aura lit up momentarily, a dazzling flash of colors like she just ignited in front of me. There wasn't a specific pattern to them, no single emotion to be seen. I felt a slight twinge of wanting to leave, something closer to giving up than fear, but quickly managed to push it aside. Whatever she was trying, she was either new or I was less easily manipulated than believed.

Standing firm, I asked, "So who *would* I ask about a couple deals on the west side?"

The Kitsune's pleasant demeanor cracked, however briefly, to express a little frustration at my question. Again, a flurry of colors radiated from her and I felt the desire to just walk out and leave them be. Again, I pushed it aside. Marionette might have had me walk out without a question, but this girl was trying her best to no avail.

Shooting a look to the Garuda, the Kitsune stepped back and let her giant friend move in. I took a step back and let a hand drift down near the Helios, but didn't grip at it. I couldn't remember if his people were allergic to anything in those bolts, but I knew that if he was resistant there weren't many options besides fatal. Even if the look in his eyes and the slowly building red in his aura told me he wanted to fold me like a pretzel, I wasn't quite ready to do that yet. Instead, I let the other hand drop and started to grip at the Will-O-Wisp rod at the other hip. I wasn't quite willing to shoot him, but blinding him definitely felt like an option.

"That's enough," a woman's voice called out, immediately snapping the other two to attention.

I took a couple steps back to make sure I was out of arm's reach again before I looked for the source. Catching sight of her beyond the other two, I was momentarily stunned by the person who demanded their respect. A slightly pale Asian woman with raven black hair in a silk dress walked up behind them with notable grace. The visor's readings reflected something similar to a Vampire, so likely a Jiangshi, but I was getting more than that out of the way she walked. Her features suggested someone in my age range, even if anyone here could have been timeless, but if she was a Jiangshi those elegant movements took a lifetime of training.

The "Chinese hopping vampire" of lore, Jiangshi have always been known for agility but not particularly grace. Like the western Vampires, their bodies were always trying to proactively repair themselves. But the slight chemical changes between the two means the Jiangshi have a spring-like tension behind every movement. The young tend to hop to control this tension. But this woman, gently swinging while lightly stepping past her enforcers, showed zero sign of the power she was suppressing. She was at least a century old, and probably a lot more than that.

The Kitsune bowed to her as she passed. "Lady Zhang."

And then I knew all my guesses were right. Zhang is one of the most common surnames in the world, but I'd familiarized myself with all the heads after a couple encounters with the likes of Dante of the Locusta. Not only was she a Jiangshi, she was ***the*** Jiangshi in this part of the world. Shih Zhang was the daughter of the previous head of the local Tong and the boss since the very conflict I was suddenly investigating. Her name sounded like a play on words in the traditional order, but rumor was she'd been named after an old rival of her father from the early 19th century – the pirate queen Ching Shih. Legend was he was hoping his daughter would strike fear into others the way his rival had long ago.

She definitely looked like trouble from where I was standing.

However, despite her imposing presence, she greeted me warmly. "We welcome the ACTF and are more than happy to help."

The other two looked dumbfounded but did nothing to voice their dissent. The Garuda, powerful as he might have been, gave Zhang a wide berth like an apex predator just walked through. The Kitsune, still trying her best not to break her calm façade, mirrored her master's posture and stood in formation with her. Giving them a once over, I released the grip from the Wisp and returned the gesture with a bow of my own. I'm not sure if that was the proper etiquette or not, I just knew the woman in front of me was in charge.

Zhang turned and started walking back the way she came, nodding back to me as she did. "Please, walk with me."

I followed her, once again impressed with how well she was moving for a Jiangshi. Honestly, the thought occurred to me that's why she wanted me to walk with her. On the one hand, it was a disarming move, on the other, it was also a total power move for a Jiangshi.

Slipping past her guards, giving them both a parting glance before passing through the next door, I asked again, "Would it be possible to get information on a real estate deal carried out around Pioneer Square?"

Zhang led me through a luxurious apartment with the flair of old-world tradition meeting new age comforts. Antiques as old as anything in the hallway decorated the corners of what I assumed was her home. I assumed they belonged to her father, a man who was thought to have been around 1400 years old, but some had an aesthetic that felt more like what I saw in the print along her dress. Regardless, I made mental note not to get in trouble in a room where anything that broke was likely worth more than a year's salary. Thankfully, as that idea started to creep into my head, she walked out onto an open-air walkway wrapped around the building with a view of the city skyline in the distance. If she decided to hurl me over the rails, I wouldn't be around to pay for anything.

She stopped to look over the rail for a moment, like she heard my thoughts, then smiled my way and started walking again. "We haven't had many holdings in Pioneer Square for some time – not since resolving a few disputes."

Keeping a few steps behind her, I said matter-of-factly, "Gang wars."

A brief, quiet laugh escaped her before she said, "Tongs across the country are community organizers and legitimate political organizations, we do not take part in gang wars anymore."

"Human Tongs," I remarked. "The Jiangshi Tong have been tied to the Immortal Triads since the start."

Surprisingly, she nodded in agreement, saying, "Under my father, that was true. He was dedicated to the old ways and protecting our community through any means necessary."

"But not you?" I asked sarcastically.

There was a momentary hitch in her step, a subtle lowering of her guard, and she turned to face me. Part of me was getting ready to dodge, watching her hands to make sure she couldn't grab at me. But after a moment she exhaled sharply through her nose and smiled again.

"My father," she started, halting herself and lowering her eyes to the floor. For a moment she stared down, visibly reconsidering her words before continuing fondly, "It is hard to let go of the past when you're over a thousand years old."

I'd known a few immortals. It was true they could be a bit stubborn. Thinking on my own, I empathized. "Yeah, I guess it would be."

Gathering herself, she started walking again and continued, "I'm not young by human standards, but I've lived most of my life in modern society. I saw the opportunities in going legitimate."

Hearing the heavy footsteps behind us, I looked back at the towering man following at a distance. Adjusting my glove, I asked, "So then what's with the muscle?"

In a vaguely mocking tone she answered, "What legitimate organization doesn't have security? They were my companions and guardians long before I took my father's place."

Peeking back at them, I mused, "Diverse bunch."

"I have traveled quite a bit and have lived throughout much of Asia," she said. "You can find the Garuda anywhere Hinduism or Buddhism spread and the foxes can be found throughout East Asia."

I considered for a moment she might have been telling the truth. The Tongs were ostensibly formed to help immigrants from the start. Today, that's exactly what most of them do. It wasn't unusual for wealthy or influential people to have personal guard. What if the Jiangshi learned from their human colleagues after all?

"All right," I said, "then you wouldn't mind telling me what happened in Pioneer Square."

Nodding along, she replied coolly, "We were offered a deal that worked for everyone. The Triads were pressuring us to retreat to 'secure assets' while the Locusta were intent on controlling the Undercity."

"So you sold everything to the Locusta?"

Shaking her head, she stopped and leaned on the rail, looking off in the direction of Fangtown. "Not directly," she said, "but I have little doubt that's who eventually took ownership."

I'd figured that much myself, but something nagged me about the idea. Keeping my distance from that rail and a couple more steps back for good measure, I asked, "But you initiated those deals?"

Studying me with a hint of Elf-like mischief in her eyes, she seemed amused with me as she turned and corrected, "No, we were approached by a third party - a business attorney facilitating a series of deals to divest the Third Avenue Hunt from the area. He was a Gangsi, a Korean Jiangshi, so my father was almost receptive to the idea. I sealed the deal when I took control."

A small part of me screamed in a dark corner of my mind and I idly flexed my hand as my arm started to ache. Hesitantly, I asked, "Who?"

Eyes shifting a bit, face in deep concentration, she muttered, "Ah, what was it?"

Watching her anxiously, I had a bad feeling I knew what she was about to say. And then, again like she could hear my thoughts, her eyes lit up like it popped right into her head on cue.

"Ah, yes, that's right," she said. "It was Cho, Daniel Cho."

Chapter 9
Retro Hallways

Hearing Danny's name again after all this time was an unwelcome surprise. Honestly, though, it shouldn't have been. An attorney for former Hunt members who helped them go legit and stay that way? A man who'd been working for the same employer as Marionette? A man murdered by someone working as a hitwoman for the Locusta!

On the one hand, it all made perfect sense. On the other hand, the one attached to my aching arm, I hated the idea that he wasn't just some innocent bystander after all. I had to know what happened in the Undercity. I had to know if that was the reason he died.

Driving across town again, I ran a mental checklist of reasons I could imagine for wanting the subterranean levels of Fangtown. It was a good place for operating out of public view - that was obvious. But you didn't need the entire space for that. It had a maze of passages that weaved inland from the shoreline, so it could be useful for smuggling. But, no, they already had a sophisticated operation for that to begin with. It couldn't have been as simple as just wanting the competition out because the Tong were getting their orders through the same game of telephone the Locusta were.

Whatever it was, I knew it had to be worth eliminating all the witnesses.

The Undercity was something of an open secret. People who were comfortable with the idea of Fangtown expanding beyond its relatively small space found the old Seattle underground converted into a newly thriving neighborhood. Meanwhile, for people who liked to ignore Fangtown existed, it was easy to pretend these subterranean levels remained old ruins of a bygone era. Either way, the space was perfect.

The Alters had completely renovated what was once broken-down relics of the past. Historical sites, once part of tours, had now been restored to their old glory and given new life. The condemned parts of the underground, long deemed too dangerous for regular visits, were now rebuilt, reinforced, and expanded. Though the permits were all cleared and the construction was overseen by Argyre's engineers, it was never really known just how far those tunnels now spread. More than a few had gotten lost in the years since that expansion. It was a good place for your secrets.

Parking outside one of dozens of entrances, I did another equipment check. My shades were secured, rods were prepped, and the Helios charged and fueled. Adjusting the cuff of my glove, I flipped the silver plates of my gear on and off to make sure they were working but didn't leave them active. Down in the Undercity, there was always a chance of a narrow passage filled to the brim. I didn't want to burn anyone that didn't deserve it.

It was during that equipment check that I noticed something in my rear view. A towering figure in a hooded coat stepped out of a van parked about a block behind me, the outline of a shorter driver lit up by passing car lights. Though the hood was doing surprisingly well to hide his face, I could recognize the sheer mass of Zhang's Garuda.

The "legitimate organization" had me followed.

Pretending I didn't notice them, I stepped out and walked towards a covered stairwell with a sign reading "Paradise Pass". The structure over the stairs was made of a frosted glass with a faint blue hue and a fancy frame mimicking wrought iron. I knew it couldn't actually be iron because more than a few Alters would have complained. Likely it was some sort of composite that could stand up to the likes of a drunk Minotaur or the eagle currently trying to make himself look smaller in my wake. Either way, it did its job: it was pretty, functional, and that glass probably filtered UV light.

Despite being a place that couldn't have witnesses, I found the area involved in the real estate deals to be pretty active. Thumping dance music echoed from down a long tunnel out of what seemed to be a club at the far end. Shops lined the walls on either side, from a new age apothecary to a small hole in the wall selling a variety of meats on a stick. A wide variety of humans and Alters wandered the passage between them all, several looking a little unsteady with a faint yellow aura on the visor. More than a few of them caught sight of me and quickly turned away.

"Oh great," a rough voice complained from below, "just what we need around here."

I looked down to see a relatively young Satyr sitting on the bottom steps, giving me a dirty look with a jug in one hand and corkscrew in the other. He wore a small jacket with visibility patches and strips stuck to it, the logo of a tour company across his back. A pair of hoof-like shoes sat on the step next to him, an empty wine cup sat in his lap.

He started to put away the cup and the corkscrew, muttering under his breath, "trying to relax."

I waved and kept walking down the steps. "Not starting anything if I can help it."

Continuing on my way, I soon realized the opportunity that presented itself. Looking back, I nodded to him and asked, "Is your tour local?"

Hesitating as he was pulling out the corkscrew again, he stared for a moment before answering, "Yeah, what of it?"

"Anything down here the Locusta wouldn't want me to know about?"

Annoyed, he snapped back, "Why would I take the risk of telling you?"

He had a point. He really had all the leverage at the moment. Even though he was about to be publicly intoxicated, the ACTF policy on that was effectively: "not our problem until you break stuff". Unfortunately, that meant that there was nothing I could really offer him within reason. Would the truth be enough?

Then it struck me: he was a tour guide.

Crouching while facing him to get eye-to-eye, I pulled my shades off and folded them up. I reached into one of the pouches on my belt and pulled out the hand-link, bringing up the profile of the guide I saw in my last search. He wasn't very old, probably fresh out of college, and I was willing to bet the Satyr worked here around the same time. Showing it to him, I asked, "You know him?"

He hesitated, an annoyed scowl on his face, before finally relenting and looking up. His expression soon softened dramatically and he lowered the jug to the floor.

"Yeah, that was John," he said in a distant, concerned tone, "worked with him a couple years. He showed me the old historic sites around here."

I nodded and returned the link to my pouch. "For some reason, someone killed him and I think it has to do with this area of the Undercity."

His face sank with a great weight behind his expression. One of the deepest, saddest frowns I'd seen crossed with a look of genuine fear in his eyes. It was one of those expressions that didn't require a visor's help to fully decipher. It wasn't just remorse for a fallen friend, but a realization they walked the same passages. For all he knew, it could have been him.

"There's," he stammered, "there's secret doors all over the place. A lot of these shops were built into old access tunnels or in gaps between the old buildings. I don't know what's in them, but they're everywhere. Though, I heard something once…"

As he spoke, a great shadow appeared at the top of the stairs. The looming figure of the Garuda towered at the entrance, backlit so the hood prevented his features from shining through.

Standing up and stepping back, I whispered to the Satyr, "Tell me to fuck off."

He stared at me, puzzled, before hearing the heavy footsteps up the stairs. Understanding dawned across his face as he piped up, "Fuck off, shuck."

I had to admit, I wasn't prepared to be called "shuck". It wasn't exactly common parlance, an old Alter term for vampire hunters based on a legendary black dog. I thought no one used it anymore, it was only now I was realizing no one used it in front of ***me***. And he put such bass into it too – like he'd been wanting to say it to an agent's face for years. The look on his face as he realized I was caught off guard was kind of funny though.

"Wow," I said, putting my visor back on and starting to back away, "have a nice night, I guess."

As the Garuda and Kitsune came closer, it grew harder to focus on their shadows. They weren't making a major effort to stay out of sight, but she was doing her best to push away our attentions. The Kitsune technique was similar to a Witch or a Succubi: a mix of chemicals and hypnotic suggestions, little motions and whispers pushing you while they put out a drug that made you very receptive to what they were saying. The fact I was starting to lose some focus meant she was putting her all into it and they were getting close enough for it to work. But still, it wasn't quite enough to hit me with as much force as she hoped. I kept walking anyway, looking back only to see the Satyr go blank as they passed.

I muttered and shook my head to keep up the act of being annoyed by the "shuck" comment and walked straight down the passage. He'd given me a start, but I couldn't risk anyone knowing that. Scanning around, I peered through shop doors as I passed, doing my best to look nonchalant to anyone inside. With secret rooms behind some of the shops it was safe to just start looking for secret doors and chemical marks. With luck, they might've been like the ones in New Skids.

Although the marks used by criminals in some of the seedier parts of town were visible to the visors, they were still well concealed to anyone else. Human senses could never pick them up, even some Alters weren't quite able. Finding one usually required the right friends or a good tip. Fortunately, the Satyr turned out to be just that.

Shining softly near the ceilings, I could make out faint signs written in Elvish script in a handful of shops. My Faelish, however, was a little rusty. So often I'd seen the script used to spell modern languages, I'd let my understanding of their actual language lapse. I knew the hand-link could manage it, but I couldn't risk taking it out. The visor, great as it was, also lacked the functionality to translate for me.

Hesitating in front of a shop selling crystals, I wondered if a black market was worth a coverup. This wasn't just a few witnesses gone, and they seemed more than happy to let regular people wander through the place. It lacked security and it lacked secrecy. They were, despite the invisible signs and hidden doors, very much exposed to the outside world. Pulsing beats from the club at the end pulled my attention away from the sparkly little shop and towards the dark, smoky room full of strobing lights and a herd of people.

Maybe being in plain sight was part of the point.

I tightened my gloves and made sure everything on my belt was secured. Most of the gear required system approval to be armed and fired, but I still didn't want to risk someone grabbing anything in a crowded room. It wasn't so much they could be dangerous, not with the Oracle watching, but I didn't want to have to fill out the paperwork for "someone swiped my particle gun." Finishing my quick once-over, I crossed the threshold into the dark space and into the path of a Minotaur just around the corner.

It was actually surprising to see him there, down in a maze of tunnels, emerging from the shadows only slightly lit by a recessed light overhead. The position of the light made his already unique features ever stronger, horns creating an impressive outline, jaw square enough to use as a level. Most Minotaurs didn't actually look like cows, like most Garuda didn't usually look like actual eagles, instead more like the archetypal demons. But it didn't much matter when one was looking down on you.

Turning to face him, I adjusted my shades and looked up at him with that long-trained expression of authority. No words were exchanged, just a long stare down as we sized each other up. He was wondering how much shit he'd be in for letting me pass. I was wondering how much shit I'd be in if he decided not to. It was funny, really, trying to stare down someone nearly twice my size with literal horns on his head. Like the Garuda following me, this guy was probably well out of my weight class. Still, Lucian taught me long ago never to let someone know that.

Letting out a loud snort and reaching over, he pushed the door open for me and waved me in. I don't know if he thought I was harmless or too much trouble for his time, but it didn't much matter. Nodding to him, I took the offer and entered a room smelling like a blend of every kind of cologne, perfume, and liquor you could imagine pressed into what had to be the hottest room in the Undercity.

Under the strobing lights, few people stood out for long. The visor started to adjust, lightening up the shadows and dimming the bright lights, but they were still mostly a blur on the dance floor. It was an eclectic mix of people at least, humans and Alters alike packed like sardines and rubbing together in ways that at least a couple of my friends would approve. As for me, it was a reminder I needed to get out more because I was well outside my element.

Aside from the usual scents, I could pick up various Alter musks in the mix and the visor was more than aware of pheromones drifting over the crowd. The music also had that underlying subliminal beat I'd learned from the basement level of the Moirae. I closed my eyes for a moment, letting myself feel the music I couldn't quite hear. I had to admit, letting it flow through me, it took me back to that first time someone showed me how to do it. In that brief moment, memories of a gentle face under neon lights came to me and I felt some of my tension lift.

Once again, I was reminded to put my earplugs back in.

Rolling my shoulder and opening my eyes again, I walked around the edge of the room and got back to work scanning for hidden doors. Understandably, this place had done better to conceal something like that. The walls were actually covered in glowing murals like the kind found on the Fangtown streets. If there were hidden markings, they blended well into the design. Meanwhile, constantly strobing lights made it hard to focus on anything at a distance. If I was going to find something, I'd have to stare at the wall a few feet at a time and hope for the best.

So, I stood to face the wall, staring at it for a few moments to search for something out of place. Then, I moved a few steps further down the wall and did it again. This, of course, meant looking like the greatest wallflower to have ever grown. As I came closer to the bar itself, the look on the Succubus' bartender's face let me know two important details. First, I was weirding her out. Second, that probably meant she had no idea what I was looking for.

"Uh, what can I get you?" she uttered, eyebrow raised, doing her best to radiate pheromones to chill me out.

Turning to take in the rest of the room, I tried to think of a sane reason to stare at the walls without tipping my hand. It was harder than you'd imagine. "Well," I started, trailing off while waiting for my thoughts to catch up. Turning back to face her, seeing a growing smirk, I went with the only thing that came to mind.

"I was checking the walls for chemical traces."

Laughing, she waved. "Good luck telling the difference. But were you looking for anything in particular?"

Thing about Succubi is that the effect they give off when they're trying to manipulate you isn't quite like the push you'd get from a Kitsune or Witch. In my dealings with Trey and other Incubi they never took the time to try to manipulate me. But, given her profession, I figured she was used to turning on the charm for tips. Gradually, an already beautiful face started to seem unreal and the rest of the room started to seem more distant.

Biting the inside of my cheek, I looked away and tried to think of an answer for her. The sudden pain helped bring the room back into focus but also did nothing to actually help me think. Worse, as I stared out over the room, I was starting to see more alluring figures in the mix. Scanning the crowd and taking in just how many Succubi were actually in attendance, I caught sight of something I didn't expect.

Weaving through the festivities with remarkable ease, Marionette made her way across the club. She hadn't seen me, I don't think, but I wasn't sure she was all that concerned either. Her aura was brighter than anything I'd seen from her and radiating like a rainbow-colored fire that flowed off of her. The way she was moving, the way others were moving around her, had that familiar detached feeling like they were hardly even aware of each other. Then, as a dancing woman bumped into her, she pivoted and stepped around the woman with calm and finesse. The dancing woman didn't miss a step, didn't pull away, and didn't even look back.

I think I was the only one that could actually see her.

I lifted my shades and peeked, seeing if it was just the visor's work. She was still there, staring ahead with great focus, weaving past the dancing masses. I couldn't believe it. The bartender faded from my attention as I started walking towards the dance floor, stopping at a rail separating it from the rest of the club. Gripping at the rail, practically wringing it, I watched her make her way for a stage up front.

What was I supposed to do? Lucian and Dulaf were adamant I shouldn't chase her. But right here, right now, I could actually see her. A dozen possible routes raced through my thoughts. I could call Lucian, Dulaf, put in a call for a SOL team, maybe even ask the Minotaur for backup. Maybe the Succubus would be immune if I asked her. But then she could try to push everyone else and this was the one time I was finally able to see her plain as day.

Before I knew it, I'd vaulted over the rail and onto the dance floor.

Chapter 10
Angry Yardbirds

The bartender yelled for me to stop but could do little to stop me. Others turned to the voice, scattering as I landed and started my march through the crowd. People didn't seem to notice Marionette, but they were definitely noticing me, several practically leaping out of my path as the badge caught their sight. Hearing the commotion, Marionette broke her focus on the stage and glanced back into the mirrored surface of my visor. For a brief flash, under those strobing lights, I saw a hint of panic on her face.

Picking up her speed and actually pushing people out of the way now, she fled for the stage as fast as she could. I gave chase, forced to weave more as people filled the space again like water in her wake. The way they moved was almost like she was pushing the crowd closed behind her, putting them shoulder to shoulder where there used to be at least a few inches to move. I had to do my best to shuffle around them, getting slowed by the wall of humanity quickly forming between us. Clearing a couple of taller people, I looked up to see the back of her head as she climbed onto the stage, passed the DJ, and disappeared into the back.

Frustrated, I actually shoved a man aside as I broke off into the best run I could manage. Colliding with several along the way, I quickly cleared the crowd and rushed the stage. But, before I could climb up, a couple beefy security guards stepped in my path – ironically not Minotaurs like their friend out front. To my left stood a Viking-looking dude I quickly realized was a Werewolf, to my right a mountain of muscle who seemed to be human but had an aura so yellow I was confident none of it was natural. Either he was a school bus or had taken enough drugs to make up for it.

I tried my best to explain myself, but even I couldn't quite hear my voice over the sound of the music blasting from the speakers just behind them. The DJ, oblivious to the woman that just sprinted across his stage, continued on and seemed more interested in the little dance I was having with security. Flipping my silvers on quickly warded off the Werewolf as the Bus moved in on me. Sprinting through the momentary gap, I dove onto the stage and scrambled to my feet before meaty mitts could grab at my ankle. The DJ, to his credit, was still undeterred as me and at least 500 pounds of guard rushed past him.

Backstage, I found a tiny room full of equipment for a live band and a couple doors. Giving them a quick once over, feeling the floor at my feet shake from the dudes about to barge in, I considered which one Marionette went through. Moving to the one on the left, I stopped as I caught sight of a sliver of light that would've been too dim without the visor. A third door in the room, against the back wall, was revealed to me by the slightest crack. Looking up, I could see a black-market sign – a Faelish word for "welcome" painted like the other marks.

Studying the door directly ahead of me, lacking a knob and having a push plate like so many Alter establishments, I kicked it open to give it a good swing before reaching for the crack of light. Feeling around quickly, I found a small gap in the wall just about the size of a handle. Pulling the hidden door open, I ducked inside and closed it behind me just as the sound of the two large men thundered into the room and rolled right for the left-hand door.

Making haste to get a lead on them, just in case they knew about the third door, I started walking down the new hallway beyond. A green door with frosted glass panes sat at the far end, stylized script across the wood frame marking it as "The Gilded Cage". Like the door I kicked earlier, it lacked a knob and had only a simple push plate. Nudging it open slowly, finally drawing my Helios, I edged cautiously into the shop. As a bell rang overhead, I slowed at the amazing sight revealed to me.

Constructed with what seemed to be wood panels and a sturdy wood frame, The Gilded Cage had a strange old-world charm to it. It was an odd contrast to the club behind us, but the spectacular part was what it stored inside. Along every wall, up on shelves, stands, and hanging from the ceiling were various cages made of iron, silver, and one that looked to be carved straight out of a block of jade. Inside the cages, hundreds of eyes stared at me from the shadows. Though dimly lit in some spaces, I could see the outlines of creatures I was sure didn't exist anymore, and colors that required me to lift my visor for a moment to confirm it wasn't a glitch on the auras.

The shopkeeper, short in stature but with a remarkably large head and wild, unkempt grey hair, peeked just over the counter. His pale, weathered features and craggy skin gave me the rough idea he might have been a Spriggan – a relative of the Gnome-kin that was rare in this part of the world. A wry smile crossed his face as he nodded to me.

"Don't have many of your kind here," he said. "But I'm sure we can find you something worth your time."

Lowering my gun, I searched the room for any sign of Marionette. I approached the counter, continuing to search, before peering over at a cage to his side as it came into view. A brilliant red bird with a golden sheen perched nearby, the colors shifting and practically dancing like flames across its feathers at different angles. If I wasn't sure about the legality of the rest of the creatures in the room, that bird showed me just how deep into the black market I'd stumbled.

"Is that a phoenix?" I asked.

He chuckled and patted the cage. "That it is. But don't think of burning it – that part is just a myth."

Spriggan customs were notoriously shady throughout history. Like Goblins, who they often lived closely with, many of them had a worldview that was "objectivist" at their best and "anarchist" at their worst by modern standards. To put it loosely:

they weren't fans of being told what to do. Finding one in a black market was not much of a surprise. Finding one with a phoenix ***definitely*** was.

Grimacing as I realized I had more important things to worry about, I asked, "Did anyone else come through here? Do you have a back door?"

"Oh, yes," he said brightly and gestured to an open archway, "Another customer went into the back to look at the pixies."

I was frozen midstride by his words. Turning back to him, I echoed, "Pixies?"

"A very fine selection," he beamed, "one of the best in the world, in fact."

Homo alatus minimus, the "tiny winged man" or common pixie, is one of the few Alters not to be legally classified as human. Descended from Homo floresiensis instead of Homo sapiens, they long ago evolved to be only a couple inches tall with wings, intelligence comparable to a raven, and a severe contempt for the technology that formed modern civilization. Spriggans had long been known as the "guardians of the fairies" in folklore. In truth, they were the "jailers" of the fairies – a practice made very illegal at the founding of Argyre.

Reacting to my concern, he chided, "Oh come now, they're tiny giggling bird monkeys that sit on your shoulder and eat berries. How are they different than any other creature in this room?"

Going over the list of reasons this guy was going to jail, I almost didn't hear the metallic click of several iron latches being opened. Hearing the rising giggle in the next room, like the sound of river otters going for the kill, I felt chill run through me.

"Oh shit."

Fun fact: pixies are incredibly sensitive to the electromagnetic spectrum. It's the reason iron messes them up. It's also the reason why they seem to hold a grudge against electronics – especially anything transmitting a signal. That's why they came out of the wood work during the World Wars under names like "gremlins" and "foo fighters".

Another "fun" fact: every ACTF agent is carrying at least four wireless devices at any given time and, due to limited space, usually keep anti-pixie gear in the trunk of their cars.

Running from the shop repeatedly screaming "fairies" isn't one of my proudest moments.

Clearing the green door and sprinting down the hallway, I heard the glass panes shatter as the giggling swarm charged through. The beating of their wings and high-pitched laughter tempted me to look back but also told me it was a bad idea to slow down. They were coming for my equipment and I was sure they weren't above taking pieces out of me to find it. Instead, I turned my shoulder into the door ahead of me and charged through with all my might, swinging it open right into the face of security. As one fell to the floor and the other staggered back, their swearing and demands for attention were soon replaced by panicked gasps and the sound of a body builder doing his best to roll away from the swarm.

Into the strobing lights and pounding music I burst onto the stage and practically dove from it into the crowd. The closest people gave way this time, but only for few inches and only so I wouldn't land on them. Everyone's attitude soon changed as the flurry of colors erupted from the back and scattered across the room. Lights, speakers, turntables, and anyone unfortunate enough to be close to one soon became targets as the pixies were unleashed on the club. The music finally stopped, replaced by high-pitched squeals as tiny people discovered the switches. Finally looking back, I saw the Werewolf guard now being tormented by a dozen before tumbling from the stage while the nearby DJ helplessly flailed at the tiny terrors.

I didn't have time to appreciate my luck, however. The room was full of wireless devices of every kind you could imagine and the pixies quickly decided to tear into everyone else. Part of me considered leaving the room and going to get my gear, but another part realized I couldn't let the mess go unchecked. Pulling a rod from my belt, I adjusted a Will-O-Wisp and held it over my head like a torch. Triggering it, I sent out an EM field so strong that the lights flickered. Dozens, maybe even hundreds, of tiny faces turned to me and the blinding flare over my head.

The Wisp had two advantages. First, the field was so strong it easily outweighed anything else in range. Second, it would short out anything close enough to get someone else hurt. Effectively, I went from one of hundreds of targets to the only one worthwhile, and they all homed in on that like the world's most cheerful missiles.

Turning and sprinting for the exit, I carried the Wisp upright for only a few seconds before opening the front of my jacket and stuffing it inside. The double-breasted coat would keep the rod snug against me and protect everyone from potential UV flares. Meanwhile, my equipment was probably the only technology actually hardened against the EMP it was churning out – a theory confirmed as I exited the club into a tunnel of flickering lights and lost signals. The crowd outside, confused by the lights, stood around blankly until the rush of giggles alerted all of them to get the hell out of the way. Parting like the red sea, a completely clear path presented itself and I ran for all I was worth to the stairs.

No matter how much speed I might have had, the pixies had me on the straight away and there was no getting past that. Halfway down the tunnel I was getting grabbed at by dozens of angry, giggling bird monkeys who quickly started to dig into whatever they could find. Like the Nosferatu, their wings stemmed from the wrist, leaving little clawed fingers to grab hold of whatever they could. It wasn't long before they yanked my visor off and started going for my eyes. Though they all hurt on some level, I couldn't help but focus on the one that gripped at my eyelid and held on for dear life while repeatedly kicking me in the face.

I swear I have never backhanded someone that small before, and I felt bad for a moment, but I'd do it again.

My Satyr friend saw me coming from a good distance and sprang up the stairs like the surefooted mountain goat he resembled. I chased him up the stairs, taking the steps two at a time just as he did, using the rail to make up for my clumsy human feet. With tears, feathers, and some pixie spit in my eyes, I could barely make out the fuzzy form of the Satyr reaching the top and bolting to the right down the street.

In the couple bounds I had left, I tried to remember which direction I parked the car and realized, if the Satyr knew anything, he ran the opposite direction of my car. Turning left, I stumbled and nearly ate the pavement, catching myself and looking up at the welcoming white and black blob that I hoped was the hearse.

I screamed "riot control" at the car while running past it, feeling the car's siren scream rolling through me as it scattered the pixies like a water hose blasting ants away. The trunk took an eternity to open as they started to regroup, now angry at the car as well as me. But before they could get back on top of us, I pulled a metallic frisbee from the trunk and whipped it into the middle of the swarm.

The Roswell anti-pixie disk whirred to life as it passed through the center. Pixie eyes turned and dilated as the sparkly disk flew by and broadcast a strong EM field. Losing all interest in me or the car, they turned on the interloper among them and tried to take the disk out of the air. The trap sprang as they closed in, a cocktail of herbal extracts blasted on them as it unleashed the pixie equivalent of mace into their faces. Tiny screams pierced the night as the whole flock fell from the air and writhed around on the sidewalk chittering and squealing. Reaching into the trunk again, I pulled out a handheld version of the mace in case they rose again. Met with the view of them rolling around as my vision cleared, I clipped it to my belt instead and took a moment to savor my victory.

I'll admit, from the outside, it probably didn't look good that I was laughing at their pain.

Another time, another place, I wouldn't have noticed the surprisingly fast behemoth out of my peripheral vision. I'd taken my eyes off a giant once before and I'd long ago learned to make sure my back was never more exposed than I was ready for. As that eagle shaped figure eclipsed several lights, I instinctively dropped and rolled aside as a fist the size of a melon punched my car. Taking a knee, I looked up at a seething Garuda and the crack he just put in my heavily reinforced window. An instant before I could pull my Helios, however, I had a flurry of red hair and the outline of a surprisingly fluffy tail lashing in front of my face. My hand released the grip as I saw the Kitsune desperately trying to pull him away.

"This isn't what we're here for!" she cried out, hanging from his arm like a strange bracelet. "She just wanted us to follow!"

Having that extra moment to read the area, I could see the glossy look in those eagle eyes and the vacant stare he had. He couldn't hear her; he could barely register she was there. She wasn't about to give up though, and even though the visor was gone I could smell an alluring scent building in the air around us. She was doing her best to try to sedate him and it was getting nowhere. With little hesitation he cast her aside with a simple whipping motion and lunged at me again.

Realizing the situation I was in, I sprang back from him and tried to scramble to a better position. The Helios was on crowd control, it wouldn't kill him if I fired center mass or into a limb, but I knew it wouldn't stop him – not without ramping it up. Given the look in his eyes, I didn't want to do that but, like in the Plaza, I wasn't above blinding him. Reaching into my coat while trying to stay just out of his reach, I pulled the still pulsing Wisp and chucked it at his face.

I felt a powerful shriek just narrowly above the earplugs' frequency reverberate through my bones. He stumbled and nearly fell on his ass, only barely catching himself on my car. Seeing that moment of opportunity, I reached for the Helios and got ready to kneecap him. Unfortunately, before I could draw, he grabbed at my coat and hurled me with enough force to send me tumbling over the car's roof and crashing down to the pavement on the other side.

I landed more gracefully than when I was thrown by the poltergeist, but that didn't mean much with a screaming eagle man on the other side of the car. Peeking through the windows, I could see him stand fully upright again at the other end, giant mitts he considered hands pushing up against the side of the car and rocking it my way. Finally drawing the Helios, I sprang back up to my feet just as the foxtail once again emerged from behind him. Leaping onto his back, the Kitsune started trying to peel him away from the car but looked like a small child riding her father's back. The Garuda, barely fazed by this, grabbed her arm as it got too close to his neck and flung her up and over with the same ease he did to me.

There was a split-second choice to make. I could either back up, let her crash, and take my shots at the big man, or I could try to catch her. I admit I'm still not entirely sure why I put my arms out, but soon they were full and I fell with her to the blacktop. Dazed from her sudden flight, she looked just as confused as me as we made eye contact and both tried to process my decision.

Shaking it off, I asked hurriedly over the sound of the car starting to tip again, "Will the Helios slow him down?!"

She shook her head, looking back at the rising frame and muttering, "Not unless you go full power."

He had the car up on two wheels with amazing ease. Admittedly, it was hard to tell if he was straining with the eagle face but it still looked effortless. Memories of the last time my car got flipped flashed before my eyes. Worse, the pixies I'd worked so hard to stun were starting to recover and several encircled him like a halo of birds orbiting their new king. I was running out of options.

Then again, they weren't really birds.

Pulling the hand-link from my belt, I started searching through its functions as quickly as I could. The Kitsune, probably being the smarter of us, got up and ran like hell away from the car. But what she didn't realize was that the hand-link could be used for all sorts of little communication tricks including being a wifi hotspot and a jamming device. I rarely used it, you generally didn't need to cut communications, but that wasn't what I needed it for tonight. Turning it on, I slid the link across the pavement and under the car, letting it broadcast what had to be the most annoying signal next to the Wisp.

The Garuda didn't notice the frequency, none of us could, though I imagine a few phones and computers that survived the Wisp were now showing brand new symptoms. But the pixies? It was hard to ignore them as they turned on their new king like a feathered inquisition. Watching a tiny feathered doll throw all her weight behind a right cross into someone's eye was kind of funny from the outside. Still, pangs of sympathy washed over me as the big man shrieked and started to get mauled by vicious little hands. He dropped the car and flailed fruitlessly through the air, his cries mingling with the haunting giggles and tiny shrieks surrounding him.

His movements slowed, his posture starting to slump, beak agape as he fought to catch his breath. I'd seen the posture in the cage before. Big man was short on cardio and, even if the little guys couldn't cause real injury, he was getting gassed. Screaming in frustration, he started to flee and stumbled into an alley with his petite assailants. For what it was worth, even gassed, I'd rarely seen someone his size move that fast.

The Kitsune stood and watched me from just across the street, her tail fading from view as she focused on it again. Her composure returned, but the bewildered look in her eyes remained. She probably couldn't be trusted since I still didn't know why they'd been there. If not for the fact her partner whipped her through the air, I would have left it at that.

"You good?" I asked while securing my gear again.

Brow briefly furrowing, a subtle frown on her lips, she nodded. "I apologize, I do not know what happened there."

"Yeah, I think I do," I mused while holstering the Helios. "I think you got out-witched there."

"Out-witched?" she echoed, frown deepening. "I don't appreciate the association."

Raising an eyebrow, I tried to choke back my incredulity and get back to sorting the mess. I shuffled over to the car and peeked under it to see how my hand-link was doing. A small gang of pixies had detached from their swarm to take their aggressions out on it, stamping and punching at it for all they were worth, losing their balance as the signals continued to disorient them. It was like watching drunk toddlers trying their best to teach the link a lesson.

Getting up and going back around to the trunk, I started fishing through other gear for pixie control. The Roswell was usually good enough for stopping an attack, but it was a short-lived deterrent. If I was going to get my hand-link back I needed an actual repellent. Pulling out a tube about the size of a flashlight, I got back onto the sidewalk and started to edge my way over. Though they're hostile to modern electronics, pixies have a whole different relationship with permanent magnets. Opening up the tube, I pulled a stack of neodymium magnets and just set it in the gutter near them. Hissing and chittering, the gang scrambled out from under the car and took flight.

Reaching under the car, I felt around for a bit and pulled the link out. It was cracked and scuffed despite the sturdy construction. Then again, seeing my own reflection, I wasn't looking so great either.

Drawing my attention again, the Kitsune stood over me with her hands on her hips, demanding, "What kind of 'Witch' are you tracking, anyway?"

Eying the damaged link, turning it over in my hand to check the rest of the case, I thought about how little I knew of the woman I was chasing. "You know," I trailed off, hesitating as my thumb floated over the program to search her profile.

"Maybe it's time to find out."

Chapter 11
Earlier Interactions

The idea of hitting that command was heavier than it should have been. In fact, despite everything, I decided not to at the moment and instead walked back into the Undercity. The Kitsune, still demanding answers, followed me as I strolled through the carnage.

Shops were only half lit, the overhead lights were mostly gone, and not all of those were due to the Wisp. Broken glass littered the floor, mostly from busted bulbs, now being swept into mounds along with a rainbow of feathers. Quite a few dirty looks were pointed my way as employees looked up from their mounds. In one of them, I managed to find my visor which I picked up and dusted off along the way. Putting it back on, little hand prints dotted my field of view like a strange cutesy image filter applied over the world.

We entered the club to find most of the crowd gone and the staff doing their best to recover. The security guards glared as I entered, the Werewolf holding an icepack over his head while the other guy applied band-aids to the tiniest of cuts. The bartender, off behind her counter, had the least damage to clean since the swarm chased me before they could get to her. Still, even she had visible tension as I came by.

"The fuck you want, man?" the Werewolf barked at me, fur growing in like an aggressive five o'clock shadow.

Seeing a few more hints of a transformation like tension in the muscles around his jaws and a general swelling around his cheeks, I decided to give him an answer this time. The visor was telling me he was angry but not recovering and an answer from me could only help. Besides, whatever happened in that shop,

Marionette was long gone. Adjusting my coat, I stood firm now that I wasn't trying to catch anyone.

"A woman wanted for questioning in a murder investigation ran past you," I said calmly. "If you check your security cameras, you'll see her there when you couldn't see her before."

The guards eyed each other as silent confirmations before the bus piped up, "So some invisible woman ran by? How?"

"She's a Witch," I replied, "and probably one of the strongest ones in the area."

The Kitsune at my side, nodding along, declared, "She pushed a Garuda I had with me."

The Werewolf, aura calming but still looking terrible, asked, "Aren't those guys supposed to be immune to chemicals?"

"Poisons or toxins, yes," she answered matter-of-factly, "but they can be swayed."

Climbing up onto the stage again while they talked among themselves, I walked to the back and fished out my cuffs. You could practically feel the room tense again as the polished finish of the distinctive ACTF cuffs caught the light. For some I figured the question was whether hell was about to break loose again. For others there was the concern they'd previously tried to interfere. Whatever their concerns, everyone's shoulders relaxed and no one tried to follow once I passed. As I entered the back stage area, one muttered the name of the Gilded Cage with a clear understanding.

I found the hidden door still partially open, sounds of a sweeping broom echoing out of the corridor beyond. The Spriggan swept up the debris like every other merchant in the area with a short broom that was still just a hair too tall for him. He grumbled and muttered about getting locks for his cages, then looked up to see me approach. Like the others outside, he caught sight of the cuffs almost immediately and dropped the broom, holding his breath and flexing to expand his form like a spooked animal trying to look big. Honestly it was kind of impressive, his head and upper body inflating to a size I didn't figure possible.

Unfortunately for him, I'd just dealt with a guy who could crack bullet proof glass so I wasn't exactly intimidated.

Holding up the cuffs, I said dryly, "You really think we didn't consider expansion?"

He started to deflate as I said it, quite literally in this case, with the sound of whistling air flowing out of his nose even as I was cuffing him. It wasn't the most dignified sound, especially since it was quickly starting to sound like a deflating balloon. As fast as he was able to inflate, the reverse process was painfully slow and hard to get through with any dignity for either one of us. But, somehow, there was still a little more dignity to lose.

Generally, you just escort a suspect to the car by their arm so they can't run away. But with our height differences, there was no way around it. Taking a moment to close the door and lay a Halo strip at its threshold, I picked him up and walked out.

We were met with snickers as I stepped out onto the stage carrying the small, puffy man as his noises gradually went from party balloon to whoopee cushion. The guards moved aside and let me pass without question, covering their mouths to stifle back their laughs. A few others even applauded. Only the Kitsune seemed to keep her calm as I hopped off the stage and the Spriggan made one last sputtering exhale.

"Is this really the time?" She asked sternly while following us out of the club.

Trying my best to remain stoic, I replied, "It was either I arrest him now or we start a manhunt after he ran. The animal control division is going to have a field day back there."

Her eyebrow raised, the once again invisible tail audibly swishing, she asked with a light growl, "Why would the ACTF have an animal control division?"

"Long story," I answered bluntly as flashes of 'Peaches' flew through my mind. Glancing down at the sound as her skirt settled into place, I clarified, "Not for you, mind."

A deadly glare awaited when I looked back up.

"Probably that Nosferatu not long ago," the Spriggan commented, now fully deflated and sounding reasonably normal again.

I raised an eyebrow, shrugged and raised him while nodding his way. She peered between us before rolling her eyes and glaring straight ahead with her arms crossed.

"You're still wasting your time," she muttered, "that Witch-"

"Was long gone before I even got to the street," I interjected.

Hopeful, the Spriggan asked, "Would you be willing to give me a break if I had some information on that?"

"Depends on the information," I said. "Though I'm not sure you'd have anything good."

Clearing the stairwell to the surface, I hesitated and checked the shadows for any signs of giggles or colorful feathers. Most had chased the Garuda, but I had to be sure they didn't come back.

"She grabbed some feed on the way out," he said, looking up at me. "Unusual stuff unless she owns a phoenix."

Carrying him to the car, I sat him on the curb as I opened the door. There was a chance he was snowing me for a bargain, but the remark about the phoenix made me wonder.

"Alright," I said, warily, "what'd she take?"

"Bag of phoenix feed – some insect meal seasoned with a little cassia-bark, cinnamon, myrrh, and a couple other strong spices," he answered matter-of-factly. "Nothing but a phoenix can really stand the stuff."

It was definitely an eclectic mix, but I also recognized the stuff he was listing had a strong odor too. Shooting a look to the Kitsune, I wondered if she would know anything about western witchcraft.

She met my gaze, shrugged, sighed, and commented with a touch of disdain, "Those are generally used to reduce inflammation. Witches tend to use them when they expect to over-exert themselves."

Looking down at the Spriggan, seeing the shit-eating grin on his face, I had to admit it was suggesting her next move if not where she was going. Unfortunate for him, I needed to know where she was going, and he was soon being lifted up and into the passenger seat.

"Wait!" He protested. "I helped!"

Nodding just before the box snapped shut around him, I assured, "I'll put in a good word for you at the hearing."

Through the box I could still hear the yelling, muffled through the case and nearly silenced completely as it all slid under the dash. It's not like I was going to just let him go, the pixies alone were enough to trash a whole neighborhood, but I could at least help him get a reduced sentence. If that wasn't good enough, he'd just have to practice his intimidation skills in Acheron.

As I closed the door, I turned right into a waiting Kitsune. I knew she was back there and had kept all the dangerous gear angled slightly away from her, but I hadn't realized how close she'd actually gotten. The visor, still a little smudged, didn't show much activity from her either. She seemed reserved, if anything, like the events of the night were sinking in and she'd realized it was time to tell Zhang that they'd lost a giant bird in Pioneer Square. She lingered for a moment, took a cleansing breath, then held out a card in both hands while making a light bow.

Staring at it, likely looking stupid as I did, I hesitated for a moment before pulling out one of my own. Taking her card and giving her mine, I awkwardly bowed in return. I'm not sure if that was the right thing to do, but it seemed polite enough. After a couple years of dealing with the more "organized" side of the Alter community, I'd been shot at, thrown through walls, and put in more than a few uncomfortable holds. This was my first exchange of business cards. It almost felt wrong not to bow.

"If you manage to arrest my friend," she said, "I would appreciate a call."

"Yeah, sure thing," I trailed off while scanning over the card, "Akemi."

She bowed again, flashes of red in her hair and in a faint haze behind her hinting at the unseen traits she was back to hiding. "We will be in touch, Agent Leone."

I watched Akemi leave, tucking the card away in my pocket. I still wasn't quite sure what to make of her, but it was clear she didn't have control of the big guy. Sadly, I was pretty sure I knew who did.

Climbing into the car, surrounded in the sounds of the Oracle system booting up and the muffled protests of the Spriggan in the box, I reached over to the terminal and started entering the various requests to the system. The Oracle had already marked them as points of interest on the map but it was always procedure to confirm her information in case of a false alarm. In a case like this, the confirmation was probably necessary to prove the poor girl didn't have a seizure in there. Animal control needed to sweep the shop, patrols needed to keep an eye out for a Garuda and a swarm of pixies, and Lucian could probably use an update on Marionette. All clustered together on the map, it looked like quite the party.

Akemi's questions about Marionette rang through my head as I worked. The icon for her profile hovered out of the corner of my eye, taunting me just off to the side. With a quick tap I could get an idea of who we were actually dealing with. The sound of the system and the Spriggan faded into the background as my hand hovered over it. Any other time, I probably wouldn't have even thought twice.

I couldn't fully understand my hesitation. I'd already decided I needed to see it after my tussle with the Garuda. I'd had a lot of time to consider options on just who exactly Marionette could be. I'd considered she'd been a relative of Janice Grey at one point. At another I'd thought, maybe, she might have been another plant working for Rufus. I'd also considered that she may have just had one of those faces from time-to-time. But never before had I actually stopped to sit with her files.

Part of it was clearly that she was pushing me, but something about that didn't fully sit right. If she did push me to not think about it, why did it linger? And if she could control me that well, how did I just see her down in that club? It felt like there was something else. Maybe that's what made the others nervous.

Maybe the fact they were nervous was the reason ***I*** was starting to get nervous.

Still, for as long as I felt like I was just sitting there, it was only a second at most. The hesitation probably wouldn't have even been noticed if someone else had been there. I mean, anyone that wasn't currently screaming in a box. Before the feeling had even fully passed, I exhaled slowly, decided to take it on the chin if anyone got mad, and unlocked the mystery that had been hovering just out of the corner of my eye for a couple years. Whatever hesitation I might've had, some part of me was always eager to figure it out – eager enough to resist her manipulations.

Soon, even that part wished I left it alone as a deep, cold, hollow feeling radiated through my body.

It didn't take very long to understand why everyone wanted me to avoid following this side of the case. There'd been others in the past where they trusted me to follow through despite my personal hang-ups. But this one had problems in it that I couldn't have ever imagined. It sat there at the top of the first page of the complete profile: a line that explained everything with a stark, brutal honesty.

I'd met her before. I knew Marionette from a time before I'd ever considered putting on the uniform. Memories of seeing her started to flood back to my mind as I sat there feeling completely alone with those files. I'd seen her in a crowd during a fight I'd lost to an unregistered Alter. I later bumped into her just outside the hospital where my grandmother died. The two of us stood in a cemetery on a cold, unforgiving day while most others had gone inside. She was around at a time in my life when I was too preoccupied to take notice.

We never exchanged names; we never even spoke. When I asked my grandmother if she recognized her, I was reminded to focus on what was important. And that's exactly what I did. And because I stayed focused, those little encounters just bled away. I didn't recognize her at all when we met again years later. I still couldn't recognize her now. Yet, knowing who she was now, connecting the dots in my head, I couldn't help but think back on my very first memory of Marionette.

It was a lot further back than I would've liked. I would have loved if the first time was in that arena. But I couldn't be so lucky.

I was actually a child – not even sure how old I was at the time. I know I was old enough to run around, but young enough to not realize when I shouldn't be. I know this because I was charging headlong through a room that had way too much furniture and not enough room for a clumsy kid to make the corners. I'd hit a rug and spun out like a miniature racecar driver without the car, crashing like a ragdoll into a corner stand and knocking over a lamp.

The thing shattered, practically exploded, and I bawled my eyes out like it was the end of the world. I wasn't hurt, just scared, embarrassed and worried someone was going to come down on me for the lamp. No one came to punish me, though. Instead, a hand came down, took mine, and lifted me to my feet. She picked me up off the floor, checked me over for bumps and bruises, and brushed the hair out of my face before carrying me to the next room over.

Sitting me in a chair at the kitchen table, she tried to coax a smile out of me. She nuzzled me and cooed to me like you would a toddler. Our noses touched and I momentarily paused my sobbing to look into her eyes. Thinking back on it, I couldn't imagine how I could forget that face. It wasn't the same anymore, but her eyes were. They were unnatural but beautiful even then - a brilliant but calming shade of green that almost returned my little soul to sanity. I guess it's just too hard to remember details like that when enough time passes.

It's funny, in the years since I met her again, they were sometimes blue. Colored contacts didn't seem like much of an issue, so I just ignored them over time. But now I had to ask: was it all just to hide from me?

Even staring into those eyes as a child, I still couldn't completely calm down, unable to control my emotions at that age. She was still relatively new to all of this too, so she offered up a treat to me as a quick and easy tactic to soothe a panicked child. She'd do that a lot in the times I could remember. She grabbed a box from a cabinet above, took out a toaster pastry and put it into an old piece of crap that was amazingly still working up until a couple years ago.

That file laid out so many answers while opening so many questions and reopening so many old wounds. I hadn't even gone into detail yet because that first line was enough to split open my whole world. It was just her name and a list of aliases, but one of those aliases was Marion Leone. No one expects their mother to get younger. No one is expected to recognize their mother's face from before they were born.

Chapter 12
Evocative Enemy

A lot of things made sense real fast in that time. First, the fact I never fully let it go and could see her was probably some latent ability. Second, the reason why I kept running into her was because she was literally following me. Third, the reason why I never knew any family from her side was because most of them had probably died before Washington was even a thing – the man, not the state. Unfortunately, that last thought made one other thing painfully clear.

My grandmother, the only family I had for years, knew damn well where she was.

After what happened to my dad, I remember once asking my grandmother what happened to my mom. I wondered about her more often than that, but the first answer was all I ever really needed to hear. My grandmother was a sweet woman but didn't hold back any disdain for the woman that walked out. She told me bluntly she didn't know where my mom was but that she figured it wouldn't have mattered even if she did. Now I had some idea that only half of that was true.

I drove away from that neighborhood long before anyone else showed up. Sure, I had a prisoner in the box and needed to book him, but that wasn't the reason why. The idea that Lucian also knew my mother was out there, that she might have been toying with me, and he didn't tell me was too much. I couldn't face him with that information just yet. Besides the years of trust that I just felt breach, I couldn't really risk that I might have hauled off and punched him.

Only part of it was really about him. You have to understand, in only a minute I just found out that every mentor and parental figure I'd had since I was a kid had been lying to me. I knew they probably had their reasons, but those reasons suggested they didn't trust me either. What did they think I was going to do? Join my mother in some criminal empire? Worse than that was the fact I now needed to do something I ***knew*** no one would agree with. I needed to catch her myself and confront her before anyone else could. I knew it was irrational, but nothing seemed rational in the moment.

It wasn't necessarily the fact she'd abandoned us when I was a kid. It wasn't even the fact she was family and there was some sort of honor attached to the whole thing. It was the fact she had been trying and failing to make me ignore her this entire time and everyone else was content with helping her do it. I needed to prove to her and everyone else that she couldn't control me like that. I wouldn't let her.

On the way to the HQ, I kept peeking back at the file at every intersection. Morbid curiosity and a genuine need to find clues kept drawing my eyes to the screen. Known associates, former addresses and criminal history painted a colorful picture of what kind of person she was. And, frankly, my mother was sketchy.

She'd been constantly near situations but never in the middle of them. More than once she was a person of interest or a witness to a case while appearing to have airtight alibis. Everything from fraud investigations to missing person cases stretched back decades as she weaved her way from one lifetime to the next. Sometimes, missing person reports even seemed to be her under a different name. This wasn't someone who would have gotten caught red handed under most circumstances. In fact, if anything, the file read more like someone out of the CIA. As strange as it sounded, her record was way too clean for someone who'd been in all the places she'd been.

Worse, one of her known associates before she met my dad was Rufus Plagas.

By the time I reached the garage I knew anyone who was keeping an eye on this case would have also likely known about me opening the profile. The Oracle recorded everything like that.

Usually that wasn't a problem. The issue this time was that meant ancient forces were lurking in the shadows waiting to drag me to an intervention. Fortunately, the line to booking had cleared and the Spriggan didn't have much of a choice about our pace. Double-timing it through the garage while he thrashed around in my hands, I hauled his uncooperative ass to the second elevator like a piece of carry-on luggage.

A couple voices rang out as I passed, most just greeting me or laughing about my cargo, but I let them fade into the background noise and pretended not to notice. The only voice of any real concern would be Dulaf if I heard her. Of all the people who could be waiting for me, she was the one most likely to get me to stop. Not that she could get my attention better, just that she was an Argyrean level athlete and was unlikely to take no for an answer. So, it was some relief that when I did see a pair of bladed ears and chestnut hair it was through a crack in the closing doors as she emerged from the other exit.

The prisoner transfer entrance was a kind of funhouse mirror version of the office entrance. Whereas the entrance I used most days was meant to keep people from sneaking in the back door and breaking into the offices, the one to holding was focused more heavily on keeping people in. The corridor was structured like an airlock, a series of smaller chambers with shutters between them like a smaller version of the gates down in Limbo. The usual biometric scans were there too, reading both of us and getting my passenger's file started by bringing up his profile.

"Welcome Agent Leone," the Oracle's voice echoed from the walls, "preparing system to process Spriggan suspect Burrows, Jowan."

The elevator required the usual scans to get it to move, descending from the garage level and into the deeper holding stations. The elevator car was a whole different beast too with a bulkier, reinforced door, a second set of UV lights for emergency pulses, and speakers equipped to set off a Banshee shriek inside. I had to put the Spriggan down to give a hand print scan, but it wasn't like he could have gotten through the door. I was pretty sure it would have taken a couple explosives to do that.

The ride down was quiet; my companion finally deflated enough to breathe like normal. Usually that would have been welcome but I didn't necessarily want to be left alone with my thoughts at the time. How was I supposed to react to all of this? Did they hope I would just go along with the mystery forever just because I used to have a similar game with Trey? Then again, maybe they had a reason.

Maybe grandma had one too.

As the doors opened down in holding, the calmest place in the building despite its location, I was almost too preoccupied to remember Jowan cowering in the corner. It wasn't every day I had to actually pick up the guy I was escorting and, strangely enough, he was actually waiting for me to do it by this point. Half a step out the door, I caught sight of Joe the curate sitting behind his desk and remembered what I was here for. Quickly backing up, I hoisted the little guy off the ground.

Chuckling, Joe punched a few things into his terminal and commented, "One of these days they'll figure out a way to make that look more dignified."

"The perp walk is a time-honored tradition," I said while walking up to the desk, setting Jowan back on the floor as gently as possible.

Shrugging, Jowan complained from below the desk, "I suppose I get it, but believe me – it won't soon be forgotten."

I shot a look to Jowan at my feet and gave him a moment to realize he just made a thinly veiled threat at the mouth of Acheron. He was literally already in a deep, dark hole and there was a mile of shaft still to go.

Returning my gaze, he took a second to process before correcting, "I mean I'm gonna sue!"

Shaking his head, smirk across his face, Joe asked, "Is this Burrows?"

I nodded along, keeping my eye on Jowan now that he'd started to show some of the old Spriggan vengeance.

"And he's in for," Joe trailed off as he went through the Oracle's report, "smuggling, trafficking, dealing in illegal animals, and operating a pet store without a license?"

Jowan hopped repeatedly to peer over the edge of the desk, frantically protesting. "Hold it! I have a license!" he said. "I just might have lied a little about the extent of my operations."

Joe's eyebrow raised as he made a few keystrokes and murmured to himself. Jowan's expression slowly shifted as he realized it was a good time to shut up. I just grinned as I amused myself watching the guy threatening a lawsuit keep digging his hole. Still, I remembered our deal before he went into the box.

Reaching down and patting his back, I spoke up, "I'll put it in my report you cooperated and assisted in another case."

Jowan looked over his shoulder and settled down, fully deflated both inside and out.

Joe nodded along, asking, "Want us to handle the processing while you fill out the report?"

For other organizations, half the act of arrests was a pile of paperwork large enough to be considered inhumane. For the ACTF, reports were really just a way of confirming the Oracle's account as a safeguard against any potential mistakes. I didn't have to be in any specific place right away. I could stick around to process Jowan or I could go find a nice little hole to hide in with my reports. But, as Joe was asking the question, I could already feel the call of another option altogether.

Down in Joe's "office", nestled between several different wings, I had four doors I could have used. To my right, I could walk out through the psychiatric ward and sanctuary and up into the bullpen where I could pick out a desk and wait for someone to bother me. Directly ahead I could have walked into the holding center where we kept people before they were sentenced and handled questioning. Behind me was a relatively quick escape to the garage and out into the open world where I could file the report digitally from anywhere in the city. Unfortunately, as parts of Marionette's profile continued to rattle in my skull, the door to my left was practically screaming for me.

"Actually," I said hesitantly, eyeing that door, "I think I need to go talk to someone down in Acheron."

Joe gave me a knowing look. "Need to ask the devil some questions?"

There was a weight to the question that hadn't been there in a while. I'd felt uneasy talking to the man before, when the Aegis patch on my coat was new and the shoulder under it didn't occasionally ache. I'd gotten used to the song and dance with Rufus Plagas in the time since. I'd seen with my own eyes that he couldn't get through his glass cage and it'd been ages since they let him actually keep real scissors on hand.

Why did this feel like the first time again?

Taking a moment to clean the smudges off my shades, I chewed on the thought for a couple seconds before putting them on and nodding to Joe. "More than a few," I said, starting the deceptively short walk into the prison.

"Glutton for misdirection," Joe commented as he walked around to fetch Jowan.

My fist clenched for a flash before I caught it and realized why the feeling had come back. I wasn't intimidated by Rufus, not anymore. He would always be creepy, and I couldn't figure out how he kept so much control over the world above, but he couldn't hurt me directly. Sure, he might be able to get at me indirectly, but that was true whether I was in the room with him or not. No, the real problem was that, for possibly the first time ever, he was the person most likely to tell me a version of the truth without much hesitation. After all, at the moment it was a mound of salt to pour into open wounds.

I relaxed the hand and flexed it a couple times before idly adjusting the cuff and absently confirming my silvers were on. I wouldn't need them down there, but having them flipped on felt right at the moment. A sense of control, maybe?

Stepping on through the door, I took one last look back at the others and nodded to them both. Joe returned the gesture but Jowan had no intention of even looking my way. I couldn't blame him. Well, I could, but I could at least understand the animosity.

As they shuffled through their door, I let mine close and turned to face the entrance to the mile-long tunnel into Acheron. It was well-lit but still seemed darker than usual despite the curate on the other side reading from an old print copy of a horror novel with no reservations. And there was no reason for it to seem so dingy at the moment – it was so sterile there I couldn't really even pick up any discernable scents. It was just the great stretch of tunnel that seemed so much greater and darker than usual. And in that moment, looking at the far end of the lift, I could hear the dull hum of the electronics around us. For the first time in a long time, stepping onto that lift, the whole place just felt ominous.

Chapter 13
Secret Affairs

Down the winding tunnel we rode, passing the series of windows overlooking the various levels. Though I'd gotten used to talking to Rufus himself over the years, I was still fascinated by the show afforded by a relatively slow descent. The usual suspects amassed in the commons. The higher levels, mostly populated by non-violent offenders who did things similar to Jowan, were always a little calmer than the ones below. You could see the people trying to pick up a trade or enjoying a hobby. Hell, on that night I could even see what looked to be the beginnings of a book club while several guards watched on with a bit of interest.

Gradually, descending through the levels, you could feel the rising tension. The way we stacked our prison prevented things like riots or gang wars. The more violent your offense, the deeper you went and the fewer you could directly interact with. There was really only one person in solitary, Rufus himself, but the others weren't grouped together in a way that could open up to harm. When I first got started, I didn't see much of a difference, splitting up the populations so strictly. But over the years I'd grown to appreciate that the guys who really belonged here never had a chance to hurt or corrupt the guys who were just…passing through.

By the time I was only a few levels from the bottom, I saw one example of corruption sitting calmly in the general population as Dante from the Locusta watched us pass. The orange jumpsuit with the distinctive markings for his level wasn't quite as fashionable as the suit he was in the last time I saw him. He'd had to take a less expensive and easier to maintain haircut with a near complete buzz around his head. But despite these changes, I could still see his old role in his posture and the way he seemed unfazed by his surroundings. Dante, like Rufus, felt in control even down in the pit.

That was exactly what bothered me most about both of them.

At the bottom, I found the lounge full of guards as they took their usual break between watches. The place was always a little musty, like a locker room with the heat turned up just a bit too high. Part of it was the fact we were hundreds of feet below the Earth and any miner could tell you that was never a comfortable place to be. Another part was the fact that the reduced floor space and increased security meant that this room was full every hour of every day without exception. Even with the air-conditioning cranked to the max and air fresheners mounted in the walls, there was no way to avoid it smelling like a dozen sweaty dudes in full body armor.

None of them even bothered to get up as I emerged from the lift. A couple looked up to see who was coming and confirm whether or not they should even consider rising. It wasn't worth it half the time anymore. The security had long ago been beefed up even down here, doing a full skeletal scan of me as I stepped through. So, seeing as it was me and that the body scan confirmed I wasn't a Shifter this time, they went back to their mid-watch activities.

Watching them would give you the impression it was a cushy job if it weren't for the smell, cramped space, and the fact a man they called the "Devil of the Ninth" was on the other side of the door. A few of them were watching baseball, another was eating what I guess would be considered "lunch" for people like us, and the rest were off in their own little worlds with tablets and phones. One man in particular, grizzled, scarred, and as hard as you could be from years down in Acheron, swiped through surprisingly flowery furniture designs on his screen.

"Find anything you like, Pete?" I asked on the way by.

Looking up, his seemingly permanent scowl cracked for just a minute to form the slightest of smirks. "The wife was thinking some contemporary monochrome shit," he rumbled, "but I see enough steel walls at work."

I grinned and patted his shoulder, heading through the next set of doors to the unreal vault beyond. Echoes of classical music and the faint smell of allium extracts greeted me almost immediately. The dim glow of the threshold lights and the curtain of chemicals lit up like an aurora through the visor against the dimmer than usual glass box.

Rufus wasn't asleep, it was far too late in the night for that, but he wasn't keeping himself too busy at the time. The music seemed to be coming from the compartment he seemed to consider a den, an old scratchy quality to it suggesting very old vinyl on a player old enough to be worth a fortune. I used to be shocked about how comfortable his place was. Now I was just annoyed they let him have a player with a functional needle.

Several guards hovered at corners along the surrounding catwalk while another followed me at a distance. By the time I reached the usual alcove I was acclimated to the smell and my visor had corrected the light levels enough to see Rufus' figure slouched in a chair with a glass in his hand. He glowered through the dark, looking vaguely in our direction but not focusing on us, before taking a hefty drink from his glass and setting it aside. Refusing to rise, he merely waved his newly free hand in a dismissive gesture and called out from across his little glass apartment, "What the hell do you want this time?"

There was a thing about talking to Rufus that took a while to understand. Somehow, he knew more than he was supposed to. Somehow, he was seemingly in constant communication with the surface and could track things that even we weren't always aware of. But on more than one occasion he'd needed to have direct contact with someone from the outside. I used to take it for granted he knew everything, but something started to dawn on me. At least some of the time, he discovered things because people had asked him about it. I needed to wade into the waters instead of being direct.

Knowing this, I said only two words as loudly and firmly as I could, "Marionette Corbin."

His eyebrow quirked, his aura sparked, and he sat taller in his chair. I couldn't be sure how much he knew from that, but I knew he had something of an idea. Chuckling, he mused smugly, "That took longer than I expected."

I didn't resist clenching my jaw. We were too far apart for him to get a really clear view of me through all the reinforced glass. But at the very least he was giving me some confirmation.

"So, you know what's going on?" I asked tightly.

Standing and starting to weave his way through multiple doors like a ghost drifting through an old house, he replied, "At the moment? Not entirely. But, despite being one of the best in the business, Marion's luck had to eventually run out."

He called her Marion instead of Marionette. For most people that would have a fifty-fifty shot of just being a diminutive. With Rufus, I knew damn well what it actually meant.

"You know her?" I asked for confirmation.

Coming to a stop in front of me, sharp features highlighted by the ambient light, he bared his fangs in a toothy grin and answered, "You mean to ask if I know your mother?"

Restraining myself wasn't easy, but I think I managed. Even with a barrier between us, the man was good with cutting remarks and digging when he found a soft spot. Doing my best to be stoic, I asked, "And how exactly do you know her?"

Despite my efforts, I could see on his face and in his aura that he was amused with my reaction. I'd never exactly practiced my poker face in a mirror, so I wasn't sure how good it was. All I knew was that the toothy grin remained as he said, "Marion has always been a valuable asset to those who could afford her since long before she came here."

"And what kind of asset is she?"

The grin faded as he lowered his eyes to the floor before a new smirk crossed his face and he answered mockingly, "If I told you, I probably couldn't use her again."

I kept my cool despite his tone. I knew he would talk to me like this, especially given the subject. It's not like it didn't bother me. But he and I both knew there was really nothing I could do to him where we were standing. On the other hand, if I could punch through Vesperadin laced glass like that Garuda, I would have.

Against my better judgment, I asked, "Were you using her services when she met my dad?"

Even as the words left me, I knew it was a mistake. They slipped out and instantly his toothy grin returned. It was hard to read just what was behind that smile, even the aura not giving me much more than a strange, twisted joy. It read like the conversation excited him. Everything about how he was acting felt that way. It was the kind of thing that would have lingered if the next words out of his mouth hadn't put it all into context.

"Whoever said that I was the one who sent her?" he asked.

"You said you've used her services," I answered, trying my best not to give him more to work with.

Shrugging, he started to back away from the alcove. "Yes, I did," he said, "but that doesn't mean I had anything to do with their meeting."

Oddly enough, I believed him. If he had anything to do with their meeting he probably would have gloated. Every encounter we had showed he was willing to take credit when due. And, to be honest, that was kind of a relief.

"Of course," he continued, turning a corner into a room set up like a study, "I wasn't the only one using her services."

That sounded more like him.

Bitterly, I finally took his bait and asked, "And what's that supposed to mean?"

Browsing his books, one hand behind his back as he traced the fingers of his other hand along the bindings, he didn't answer right away. I couldn't read the titles from where I stood, but I could see that they ranged a great many eras. Some were leather bound and had the wear you'd expect on a particularly old book. Others seemed to have been published within the 21st century.

Whatever they were, they had his full attention until he spotted one that couldn't be much older than me.

"Tell me," he started, pulling the book from the shelf and beginning to thumb through it, "are you familiar with the idea of Mitochondrial Eve? The most recent common ancestor of humanity?"

I did, actually, but that didn't mean the question made sense. I'd actually heard about it twice in my life: once in high school biology and again in the academy's science classes. Both times I didn't quite understand the importance of the topic, but the musk of my Sasquatch instructor from the academy had left deep marks on my memory. Still, feeling like he was trying to lead me off the path, I wasn't about to play along.

"Rings a bell," I said, crossing my arms, "but that's not what I'm here to talk about."

He drifted back over with the book in his hands, tilted enough that I still couldn't make out what it was. As he came closer, I could catch "biology" along the spine for a moment before he snapped the book shut, a finger resting between pages, and lowered it behind his back.

"Did you know," he started again, pushing ahead, "that there was also a Mitochondrial Lilith?"

Starting to let my irritation slip, I snapped, "What the hell does this have to do with Marionette?"

Unfazed, he continued on. "Did you ever consider why Alters are so rare, what it is that keeps our numbers low?"

"No," I rebuked, "and I don't care right now."

"You should," he said, "because it has everything to do with why your mother was sent to meet with your father."

Stepping back, I considered just leaving. He was on one of his tangents again and wouldn't have anything useful for me. Whatever was going through his head, it was just about fucking with me instead of giving me what I needed. The only thing keeping me in the alcove was the fact it was the most anyone had actually admitted on the subject so far.

Taking my hesitation as an invitation, he carried on, "Alters are a part of the gene pool, our traits passed down from one generation to the next. Some traits are recessive, others are dominant. Maybe you have the gene for immortality, or regeneration, or incredible strength. Enough of the traits in the right combinations and you fit into a certain breed. But what exactly triggers the actual transformation?"

He raised the book again, opening it to a page about mitochondria and the various functions it carried out.

"All active Alters are the descendants of Lilith."

Shaking my head, sighing, I turned to walk away, muttering, "So what?"

"Mitochondrial DNA is matrilineal," he said louder. "You're also a descendant of Lilith."

I stopped dead in my tracks. I shouldn't have, but I did. Looking back at him, I only hoped the mirrored shades kept him from reading too much of my face.

"Long ago, though I can't remember how long anymore," he said distantly, the grin fading from his face and twisting into a frown of disgust, "I almost had an army of Alters greater than any ever made. An Empyreal stopped me before I could finish my work."

The story felt familiar. I recalled a fable Lucian told me once before, and complaints from Dulaf about biological warfare. Now it was sounding like they might have been the same thing.

"He didn't survive," Rufus continued, "at least I don't think he did."

Steadying myself, I turned to fully face him again and set my shoulders. "Get on with it, Rufus," I demanded, "get to the point."

His frown grew, an open disdain for me flashing across his face and his otherwise controlled aura.

"What if you could have a trained Empyreal soldier?" he asked. "How far would you go to keep it at the ready?"

No matter how dumb he might have thought I was, I was catching onto his implications and didn't like them one bit. Getting a little bass in my voice, I replied, "It'd be impossible."

"Not at all," he said. "All you would really have to do is ensure that the bloodline didn't lose the necessary traits. Every few generations you would ensure beneficial traits were added into the gene pool. Follow the right branches, keep repeating the process as long as necessary."

Something about the tone in his voice was unsettling. For once, as he was saying those lines, he wasn't smug or condescending. It was confident but matter-of-fact. I wouldn't put it past him to be able to fool the visor or even an Oracle face-to-face. But for right now, they believed him and I was having a problem disagreeing.

"And, of course," he remarked, "the mother would have to have the right mitochondrial DNA."

"This is bullshit," I growled.

"Face it, boy," he replied, "you didn't dig far enough into her known associates."

He turned around and started walking back to his den and the old record player, book in hand, a spring in his step. Weaving through the doorways, he spoke up loud enough to be heard through glass walls and scratchy music.

"I wasn't the one to send her to meet with your father," he said bluntly, "Lucian was."

Chapter 14
Deep Need

I couldn't get out of there fast enough. I didn't go to the bullpen, I sure as hell didn't go through the sanctuary, and I turned off all means of communicating with me just long enough to put a couple blocks between me and the building. The car was being tracked as always, as was my badge, so I knew I couldn't get away for long. All I wanted to do was sit somewhere that wasn't a quick walk away. Unfortunately, with dawn not far off, the only place I felt comfortable sitting down again was the Ahab's by my apartment.

Sometimes I'm not as creative as I'd like to be.

There weren't many there at that hour and my usual table was open. My friend Trey was manning the counter and the look on his face suggested I wasn't looking my best. Still, he didn't ask any unusual questions and just gave me my coffee, my cookie, and my space. Since I was still on the clock, I had to at least make a show of working and opened the program to file a report remotely on my hand-link. While not the most thrilling of tasks, it at least gave me something to think about other than the load Rufus just dumped on me.

As soon as I left his vault, I checked the hand-link to confirm some of what he said. Lucian really was in the list of known associates. Not only that, but the time periods lined up as they apparently knew each other in the early 1990's in New York and she made contact with dad in Washington about ten years later. It was a big enough window that it could have been coincidence still, but something told me digging into the files any deeper was just going to make me feel worse at that point. In fact, by the time I reached Ahab's, the frustration was palpable as I realized I'd handed the Undercity lead over to Lucian. If I had any chance of catching up to her myself, I probably gave it up right there. So, I spent the next hour nursing my coffee, scribbling out my report, and trying my best to get lost in memories of pixies and the atmosphere of the shop.

I hadn't really considered it too much, since I wasn't exactly a "morning" person, but the shop was always one of the few places where I had some sense of Zen. I don't know if it was the aroma of the coffee, blood notwithstanding, or the subtle vibes of the Alter jazz. It could just be a place I associated with caffeine. Maybe it was the way the murals outside glowed through the window by my usual table after the sun set. It was even possible I just had nostalgia for the days I would come here for a chance to bump into certain people.

It was ironic, really, because it was also a place where a Shapeshifter twisted me around and made me question my sanity not that long ago. Hell, the guy at the counter and I used to have a long-standing game built around secrets. And, almost on cue, that friend was soon hovering over me as I started to stray off the path of reports and jazz and into the woods where people fed me bullshit.

Sitting across from me, Trey rested his elbows on the table, leaned over and said, "You're having one of those nights again."

I minimized the report with a tap of the stylus and sat back. Technically I was in the middle of an investigation. Maybe it took some personal turns that meant I should back off, but it was still not something to spread around. Then again…

"I found my mom," I said sullenly, taking a long drink of cold coffee.

"No shit?" Trey exclaimed. "How long's it been since you saw her?"

I had to bite back the genuine answer. It hadn't been long at all, apparently. But that was still too much information to share right now.

"I'm not even really sure how old I was when she left," I said, hoping he didn't notice the dodge.

He nodded along, sitting back himself and saying with an understanding tone, "My dad left back in the 30s, never really saw him again. I don't really even remember his face anymore."

I felt a little bad, but I had to ask, "Which century?"

Without missing a beat, he smirked and replied, "20th."

It was easy to forget how many people I regularly dealt with were biologically immortal. Trey looked like he was in my generation, maybe a little older, but the man was at least a century ahead of me. Which, to tell the truth, raised a lot of weird questions I usually overlooked.

"Tell me," I started, taking a moment to find the right words, "if you've been around that long, why are you still a barista?"

He slowly scanned the shop around us, smiling at some people sitting at another table, and answered fondly, "I like people, I had enough money to start a business, and there are fewer fights to break up than a bar."

"Wait," I sputtered, nearly choking on my coffee, "you ***own*** this place?"

He chuckled and nodded. "I was there when the first Ahab's opened, thought, 'I could run a blood bar'."

I could feel my brow furrowing as I chewed on the thought. Why would any immortal choose to be "the help" after a century? Guys like Trey were probably common.

"Why wouldn't you let everyone know that?" I asked.

He shrugged, waved it off, and said, "The immortals among us, we've spent decades trying to keep anyone from noticing us or asking too many questions. It makes secrets second nature to us, even when we don't mean to."

It might have been enough to explain why they wouldn't have said anything. If I'd heard it out of him even an hour earlier, I might have even been satisfied by it. But what if Rufus was actually telling the truth for once? Was I here to be a piece in their millennia long game of chess?

Without really meaning to, I muttered, "And manipulations."

Taken aback, Trey interjected, "Hey, I thought we were cool about the Incubus game."

Realizing I said it aloud, I glanced back up at him and felt the heat in my face. Shaking my head, I assured, "No, no, that wasn't about you. I've been having problems with other…"

I trailed off, the words I was about to use not really feeling right in the moment. If it was true, were they really even friends?

Seemingly seeing the distress on my face, Trey commented, "If it was your mother, I'm sure she had some reason."

Hearing him say it, I tried to stop myself from picking apart the various "reasons" she might have had. Idly running my thumb up and down the side of my cup, I couldn't help starting to drift off into my own little world. Would I ever really understand why she did any of it? Lucian was on her trail and I'd given him a head start. He'd been tracking down Witches since before most modern countries had names. And, as much baggage as I was bringing to the table, no one was going to let me talk to her until long after she was in the pit.

"Seriously, man," Trey pressed, "you okay?"

I broke from the train of thought and looked up from the cup again, considering just how much of the line I could walk before crossing it. But, thinking about Lucian, I realized it wasn't really my investigation to worry about anymore.

Sighing, I answered, "My mother's on the run right now and I don't think I'm going to have a chance to talk to her about any of it."

"Gotta back off because she's family?" he asked.

Shaking my head, I replied, "Not technically, no. No one's officially pulled me off of the case yet. But Lucian's taking point on it and I'm not going to be able to catch her before he does."

Lacing his fingers together, Trey stared at the table for a minute before giving a single nod and remarking, "I guess if you can be okay with it, might as well just sit back."

"I wouldn't say that I'm okay with it," I protested, "but I don't know how I would even try to find her before he did. He was the one who taught me how to track people in the first place."

Trey's posture changed, the lighter tones he spoke with disappeared, and for a brief moment I could almost see the immortal in the barista as he said, "Knowledge isn't stagnant."

"What do you mean?"

"Knowledge isn't stagnant," he repeated, "there's always something new to learn or a new way to understand. He might have taught you everything you knew about investigations when you started, but that doesn't mean you haven't learned anything without him. He's immortal, not omniscient."

A half-hearted smirk crossed my face. "That's still a huge gap in experience."

He gave a single nod, then said with an almost sage-like tone, "If he was a good teacher, he taught you most of what *he* knew too."

"Yeah, I guess he would have," I said, trailing off, my eyes starting to drift towards the window.

"Look, Nate," Trey said, the familiar tones starting to return, "if he taught you well enough, you know what leads he's going to follow."

It was a simple point, but enough to snap me at attention again.

"So," he said, the beginnings of a smile forming, "find the leads he wouldn't know to look for."

Watching him for a moment, knowing he had a point, I asked hesitantly, "What leads could I have that he doesn't already?"

"Well, hey," he said, reaching over and lightly slapping my forearm, "she's your mom, right?"

He was right. Simple as all the points were, he was like a splash of cold water in the face. I was spending so much time revering the guy that I didn't consider the fact that, somehow, I already found her accidentally once by following a different route. How many routes to her were buried somewhere in my head already? How much did I know about her that he didn't right now?

I finished my coffee and stood back up, gathering my things as quickly as I could. Trey smiled at the sudden energy, then got up himself and patted me on the shoulder before heading back to his counter. He'd been my friend for a long while, certain outbursts and games notwithstanding, but it'd been the first time he gave me some real genuine advice. Though, watching him walk and seeing the casual, laid-back stride return, maybe that was all part of his smokescreen.

"Hey, Trey," I called out, "thanks."

Peeking over his shoulder, he grinned and gave a quick bob of his chin. "No problem," he said. "I hope you can find her again."

I nodded back, donned the visor, and marched back out into the night and down the block to my car. While he didn't give me anything really solid to work with, he did give me enough to start the gears turning in my head. Was there an insight into her that I had that others wouldn't? Lucian knew her back in the 90s, but it was in another state, practically another life. How much interaction did he have with her since then?

Getting into the car and watching the displays light up, I went right back to her file and started to sort through it. She had the phoenix feed, something that Akemi said would be useful to reduce stress and inflammation. That suggested Marionette was going to be doing something big. And for a Witch to do something big, even something like her poltergeist, she was going to need a coven.

Witch covens were a little tougher to classify than other organizations. Though some would be involved in criminal activities, they organized and acted much more like secret societies than gangs. In fact, several of the most notable secret societies started as covens and slowly migrated into something else. The Illuminati, as much of a joke as they'd become, started that way before chapters started to let humans in. But, in their raw form, a coven was much more organized and tightly knit than others. She was likely to turn to them for help in a time of need. But would the coven ever help her openly? I wasn't so sure.

Checking her known associates and Lucian's current activity, he was on a similar path. His trail was weaving through the city from one coven member to another in a systematic fashion – a couple seeming to get word ahead of time and trying to move clear to no avail. Watching the markers moving across the screen, a thought started creeping forward. If Marionette's closest friends were all members of a coven, maybe I'd met some of them.

Concentrating on what little I could remember from that short time after we moved to Seattle, before she left, I tried to focus on faces long forgotten. I know I'd spent time with my mother's friends. Faded memories of old wood floors, antique toys, and the sounds of women chatting crept from the dark corners of my mind. Intermingled with these fragments were flashes of faces and people that I never saw after she left. They weren't family, I don't think, but she acted like they might as well have been. It felt like they were the closest things she had.

And I couldn't remember any of their damned names.

Trying desperately to remember any of them, I brought up every profile from the coven and moved them up to the windshield where I could see them large as life and in full HD. Practically surrounded by them, I scanned every face for something I could recognize. There were dozens of them, men and women, of seemingly all walks of life. I saw little old ladies from Trey's day next to what looked like college kids born in the original US colonies. There were seemingly boring researchers situated next to TV personalities. But the faces from memory, the blurry social group I saw from ground level, were nowhere to be found.

Was she part of more than one coven? Was that even allowed? Or were our records of her coven somehow incomplete?

The possibility led me to do something that would have otherwise been a wild goose chase. From time-to-time, when witnesses didn't have specific names, we were forced to cycle them through catalogues of mugshots and registrations to see if any were familiar. Sometimes, it worked, most times it wasted a full day and left everyone in the room frustrated. But I didn't need to look at every Alter in the city, I just needed to look at all the Witches.

Applying multiple filters and changing the display, I soon populated the windshield and every intact window with every Witch in the Cascadia area. Surprisingly, the number wasn't so high that they all turned into thumbnails. Unfortunately, that was partially because I was using the whole car as a screen. Understanding this, I climbed back out of the car and marched right back to the Ahab's.

Trey raised an eyebrow as I stepped through the door again, slowly turning to a look of concern as I walked over to him like a man on a mission. I could understand, it was a short turn around and I was not looking casual at the time. Plus, the last time I was this amped in his shop I tried to drag him across the counter. But this was just a supply run.

With authority, I said, "I need a large with two shots of espresso and at least three cookies."

The tension on his face broke immediately as he stifled back a laugh and went to work, commenting, "Long day ahead, eh?"

Emerging a couple minutes later, I marched right back to the car, climbed in, and drove off to where I normally parked for the day. I didn't plan on leaving it. The list was too extensive to go over on my hand-link, even on the windshield it was too much to take at once. But parking in front of the Ahab's was limited during the day and I didn't want to have to explain the ticket to HQ. So, to my usual spot I went with my coffee, some cookies, and a setup like the world's most niche dating app.

I wasn't sure how much time passed while scrolling through. After enough photos, time kind of lost meaning. But, before I knew it, the sun had risen and the normal people strolled by to their cars to start their day. A couple looked at me with an expression suggesting they'd call the cops soon if I weren't already sitting in a patrol car myself. Some calls came through to my dash, link, and personal phone but I ignored them all. I knew it was probably Dulaf, maybe Lucian if he hadn't gone straight to bed, but I wasn't really feeling like talking to either of them. Even if I did, I didn't want them to hear I'd wasted several hours going through head shots in hopes I saw someone I hadn't seen in two decades.

I was about ready to give up when one last face rolled across the view. She was blonde with blue eyes and a vaguely retro style to her hair. I knew I couldn't tell her real age from the shot, but she looked late 30s to mid-40s at the most. The catch, though, was that her face came through to me stronger than any other in memory. She owned the house in the blurry fragments. That was her wood floor and those were her antiques. I could picture her and Marionette hugging as the door opened and a piece of hard candy being offered to me as I peeked out from behind my mother. If it wasn't just my sleep deprived brain playing tricks on me, or the caffeine starting to push me over the edge, she was one of the people I was looking for.

Opening the full profile, I found three important details worth noting. First, for some reason she didn't seem to be an active member in any known coven. Second, she'd lived for nearly 40 years in Ballard, which put her only a short drive from my parents' house in Fremont after we moved closer to dad's new job. And third, despite the fact her current legal name, Linda Green, didn't ring any bells at all, a nickname of hers popped to mind almost immediately once I saw her in detail.

Nearly choking on the last sips of long cold coffee, I sat up straighter and whispered to myself, "Aunt Glinda."

The feeling of familiarity with that face was even stronger than any I had with Marionette. Despite her efforts to block out who she was, she must not have done anything to wipe away memories of her old friends. Then again, she might have tried and failed. Either way, I was growing more certain by the second that she was my mother's best friend when we first got to Seattle. She was the Good Witch of North Seattle and, despite her lack of known connections, exactly where I intended to start.

Closing up my coat, logging back into the system so the Oracle would keep track of me, I set off to the north. Hopefully, it was the kind of leap that would put me ahead of an ancient hunter.

Chapter 15
Aethereal Scene

As much as places like Salem, Massachusetts became associated with Witches, they weren't exactly the places you'd find most of them. Witches liked to play things smart from my experience, often finding the places where they could blend in. They didn't go where their eccentricities might stand out. In fact, the few times Witch trials happened to catch a real one it was usually the doing of a rival. For those who could, they would blend into the larger cities, staying closer to places of education where a few quirks were generally overlooked. Failing that, they often drifted to communities with a similar sensibility to their own. My landlady Babs picked the counter culture of the mid-20th century and never really left it behind. She wasn't the only one. But blending in didn't always require such an extreme shift.

Back in the day, Ballard was predominantly fishermen of Scandinavian descent. The demographics shifted in the time since, but the culture lingered. There was still a Nordic Museum, local Viking themed merchandise, and celebrations of Scandinavian ancestry. But what most people never picked up, even me until I was an adult, was how many old rites and rituals blended in nicely in such a place. The Seattle Witch population, though fairly evenly spread today, first clustered in the Ballard area where their trinkets and behaviors seemed like little more than new age appreciation of the local flavor. And, being a short drive from the University district, the occasional surge of seemingly young people wouldn't have been too out of place.

When I was a kid and my dad transferred from Burien up to Seattle, they decided to cut his commute in half and move into the city proper and out of my grandmother's old house. As a kid, the move didn't make much sense to me, but I was okay because we moved to Fremont and there was a big stone troll under a bridge. It never really occurred to me, being a kid and all, that my mother probably had more to do with choosing the neighborhood than my father did. Now, driving across the bridge and seeing an area of the city I hadn't been to in quite a while, I could practically feel the witchcraft in the morning air.

Then again, I'd been feeling witchcraft in one form or another for a couple days, so that wasn't saying much.

Though the GPS was sending me along the most logical route, part of me decided to confirm the old memories were legit. I detoured into my old neighborhood, which was quiet in the early morning hours and looked like I'd passed into a whole different world. The roads were narrower, the buildings much shorter, and the whole place just a little cozier. That could be the fact I hadn't really been down those particular roads since I before I even had to shave. Not that I'd shaved in a bit, which I realized about half way through town. Going home, getting cleaned up, and coming back again would have eaten up at least another hour though. So, I wasn't exactly expecting to make the best first impression on "Aunt" Glinda.

As I weaved through the two neighborhoods and made my way from my old stomping grounds out to Glinda's address in Ballard, I found more than a few sights that gave me that odd feeling. It wasn't anything particularly profound, just a few houses giving me déjà vu, a couple businesses that stood out, even a tree that caught my eye. Somehow, the whole place made me feel both incredibly nostalgic and absolutely out of place. The few people who were out and about seemed shocked to see a car like mine pass through, and I couldn't really blame them. Then again, there was an off chance they could see my haggard, fuzzy face through the tinted windows too.

When I finally pulled up in front of the house, a feeling welled up inside of me looking at it. It wasn't shock, exactly, just a stronger version of that feeling I had when I saw her face on the screen for the first time. It was like standing in front of the house of a distant relative I'd only visited every few years. There was a vague sensation like I knew where everything was while simultaneously feeling brand new. The way the porch was decorated, the flowers in the little garden space she had, and the sign over her mailbox with the Celtic knots around her name were like fragments of old dreams I had long forgotten.

At first glance I saw a lot of signs that I missed my window of opportunity or was barking up the wrong tree. There wasn't a car in the driveway and all of the curtains on the first floor were closed up tight. Walking up to the door also gave me a couple bad vibes as I saw a few wilting flowers and dried out patches of grass. In the summer that wasn't particularly out of place, but it could have meant Glinda hadn't been there for a while. Passing the mailbox, I peeked to see if there was anything inside since that was one of the easiest ways to see how long someone had been gone. Even now, after digital communication and a great deal of things going purely electronic, you'd be surprised how much junk mail could collect if you were gone even for a week.

The box was empty and the porch lacked any out of sight packages. Either she had been there within the week or no one knew where to find her. Considering even I got at least one ad stuffed in my box at the apartment building every week, I figured the former was more likely than the latter. Then again, most of my junk mail consisted of coupons for coffee and doughnuts, a local bat watchers' newsletter, and the fruit of the month club samplers Dulaf signed me up for after we met Peaches.

Her doorbell chime, muffled through the door but still easy to hear, could best have been described as "kooky". It wasn't too over the top, but it was definitely a custom bell that had a few more notes to it than most I'd seen. Strangely, despite being so unique, it was also the first thing that didn't feel familiar at all and brought a little doubt to mind. It was so whimsical, so noisy, that I couldn't picture being a toddler and not wanting to press it every chance I could. Still, with everything else looking so familiar, I had to figure it was either new or something she updated every few years.

Original or not, it didn't seem to draw any reaction from inside. There wasn't a sound, not a creaking of floorboards, not even a flutter of the curtains from someone peeking. I hit it a couple more times before stepping back to examine the rest of the house and deciding to check through a garage window. I probably looked silly hopping around the wall, but it paid off as I saw no car inside. Clearly, though she might have been around recently, she was gone right now.

Pacing slightly along her driveway, I started to draw attention from the rest of the neighborhood. There were a few murmurs and odd looks, one half neighborhood gossip and another half genuine curiosity. A police car in this sort of neighborhood would have drawn half of them out any day of the week, but an ACTF car was practically like a UFO landing. The thing that really caught my eye under the visor was the fact quite a few of their auras didn't seem all that shocked.

Raising my hand and waving to the nearest person, I called out, "I'm looking for Linda Green. This is her house, right?"

An older woman in a robe, hair pulled back into a messy bun, startled from the gesture and looked around to make sure she was the only one in my path. Nodding nervously, she called back, "I saw her leaving late last night with a friend!"

Walking closer so we didn't quite have to yell it for the whole neighborhood, I asked, "What did this friend look like?"

I could see on her face that she wasn't really ready to have the conversation. She started to straighten out her hair as much as she could and tightened the belt around her robe, muttering the whole way. Settling down a bit, she finally answered, "About her age, paler, with dark hair. It looked like she just came from an office – blazer and a skirt. She wasn't quite like the usual type to go through there."

Given her quick straightening up, she must have thought herself a sorry sight, but she was the most beautiful thing to me in that moment. I went from second guessing a drive uptown to knowing for a fact I was in the right place. Of course, I was several hours late. But, hey, locked doors and tardiness never stopped me before.

Giving her a quick handshake and my thanks, I hurried back to the house and punched a few things into the system. The Tolerance Day Treaty said the ACTF didn't have to obtain local warrants when Alter involvement was confirmed. This was mostly because of the Oracle system, which recorded literally everything we did and effectively processed warrants for us on the fly. On the surface it looked like there were no warrants at all, and that was true as far as the local governments were concerned, but behind the system was an international council of judges the Oracles forwarded requests to. Generally, we were cleared to enter the private property of an Alter suspect as it was processing with the understanding that a rejected warrant would invalidate any evidence we found. This came in handy since our suspects could do things like jump out windows, climb up buildings, or outrun cars.

However, I'd found myself in a bit of a grey area.

Effectively, if Glinda were waiting behind the door or I had reason to believe she was still around, I could kick it down like Marionette's after giving her a chance to answer. But in a case like this, since she wasn't the subject of my investigation and I knew she was gone, I actually needed to wait for the system's response for once. Luckily, that networked council streamlined things considerably. By the time I was back at Glinda's door, I already had my lock picking kit in one hand and a digital search warrant in the other.

Conflicted as I might have been about his motives at the moment, learning from a Vampire came with perks. Most guys I know would have to try to find a way to force the door open. Me, I just had to pick a standard five pin tumbler lock. It was a shady skill to know, but it was also one of those things that made everyone's life a little bit easier. Though, full confession, I could probably do it faster with a bump key but I've always kind of enjoyed the process. As the last pin was in place and the cylinder turned over, the door opened with that satisfying click and I quickly packed away the kit.

Stopping for a moment, I knocked one more time and announced myself clearly, "Linda Green, if you are present, this is the ACTF and I am entering your home!"

It felt silly, knowing she was gone and still yelling her name, but entering without declaration was a no-no in a situation like this. Waiting for a few seconds of continued silence, I opened the door and stepped through.

The house smelled of ointment, herbs, and bits of incense long burned away. Natural light flowed through the space despite the curtains closed across the front windows. It was calm and quiet aside from the boards creaking at my feet and the muffled tones of what sounded like an old-fashioned clock somewhere out of sight.

It was an older house, and the steady swing of that pendulum suggested some items inside were just as old, but the décor wasn't quite as out of date as I'd expected. The furniture itself was older, but no more than hand-me-downs you might get from your parents. In fact, most of it was newer than my couch and recliner back home.

It was only as I continued to explore that I found hints of someone who'd lived as long as my landlady or Marionette. Some of the photos on the wall, though mounted in modern styled frames, were naturally sepia toned. A few of the furniture pieces were clearly reupholstered to update their style. The first closet I came across contained enough double-knit polyester to have suggested she'd hunted disco dancers for sport. None of it was enough to confirm her age but it was enough to show she was from another era.

The living room confirmed the neighbor's account. A couple partially full teacups sat on a small table and a shawl was lying on the floor like it'd been taken off mid-stride. Glinda welcomed Marionette into the house like an old friend, invited her to some tea, and then the two of them left abruptly. One of the cups was near empty, closest to the shawl, while the other looked to be barely touched. Marionette was telling her something before Glinda jumped into action. Recalling fragments of a generous personality, it seemed to fit. Though it didn't give much of a clue what Marionette needed Glinda to do.

Looking around, the rest of the living room was littered with objects that felt like they'd fallen out of the same old dreams as the sign and the garden. She had a lamp with a glittering finish over dark paint. Her incense burners looked like mythical creatures dancing around a fire. A small dish shaped like a cauldron held candy inside, the feet of it crafted to look like they belonged to a dragon. I lifted the lid and saw the typical hard candies you'd expect in an elderly home. I was certain now I'd seen all of these before, lingering in memory, sometimes blending with memories of my grandmother. Then, I saw something that brought everything back together.

Up on an old mantle sat a relatively newer photo of a group of women with Glinda standing at the center. I reached out and snatched it up, staring at Marion to her left with an uncooperative toddler resting on her hip as he tried to chew on her hair. After a lifetime of blurry images and a hollow feeling I always tried to ignore, those days came back clearer than they'd ever been.

I'd been here. I'd sat on the old floor boards and listened to them squeak. I watched humming birds out the window feeding from a special blend Glinda called her "panacea". I was fed more candy from that dish than I could possibly remember. And I'd listened to lively conversations between eccentric women that I never understood. This was the place my mom brought me while my dad was at work when we first moved to Seattle.

This was probably where she came when she decided to leave.

Glinda's voice cut through the silence as she shouted from the entrance, "Just what the hell do you think you're doing?"

Wincing and tightening my grip, I couldn't find the words to answer her. I just turned to face her as calmly as I could and tried my best to stop wringing the frame in my hands. She stood there completely untouched by time, identical to the face in the picture

I held. The difference now was the indignant rage in her eyes followed by a slowly dawning shock.

Breathless, almost choking on the words, she covered her mouth and whispered, "Oh god, Nate."

Lowering the frame to my side, I replied coldly, "Agent Leone."

She took a couple steps towards me before coming to an abrupt stop, stammering, "You, you look so much like Michael."

The words had more impact on me than she probably knew. On the one hand, I wondered if she was trying to get familiar to make me lower my guard. It probably wasn't fair, but my job wasn't the best at building trust and nothing right now was really fair. On the other hand, I'd wondered about that myself a couple times in front of the mirror. Though I could remember my dad's last days pretty well, I always had some trouble remembering his face from before. Part of it was time and part of it was the fact the last time I saw him didn't leave the best impression. Either way, he'd kind of turned more into a presence in those memories like the woman standing in front of me.

But I couldn't let her know that, not then and there.

"I'm looking for Marionette Corbin," I said with the most authority I could.

Reflecting the tone I took, Glinda's expression hardened as she said, "I'm sure you are."

Putting the picture back on the mantle, I continued, "I know she was here last night. She's a person of interest and she's been fleeing custody for— "

"It wasn't her," Glinda interjected. "Whatever this is, that isn't the Marion I know."

My swelling contempt was almost overwhelming. Marionette wasn't the person anyone knew. She was a chameleon who darted in and out of people's lives and erased any trace of who she was. She did it to everyone, including me.

I turned to the mantle to make sure she couldn't see me crack, but I could feel it run through me like a fault-line. I'd been freaking out for hours, I knew that, but being here was harder than everything leading up to it. Failing to steady myself completely, I could hear a crack in my voice as I tried to keep that authoritative tone.

"And just who is she, really?" I asked.

The floorboards gave away her location with every step. She was doing her best to come closer without startling me but there was little she could do about the old boards betraying her. I turned my gun toward the wall as I faced her again. Part of me hoped she didn't know I did it intentionally. Another part that I wasn't proud of kind of hoped she did.

Glinda's expression softened again, eyes glistening like she was on the verge of tears herself. Her aura was one of the least guarded of any Witch I'd seen, including Babs. Right now, she was deeply concerned, but not hostile. At least it wasn't hostile if it was telling me the truth.

"Your mother has had her problems," she said, "but she's never killed anyone before."

"***Before***," I said curtly.

Lowering her eyes, chewing her lip, she looked up again with a furrowed brow and said, "Something's happening, something dangerous, and she needs to sort it out."

With a frown so severe it started to hurt, I scolded, "She could have cooperated with us, with me, and we could have sorted this out with her."

Shaking her head, Glinda walked away, scooped the shawl off of the floor and sat on her couch. I had half a mind to cuff her as her back turned, but I stopped my hand before I reached the pouch. She had knowingly aided and abetted a fugitive, I was well within my rights to do it, but there was no chance she'd cooperate if I did. I wasn't sure if that was just experience talking or memories of the woman before. I just knew she wouldn't react well and I couldn't afford to let Marionette get too far ahead of me. Even though the daylight should have given me an edge, Lucian was probably still out there despite the sun.

"Where did you take her?" I asked, walking to the other side of a coffee table and scowling down at her.

"I took her to a friend," she said, averting her eyes, "someone who could help her lift a hex."

"I want a name," I demanded.

Fidgeting with the shawl in her hands, she looked up and said hesitantly, "We know her as Orin."

"Where can I find Orin?"

She shook her head, saying defiantly, "We're smarter than that. We met at a neutral location. I just handed your mother off to her."

A spark of that personality I remembered crept through as she was defending what I assumed was part of her coven. She was feeling guilty while dealing with me, but I was still a threat to them. I could understand it, but it was the last thing I needed. My hand hovered over the handcuff pouch again.

"She's a fugitive, Glinda," I scolded.

"No," she rebuked, "she's your mother."

Glancing back at the picture on the mantle, I sighed. "If I don't find her, someone else will."

Taking off the visor, I made eye contact with her, probably with bloodshot eyes over dark circles to go with the rest of my haggard look. I should have been taking her in, dragging her back to the station. Instead, I was going to try to appeal to whatever part of her might have once been "Aunt Glinda".

"I need to talk to her," I said, "I need to know."

Quietly she echoed, "Know?"

Shrugging, I said, "Everything."

Silence fell over us again, the distant clock keeping time as we both seemed to be holding our breath. I couldn't see her aura but I could tell she was deep in debate with herself. Standing abruptly, she snapped, "Orin is old school, no one knows where she is!"

Calming, softening her tone, she continued, "You deserve to talk to her. But I don't know how to help you now. Orin's not a part of my coven or your mother's. She's from another era."

The thought of arresting her crossed my mind again, but I pushed it aside. She could be lying to me, or manipulating the situation. She might have turned right around and tried to warn Marionette. But I had a hard time picturing myself doing it, and at least she'd given me a street name if nothing else. I still took a cleansing breath and reconsidered it once again to make sure it was me and not another push. But, once that breath cleared, I found a couple more reasons to not do it and none of them were blanket warm and fuzzies slipped to me like a subliminal cue. It would lose me time, it would tip off Lucian, and it would be hard to convict. There were a lot of reasons that made some logical sense.

Besides, she wasn't the only Witch in town.

Putting the visor back on, I started walking out of the house. Glinda followed several feet behind, calling out my name to try to get my attention. With every repetition she got just a little more agitated. There was fear in her voice, like she needed me to stop and talk with her instead of following this lead on Orin. Spooked as she was, I couldn't tell if it was me or the other Witches that had her so concerned. Finally, she cried out "wait!" and I felt a sudden, unmistakable haze over my thoughts combined with the urge to turn around.

It was funny. After a couple of years of getting pushed by Marionette without notice, I suddenly recognized it like a language I'd picked up on the street. I couldn't speak it, I couldn't pick up the grammar, but I recognized the broad strokes. There was a subtle change in the tone of her voice, a few smells in the room were a little more acute than they were before, and I could feel this shift in the pressure in the air around me. I didn't know how it all worked, but I didn't need to. All I knew was that now I could see it coming, I could choose to ignore it somehow. Turning slowly to see her aura, watching that burst of colors retreat, the look on her face showed instant regret.

"You do that again," I said, "and I'm going to make sure Orin knows exactly who gave me the name."

She stepped back, clasping her hands together, stunned into a temporary silence. I gave her a once over, peered over at the photo past her shoulder, then continued for the door. She didn't move from that spot or say anything in protest again. All I heard was a heavy, gasping sigh as I stepped outside, then the scrambling sound after I closed the door.

I let her go, for now, but I wasn't so stupid as to just leave it there. Pulling the hand-link out, I punched in a request to track her electronics, her vehicle's GPS, and pull her phone records as I walked away from the door. I considered asking for a full out tap, but I didn't need something that detailed and even with the fast-tracked system that could take a while to clear. I just needed to know she wasn't skipping town and if there was any indicator of who "Orin" might have been.

Getting in the car, I tried to run a search on the alias on its own. There'd been a few Witches to run with the name. Like Glinda, it was apparently a possible name for the "Good Witch of the North" in one of the many iterations. Understandably, few went for the names "Tattypoo" or "Locasta". But the Orins on record were outside the Cascadia region or all the way up in Vancouver. Either I was in for a long drive, or the "old school" Witch wasn't recorded by that name. This either meant she didn't have a record or she was better at covering her tracks than even Marionette. Still, as I thought in the house before I stepped out, Glinda wasn't the only Witch in town. Pulling out my personal phone, I called one of the only Witches I felt I could trust anymore.

"Ah, Nathaniel," a sweet, lively voice chimed through, "why are you up at this hour? You should have been in bed hours ago."

"Hey Babs," I said, a weak smile crossing my face, "ever hear of a Witch named Orin?"

Chapter 16
Exit Routes

Babs quickly made sense of the mystery of Orin's lack of a record. Technically, though she helped criminals, nothing Orin ever did was ever actually illegal. I say technically for a few reasons. First, she tended to help people who were in shady circumstances. Second, she was operating a kind of clinic without any form of licensing. Luckily for her, and unluckily for me, no one was exactly looking to rat on their nurse.

However, a bit of a hitch presented itself. Though Babs knew the woman and knew her general location, Glinda wasn't entirely full of shit. Orin kept her location incredibly quiet and operated through something of a coven whisper network. Back in the day she used everything from smoke signals to semaphore – which I admit I had to ask Babs to explain to me. Turns out, it was communication through flags. In more recent times she relied on prepaid phones with the numbers handed out to the local covens. However, in the modern day, she'd migrated to a far cheaper method of obfuscation – direct messaging apps.

Babs wasn't specific on the reasons why Orin operated like this, but I had a good hunch. No one was ever eager to "spontaneously combust" and old habits die hard. Unfortunately, that meant I couldn't just ask for the directions to her place. Still, Babs had something for me that no one else probably could have provided: a legal name.

Aileen Hutchins was probably not her real name, given how shifty she was, but it was the one she'd been using for the last few decades of her life. It was also something she apparently didn't spread around often. But, and this didn't surprise me much, Babs was something of a local legend and was friends with just about everyone. Part of me wondered if that included Marionette but I wasn't about to pull that thread.

Luckily, while "Orin" didn't have a record, Aileen was registered. In fact, Aileen seemed to prefer to spend her days expressing her creativity as a quick cross reference showed an art gallery where she sold some of her work. Artist was a pretty solid cover for a Witch, all things considered. You could make something new every day, improve your skills steadily over countless lifetimes, and no one asked any funny questions when you ordered a bunch of peculiar powders, minerals, and who knows what else. She'd been operating out of a suburb called Edmonds under that occupation and hopefully kept her clinic relatively close. So, likely tipping off the entire system, I headed even further north.

The day shift was patrolling now and the map showed a slightly sleepier routine. It was still the morning hours, the real ones, and one of the quietest times of day. There was sometimes a bit of a spike in the winter as the two sides of the city would mingle and the population would increase just a touch. But here in the summer, the sun rose even too early for the morning people and that meant there was that brief, pleasant window where everyone could just coast around and have coffee.

Still, not all those cars were part of that blissful day shift routine.

Like my gut had been telling me earlier, Lucian was still on the move. He had to be careful with his movements, avoiding direct sunlight as much as possible, but I knew he wouldn't just disappear. Word had it that, if he really needed to, he could probably handle some limited exposure to UV after centuries of trying to work past that defect. All I knew is his unit had tinted windows and its beacon was suddenly moving due west and crossing water.

Mildly concerned, I muttered, "Why're you taking the ferry?"

Whatever his reason, at least he wasn't headed towards Orin or after me. I was sure it would bite me in the ass but I had to believe my whole morning wasn't a complete waste. I was still in the proverbial lead as I drove into the quaint little city north of Seattle.

Like Ballard, Edmonds felt like a whole different world from what I was used to. The buildings were short, well-spaced, and charming. The view of the sea and the mountains in the distance was almost completely unobstructed. The people on the sidewalk were actually smiling. A couple even waved at me.

Was it proof of witchcraft? No. But it wasn't a mark against either.

But then, as I marveled at the friendly faces and waited for the light to change, something even more unexpected came to me. A knock at my cracked passenger window startled me as an apparently middle-aged woman stood outside with a broad smile and two cups of coffee in a tray. Dressed a bit more fashionably but not quite eccentric, with dark brown hair cut a little shy of shoulder length, she wouldn't seem too out of place normally. But, if I'd been shocked before, I was now completely astonished as Orin herself stood next to the car and gestured for me to let her in.

Unlocking the door, I nodded back to her with what had to be the most charmingly dumbfounded look she'd ever seen. She laughed, eyes smiling along, and slipped into the seat next to me, transferring the cups from her tray into the cup holders.

"I had a feeling you'd be here," she said cheerfully while buckling her seatbelt. "Glinda warned me you were looking, but I assured her it would be okay."

Mildly stunned, I nearly missed traffic moving again before she off-handedly pointed to the road ahead.

"I hope you can understand," she said, idly picking up her cup and pouring the contents of a small, mysterious baggy into her coffee, "I don't exactly want people to see a patrol unit sitting outside of my home or gallery."

Gesturing to "my" cup, she waved the little baggy in her hand. I shook my head as politely as I could while stunned stupid. I'd had a Witch's brew once before and lived to tell the tale, but I wasn't about to see what she was using besides cinnamon. Though, as she was waving the bag, I did actually smell some cinnamon off of it.

Figuring where I could go with her, I did a quick once over of the map and looked for somewhere that seemed quiet enough to pull over. I'd never actually been to this particular town or in this peculiar situation. It was kind of an oddball twofer.

"We should go to the waterfront," she said cheerfully. "I try to get out there at least once a day to take in the view and listen to the water."

Lingering at the next intersection for a moment, I looked out at the water down a hill slope and relented. Turning for it, I drove well under the speed limit and quietly contemplated if there was any way for a Witch to ambush me with the sea. Maybe she knew a Siren, a Nix, or a mob enforcer. I knew I was being silly – she could just try to put me into a trance and have me sit and wait for high tide – but it wasn't every day the fish just jumped right into the boat.

With a resigned sigh, I asked, "So where's Marionette Corbin?"

She scoffed, took a drink of her coffee, and retorted, "I wouldn't have a clue, that wasn't even the name she gave me if we're talking about the same person."

"Average height and build, dark hair, bright green eyes," I said briskly, "and possibly carrying feed for a phoenix."

A short, barely restrained chuckle escaped her before she commented, "She said her name was Victoria Foucher."

I tried not to raise my eyebrow above the line of the visor, but I don't know if I managed it. It was a brand-new alias, again, and not at all like the two before. I had to figure she would make one soon, but I'd never actually seen how fast she moved on these things.

"Did she show you ID?" I asked, bemused.

Shaking her head, Orin replied, "Not intentionally, no. Though, I'm starting to think she intended it that way."

"What's that supposed to mean?" I pressed.

"Well, when she opened her pocket book to pay me," she answered with a tone of admiration, "I saw her name on the cards inside."

The answer to my questions was incredibly clear: Marionette was either one of the greatest escape artists I'd ever met or mommy was a con artist from the start.

"Fine," I grumbled, "where'd 'Victoria' go?"

Aileen, Orin, or whatever she wanted to be called stared out over the sea as we approached it and quietly sipped without answering me. I wasn't about to start shit in my car, even if there was a manual button to close the box around her if I needed. And, despite the peculiarity, I couldn't look this gift horse in the mouth provided no one attacked the car once it came to a stop. Finding a spot near a grassy little park overlooking the water, I parked and started adjusting my gloves in case I had to come out swinging.

"You agents are always so high strung," she said, setting her cup in the holder and spinning it around so the logo on the side was facing her. "You need coping mechanisms."

"I'm chasing a murderer," I chided, "it's not time to relax."

Shaking her head and rolling her eyes slightly, she gave me a faint smirk and replied, "I don't know what she did or didn't do, but I know she's long gone now."

"Where?!" I demanded.

Sitting back, she silently raised a finger to point towards the horizon over the sea.

Looking out over the water, dots quickly connected. Lucian wasn't the only one to take a ferry and both of them were headed west. Somehow Lucian knew where she was going before I did. Did someone in her known coven have information Glinda didn't? Did Glinda screw me? What did I miss that Lucian saw? Unfortunately, the one person I could ask at the moment wouldn't have known. I needed to figure out Marionette's endgame and stop chasing her trail.

That's when it clicked.

It struck me so hard I had to wring the wheel so I wouldn't spook the Witch in my passenger seat. She was on the run and needed to get out of the country. If she was having to do it through publicly accessed routes, she only had two ways to enter Canada. It was an easier trip to just get on a train and head into Vancouver, but the ACTF has offices in the Vancouver metro area. The only route where she could theoretically dodge us was…

"Victoria," I sighed.

Aileen raised an eyebrow and looked at me, gesturing over her shoulder with an offhand wave. Reassuringly, she said, "There's another ferry leaving in half an hour; you can take the car aboard."

There wasn't any way around it. I was going to have to wait for that ferry. Even if I tried to get moving immediately there wasn't any route that could get me to the other side of the sound in less time than it would take for a ferry across. On the upside, it gave me time to figure out what was going on with the reportedly elusive Orin.

"Why are you cooperating?" I asked, suspiciously inspecting the cup she placed in my holder.

"Well, I knew you were going to arrive," she said, "and I didn't want to have a scene anywhere that connected to me."

Picking up the cup, I grabbed a sugar packet from the tray and then a small stick from a pocket. Going through the routine of acting like I needed my coffee well stirred, the stick was actually a chemical test for drugs that I'd started to make sure to carry around. You'd be surprised how many cups of coffee I get offered and how often my dumb ass was tempted to take them. But the stick let me test without trying to use the visor and staring so long into the coffee that it looked like I was trying to see the future.

Idly as I continued to stir, I remarked, "You said something like that before, but isn't telling me she got on a ferry some sort of breach of the code?"

Shaking her head, pursing her lips, she made a little dismissive wave with her fingers. "The code doesn't much care what I do or don't say after she leaves," she said, "only that I don't harm her while she's in my care."

"And what was she here for?" I asked, continuing to stir like a man with OCD.

Shrugging her shoulders and giving me an unconcerned look, she said, "there was some sort of hex on her, a mental one. Lifting one is a bit like an exorcism and took a careful hand. I don't know the specifics; I just know tomorrow I need to go to the spa so when people see my youthful skin, they'll just think it did me wonders."

Glinda had said it was some sort of hex, and apparently that was something Orin specialized in. Whatever it was, it required heavier work as I started to note hints of cinnamon in the air again. When she first got in, it was overwhelmed with the sudden introduction of coffee. I'd thought it to be something she blended in from her little baggy. Now it clicked for me that she'd been around the phoenix feed, possibly even used it. She knew what she was doing – they both did.

"Still," I mused, lifting the stick to discover the coffee was clean, "you wouldn't want word getting out about something like this, I imagine."

Sitting a little straighter, she answered with a smug tone, "You'd be surprised how often Aileen Hutchins has assisted while Orin wasn't looking."

Suddenly I was starting to understand just who was sitting in the car with me. It wasn't just that she didn't have a record – she actively worked to keep herself clean whenever something came towards her. I'm sure there had to be times she would have kept something covered. Even in this case, she was just pointing to a horizon and leaving it at that. It was absolutely devious.

I exchanged cards with her, of course.

Climbing out of the car, Aileen strolled out onto the grass. It was probably the most leisurely anyone's ever walked away from a patrol car before. At least, discounting the odds this wasn't her first time. Getting ready to head up the street to the ferry, I stopped just as she turned to face me again and waved for my attention. She gestured for me to roll down the window, then shielded her eyes from the morning sun.

Calling out once the window was down, she said, "By the way, she had a bag with her when she left. I think it was a change of clothes."

Leaning her way, I yelled back, "Yeah, she's been in the same clothes for over a day!"

"You don't understand," she said, waving lightly as she turned to enjoy her morning seaside walk, "she's trying to disguise herself!"

Seeing her walk off like the most innocent person in the world, I wondered how many times the infamous Orin had done this in the past. Was she simultaneously the witching world's most prolific exorcist *and* informant? Turning for the ferry terminal, I knew I'd have an unfortunate amount of time to chew on it.

Chapter 17
Altered Ship

Once I was across the sound and back on dry land, I had to speed along to catch another ferry. For several hours, driving along a highway surrounded by grassy slopes, trees, and brief glimpses of small towns, I chased Lucian's marker to Port Angeles like a cat chasing a laser pointer. Whether he knew I was behind him or not depended entirely on whether or not he cared to look at the map. We were the only two out there until Port Angeles and it was impossible not to see me mere minutes in the rear view. To be honest, I had to speed a little to get that close since he figured it out first. I should have been the one with the lead, but I wasn't considering the fact she was fleeing the country.

We had an ACTF station in Port Angeles, but it was a relatively small one that rarely saw real action. Mostly it was meant to handle random sightings out on the Olympic Peninsula and a theoretical worst-case scenario where everyone had to bug out of Seattle. In fact, most of the activity they'd had lately was our fault as we failed to drag in what could only be described as Frankenstein's super-soldier. Now, they spent most of their time coordinating with the local forestry services to make sure the big foot tracks in the mountains were just run-of-the-mill Sasquatch. This translated into a couple things. First, most of their agents were in the mountains at all hours of the day. Second, they weren't exactly ready for something small and crafty.

Strangely enough, I wasn't the only one to make that assessment. Even as his marker crossed through city limits, the local branch of the system remained fairly quiet. For some reason, he wasn't telling them about Marionette. Was he worried they couldn't take her, or that someone else would get to her first?

No, even if what Rufus said was true, that wasn't Lucian. I knew he had his secrets, like where he would go every few years or why he was never promoted above lancer. But there was always a code of honor for what he was going to do. There had to be a reason beyond the cynical crap that had been infecting my thoughts. He might have even felt like it was his responsibility to bring her in, just like me.

Accelerating over the speed limit again, I raced for the city.

Though I'd been there on serious business before, Port Angeles wasn't exactly the place you'd expect such a chase to happen. It was just a hair above the line between town and city, far removed from more serious events until Patch moved into the neighborhood, and had an Alter population so low that we didn't even bother constructing a full HQ in the area. It had that small town vibe, but was covered in small Argyre funded projects that avoided drawing too much attention to themselves. The project of interest that day was the upgraded ferry facilities along the waterfront.

The town had always had a ferry line crossing the border into Canada by way of Victoria, BC. Back in the day it had multiple before a couple shut down. But when Argyre went public they quietly funded a massive upgrade of the ferry lines and the station. Gone were the simple one-story buildings supporting a small passenger-only ferry and instead was the Argyre bankrolled terminal with multiple boats operating lines that no business in their right mind would have operated normally. But for Argyre it wasn't about profit, it was about escape routes. The irony wasn't lost on me that a fugitive was about to use one.

The terminal was one of the newest and most expensive buildings in the city. It was designed with an ACTF aesthetic but did its best not to look aggressive about it. The result was what could best be described as a series of waves frozen in time as they crested over the shore. It didn't much care to keep hostile Alters out, like the black tulip of the headquarters back home, but instead focused on keeping local authorities from being able to drop teams onto the roof as the armored gates slammed shut in their face. To the untrained eye, it was just pretty, but that was generally how Argyre liked it.

The parking garage across the street from the terminal had similar hallmarks despite its mundane appearance. It wasn't anything too in-your-face, just a few little hints most of the world wouldn't notice. The gates over the entrances to the garage were constructed from the same material as the security gates over Acheron. Each ramp had gates too, as if certain floors needed to be locked down. Emergency lighting strips were installed into places where they wouldn't see much use at all unless the power was suddenly cut off and all natural light was blocked out. Lower levels were dug much deeper than should be necessary, tunnels going straight to the terminal without ever risking a hint of daylight on the way. It was nothing too extraordinary, just enough to show it for the fortress it really was to those who recognized the architect.

Frankly, I'd say it looked more like an ACTF station than the one Port Angeles actually had. Then again, that was probably why the two were positioned so far apart.

I could have parked just about anywhere, with most of the floors only a quarter full at most, but I kept searching for a particular vehicle on the way. Finding his car felt important even if I knew Lucian was a good clip ahead of me already. Part of me was hoping he was standing and waiting for me. Instead, I found his empty car in a sublevel not far from one of the tunnels. Parking next to it, I idly checked my gear while staring holes through his car. After a second, I stopped and looked at my hands – silver plates active and my finger resting across the activation strip.

What the hell was I planning to do?

Most of it was just reflex. Every time you enter an unknown you do a gear check; it was just training. But the silvers weren't for Marionette. Witches don't have that allergy. Was it just idle reflex or was I expecting to punch someone sensitive to them?

Flexing my hands for a moment, I decided to leave them on in case Marionette had help and hopefully not to punch my old mentor in the face.

Getting out, I started the seemingly long march down the tunnel. It was constructed with the same airlock-like design as the headquarters' entrances but far wider than any of them. It wasn't designed to throttle people, but rather ensure that only the right people were getting in or out at any given time. Multiple security doors stood at the sides of the room, thick enough to be mistaken for supports but resting atop rails and grooves to let them slam shut. I'd imagine once they were closed it would take hours to make any progress, forcing anyone who tried to go after the surface structures through the port. Sometimes I would get so used to Argyre's approach to security that I'd overlook their penchant for backup plans and fail-safes.

Sometimes I'd forget they liked to be ready for anything.

As I approached the terminal itself on the far side of the tunnel I was greeted by a warm light. It wasn't sunlight, obviously, but the lowest levels of a terminal more complex than anything this side of Seattle. The lights above were similar to the ones down in the HQ's sanctuary, creating light as strong as natural sunlight but with all of the UV filtered out. The walls were covered in screens rotating through views of all the places the ferries would go at a definition so high you could practically touch them. Benches lined the center of the passage, facing out towards those scenic locales, stretching all the way from the entrance to a set of escalators hundreds of feet away. Between the benches were arrangements of plants, flourishing under the artificial light – in part because they were so strong and in part because, as my visor told me, they were genetically modified themselves to make the place feel fresher.

Past all of it, one figure stood apart from all others like a statue carved from obsidian and inlaid with gold. Lucian seemed so much taller than everyone there as he walked in full uniform with a SOL helmet covering the last bit of him the uniform couldn't. He weaved past the crowd with little effort, almost like

Marionette, but more due to personal grace than to the subtle mental nudging she used. She was a whisper on the wind – he was a specter.

I was a bull in a China shop.

Sticking two fingers in my mouth, I whistled so loud the place momentarily came to a dead stop. Eyes burned holes into me with looks of annoyance and confusion. But none of those mattered, only the distant reflective visor of the helmeted man as it turned to face me.

Not even waiting for me to get to him, he opened a direct channel between our badges to start lecturing me. "You shouldn't be here, Nate," he said. "I know what you think you're doing but you can't be involved in this."

Marching past the continuing glares, I refuted, "I'm already involved, it's up to you whether we cooperate or not."

As I approached, my reflection growing in his visor, it was nearly impossible to tell what was going on inside. The uniform and the helmet had covered him so well and he remained so still that even the visor was struggling to get strong reads on him. It was more like a void in the reads than your typical suppressed aura. He wasn't just blocked from the light: he was completely sealed. Standing directly in front of him, all I could see was the infinite reflections of his helmet and my shades face-to-face.

"Don't make me pull rank," he said, muffled now that the channel closed.

Frowning, I replied, "Don't make me ignore it."

One of us might have been bluffing – maybe even both of us. Truthfully, I wasn't sure if I was at the moment. I was tired, visibly worn, and running on little more than caffeine and fury. Anyone else standing in front of me would have been in for a rude awakening. But, besides the fact he could probably throw me back to the entrance from where he stood, I wasn't really sure if I wanted that. No matter what Rufus had said, I didn't want to be standing there. I was there because I needed to be.

Quietly, I broke the silence, whispering through a clenched jaw, "I need more than a couch and a toaster."

Bruskly, he replied, “She’s a powerful Witch, a professional, and— “

“And she has a hard time manipulating me,” I interjected, “I was the only one who could see her in the club.”

Though I couldn’t see his face behind that visor, I could imagine it pretty well. After years of dealing with him, I knew the look he got when he was conflicted. He wasn’t given to extreme expressions with a face that often looked like it was carved from marble. Instead, it was a very subtle frown, the slightest hints of a furrowed brow that could disappear behind a pair of shades, and a slight lowering of his chin. Early on, I never noticed, but the visor always caught it for me. Now, I just pictured the face since even the Oracle wasn’t sure what was behind that helmet. Then again, if he was angry, the brow and frown were a lot worse, his chin was up, and he was calculating my weight so he could figure the arc to clear the plants on my way to the door.

It was a tough call.

Muffled by the helmet, I heard a grunt and sharp exhale escape him before he muttered “fine” and started walking for the escalators again. “But remember,” he said as he stepped on, “if you start to feel anything unusual— “

“I know, I know,” I interrupted, jogging to catch up, “scream to assert dominance and keep firing until the bugs stop swarming me.”

Even through the helmet, I could feel the icy stare.

“Kidding, kidding,” I said, having the first real grin on my face for a couple days.

His shoulders relaxed as he turned to look back to the top.

“Don’t be ridiculous,” he said matter-of-factly, “you jump into the water.”

My grin grew for a moment before a chilling thought crossed my mind.

“Wait, seriously?”

He didn't answer, of course, only silently riding to the top and watching for something ahead. As he stepped off the escalator, he finally said, "Just try to be careful."

"She's just a Witch," I said, scanning the area immediately around us. "I've ran into several today alone."

The floor above was much more open and expansive. Skylights and windows provided natural light but had a faint tint over them to filter out the UV like the lights below. None of the windows faced towards the city itself, or even out to the parking lot, instead facing out over the waterfront where four piers could be seen stretching out ahead of us. The ferries were just unloading their previous passengers, a larger one capable of carrying cars docked at the most eastern edge unloading a surprisingly large number of Argyre designed vehicles. But the ferry to Canada itself was dead ahead, a sign above its corridor letting us know we had less than half an hour before it would be off again.

I caught my reflection in the back of Lucian's helmet as it moved very slowly and systematically to sweep the floor. Though he could probably take it off inside the room, I could understand why he wouldn't at the moment. Besides the risk we might have to run out across the surface, there were a couple other advantages to that polished dome. I'd worn a functional SOL helmet before so I knew it had a better visor than the shades I was wearing and I could only imagine what sort of information it was picking up. Not to mention, if it could take a hit from a Nosferatu, it could probably survive a flying lamp or two.

With a strange emphasis to his tone, he said, "Marion is more than ***just*** a Witch."

The way he said it had that air of familiarity, of knowing, in the way that Glinda had in her living room. It was a distant, nostalgic tone like he was dredging up memories of someone who stood out more than Marionette ever seemed to do. Hell, he was using an older alias.

"Currently named Victoria," I stiffly corrected.

"You got her current alias?" He asked, only barely audible through that helmet over the sound of the sea and the terminal crowd.

I picked up the pace to walk alongside him and nodded, replying, "Victoria Foucher."

Though I couldn't quite hear it, I saw the little jolt of an amused snort escaping him as he said, "Of course it's Victoria."

"It seems a little on the nose for where she's headed," I said.

"Well, that" he added, "but it's also the feminine form of her favorite author's name."

I nearly missed a step when he said it. I realized they'd known each other. But he really ***knew*** her and I wasn't sure I was ready for that. You don't know the favorite author of a passing acquaintance or someone who you only work with occasionally. That's something you know about a friend or…

"You two didn't," I started to ask before trailing off.

He didn't act surprised and his muffled voice didn't waver as he responded, "No, it was never like that. Our arrangement was... unique."

Halting in midstride and turning abruptly my way, it seemed to hit him what had to have been going through my mind. He reached for the visor of his helmet momentarily before hesitating and reaching out for me instead, resting the hand on my shoulder.

"I don't know what you were told," he said solemnly, "but it was never anything sinister."

Like I thought, he was going to say he had the best of intentions. But that didn't clear him as much as he'd hope. There were still questions that didn't care what his intentions were. I just didn't have the time to ask them yet.

"And we'll talk it over later?" I asked.

He nodded, squeezing my shoulder, then continued on ahead. As tightly sealed as he was, I just had to hope he looked sincere under it all. I was putting my trust in him and he was doing the same by letting me be there. It had to be enough.

We marched to the Victoria-bound ferry and gave everyone we passed a quick once over no matter what they might have looked like. I didn't know how easily Marionette could disguise herself, at least not without resorting to subliminal messages and disappearing acts, but the fact Lucian was doing the same made me a little more confident. Victoria was who she'd be arriving as, but not necessarily who she'd be boarding as.

Though, that did make me realize we had at least that much to go on. Taking out the hand-link, I ran a check for Victoria's passport and hoped it existed somewhere on the US or Argyre databases. Soon a vaguely familiar face appeared on my screen, makeup concealing her features in a way I'd seen only in online tutorials. She was blonde on the passport, somehow seamlessly, and even managed a tan that didn't look sprayed on. More than that, it was an American passport with no associated Alter registration or Argyre citizenship. Given the way she hid her aura for all that time, there wouldn't be any way to spot her on the other side without stopping her for a genetic test.

In short, once again, Marionette might've had a past life in the CIA.

Passing the profile from my hand-link over to Lucian's gear, I started searching the crowd for blondes and hoped for a sign of a cheap wig or bleaching agents among the crowd. In a bustling transit hub that was a bit like searching for a needle in a haystack, but the visor could close some of the gap. Though it focused on the biometrics of a person more often than not, it was always keeping track of chemicals in the air too. More than once, I learned that was a bit of a double-edged sword. Here, it was helping me parse the difference between naturally bad hair and the kind you had to buy. There was a wave of chemical traces out there, but nothing particularly damning: hairspray, gel, and conditioners formed a light haze over the top of the crowd. Nothing was particularly fresh or extreme.

Firmly, like he knew, Lucian asserted, "She's going to be wearing a natural hair wig, Nereid makeup, and wedge shoes."

The natural wig made sense, and the Nereid makeup would be water proof to keep her new face intact, but I had to ask, "Why the shoes?"

"Old trick she picked up before you were born," he said, picking up the pace as he took a more authoritative march down the corridor and to the pier. "Carrying a bunch of vials of herbs and oils draws a lot of attention and can't get through most security, but you'd be surprised what a Witch can do with some essential oils soaked into cork."

The crowd grew thicker halfway to the ferry, bottlenecked by a full body scan. I almost got into line like a twit before remembering the security was on Argyre's payroll. Lucian bypassed the whole thing without so much as a word, angering multiple people in the crowd and spooking the others as he continued at his determined pace. I lagged behind, producing my hand-link for the security to quickly ask if anyone had seen the blond woman on my screen. Of course, no one standing at the line had, but someone sitting behind the scanner a good dozen feet away spoke up in a nasally, congested tone.

"She looks kind of familiar," he said, sounding miserable with every syllable. "Maybe a couple days ago?"

I nodded and didn't bother to explain how that wouldn't be possible, instead just hurrying after the dark phantom in the distance.

"Congested guard back there confirms she looked familiar," I said, tucking the link away as I caught up.

Lucian nodded, not uttering even a sound, as he lifted his hand to point to a group boarding the ferry and a blond woman in a casual summer outfit half way across the ramp. Despite the distance between us, the noise and movement of the crowd forming a wall of activity between us, she turned to look our way. For that one moment, the waves of humanity between us didn't matter and we stayed silently locked on each other. Then, in a flash of activity across her aura, something shifted in the air.

She continued up the ramp with urgency to her pace as a man further down the ramp bumped into another man in front of him. It wasn't a severe bump, barely even visible, but in an instant the second man's aura turned brilliant red and he turned with a tremendous fury. Soon the two of them were screaming and shoving at each other on the narrow path, then jostling and colliding with others on the ramp, setting a chain reaction of sudden, irrational anger that rolled through everyone behind "Victoria" as she boarded the ferry.

An exasperated "shit" escaped Lucian's helmet as he dashed for the ramp, weaving between people.

"It's a ferry," I remarked, running in his wake to navigate the crowd, "she's not going anywhere!"

"Just one problem," he said while picking up speed, "you're assuming the crew won't leave without clearing the ramp!"

Mere seconds later, the ferry sounded a horn and the engine started to rev. The ramp, thankfully, started to back away from the ferry as the people on top were clear and the people at the bottom were quickly falling off in their mad tussle. The mooring lines, on the other hand, now went taught and caused a tremendous groaning noise as the ship fought to get free. A terrible groan built between the ship and the pier, echoing in a way where you couldn't tell which side was straining worse. But the real racket was the sound of the raucous crowd ahead.

Lucian went low and sprinted across the pier like an Olympic athlete. Meanwhile, I did what I could just to keep up and stay in his wake. I didn't do too shabby, the crowd that got out of his way didn't have time to close in my path, but we can't all be built like iron gazelles. And there really wasn't much I could do to match it when he effortlessly jumped a dozen feet and vaulted over the rail onto the ferry's deck.

Nope, I had to use the retracting ramp and the power of positive thinking.

Bobbing and weaving through the crowd, deflecting a few stray punches, I did my best not to get dragged into the chaos Marionette left in her wake. Most of them weren't reading a natural red – instead sporting a blend of shades that made it clear something touched them. The clearest view I got in the mad dash was the woman who lunged nails first at my face while screaming like some sort of bird of prey. Catching her wrist and pivoting around, I had a split second to notice the yellow running along the edges of her otherwise blood red before I hip tossed her into the deck behind me. It wasn't much, but it was enough of a reason to shift my stance to ensure she wouldn't land head first and hopefully wouldn't take too much of a bump on the way down.

It still sounded like I was murdering her in the process, though, as she went down like a screaming firecracker and sold the drop like a professional wrestler.

Over the screaming and scrambling, a distinctive crack sounded like a whip snapping overhead. I looked up from the not-quite-banshee at my feet to see the mooring lines lashing through the air overhead, cut clean near the ferry and sent flying out from the sudden release over the rest of the crowd. A member of the crew stood on the deck near the mooring reel, vague look on his face like the one Kate had when she was holding the gun. Suddenly, the ferry was getting away much faster.

I released the raptor's wrist and bolted for the ramp, the first two puppets still dancing away as they tried desperately to hurl each other over. I could have probably restrained them both, they were human and not in the best of shape, but I didn't have the time. Judging the place like a parkour obstacle course, I got a quick assessment of their footing, the rail, and the angle of the ramp before sprinting at them for all I was worth. Going full bore, I hopped, grabbed at their shirts, and then yanked them back while using them like a makeshift pommel horse. It wasn't the prettiest gorilla vault, and I heard one of them clang against a rail while they fell, but I stayed upright and my feet landed on ramp instead of someone's face so I considered it a win.

Despite that, the rear of the ferry cleared the ramp before I could catch up and the gap was opening faster with every step. By the time I reached the top, the only thing I had left to carry me over that gap was adrenaline, caffeine, and dumb luck. I crashed chest first into the back rail and damn near bounced off the thing, narrowly managing to hook an arm over the top and cling for dear life. Even through the padded, armored jacket, I could feel the sting in my ribs from both the impact and the impromptu cross-fit session.

Hauling myself over the rail, I flopped to the deck and took a moment to work out the stitch in my side. The crowd on the lower deck was full of glassy eyes and slightly discolored auras as they created a small wall of humanity ahead of me. It hadn't occurred to me during the run, but I'd lucked out that it wasn't a car carrying ferry. Maybe Lucian could take on a car, but I usually did my best to stay in my weight class by at least a thousand pounds and a Buick wasn't in the cards. Though, listening to the mad tussle on the deck above, I got a feeling Lucian was running into a whole other problem: a Buick could take a punch but tourists couldn't.

Staggering to my feet, the crowd stared blankly at me before a few started to shamble my way. The vacant look behind their eyes was unnerving. Had I never met an actual Zombie, I would have made the comparison, but I'd never seen this particular look on a real Zombie's face. This was more like aggressive sleep walking or the look of an angry drunk in the midst of a black-out rampage. The shambling grew more hectic, the group bumping into each other and jostling for position to grab at me. On the next deck above I could hear a similar thunder as Lucian ran into a horde of his own.

Despite this, I was more concerned that the world was starting to blur around me like I'd walked into the same stuff that hit them.

Thankfully the handful in front of me weren't exactly coordinated in their half-awake state. Their movements were a little sluggish, their hand-eye coordination was way off, and I wasn't entirely sure they knew why they were grabbing at me. I looked for an opening and took it, dashing between a couple middle aged tourists and passing them with relative ease. Had there been more, even in that state, I might've been in some actual trouble, but the lower deck was spacious and left plenty of openings. The upper deck, on the other hand, was growing noisier with every passing second.

Weaving through the crowd and slapping away stray grabs, I rushed the stairs as the upper deck had grown into an all-out brawl. The crowd, stomping around like inconsiderate neighbors, was snarling and screeching like a pack of rabid animals as they centered on what I assumed to be a lithe Vampire doing his best to stay calm. Lucian could have cleared the deck with ease, but not without putting a few of them in the hospital.

Despite his restraint, I saw a 300-pound dude in a Hawaiian shirt fly over the crowd like a cheerleader and heard the tell-tale crack of someone else being forced to eat deck-boards. Just as I imagined, the real battle was between their numbers and his mercy. Still, as floral print tumbled out of sight and the man who face-planted in the center crawled out from under foot, I was tempted to go around them and continue the hunt for Marionette. Really, I would have if not for a familiar helmet flying out of the mob and bouncing across the floor.

Lucian could take the pack – the sun was another story.

Fetching one of the rods from my side, making sure my earplugs were in, I called out "Banshee!" before whipping it through a couple legs and making a run for the helmet. The scream caused the mob to scatter as several snapped out of their trance and others became too disoriented to focus. Soon, as the crowd thinned, Lucian punted the rod and sent it flying into the harbor. Fetching the helmet from the deck, I hurried to give it back to him only to find it wasn't as necessary as I thought. Straightening as the screaming rod disappeared beneath the waves, Lucian stood in a ski-mask and a visor.

Looking perplexed, I gestured at the helmet in my hand.

"Extra precautions never hurt," he said, "and the helmet comes with an air filter."

I tossed it to him, shook my head, and searched the chaos of the deck for any signs of "Victoria". The top end wasn't very large and designed for open movement, but still wasn't a completely empty space. With the stairwell and restrooms providing a completely opaque column in the center, the passenger cabin couldn't be seen entirely and the control deck was amply secured to prevent a hijacking. Of course, considering we were getting mugged by vacationing suburbanites, she could've double backed on us at any point.

Hell, she might've jumped into the sea.

Securing his helmet again, Lucian confirmed, "It doesn't afford much space but she can still use the location against us. Split up."

Considering the possibility she might have slipped past me, I turned for the stairs and made my way back down. With the chaos above and the mob below, I didn't have much time to assess the people who weren't shambling my way. She could have been down there the whole time, sitting and watching me trying to shimmy my way through a grabby crowd.

Even with some time to calm, the lower deck looked like a sluggish mosh pit as the dazed and confused passengers meandered and ricocheted off each other in slow motion. They were running out of gas, almost like they were growing increasingly more intoxicated. I could feel it too, the slowly growing fog rolling over my brain, but not the rest of whatever hit them. A few hands reached for me, easily avoided with a light pivot or a couple steps to the side. But that early surge, whatever she pushed on them to make it happen, had evaporated.

I still didn't see a hint of our escape artist. There weren't any blondes, no sign of anyone in the outfit I saw, and most of the people there were in flip-flops, tennis shoes, or some boat shoes on the particularly well-prepared. The visor showed a deck full of chemically altered people, so much so that I don't know if it could have told the difference between them and a Witch regardless. Marionette's aura had been traditionally dark blue, a hard suppression by someone with years of training. But here, she could actually relax and blend with the crowd by pretending to be just as wasted as the rest. Worse, even if she couldn't, I was starting to get a little too impacted to tell the differences myself.

I wasn't going to find her like this.

Taking a moment to lean against the rail and breathe in some fresh air off the sea breeze, I took a moment to put myself in her cork wedges. There was a secured terminal in Victoria, Lucian and I were on the boat, and there was no way we wouldn't call ahead for help once we got close enough. She could try to hijack the boat and send it off into international waters, but that would just leave her stuck with us. She could try to get the crew to kill us, but they were mostly out of shape civilians and at least one of us could flip a car. There was really only one option left.

Muttering into the sound of the waves, the answer was suddenly obvious. "Life rafts."

I pushed off the rail and steadied myself. The fog at the edges of everything was growing. Whatever she put into this hex was amazingly potent and at least odorless enough to not be instantly recognized. This wasn't just about distracting us or even trying to throw us overboard. If she needed to get onto the life raft to ditch us, she needed to make sure we couldn't punch a couple holes in the thing from a distance. The shambling masses weren't just pushed, they were drugged, and so was I.

Making a foggy guess at the layout of the ferry, I headed for the place that seemed most likely to be carrying life rafts and emergency supplies. I wasn't sure the capacity of the ship, but I knew the regulations said the thing needed to carry enough lifeboats to support at least 125% of whatever it could hold. I never quite understood that, but it meant that this thing had to have a way to get off and back to shore in a pinch. And, on something this small, that was going to be an inflatable raft as part of an emergency kit. Searching for anyone looking like crew, my hope was I could slap one of them back to their senses and get them to lead the way. However, before I could find one, I got the sort of sign I was hoping for: a signal flare fired horizontally across the upper deck.

With a bright red light and hissing sound, I listened as previously slumbering people screamed and scattered before a loud bang. A flurry of footsteps charged in the direction of the shooter, followed by a loud tussle. Obviously, Lucian found something and, with one of the crew hurtling over the rail and falling into the water, I had a couple guesses what it was.

The fire, light, and sudden bang snapped the upper deck passengers out of their trance. They stampeded down the stairs and piled into the lower deck trying to escape the chaos. Within moments a second flare blew overhead, this time met with the distinctive buzz, a pop, and a blue flash cutting through the red glow as a Helios returned fire. Marionette couldn't have possibly thought she could win a firefight using a flare gun, yet that was apparently what was happening. I ran back into the crowd and started fighting my way against the stream like a very dazed salmon.

And then, I saw something pass me in the stream of people.

It was a bright orange case, below line of sight, but covered in reflective tape that caught my eye. I glanced at it for the flash it was visible before losing it again in the river of tourists. Looking over the crowd that had spilled out onto the lower deck, fighting to stand firm against an onslaught of shoves and elbows, I searched frantically for the blond in the wave of humanity. Unfortunately, there wasn't a sign of the golden wig. Knowing what I saw had to be the emergency kit, I kept searching until I caught sight of raven hair pinned up into the tightest of buns over an alabaster neck.

Pulling my gun and giving chase, I yelled over the crowd with all the strength I could muster, "Marionette Corbin! You're under arrest!"

She didn't look back, simply keeping her head down and moving like she hoped I'd lose her again. She made a beeline for the port side and started to fumble with a package from the larger kit. Nearing the rail, she grabbed for a chord and prepared to heave it into the water.

"Freeze!" I cried out, trying to keep the gun level as multiple people ran into me in their mad panic to escape the shootout above.

Even with my weapon drawn, Marionette didn't hesitate. My vision was blurring and she probably knew it. Even with the target assist, it wasn't clear I could safely disable her. Either I'd miss wildly or I'd hit something I didn't mean to. But there was still something I could do to stop her. Increasing the power, I cranked the Helios from crowd control up to max, moved to get a better angle, and steadied my aim on the mass I knew I could hit. No matter what tricks she pulled, I wasn't letting her escape again.

Watching as she sent the raft flying over the rail, I let the visor confirm my shot and pulled the trigger. With a surprising bang, case torn apart midair, the gases of the raft erupted out of the hole burned through it. As it hit the water with a heavy splash, the escaping air was soon smothered by the waves. The dying raft let out a series of bubbles as its sad last gasps before being claimed by the deep.

Spinning on her heels, we were finally face-to-face. Nearly twenty feet apart and through a visor, we weren't exactly eye-to-eye. Her aura was still guarded, despite all the shit she'd been casting about the boat. Her face, on the other hand, was the most expressive I'd seen from her since we met…the second time. It was stressed, brow furrowed, faint frown beginning at the corner of her lips. She still had her sunglasses on too, but the way her eyebrows turned gave me the impression there was an uncertainty in her eyes. It wasn't just fear, there was some sadness. I wondered if she was just upset it was me or if she was worried if I'd actually looked at her file. Either way, I knew exactly what I had to say.

"Drop the bags, put your hands on your head, and turn to face the water," I said as calmly as I could.

Complying, she said with a wavering voice, "You don't have to do this, Nate."

Something swelled in me. Was it nostalgia from Marionette using my name at a time like this? Was it resentment boiling to the surface? Or was she trying to push me again and the visor just couldn't pick it up? Whatever it was, I pushed it down and said what might have been the cruelest thing I could think of.

"I'm afraid I do, ***mom***."

Chapter 18
Limestone Yoke

For all the bitching I did to get Lucian to let me help, once we had Marionette, I felt weird shoving her into a box and I couldn't stomach the idea of having her in the passenger seat for 2 hours. Just putting the cuffs on her felt a little too surreal to me. Less reluctantly than I would have thought, I handed her over to Lucian, who had the luxury of a back seat and the stoicism of someone who's lived longer than most civilizations.

The drive back was quiet and uneventful, which was good since I needed to just tune out for a bit. Besides the sheer insanity of who was in the lead car there was also the fact that every bit of the caffeine I'd ingested had faded from my system. I had a bad habit of driving to this part of the state well after my shift to take part in crazy crusades and it was catching up to me this time. Maybe the drain of dealing with so many mind whammies was more than I could handle. Maybe the fact my last trip to Port Angeles involved an angry mountain of muscle meant I had more adrenaline to keep me alert that time. Either way, the street was getting *real* same-y and the lack of changes was starting to make me zone out.

The upswing was that a monotonous road was the best time to turn on the self-drive and let the car go. Normally you wouldn't catch me dead using the thing, but there wasn't anyone around and *undead* felt like a loophole. I never quite fell asleep. Years of nocturnal living, stress, and more than a few coffee pot binges had rendered me a bit of an insomniac anyway. Instead, I spent most of the time focusing on the subtle changes in the scenery, thinking about how much I resented every minute of this situation, and doing my best to ignore the calls coming through the dash from a certain Elf. With every passing attempt I became more and more aware that I'd ditched her in a hissy fit.

Despite understanding that, it was about the twelfth time and half an hour outside of Seattle when I finally decided to pick up.

"It's about damn time," Dulaf scolded, the least threatening scowl on her face as she floated on the screen. "What the hell were you doing in Port Angeles this time?"

I studied her face, really focusing for the first time in at least an hour, and looked for signs. A corner of the mouth turned just right, an angle of a brow, the direction her eyes were pointing – all provided little clues. I couldn't be entirely sure just what I was looking for, but what I found was concern and I wasn't sure what to do with that.

Slightly disarmed, I replied, "I needed to catch her."

The irritation on her face, that unthreatening scowl, melted into outright concern as she listened. Leaning towards the camera she asked, "Was that a good idea?"

It probably wasn't, but I wasn't going to admit it as I answered, "I needed to see her brought in."

Her ears drooped very faintly as a frown crossed her face. Quietly she assured, "You know Lucian wouldn't have let her get away."

"That was part of the problem," I muttered, briefly glowering before that thought of bailing on her crept up again. Glancing up to make eye contact with the projection, I asked with barely restrained disappointment, "Why didn't you tell me?"

She grimaced, shook her head, and protested, "I didn't know until recently."

"How recently?" I asked grimly.

Her ears sank further and her eyes lowered to the desk as she mumbled only barely above what the microphone could pick up, "He told me after you mentioned feeling strange around her the first time."

My jaw clenched and I gripped the wheel again. I'd met Marionette and felt strange a couple years prior. She'd sat on it for all that time? Then again, he'd sat on it longer. Though, that thought led to another uncomfortable question.

"How could you not know, all that time?" I asked. "He knew!"

Ears folding back like a cat ready to pounce, she snapped at me, "She worked for him decades ago! I never met her before!"

Rufus' words echoed back from our conversation the night before. Lucian had more or less confessed to it by revealing how familiar they were, but Dulaf had confirmed it straight to my face. Not that being blunt was out of the ordinary for her.

"Did he send her to meet my dad?" I asked, pushing past my fear of her response.

"Of course not!" she exclaimed, hesitating before following with a touch of uncertainty, "I don't think so."

"Rufus said some things," I murmured.

Her ears perked, picking up what I said clearly as if I'd whispered it directly to her. Sternly she scolded, "You of all people should know never to listen to that man."

Sighing, running fingers through my hair, I said, "I know, I know. I just didn't expect to find her and to find out you guys knew it was her."

"Nate," she said warmly, "I bust your balls, but we're still friends. If I'd known before Lucian told me not to say anything, I would have told you right away."

That sentence quickly snapped me into focus. Bluntly, I demanded, "Why did he tell you not to say anything?"

Squirming, fidgeting in her chair, Dulaf avoided looking directly at the camera or speaking for what felt like an eternity before she answered, "He said she was dangerous to you."

Turning off the self-drive, I took firm grip of the wheel and drove the rest of the way practically in Lucian's trunk. The rest of the conversation with Dulaf went fine, I realized she was just trusting Lucian and she spent most of the time making sure I was okay. Maybe she was full of mischief, but she was right: Dulaf is nothing if not brutally honest.

The problem was the man with millennia of secrets.

Lucian wasn't oblivious to it either. Once we entered the city, he started giving me ample warning on when he was going to come to a stop so I wouldn't end up in his back seat. It was actually kind of considerate given the fact I was acting completely irrational. I knew where he was going, the cars were all tracked, and it wasn't like I couldn't call to confront him about something. It was less about keeping track of him than it was about the idea that he could get her out of the car and into processing before I could intercept. I'd let him take her in, but I suddenly wasn't cool with the idea of him taking her to holding without me. It was ridiculous, all things considered, since I didn't really think he was going to coerce her.

Frankly, I just needed to know what they meant by "dangerous".

Once we were in the parking garage, it became a mad race to find a spot before he could so that I could cut them off at the pass. I wasn't planning to rip her from his hands, or even start a scene, I was just hoping to get to his back seat before he could… somehow. So I went for the nearest spot I could find, one that he passed himself, and got out of the car with all the energy of a man who'd actually slept recently. Catching sight of where Lucian pulled in, I cut through the garage as quickly as possible. Yet, for all my effort, I found Lucian and Marionette standing and waiting for me at the back of his car. She looked utterly defeated in his grip, bloodshot eyes with subtle blue contacts quickly averting from me as I approached.

He released her and made a quick gesture for me to take her, then took a couple steps back. I wasn't really sure what to do with the gesture at first but took her by the elbow anyway and gave him a befuddled nod.

"You caught her," he said matter-of-factly.

Marionette didn't say anything as we walked, staring at the ground as we took a much more casual stroll to the holding elevator. The earlier crowd had flushed through long ago, what with the sun having risen hours prior, and the whole area was eerily quiet. Our footsteps echoed around us and drew attention to just how awkwardly silent we'd all become. I wasn't talking to Lucian because of the questions. Lucian wasn't talking to me because of the same. Marionette was just clearly using her right to remain silent and probably hoping I'd retained some of dad's best traits like restraint and the ability to separate work and family. When someone finally broke the silence, it wasn't even one of us.

"Oh hey," a smarmy voice cracked through, "it's you!"

The three of us looked over to find Mark Robinson, thankfully clothed, smiling like he'd just crossed old friends. Though he seemed friendly, the sudden burst of noise put the three of us on edge and brought us all to attention. We hadn't talked about it, but I was sure that Lucian and I were thinking the same thing just then. Mark was exposed to the same stimuli that Kate had been before she turned into a vacant sleeper agent, now he was standing right in front of us. If Marionette was at the top of the whole thing, he could be there to help her. If she was a middleman, he could've been there to tie up the loose ends. Marionette, for her part, seemed to use me as a human shield as I passed her off to Lucian and turned Mark's direction.

"We're going to need you to back up," I said in my most authoritative tone.

He stopped mid-stride and raised his hands like he expected me to go at him, assuring, "Whoa, I was just here to talk to a Lancer Nguyen about that shit with Kate! I'm not trying to start anything."

Lucian walked off with Marionette as I continued blocking Mark. Sure, it was messed up to think I was acting as Marionette's meat shield, but it was unlikely Mark's skinny jeans could conceal a gun capable of getting through an ACTF jacket. His aura was a little agitated but calming down, like our sudden movements spooked him. Besides that faint edge, though, everything looked pretty clear.

"What'd Nguyen need to know?" I asked, watching his hands like a hawk.

He lowered them but kept them in sight, shrugging as he answered, "Just who we ran into; she was saying something about covens." Bringing his hands back up for a moment, halting as he saw the light twitch across my shoulders, he added, "I thought this was about that Siren. Do Sirens even have covens?"

I had a bad habit of answering questions like that, usually for people who I thought I could get more from. But in Mark's case the boilerplate response came out like a prerecorded message. "The ACTF follows all potential leads over the course of an ongoing investigation. We can't give any details on the current status of the investigation, but rest assured that any and all possibilities are being treated seriously."

A subtle jolt rolled through him as he silently scoffed with the biggest smirk. "Holy shit, that was like talking to the hologram girl upstairs."

Glancing over my shoulder, I watched as Lucian and Marionette crossed the threshold into the holding elevator. Shaking my head, I looked back to Mark and gave a half-hearted wave before turning to follow them. "Take care, Mark," I said, picking up the pace, "try to stay away from anything mind-altering."

Derisively, Mark muttered, "yeah, whatever man," before skulking off to wherever his car was parked. I didn't need to watch him anymore now that Marionette was safely underground, but I did track the sound of his footsteps and made sure it sounded like he was headed away. He wasn't in as much of a hurry as I was, but he was still making good time in the opposite direction. Regardless, as I reached the elevator, I felt almost compelled to look back and make sure he was getting lost.

I caught him just before he ducked into a candy apple red Pyrois Marathon convertible. And, stupid as it might sound, I stopped to watch it pull out and drive away. Worse, it wasn't out of paranoia by that point, it was because I recognized the car. For most people it was just a shiny red car, likely to draw the attention of gear heads and the easily impressed. For me, who was a little of both at times, it was more than that: it was a ***Marathon***. It was like seeing a unicorn – and those things have been extinct for hundreds of years.

Despite the advent of infrared solar paints and advances in ultracapacitors, even Argyrean built cars have range limits. The efficiency of the things is great, but Elves can't break thermodynamics no matter what the stories might tell you. The ACTF's cars are probably the best out there, able to last a week's worth of shifts on a single charge even in the coldest winter, but even they wirelessly recharge while parked in this garage. Pyrois, Argyre's top manufacturer, built those cars and a lot of their reputation was tied into the fact they made electric cars that could do all the shit ours do. But there was a catch: ACTF cars use a proprietary power cell based on the same tech that powers the Helios.

It didn't look good when wealthy dipshits kept running out of juice while trying to go cross-country in their fancy new cars.

The Marathon was an attempt to fix that by using the most advanced consumer grade tech they could manage. Pyrois was never super open about what they stuffed in it and only ever marketed it as "Marathon cells". I heard rumors it might have even been stuffed with diamond batteries. Whatever it was, it was expensive as hell and didn't get any better with scale. Last I'd heard the damn things had a production run of less than a thousand. Yet there Mark was, smug as hell, driving by slowly like he wanted to rub it in. It was like seeing a unicorn ridden by an asshole.

As that sparkling red unicorn drove out of the garage and up to the surface, I turned my attention to the elevator and the more pedestrian assholes. Mark kept me long enough for them to go down and for the elevator to return, but Lucian's behavior had put me in a better place. Maybe he had secrets, but he wasn't trying to pull anything right now. Still, I couldn't help wondering what kind of conversations they might have had when I wasn't there to listen. Were they familiar and casual? Were they trading barbs? Were they reminiscing about fond memories in romantic locales?

That last thought made the elevator ride a lot more claustrophobic than it should have been.

When I finally caught up to Lucian, he stood across from the day shift curate without a sign of Marionette anywhere. The faint frown on his face was almost imperceptible, but easily read from across the room by anyone that'd known him long enough. As I approached, it deepened and started to cross into the range that would be obvious to anyone else. His aura, meanwhile, looked just as uncomfortable and radiated minor irritation in a sunset hued glow around the edges that stood in stark contrast to the icy blue-white he'd normally sport.

"Man," I groaned, "if you're about to say she escaped we're going to have problems."

Shaking his head, Lucian rested an arm over the helmet he left on the curate's counter, gesturing to the terminal screen just beyond as he said, "Word came down from Alston."

"Alston?" I parroted, circling around to get a look at the screen.

Adjusting his position to give me a clearer shot, Lucian continued, "We've both been pulled from the case."

The initial shock of the long stony arm of the law reaching out to slap us away left me speechless as I hastily read the details on the screen. It was there clear as daylight as Alston's orders pulled us off for being too close to the subject. On the one hand, I kind of expected an official judgment against me eventually, especially once reports started to make their way up the chain. On the other hand, I was actually surprised to see Lucian pulled too.

Shooting him a look, I asked, "Just how damn close were you?"

"Not close enough for this," he answered bluntly, picking up the helmet and starting back towards the haven. "She filled a specific role I required a few decades ago, one that made us very familiar but not intimate in the way you might be considering."

Following him down both the corridors and what I suspected was a pretty deep rabbit hole, I asked, "What kind of role is that?"

Walking through the hulking security gates separating the secured wings from the safe haven, we passed the armed guards and into the idyllic gardens beyond. Lucian stepped off the path and walked across the grass into the simulated, carefully filtered sunlight. Turning his face to the sky, he squinted as he watched the surreal floating landscape above and the light streaming through the virtually hanging gardens. It didn't occur to me right away, but the shelter's environment was probably like some sort of witchcraft to the ancient man in front of me. After all, how often does a Vampire get to stand in the "sun"?

"There are certain difficulties," he started solemnly, turning his attention back to me, "in being immortal."

Cryptic as they were, there was a weight to the words, like an unseen burden looming behind them. Studying his expression and his aura, I could see a hint of weariness in his unnaturally bright eyes.

"A lifetime ago, I hired a woman named Miriam to help me with one of those difficulties," he continued. "She helped me sort some," he trailed off for a bit before making a light sweeping gesture with his hand, "clerical matters."

Taken aback by the look on his face, I almost felt bad for pressing. "You know that's still pretty vague."

Nodding and starting towards the housing section of the sanctuary, he said thoughtfully, "You know, you're right. Come by my house sometime this week and I'll show you."

Watching him retreat to the safety of a comfy little guest apartment so he could hide from the bright light and my burning questions, I called out, "What about right now?"

He chuckled and glanced up, squinting against the glare of the heavens before putting on his shades and replying, "I'm not sure this is the best time for me to leave the building and you could use some sleep and a shave."

Reminded of my disheveled look, I activated the silver on my gloves and glanced down into my increasingly rugged reflection. Honestly, besides the cuts and bruises, I was starting to think it didn't look so bad.

"And a shower," he added, continuing his escape, "most certainly a shower."

I couldn't tell if he was screwing with me, but I couldn't help taking a quick sniff as he said it. I didn't smell anything too out of the ordinary, just my deodorant and the ghost of a few thousand coffee beans, but I didn't have the nose of a hunter. It had been a summer night and some change in a heavy black uniform… and there was some running.

Damn it, I was probably nose-blind to it.

Retreating myself, I cut through the complex to the locker rooms I rarely used. Living so close, I generally just got dressed at home to avoid the evening rush. But leaving the building felt like a step too far. Maybe I could catch wind of what was happening to Marionette if I just stuck around. At the very least, I kept some supplies for the uncomfortably common occurrence of "too banged up to go home" so I wouldn't have to raid someone else's locker.

Of course, as I opened that locker, I found little more than some bare bones supplies. I'd spared *every* expense in stocking the damn thing as I looked upon an off-brand toothpaste, a travel toothbrush, and a bar of soap on a rope that I couldn't even remember buying. Picking it up and giving it a quick sniff, I wasn't even sure what it was supposed to smell like. It wasn't anything I'd normally pick, some sort of floral blend that I couldn't quite place. But, at the same time, beggars can't be choosers. Shrugging and taking off my jacket, I just chalked it up to getting the hang of things well enough that I didn't need to use it so often.

As the hot water ran over my head, I could feel the cobwebs getting dusted away and the haze lifted around me. Maybe it was the lack of sleep, or the constant bombardment of chemicals, subliminal cues, and unpleasant questions, but it was the clearest my head had been in hours. And, in that moment, alone with my thoughts and the sound of the falling water, I started to process something that had escaped my attention for far too long.

If Marionette was the one tying up the loose ends, killing people involved in these old underworld deals, why was she even in the Undercity when I got there? More than that, why was she suddenly getting her own hands dirty? If she'd been able to coordinate the deaths of multiple people across the country, and had the ability to arrange for people like Kate to just take the shot and then the fall, couldn't she have done that for Angelique? Something had changed between the time Kate pulled the trigger and the time Marionette went to that theater. Something had pushed her from the proverbial backstage to the literal.

As I was getting dressed again, the internal debate raged on. I was being firmly told to back off by a man who was both the rock and the hard place. I had already been gently waved off by my closest friends and colleagues. Dulaf was actually worrying about me, which was never a good sign. Yet, I was at the edge of something. Lady Zhang was concerned enough to send her guards after me. The Locusta seemed to be involved, and quite a few people had been wiped off the board – including at least one by Janice Grey.

Some people believe that it's better to ask for forgiveness than permission. I'm apparently one of them.

Cutting through the building, I took a mostly straight path from the lockers to holding with only a few minor detours. In the armory, I replaced the Wisp and Banshee I'd used over the night so I wouldn't have to dip into my trunk. In the bullpen, I checked to see if Nguyen and Ramirez were still around to ensure I wouldn't accidentally bump into them. And, most importantly, in the forensics labs I raided Dulaf's coffee pot since I knew from experience it basically contained a combination of cinnamon and rocket fuel. Though, as I topped off my cup, I saw a bolt of chestnut hair out of the corner of my eye as slender ears slowly folded back.

"Stealing from my pot is a good way to lose a hand," she chided while drifting into my line of sight. "Besides, shouldn't you be going to bed?"

Taking a long, defiant sip, I replied, "I heard if you drink caffeine immediately before a power nap it makes you more rested."

Her eyebrow quirked, one of her ears going with it, as she snapped, "Sounds like bullshit to me."

I shrugged, preparing to snow her with the description of an article I only read the headline for, but hesitated as I watched her expression shift. Suddenly both ears perked as she sniffed at me like a curious cat.

"You used my soap," she commented with a grin.

"*Your* soap?"

Grin widening, she stepped back to look me in the eye again. "I gave it to you the night that drunk Werewolf marked you downtown," she said.

Suddenly the fact I couldn't remember buying the soap made perfect sense: I hadn't. It'd been a bar of soap that Dulaf had handed me after a drunk Werewolf pissed all over me outside a bar. But that raised whole new alarms.

Bemused, I asked, "Where'd you get it?"

Beaming, she answered, "I made it!"

"And what do I smell like, exactly?" I continued.

Winking as her ears bobbed, she said, "Don't worry, you just smell like flowers, it wasn't a prank."

Turning to walk away, she returned to her station with a spring in her step. I sniffed my arm to see if there was some hidden trap in the mix, but still smelled only the mysterious floral scent. Gifts from Dulaf generally came with a joke or a prank involved, from copies of Jack and the Beanstalk to the bat watching newsletter, they usually had a punchline. But now I had to wonder what the chemist could have slipped into a bar of soap.

Did she reclaim her territory like some predator in the woods?

Laughing from across the room, she waved to catch my attention again. "Don't worry," she insisted cheerfully, "the joke was just that you stunk."

Or maybe I was overthinking it.

Setting it aside, I topped off my cup and continued my trip to holding. If I was assertive enough, I could probably convince the curate I was meant to be there and get in and out fast enough that no one else bothered to ask any questions. I just needed to make it sound like something the commissioner might have yielded on. I could just say she had information about another investigation I was working on. After all, she had been working at the Moirae as long as I'd known her... this time. It would be perfectly plausible and, on my way down, it felt like the right way to go. So, as the doors of the elevator opened, I donned my visor, set my shoulders back, lifted my chin, and stepped out with all the confidence I could.

Unfortunately for me, I stepped right into the line of sight of Commissioner Alston himself, who watched me exit the elevator with a look of irritated disbelief that said he knew instantly what I was there for. His aura was a steely light blue, calm if inhuman and every bit as stoic as his stony face suggested. With that calm demeanor, he dismissed me with a simple grunt and a point of his finger back to the same elevator I just came out of.

A more obedient lad would have spun on his heels and stepped right back through the doors before they could close again. Instead, I resorted to the tactic that most suited me and simply played dumb.

"What?" I asked, glancing over my shoulder like I expected to see something behind me.

Again, he grunted, not even humoring me with a conversation, and turned to walk into holding himself. Though he didn't reply to my feigned ignorance, he really didn't have to. When every footstep sounds like a hammer hitting pavement and your shoulders have to pivot to pass the door frame, people usually know to fuck off. However, I'm paid specifically to ignore such clear markers and barrel right towards the angry behemoths. So in his wake I hustled along like a yapping Chihuahua chasing a Doberman down the block.

"It's funny running into you sir," I said, following just outside his lengthy arm's reach. "I was wondering if it would be possible to reconsider pulling me off the Marionette case."

Massive boots continued to pound the ground, sounding above even the chatter of the guards in the next room over. He didn't turn my way, he didn't make a sound, didn't even give me another grunt. Instead, he just continued marching onward unfazed. The tiny mosquito at his back didn't deter him in the slightest, nor the howling from the fairly stuffed cells along our path. In the distance I could see a pair of curates at the door of the interrogation room and realized that's exactly where we were headed. Moments later, a still silent commissioner stepped into an observation room adjacent to interrogation and stopped by the two-way mirror overlooking a curate strapping Marionette down.

Lit only by the glow of the next room over, the near-literal granite features of Alston were enhanced by the shadows creeping into every crack and crevice across his face. He crossed his arms and watched on as the curates made damn sure that Marionette was being secured. Unlike Kate, who was a Witch but in a sorry state, Marionette actually posed a risk worth full procedure. The curate inside the room was being monitored by another at the door while a third kept his distance in case either of the others were compromised. For any other situation, it probably would have seemed extreme for someone weighing half as much as any of them. But in this case, you really couldn't be too careful.

"You know, sir," I said, taking one last good drink before setting my cup aside, "I'm partially immune. You could observe while I question her."

Steely grey eyes turned my way, cold in a way I'd never seen them before. Had it been anyone else, I would have been unnerved by that gaze. But on a man like Alston, who was stone faced by default, I wasn't too concerned to see a slight variation in his naturally stern demeanor. Still, it wasn't exactly the most encouraging sight.

Looking back out to Marionette, watching as the curate finished and started to leave the room, I considered cutting my losses and asking to at least stay in the observation room. I had questions for her that no one else would ask, true, but I could probably try to visit her. There was no guarantee that she'd be willing to see me, but it was better than repeatedly throwing myself against the living wall to my right.

"I understand why you want me to leave, sir," I said, "but I'd like to at least be able to observe."

We exchanged a look, me probably pleading, him most definitely disapproving, before he silently marched out of the room. It wasn't exactly an audible no, so I probably could have stayed, but at this point I needed to be sure where the lines were drawn. Turning and following him out and around to the interrogation room, I pleaded again as he entered the door.

"Sir, please, let me observe."

Through the door, barely visible past the giant frame, I saw Marionette's face and felt a sudden, intense sinking feeling. Her aura wavered between colors rapidly, more than I'd ever seen it change before and even into colors I hadn't seen in someone who could pass for human. It wasn't a natural reaction. Whatever was going on, she was definitely doing something as she rapidly glanced from me up to Alston and back again. So, despite the giant wall of "no" he'd been broadcasting, I followed the commissioner into the room.

As the door closed, an uneasy silence swelled in the room as Alston stared me down like I'd just kicked a dog in front of him. Somehow, I was given an opportunity to explain myself before he could toss my ass out the door. All I needed to do was find the right words to convince him that he should totally trust my gut feeling in this instance. Sputtering a bit as I tried to get the words out, I scanned Marionette over again to get a feel for what she was doing. But, as I looked her way, Marionette's attention was firmly locked on Alston as a look of pure dread crossed her face.

Exploding through my peripheral vision, coming across my face like a wrecking ball, Alston's fist turned the whole world black.

Chapter 19
Haphazard Escape

The next minute was a surge of panic and adrenaline as I had to fight my way out of the grip of a living statue in a room with nowhere to run. Somehow, we even managed to dislodge what I thought had been a secured table as I tried desperately to gain some leverage. Thrashing in his arms and doing everything I could to keep him from crushing me like a bag of chips, I eventually resorted to head-butting the man in the nose as hard and as frequently as I could in some far-flung hope that his nose was softer than my skull.

The sounds of his nose breaking caused some of the most conflicted emotions I've ever had. On the one hand, it meant I was going to live. On the other hand, that condition was subjective and still possibly temporary. On a blurry third hand I just discovered, I was probably about to be fired and arrested so I might as well punch out.

As he dropped me, I spun and swung for all I was worth into his face. In fighting they call it the puncher's chance: the idea that, no matter how outmatched you might be, if you're lucky you just might hit the button and end the fight with a knockout. So, when I threw that punch, I did it with every ounce of strength I had in me. After all, if I hit him with anything less, he was going to grind my bones like a mortar and pestle. With great relief, I watched the giant man topple and looked blearily at Marionette.

As steady and clear as I could, I demanded, "What did you do?"

Shocked, eyes red and on the verge of tears, she protested, "It wasn't me; I could feel something was wrong and I was trying to snap him out of it!"

“Why would you do that?” I asked, reaching for my belt.

Her eyes darted down to my hands and back up again as she answered, “Obviously he was sent to kill me!”

Walking up to her, I stared into her eyes while they started to come back into focus. I’d been spending the last couple days pissed off about her lying to me and making others do the same. But looking into those eyes, I saw some genuine terror. Hopefully, this time, it wasn’t an act because I was about to do something extra stupid.

Pulling out a set of keys, I unlocked her restraints and helped her out of the chair. I was sure that this was being forwarded to the security stations and that we weren’t going to get very far. Regardless, it felt prudent to get the hell out of the interrogation room before the commissioner got up. If she was telling the truth and he was under someone’s control, it was probably a very bad idea to be there when he woke up. If he wasn’t under someone’s control, it could have been argued to be an even worse idea.

Relieved, she stepped around me to look down at Alston and said, “I could feel it from him as soon as he stepped in, the touch. He’s been entranced, but I think--”

The rest caught in her throat as I pulled her hands behind her back to cuff her again.

“What the hell are you doing, Nate?” she squealed, trying to pull free.

“I’m going to believe you,” I said solemnly, “but I’m not about to trust you.”

Nudging her along to the door, I caught sight of myself in the mirror and saw hints of early bruises forming on my face and a red mark where the visor cracked across my cheek. With one good punch and a bear hug he’d left a hefty mark on me. But, while it gave me pause, it also gave me a chance to realize that I had a surprising amount of extra time to cuff her and move things along.

“The curates should be swarming us by now,” I muttered, kneeling to fish through Alston’s things to see if he had a visor of his own.

Marionette, still fuming, glanced up at a camera and snorted, "Maybe he cut the feed."

Looking up at the same camera and donning my "borrowed" visor, I mused, "Maybe he did."

Even if the actual alarms weren't sounding, the ones in my head definitely were. The commissioner, highest office in the building almost literally and figuratively, was compromised and somehow the Oracle wasn't sending in every curate in the building to tackle me. If he could cut that feed then who knows how many others had been compromised in the building. The question would be why and how many of them were ordered to kill Marionette on sight.

Grabbing her arm and escorting her out of the room swiftly, I took Marionette down the long hall. Marching her at a steady clip, I kept my eyes locked on the door ahead of us and started to grip at the Manticore rod at my belt. The next section was processing and offices, filled to the brim with curates. If I had to go down swinging, their helmets could block the Banshee or the Wisp. But a pack-buster, while blocked by most of our clothes, had that puncher's chance of hitting exposed skin somewhere. Letting go of her arm and grabbing the back of her shirt and case I had to shove her to the floor, I led Marionette through that door and braced for the worst.

Several faces turned my way as we passed through, eyes locking on us, then turned back to what they were doing. No one was geared to go or showing any sign of tension at all. No one seemed to even be aware something had happened. Instead, we just walked through unaccosted as if the commissioner wasn't sprawled across a concrete floor somewhere in our wake. Briefly, I glanced at Marionette's aura through the visor to be sure it wasn't her manipulating the whole room.

To my surprise, she looked as confused as I did.

Passing through, the curate at the reception desk looked up with the same relative disinterest and only went about bringing up Marionette's profile on his terminal, asking, "Where's the prisoner going?"

Though I wasn't prepared for questions, my inner bullshit bubbled to the surface as I answered, "We're working cooperatively with local authorities, she's offering to give up state's evidence for a plea deal."

Scanning the file, the curate shook his head quickly and commented, "That's not on the system."

"Well," I started, mind racing to fill the holes as quickly as it could, "the commissioner thought there was a risk she might be targeted en route, so he's handling this low-key. He can confirm my story when he comes out, but he wanted this done quickly."

Puzzled, the curate considered my story and compared it against the file, double checking to make sure he hadn't missed anything. I knew there was a button on his display that would let him call everyone from the next room out to secure the lobby. I also knew that the door behind me wasn't particularly sound proofed so he could just yell. And I watched him with all the tension of a kid hoping his parents would believe the dog actually did the deed. But seconds later he simply turned and nodded to me as though the whole thing made complete sense. Confused or not, I wasn't about to look the gift horse in the mouth and double-timed it to the exit.

Nudging Marionette into the elevator, I turned back to look at the curate one more time before the doors closed. He sat there unchanged, smiling lightly and giving a half-hearted wave before turning back to his computer. I kept watching him as the door closed, a bored expression crossing his face as his genial grin passed. Looking over at Marionette, I checked the aura again and saw her looking up at the elevator camera as nervously as she'd looked at Alston before.

"She has to know by now," I muttered, looking into the camera myself. "The visors are giving her a feed even if the cameras haven't."

Marionette stood tensely at my side as we rode to the entrance. I gripped at the Wisp at my side in case I needed to EMP the elevator and climb out the roof like an old movie. Forget the curates in my wake, the building itself should have been trying to stop us like the hand of a vengeful deity reaching out of the sky. But the doors opened and the voice of the Oracle chimed in, "Farewell, Agent Leone."

Taking Marionette's arm, I hurried her out of there as fast as humanly possible, spot checking every corner and potential cover in the garage beyond. Like the curate rooms below, no one seemed to be any the wiser to the fact we weren't meant to be there. Only one agent even looked our way, a day shift agent named Allen that I only barely caught the nametag for as he casually nodded and walked by. Returning the gesture, I carried on silently with Marionette until getting far enough out of earshot.

"Did you do that?" I demanded, clutching at her sleeve like I expected her to suddenly teleport any second.

Glaring, Marionette hissed, "Do you think if I could shut down an Oracle I would even be here?"

Accepting her logic, I escorted her to the car and quickly loaded her into the passenger seat while I frantically kept my head on a swivel for ***anything***. I'd imagined punching some superiors in the past. When I was a cleric, I had issues with my training lancer, Stevens. But I always knew I would be hit with a discharge, a psyche evaluation, and probably jail time.

How the ***hell*** did I just get away with breaking the commissioner's nose?

Climbing into the driver's seat, I quickly ran three searches on the console before driving out of the garage like a bat out of hell. The first search was for any alerts about the commissioner being found in the interrogation room. The second was for any alerts about some sort of Oracle maintenance schedule. The third was to see if I'd somehow crossed a silver line like with Peaches and Patch. Somehow, all of them were negative and the girl behind the network was still communicating with me like an ally.

"Okay," Marionette said curtly, "now what do you expect to do?"

Driving down the block, checking the rear view from time to time, I took an inventory of the situation. Commissioner Alston just tried to fold my ass in half with the aura of a sociopath. Literally every fail safe just failed to stop me from leaving. Even stranger was Marionette sitting in the next seat over with an apparent hit on her head. My hands started wringing the wheel as I became increasingly aware of the corner I was trapped in. I needed to figure out who put us there.

"Why are they trying to kill you?" I asked.

Sitting back, staring at the road ahead, Marionette sighed and answered in a defeated tone, "I have no idea, those bastards Salem'd me."

Glancing briefly between her, the road, and the rear view, I asked, "What the hell does 'Salem'd' mean?"

She was fidgeting in her seat awkwardly, shifting her shoulders in a strange way, face deep in concentration. Maintaining that focused glare, she replied stiffly, "They wiped my memory, forced me out, and left me as a scapegoat."

Taking a longer look, I watched her squirm for a second before the road called my attention again. It was frustrating to learn there was actually a term for what had been done to people like Kate. You don't give a name to something you've just thought up, and you sure as hell don't give it a name referencing something from a couple hundred years ago.

"You're saying they did the same thing to you they did to Kate?" I grumbled.

"I can't remember a 'Kate', but probably, yes," she hissed, suddenly lifting newly freed hands from behind her back and turning her attention to the remaining cuff.

The sight of her newly free hands startled me, my car damn near kissing fenders with another on the road. There wasn't really any way to respond to it either, what with the fact more cars could be in my rear view any minute now. In fact, as the displays flashed by and my visor alerted me to a couple traffic stops on the map, I realized something uncomfortable. Taking us as far from the headquarters as I could, I drove up to one of the entrances to the Undercity and came to a stop in front of it.

"Get out," I ordered, climbing out myself without waiting for her response.

Marching around to the back, I opened the trunk and started to strip my gear. As Marionette joined me, I threw my gun belt, badge, and visor into the trunk of the car and started sorting through the rest. Most of the trunk was useless to me at the moment but still presented some options.

Breaking through my train of thought, Marionette demanded, "What the hell are you doing?"

Continuing to strip and sort gear, trying my best to catalogue everything in the car, I replied sardonically, "Look, I don't know if you've realized this, but that angry mountain with the charming smile was the commissioner and he just tried to crack me open like a lobster. For some reason our system hasn't noticed I used my head to try to make him look like the Sphinx. But, when he gets up, he's going to be ***real*** angry and he'll tell the girl that haunts my car to shut it down so they can march a whole squad of agents up our asses."

Exasperated, Marionette shouted, "Fine, abandon the car, but we might need the rest of this shit! At least keep the gun!"

Whipping around to face her, I snapped back, "Any time I use the gun it tells the system where I am, what I'm doing, and why. Half of this shit is tracked and networked! The badge alone gets upset if I breathe wrong!"

Most of my uniform was thankfully safe to use without drawing the Oracle's notice after a couple adjustments. Untuck my pants from my boots to cover up the noticeable armor. Stuff my gloves into my pocket. Untuck my shirt to look a little sloppier. The only thing really standing out too much was the coat. It was covered in markers and the armoring made it a little too stiff. Unzipping it, I started to remove the hardened Vesperadin inserts and tossed them into the trunk with the rest of it. Still, even if it didn't have that same rigid outline, the tell-tale silver plates and patches made it too obvious. Looking it over, I lingered over the Aegis patch identifying me as a full agent. It was purely symbolic, but it still meant a lot to me. Unfortunately, for now, it was a liability and demanded I turn the coat inside out to hide it from view.

Tying that around my waist, using it to cover the rods strapped to my leg, I started to stuff as much as I could into my pockets. A pair of handcuffs, a halo strip, and a spare Helios clip in case I needed a power supply were all I could fit in what little space I had left. Looking over a billyclub, I considered whether I should swap it with one of the rods. Because they were disposable, the rods were tracked by the badge rather than on their own, so I could keep them, but this case had already put me in a fist fight I wasn't quite ready for. Deciding some crowd control was more useful than a telescopic stick, I shook my head and closed the trunk before turning to face Marionette again.

Seemingly concerned, definitely agitated, she asked, "So then what's your plan?"

Looking at the entryway beyond, I nodded to it and grabbed her by the elbow, guiding her to the stairs.

"You know your way around," I said, "so let's lose them in the underground."

Chapter 20
Nice Trades

I'd been to the Undercity several times over the years. There was a strange cozy, nostalgic feeling in most areas as you wandered down historic paths in a place fully shielded from the elements. But in the seedier parts, that lack of space took on a different feeling. On top of that, the feeling changed even more depending on what brought me down. Uniform on, there was a feeling of things lurking in every shadow and trying to avoid my attention. Uniform off, the place was alive in a whole new way.

For some, I was probably prey, for others, a mark, and for a third group something in between. Furthermore, unlike the Fangtown above, the Undercity had no reason to sleep. There was no sun here and the daylight hours meant there were more than a few humans like me wandering into the honeypot. Though most of the unnaturally bright eyes turned my way were probably licensed, that made them no less predators as they stalked the passageways. Unfortunately for them, in my half-dressed state, Marionette at my side, I wasn't too keen on letting my guard down for anyone.

"Okay, we're down here, now what?" she demanded, yanking her arm free.

"We need to make ourselves scarce long enough to figure out who's trying to kill you and why," I mused, turning my eyes to the ceiling as the light around us turned a dazzling array of colors.

Marionette glanced up briefly with me. The ceiling in much of the Undercity was decorated like the walls of the Fangtown above. Antique light fixtures were carefully refurbished, supports covered in elaborate façades, and murals painted across the ceiling like some sort of other worldly Sistine Chapel in the areas where the ceiling was big enough to support the work. In this passage, one of the few tunnels to retain a skylight, stained glass tiles depicted an Empyreal divided down the center with angelic and demonic features as she stood on water. The glass was probably meant to filter out UV light and provide some mood at the same time. But despite all of that, it wasn't the reason I was looking up.

"A lot of sections down here don't have cameras outside the shops," I continued.

"Most of the property down here is private," she commented, turning my way, "for purely legitimate reasons, of course."

"Of course," I echoed dryly. "You seemed to know the area down here pretty well, even the sections that aren't fully public."

Almost sarcastically, she repeated, "For *purely legitimate* reasons."

Doing my best to just talk through the moment and ignore her tone, I said, "So you know ways out of here that won't put us right next to a patrol car or in front of a new set of cameras."

She studied me for a second before nodding ahead to one of the narrower passages. Using the Undercity to get past the watchful eyes of the ACTF wasn't exactly a new idea. Once the tunnels were renovated, expanded, and reinforced, every smuggling operation you could imagine started trying to map out new routes through the city – particularly since the Undercity created one hell of a bridge from the shoreline to downtown. But, for obvious reasons, I was never privy to the details of those routes.

Yet, somehow, Marionette was.

"We can probably get to Downtown without notice," she remarked, looking around us as if to get her bearings. "Though we might need to squeeze through some Goblin routes."

"Goblin route" was a glorified term for a crawl space, generally too narrow for most people to pass through at a brisk pace but perfect for anyone the size of a child or one of the Gnome-kin. The Goblins weren't particularly fond of the sunlight and had a knack for concealing their construction work. It was great if you needed to get around without being seen, but generally took a full-grown man about three times longer and multiple moments of panic to pass through. At least for once I didn't have to go through it with full gear – though I regretted keeping the low-grade explosives.

The mental image did inspire a thought, though, and I asked, "Is there a pub along the way?"

Marionette's eyebrow rose and she scolded, "I don't exactly think this is the time."

"It's the perfect time, really," I quipped, "but that's not why I'm asking."

"I suppose there's the Emerald Den," she answered, contemplative.

"Is it 'Emerald' because of the city or Leprechauns?" I asked.

"A little of both, really."

A faint grin crossed my lips as luck fell in my favor for the first time in a couple hours. "Perfect," I said, "lead the way."

The trip through the tunnels was thankfully not too difficult along that particular stretch. The pub was too popular to be lying between crawl spaces and old sewer lines. In fact, standing in one of the more open spaces below, it was both literally and figuratively a pillar of the community as the building it was a part of was doing more than its fair share of holding the ceiling up.

Whatever it might have been above ground, below ground there was no question as to what it was. Under the archways and between the support columns reinforcing the tunnels, the basement level had the façade of an Irish pub with vibrant green trim and subtle gold accents. A hand painted sign matching the façade's colors bridged the gap between two supports, particular care taken to make sure the name sparkled under the ambient light like the gemstones it was named for. A sign hung in one window advertising Guinness, another for Clobhair Ale the next window over. The doors had push plates waist high for most while a second set were placed closer to the knee for the shorter patrons. And as we approached, we could hear the telltale singing of diminutive drunks well off key and only God knows how many drinks in.

I didn't have my phone or link with me to check the time, but I was pretty sure they got an early start.

The pub was packed for the middle of the afternoon, an eclectic blend of humans and Alters alike standing shoulder to shoulder in a relatively cramped space while mugs of various amber fluids waved through the air. Marionette hesitated at the door while directing a questioning look my way. Gesturing with a finger for her to give me a moment, I scanned the place for the one thing I really needed there.

Easily missed in such a crowd, not doing much to take notice and incredibly subdued for the environment, sat a man with fiery red hair and a well-fitted suit. Though there were plenty of other Leprechauns there, he was the only one dressed like a professional in a sea of revelry. In fact, given the way he watched his tablet between sips, I had to figure he ws still technically on the clock despite the fact he was literally holding a beer. My only hope was that, as high dollar as his suit was, he was part of the group I hoped him to be. Approaching from behind, I could see over his shoulders exactly what I hoped to find: stock charts.

"Excuse me," I said, circling the table so he could see me. "You wouldn't happen to know a Desmond Kelly, would you?"

A blazing red eyebrow quirked as he lowered the tablet and gave me a once over. "That I do," he said, "and what's that to you?"

Pulling a chair over and sitting across from him, I leaned a little over the table to speak quietly without being washed away in the noise, "Are you part of the same company?"

He set the tablet down, tapping it to lock the screen, and sat back with his mug. "That I am," he said. "But, once again, what's that to you?"

Feeling a little less inclined to keep it quiet while watching his body language, I sat back and crossed my arms before speaking up. "My name's Nathaniel Leone," I declared, "and I'm on the ledger."

The little man's demeanor changed dramatically as he sat straight and set his mug aside. He took a second to straighten his scarlet tie before reaching for the tablet and lifting it so it could see his face. I watched him as the screen unlocked and he scrolled through a few things, seeing little twitches in his eyebrows as he navigated through what seemed like a lengthy series of procedures. For a moment I even wondered if Desmond left me off of it after our little deal. But eventually both eyebrows raised and emerald green eyes shot me a piercing look.

"Says here you got your favor," he commented, dimming the screen before putting it down again so I couldn't make out the other names on the list.

"I did get a favor," I replied, leaning forward again, steepling my fingers like some sort of supervillain, "but I'm owed two more."

Glancing at the screen again and looking back up, he protested, "And why would we give you that for a single piece of advice?"

I wondered just how much information that screen actually had on what happened. I'd given Desmond a hot tip on the fact a certain pharmaceutical company was under investigation not that long ago. He'd given me information on that company in return. With most people this would have been the end of it, but there was a certain code of conduct when dealing with a Leprechaun.

"The Ash Treaty specifies a share of the pot or three favors," I said. "I've got one under my belt, I'm calling in the rest."

His fiery little brow furrowed and the corners of his mouth momentarily twitched into a scowl. Adjusting the cuffs of his coat roughly and then picking up the tablet again, he asked, "And how would you be knowing something like that?"

I could have answered with some long-winded explanation of the Ash Treaty signed by the Faelish back when the written word was rare, but there was an easier response. Reaching into my pocket, I fished out my gloves and slapped them onto the table like an open challenge. Green eyes flicked about as he quickly assessed them and realized what was in front of him.

"Oh," he uttered quietly, "suppose you'd be knowin' the laws then."

Sweeping them back off the table, I hid the gloves away again and took a quick check of the room to make sure no one else got a good look. Seeing no other eyes turned our way and that the closest people other than the Leprechaun fellow were sloshed beyond reason, I returned to my Machiavellian pose and watched for his next move. Studying the tablet once again, he eventually nodded to me in concession.

"So, what'll you have of us?" he asked, a strange new glint to his eyes like I just awakened the mischief in his soul. "You didn't provide much for this trade, so I'd hope you weren't looking for too much."

That was a blatant lie, seeing as the company in question was at the leading edge of some organ transplant technologies. Shorting their stock had probably netted at least Desmond a giant payday. In the ancient times, Leprechauns were isolated creatures who didn't cooperate. But, as the world grew more sophisticated, the miniature moguls realized the power of their collective might. Thus, Leprechaun firms were not exactly like the standard brokerage. They didn't just run the standard financial markets; they also bought and sold the favors owed. On the one hand, this could prove to be risky if you took the wrong favors from the wrong Leprechaun. On the other hand, before it existed the little shits had to show you to their life savings to get out of a bind. In this man's case, the price was simple.

"Four clovers," I declared matter-of-factly, "I only need four clovers."

His voice rose sharply as he mocked, "Clovers? What would someone like you be needin' with clovers?"

"Doesn't matter," I interjected, "but that's what I'm asking for."

His brow furrowed again and his finger started to idly tap the corner of the tablet as he replied, "And why would you be thinkin' I'd be walkin' around with clovers of all things? Who even needs them in this day an' age?"

"Oh please," I chided, "cut the crap, we both know you've got a pocketful somewhere in that suit."

Darkly, the whimsical voice sank into a growl, "Four's a big ask on the spot."

Studying him, taking in the expression carefully now that I had to rely purely on his face and not on his aura, I considered how serious he was about that threatening tone. Clearly, I had the reach advantage, but a bar fight with a Leprechaun was never a fun proposition. Thankfully, there was an alternative.

"Four and I consider the favors clear," I said, "we'd be even."

The scowl melted away faster than it appeared, a look of intrigue taking its place. Opening his coat, he pulled a small jingling pouch from an inside breast pocket. He unclasped it and peered into the tiny purse before carefully reaching in and plucking out four gold coins imprinted with a simple representation of a four-leaf clover, every leaf taking an equal amount of space on the coin and evenly dividing each into four pieces. Biting one and nodding to me, he tossed them to the table and held out his hand like Mephistopheles.

"Four bits for a clear ledger," he said, "just close the deal."

The Leprechauns had long left behind the pots, but they'd never left behind the gold. When the rest of the world ended the gold standard, it made the wee folk rich beyond imagination. Suddenly their gold, already a precious metal and more money than most had, was gaining value every passing day. It was only a matter of time before they turned it into a financial empire. But while everyone else was fine with the new way of money and they certainly benefited from it, the Leprechauns never trusted a currency that wasn't backed by something. So, faced with a world that no longer worked on gold coins they did the only logical thing: they minted their own.

Staring at his hand, I started to reach but paused half way across the table. "Before we shake, one more thing."

Reaching for the clovers, he snorted. "Should have known."

"Hold up," I said, waving him down, "I just want to know the nearest G-Mart."

His eyebrow rose again. "You wouldn't be tryin' to arrest no one, would you?"

"Of course not," I assured, "but I need somewhere to spend them, don't I?"

Reaching out again, he nodded over his shoulder. "There's one behind the pub itself," he said whimsically, "just turn to the wall once the façade fucks off and real brick shows."

Nodding, I reached over and took his hand to seal the deal. He grinned and returned to the ledger with a sort of excitement. I wasn't one hundred percent on what happened behind the scenes of their little exchange, but I could see gears turning in his head. Hopefully I hadn't somehow screwed over Desmond in the process, but I'd just have to cross that bridge when I got to it. In the meantime, I snatched up the four pieces of literal Leprechaun gold and hopped up to leave again.

Confused as hell, Marionette joined me again on the way out. "The hell do you need clovers for?"

"Do you really think we can use credit cards now?"

She glanced down at the hand full of coins and nodded. "You're right, even Victoria's compromised."

Despite how much experience she probably had, the way she said it made me think this was the worst one of her escapes had ever gone. Maybe a little bit of that was pride for bringing her in. Still, the way she said "even" made it feel like Victoria, as silly as the name choice felt, might have been the fallback position.

"Never expected to be this bad off?"

She silently watched the floor as we exited the pub and went around the corner. Without the Oracle's senses backing me up I could really only make an educated guess. But, based on what I saw, there would have been the colors of uncertainty and probably embarrassment. Either way, she wasn't eager to reply as we followed the façade until it "fucked off" as instructed.

The border between the façade and the naked brick was a hard, unmistakable line. The brick was old but well preserved in these underground spaces. You could see mild weathering from the years it was actually exposed, long ago, but it had been shielded for quite a while since. Still, despite that unintentional time capsule protecting it from the elements, the surface was a little rounded, the colors faded, and a few minor cracks showed the stresses of the simple act of standing for who knows how long. Despite restoration efforts, you could tell how old it all was except for one particular patch that was the reverse of everything else.

Stained to match, sanded to artificially weather the edges, one whole section of the wall was newer than the rest but made to look old. Only a foot and a half wide but tall enough for a regular person, the section was narrow and disguised enough to possibly go unnoticed. In fact, if I hadn't been paying attention, I likely would have walked right by. Ironically, with all their efforts to age it appropriately, the giveaway was a single brick more weathered than any other across the entire wall.

Pushed at repeatedly over the last few years, a faint hand-sized impression marked that lone brick. For most bricks the simple act of being slapped probably wouldn't have left a mark. But this was a Goblin door and these were no ordinary bricks. Resting my hand over the groove, I pushed and found the wall lighter than it appeared, a hidden door sliding open between the pub and whatever its neighbor happened to be. It swung with some effort into a recess beyond and exposed an incredibly narrow, claustrophobic passageway with minimal lighting that ended with a sudden turn into an unseen space.

"Well," I started, hesitantly, "this seems to be the place."

Assessing the narrow passage, I guided Marionette in ahead of me. Part of it was just force of habit: ladies first was one of the few things my dad taught me that stuck. But the other part was that if anything else was going to get stuck I'd like it to be her rather than me. Regardless, it wasn't really much of a challenge for her as she was very nearly able to walk normally within. I, on the other hand, needed to crab walk through the damn thing like the world just turned two dimensional.

Down the end of the tunnel the faint light flickered and danced about like candlelight, the smell of yet more incense greeting us from halfway down. It wasn't unusual for a G-Mart to dose the air with some aromatherapy. I imagined it was to make sure that people were nice and receptive, which was also why I imagined they were so often hidden around bars. But I'd been exposed to so many different sinister scents over the period of a couple days that I couldn't help but be more aware of it this time. Every step grew tenser as I crab-walked into what now felt like a trap.

And then Marionette started to whistle.

A weird smirk on her face, she stood at the corner between the tunnel and whatever we were headed towards and watched me shuffle along. It was a familiar tune, something itching at the back of my head like so many other memories I'd recovered lately. It evoked a sense of a dark underworld and brought back blurry images of a little man with a mustache fighting turtles. At first, I thought it was some sort of fever dream, but then I remembered the colors and sounds and the feeling of sitting in my dad's lap as he showed me how to play an ancient looking game from his childhood. I don't know if it was her intention, but for a moment I felt some of those tensions melt away.

Smirking back at her, I joked, "Punching the bricks might be helpful about now."

She turned and continued into a space about the size of a walk-in closet. "You still have that thing?"

Following her, I replied a little more solemnly than you'd expect for a toy, "It died a while ago."

There was a moment of realization across her face, a spark of understanding lit by old lamps mounted to brick walls. Maybe it registered for her how much time had passed, since it felt so recent for someone her age. Maybe it was realizing she'd made me think back on dad. Either way, she suppressed a frown and nodded along.

"I guess those old electronics were bound to die eventually."

"Yeah," I mused, studying the cramped space around us, "toaster was the last to bite it."

She approached a repurposed garage door, stopping short to glance back at me. "You kept the toaster?"

Rubbing my neck, I shrugged. "Until I set it on fire a while ago."

She shot me a look somewhere between annoyance and shock. "You set it on fire?"

Shrugging again, I replied with a shit eating grin on my face, "Viking funeral."

Her eyebrow rose and her face settled into a minor glare of disapproval like she might not have completely believed me. Funnily enough, it was the first time she really looked motherly to me. The problem was, despite that, the look really didn't have any weight behind it. There wasn't a history behind it that others might've had. I feared no punishment from this person well below my weight class. I knew that fear, I felt it with my grandmother. But for Marionette? She was practically a stranger.

Shit, was grandma the dominant force I always imagined? Or was she just bluffing based on some deep programming instilled in me from the cradle?

Shaking it off, I grabbed at the repurposed garage door and pulled it up, unleashing a faint cloud of smoke that rolled out over our feet. In an instant the space we were in was reminiscent of a college dorm or Bab's apartment on a Friday night. The smell on the smoke was an eclectic blend of the expected aromatherapy and the dankest weed I'd smelled in my life. Considering I'd gone to public schools and had been called to more than a few public intoxications, I felt confident in saying whatever he spent on that weed was too much.

With the door fully retracted into the ceiling, the Goblin was slowly revealed as the smoke evacuated his toasty little hotbox. He wore a coarse, hemp-derived shirt and a set of earrings on long elf-like ears. His rough skin and large, bright eyes gave two conflicting senses of his age, though either one would have probably been way off the mark. Those eyes, catching every bit of light in the room and glowing slightly like a cat's in the dark, were also incredibly bloodshot. Staring at us, almost through us, he took another drag off a pipe lovingly carved into the shape of a deep-sea Mermaid – the fluke nestled into his nostrils to give him proper suction. Clearly, he was on break and we'd opened the oven before he could finish baking.

"Oh god," Marionette uttered, shielding her face and taking a step back, tears welling in her eyes.

"G-Marts," I said with a shrug, "they don't franchise – they spread."

Staring up for an uncomfortable period of time, the Goblin finally lowered his pipe and asked in a nasally, rough voice, "What'll you have?"

Waving the smoke away, I examined the shelves behind him and took in just what kind of G-Mart I found. Set up as small pockets of legitimate but questionable business, bordering on a black market, a G-Mart's inventory was never fully universal. They had some staples, but rarely any guarantees. I could see some electronics, a few imports, and a couple vintage magazines from before I was born adorned with half-dressed Goblins. I couldn't quite see what I was looking for, but I figured it was worth a shot.

"I'm going to need a gPhone with a full spec camera, HobSIM, solar case, and a DAO chip."

Setting his pipe in a special holder like he was putting it on display, the impish man started to pull out components and assemble them on the counter. The gPhone was an item of borderline legality. A modular device designed with a variety of plug-and-play components: it wasn't anything spectacular on the surface. But the modules allowed for some interesting configurations if you knew what you were looking for. The HobSIM, for instance, would allow me to make calls without being traced, as it used a decentralized and almost entirely unregulated network the Goblins had constructed under everyone's noses. On the one hand, the service was terrible, on the other hand, it was as off the grid as a cellphone could get. And the DAO? The DAO...

"Not going to be able to do the DAO chip," he said before picking up his pipe again. "Those fuckers are rare lately. You'll have to use the app."

"Is the app any good?"

He took a long draw from the pipe, then shrugged. "It can be, if you're listening as a hobby like a regular old police scanner. Hell of a lag otherwise."

Picking up the phone, I studied it and considered my options. It felt every bit as legitimate as any other phone, assembled anywhere else. I couldn't tell if it was a mark for Goblin craftsmanship or a condemnation of consumer electronics, but it would pass in public. Without a reliable DAO, though, I was still in a hell of a position.

"Any chance at a dedicated DAO machine, then?" I asked.

He shook his head and frowned, a severe crease forming in his forehead as he did. "If I had one of those lying around, I could just pop out the transceiver and stick it in the phone. Damn things started vanishing lately, probably easier to backtrack than the app."

Disappointed, I put a clover on the counter and pocketed my glorified burner. I needed the HobSIM to avoid getting tracked, but the DAO would let me know how close the ACTF was getting. I'd busted guys with DAOs multiple times over the last couple years, usually wired to their car's GPS, but I had to admit it'd been a while since I saw one in the wild. Hell, until he mentioned it, I wasn't aware there was an app that could probably explain half of that. But if the app sucked, I couldn't rely on it for much.

"Price is two," he chimed in, fetching the gold coin from the counter.

"Two?!" I balked. "There's no way they're worth two clovers, especially without a DAO."

He stared me down, tufts of smoke flowing out of the corners of his mouth. “Two’s the going rate in this shop.”

Glaring darkly, I slammed a second coin to the counter and held my hand firm over it. “You want a second,” I grumbled, “you’ll show me if there’s any weapons on the hidden rack.”

Watching my hand for a moment, the little bastard took another long draw from the pipe and hit a button beneath his counter. In a flash, the back shelves retracted like the garage door before and revealed a whole new set of racks and cabinets that had been obscured from view. I was partially bluffing at the time, but the guy’s inventory seemed too squeaky clean for the usual G-Mart location. Now, with the run of the mill stuff cleared from view, a whole new inventory of grey market goods sat on display. In fact, I was kind of surprised by what he had in stock.

Despite the limited space he had to work with, the little shit’s collection was impressive. In fact, I’d go so far as to say he had himself a little museum to the evolution of Alter oriented weaponry. Most of them were antiques or collector’s items, which made them legal to have while still fairly dangerous. Others, meanwhile, were a little sketchy no matter how old they were.

I saw an antique White Fang revolver designed specifically to compensate for the inherent flaws in silver bullets. It would have gotten the job done but was invariably lethal and expensive as hell to load. Not far off from that was an Orion dart rifle, one of the earliest Alter attempts at a coil gun. It was less lethal and a hell of a lot cheaper to fire, but a rifle would be hard to get around town and, even with a coil firing it, a dart would be as effective as a gentle kiss on Alston’s skin. But then, hiding among the shinier guns of the bunch, sat one of the coolest things I’d ever seen: a Helsing CPG.

The Helsing was one of the early prototypes for what eventually became the Helios. The problem of applying stopping power to more than one kind of Alter without carrying a dozen weapons was a concern for a long time. Silver worked for more than a few but for the ones that didn’t react to that particular metal a silver bullet may as well have been a mosquito. For centuries, the Magi and R&D tried their best to streamline the tools while covering all the bases. Firing what amounted to pepperballs at high speed with magnetic coils, the Helsing allowed for a wide variety of chemical deterrents to be fired for a fraction of the energy a Helios required. Sure, it didn't have nearly as much power, but a few well-placed shots to the face could potentially make a guy like Alston stop to blink. Better yet, with the right knowhow, you could actually load it to neutralize whatever the hell made Marionette's lamp chase me.

Sporting my new Helsing and a couple clips of mystery ammo, I surrendered the second coin and made my way back out through the cramped little Goblin tunnel. Marionette, initially amused by my excitement at an antique gun, moved just a little bit quicker on our way back out. Either she hoped to escape the smoke or whatever was in those clips as I shuffled behind her. The safety seemed to be functional and I did a quick check before strapping the holster to my hip, but I couldn't entirely blame her: Helsings were older than my dad. Keeping an eye on it as I squeezed through the tightest spaces, I didn't even notice her exit the tunnel but did notice an abrupt stop in the sound of her footsteps.

Looking up, I saw the back of her head as she stood with her hands in the air. Pulling my gloves out of my pockets, I stopped to put them back on as I listened to agitated voices muffled by the narrow doorway. I couldn't see past her, but I didn't need to in order to understand what was going on. Untying the coat around my waist, I turned it right side out and slipped it on before continuing out the door. Emerging behind her, hand at the grip of my new weapon, I came face to face with the last thing I hoped to find outside: a half dozen uniformed ACTF and the distinct hum of their pistols pointed our way.

Chapter 21
Learning Squad

Staring down a half dozen Helios pistols, I immediately picked up on some good news and some bad. The good news was the guys outside that passage were a bunch of day shift clerics on their first month with no idea what they were doing. The bad news was that meant there were a lot more of them. At least I could be sure their guns were stuck at crowd control and my coat could tank several.

Unsteadily, the child that passed for the most seasoned spoke up, "Drop your weapons, hands on your head, face down on the ground."

Despite being at least a full year into the training program, I could still see the raw bits across the group. The day shift was where the very newest guys got their first exposure to the street, and it was clear across the board. Half of them didn't have their silvers on, none of them had eyes and ears ready, and the guy giving me the orders sounded like he was damn near ready to wet himself. It was almost too easy as I stepped out of the tunnel and very lightly twisted one of the rods at my side.

Placing my hands on my head, I stepped into Marionette's peripheral vision. "Best do what they say, Ms. Corbin."

As she glanced my way, I slipped my hands down my head and brought the heels of my palms towards my ears. She nodded and went to the ground slowly, slipping her hands over her ears as subtly as she could while putting her face to the floor. I watched and waited for her to assume the position, then glanced up at the one guy who seemed to have most of his shit together.

"All hands on deck?"

He adjusted his grip on the Helios and repeated without answering, "On the ground, now!"

He was aiming center-mass, forgetting to use the visor to help. Normally in point blank range it wouldn't matter much, but with his weapon in crowd control by default and my coat on, the math changed considerably. The real question was whether or not I had to take advantage.

"You should know," I said calmly, lowering to a knee, "Commissioner Alston is 65."

The ringleader, despite seeming to be the least freaked out, snapped at me, "I don't think calling him old is going to get you out of attacking him."

Their faces ran the gambit between confusion, frustration, and annoyance as I took them in one at a time. I'd hoped one of them would have remembered the ACTF number codes. Instead, I found a group as raw and unprepared as cookie dough. I didn't exactly feel good about what I was about to do.

Then again, how else were they going to learn?

Seeing that they'd surrounded us evenly and had completely failed to arrange for cover, I tucked and rolled between the two closest to me while pulling the armed Banshee from its clip. Several rounds went off around me, the searing sounds as they grazed across the jacket and the momentary flash of heat as they passed letting me know the new guys at least had some marksmanship. But, as the rod whipped through the air, the group soon realized they needed something other than their guns. Shrieking above all of us, the Banshee disoriented everyone in that tiny space and started one hell of a howl in the nearby pub. The rookies divided their attentions at that moment, some desperately trying to get their plugs in, others trying to put a stop to the rod itself, and the one who had his shit together turning to get a fix on me again.

Poor guy was trying.

Grabbing his wrist as he turned to face me and pushing the arm away, the couple rounds he popped off ended up hitting the next guy over instead of me and did little to stop my elbow from crashing across his face. The impact wasn't too bad, nothing I hadn't taken in a cage, but it was probably the first time he'd taken a real hit outside of training. He spun off, the one visor in the whole group flying away from him and giving me a sense of déjà vu, and staggered while doing his best not to topple. Kicking him from behind as he tried to regroup, I gave him a taste of the wall.

The dude that took a couple Helios rounds was too shocked to move, studying the coat to make sure the bolts hadn't shot right through him. The coat was designed to take that sort of hit, and the guns for new guys were defaulted to a lower charge, so he was going to be fine. At least, he was for the second before I pulled the Helsing and fired one of the mystery rounds square into his chest, a cloud of vapor overtaking him in a violent pop. Given his reaction and the way he started to double over, coughing and wheezing, my best guess was I just unloaded Werewolf mace on him: twice as potent as human mace with the extra touch of wolf's bane for good measure.

Behind him, the guys fumbling for their earplugs realized it was too late and raised their guns again. For their efforts they got the next couple rounds of mace, aimed a little higher now that I knew it wasn't going to kill anyone. Their pained chokes were enough to make them regret things but not enough to prevent a couple rounds being popped off from their pistols. Blinding blue bolts ripped across my coat, the hairs on the back of my neck raising as the electrical charge conducted ever so slightly through a few metal bits. Still, as their eyes burned and they desperately tried to find the kit on their belt to flush them, it let me turn my attention to the last two just as my own Banshee nailed me in the face.

Turned out one of them had a brain.

Disoriented as my whole skull vibrated, the next couple bright blue flashes peppered me as I covered my face with my arm and charged headlong into the fire. The coat could take it, I knew that, but every new hit stung just a little bit more as the heat and chemicals started to build. Blindly, I ploughed right into the closest one as hard as I could, whipping up the Helsing to fire several pellets into the next guy. Adrenaline meant neither one of us stopped, but my pellets were blinding him, and that's what I needed to close the gap between us and check him into the wall, stripping his gun from him in the process and tossing it clear.

The guy against the wall, comparatively flailing, was still trying his best to get the right grabs and holds on me. The chemicals were starting to burn my eyes too, having gotten a close-up dose of them a couple times now, and my advantage of surprise was quickly starting to fade. Their adrenaline was building, they were starting to push past the momentary inconvenience of pain, and their gear was as good as mine. A couple years earlier and he would have had me long enough to let his friends catch up. As it stood, I had to do something I didn't want to and punched him across "the button".

As he slumped, I did my best to keep his head from hitting the concrete and quickly raided his gear, grabbing his Will-O-Wisp and yanking it free. Arming it as I could practically feel the others scramble my way, I whipped it into the ceiling as a blinding flare pulsed and blew out the lights. The scream of the Banshee faded, the ruckus of the pub grew, and the rookies staggered in the dark. With the one guy closest to me out like the lights, I had gained a new advantage in the dark – another damning reason they should have had their visors on.

Thanking my luck that they'd sent FNGs, I rushed to pull Marionette back to her feet and escape down the tunnel. She resisted at first, swinging for me in the dark, but relented once it was clear I was running like hell. Dazed, winded, and already a little blinded by the residual mace, I prayed I wouldn't hit a wall as we went charging through the dark and towards a distant point of light.

"Where's the next Goblin pass?!" I wheezed out.

Marionette, still not fully steady at my side, didn't reply but did tighten her grip and take point. Now leading us through, she turned corners I wasn't fully aware were there and guided us towards blurry light in the distance. The tears starting to stream down my face were making it hard to see detail, the burning sensation becoming overwhelming, and nothing quite stood out in the array of smudged, watery colors ahead of us. It was almost so bad that when Marionette came to a sudden stop I almost couldn't tell why. Fortunately, my earplugs didn't quite filter the sound of a metal rod bouncing off concrete and you didn't need to see clearly to recognize a ping of light off a polished surface.

I couldn't tell what kind of rod it was right away, but I could tell at least from her reaction that it wasn't something she wanted in her face. Thankfully, outside of extreme circumstances, the number of options was limited. They couldn't risk blowing out the lights again, so probably not a Wisp, and the chances of civilians getting hit was too high for a Manticore. That left me with a Banshee as the most likely, unless someone was crazy enough to pull out the specialty crap just for me.

Either way, instinct kicked in and I kicked that thing back down the hallway while bringing the Helsing level with the black mass that likely threw it. Another scream ripped through the tunnel right as my eyes started to clear up enough to see something more than a color – a lancer patch drawing my attention right away, a familiar face and yet another Helios coming into focus moments later.

"Stevens," I yelled past the Banshee's wail, "we got a 65 in the HQ!"

He yelled back – his words lost in the echoes of the raucous tunnels. Frankly, it was the worst-case scenario. I wasn't in the best shape, smelling of Werewolf mace, ashes, and slightly singed Vesperadin. He was fresh, better equipped, and already kind of hated my guts from back when I was like the bozos I just slapped around. In a fair firefight, he had the edge, his gun was newer and he had a visor to help him aim for the fleshy bits. In a less than fair fight I might have had one over on him. At least, provided he let me shoot first.

Watching his hands and his mouth as he continued fruitlessly to yell commands at me, I could see the subtle twitches and the tightening grip that said he was considering it at the very least. The finger at the trigger said he was doing a lot more than considering. Stevens wasn't fond of me as a trainee, I'd say passing me off to Lucian when I got promoted to devotee was a good day for him, but he hadn't quite shot me yet. Despite my better judgment, I tried again.

"We have a 65!" I yelled past the echoes and chaos.

He nodded, and though he was a still a bit of a blur, I got a good read on his lips as he said, "You're the one."

That was definitely the worst possible response.

And then, as the firefight seemed unavoidable, I watched Marionette stroll casually up to Stevens. The Banshee had died down, though voices continued to carry out of every tunnel and drown out anything quieter than a scream. Calmly she proceeded to lean over to him and whisper in his ear. He didn't really react, not seeming to even see or hear her, but the tension in his body melted away. His shoulders relaxed, the grip on his pistol loosened, and his finger slipped away from the trigger. A visible confusion crossed his face, like he wasn't entirely sure why he was standing there, and then the gun lowered. I still didn't fully understand how it worked, but I was happy to be on this side of the witchcraft for once.

Holstering the Helsing, I started towards the perplexed Stevens hoping to try again within reasonable earshot. But, before I could get anywhere near close enough, Marionette intercepted me and sternly shook her head.

"We can't talk to him right now," she murmured, "it'd be like waking a sleepwalker."

Glancing at Stevens, watching him look around awkwardly, I could tell she was right. Even without seeing his eyes, that was not the expression of a man who knew what was going on. Frustrated, I started to follow Marionette towards the next Goblin tunnel before realizing there was one last thing I needed to do.

The smell of the mace, chemical burns, and ash were getting overwhelming and probably made it easy for a visor to track me. The coat had absorbed a lot of damage, more than I'd usually expected it to, and even the aegis patch was now hanging off of it. I didn't have anywhere to stuff it, and hanging it around my waist wouldn't be subtle with everything radiating off of it now.

Hesitantly, I took it off, looked over the burnt patches, and threw the coat to Stevens' feet.

Seeing it on the ground was surreal. Sure, I'd ditched the badge and most of the equipment, but the coat had actually saved my life a couple times. Turning away from it as Marionette beckoned for me to follow, I looked back to her as she stood with an outstretched hand from the next passage.

I took that hand and went inside, the camouflaged door closing behind us and leaving us in another dark, narrow tunnel.

Chapter 22
Electronic Underground

Sliding through those tunnels, slowly moving away from the chaos, I had time to reassess my equipment. Without the coat I couldn't hide most of what I brought along, including the Helsing which was now a giant signal to everyone that I was trouble. Seattle was never particularly fond of open carry, and the Helsing's coils and strange ammunition meant it was basically a hand-cannon. On top of that, I had ACTF rods hanging from the other hip. I wasn't thrilled with the idea of stuffing any of them down my pants.

"Give me a clover," Marionette commanded as she peeked through the next door.

Trying to peer beyond her, I saw a couple storefront windows and a few shoppers blissfully unaware of the crossfire a few blocks away.

"What are you getting?" I asked, rubbing together the last two coins in my pocket.

She shot me a look and raised her upturned hand between us. "Give me both and I'll get us out of here."

Clenching my fist around them, I plucked the coins from my pocket. Each coin was worth a little shy of a grand, and without the shootout and a well baked Goblin that would have been more than enough to get clear and cover our needs until I could regroup. But now all I could do was place them in her hand. I wasn't particularly thrilled about it but I was short on alternatives.

Nodding, Marionette slipped out of the passage and into the wider tunnel, closing the door behind her.

Standing in the dark, I took out the gPhone to see if it still worked. Surprisingly, Goblin craftsmanship was hardier than expected and it powered on without an issue despite the Wisp. As expected of a phone built to be off the grid, it was littered with software and features that could best be described as suspect. Fortunately, most of that was a matter of trying to get my money and not my identity. The phone fetched a number from a pool of available numbers on a Goblin-run VOIP service, a number that probably came with one hell of a history and was funded through clandestine means. Though it was probably fairly shady, it meant the caller ID wouldn't show my name or necessarily recognize I was the one using it.

Speaking of keeping names off the thing, I didn't want to go loading it with my contacts for obvious reasons. Though, even if I did, I didn't have most of them memorized. The ones that I did know right off the top of my head were members of the ACTF and my landlady. I'd bought the thing specifically to broadcast my situation to the right people. However, staring at the screen, I realized I wasn't exactly sure who 'the right people' were in the middle of this mess.

Lucian was probably clean, but he wasn't at his most useful in the middle of a summer day. Alston was compromised, so I couldn't count on the rest of the executive officers. Internal Affairs was usually a good place to go, but at this moment their first response would be to tell me to turn myself in before they'd listen to anything else. I wasn't particularly afraid of a holding cell myself, but it was clear I couldn't let Marionette end up in headquarters before I had this sorted.

I grunted my defeat and slid down the wall as far as the tiny space would allow, muttering, "Well shit."

None of my options felt all that promising. Could I have live-streamed the whole thing and hoped the right people eventually saw it? Maybe I needed to contact the regular authorities and hope they didn't panic at "compromised ACTF". Though, who was I kidding? At the current rate everyone thought ***I*** was the compromised ACTF!

Interrupting my train of thought, a flannel shirt soon draped over the screen as Marionette firmly presented it to me. She'd completely changed her wardrobe again, now looking like a twenty-something woman in the midst of a long day of shopping. The breezy pants and shirt of a tourist were now exchanged for skinny jeans, boots, and a blouse that was uncomfortably complimentary on her. Her hair was now tied back into a ponytail, strands of hair framing her face and an expensive looking pair of sunglasses. Hanging from her shoulder, she now sported a new fairly large bag with a brand logo on it that I hoped to never recognize. If it weren't for the features I now couldn't ignore anymore, I'd think she was a different person.

"Here," she huffed. "This won't take a bullet but it'll make you less obvious."

Flashes of my childhood sprang to mind again as that was the last time I could remember seeing a man with a flannel shirt tied around his waist. It wasn't entirely due to fashion trends, though, as I'd rarely been out in the daylight for a couple years and I was never particularly fond of flannel. Reluctantly, I decided any port in a storm and did as instructed. Besides, we were in Seattle and if there was anyone still doing it, it was probably there.

Nodding, she lifted the new bag towards me, the fattest stack of cash I'd seen in recent years stuffed inside. "Now put any of the trickier stuff in here," she said, "so you don't constantly jingle."

"Where'd you get the money?" I asked, emptying some of the random items in my pocket.

She rolled her eyes. "Obviously I cashed in the clovers for cash first."

Part of me was annoyed to think she cashed them both in without me, even though that was the obvious thing to do. Did she even get fair market value for the things? It wasn't like Argyre Dollars where the exchange rate was legally backed. Someone could scam you on gold if you weren't careful.

Staring me down, seeming to read my thoughts, she huffed again. "Oh please, I've been to more black markets than you have."

Maybe she had a point there. Then again, it was stressful to think about the fact she had a point there. For sanity's sake I filed that away in "unpleasant implications" and decided to do my best to never think of it again.

Tossing the rods and gloves into the bag and tightening the shirt around my waist, I made sure the gun was concealed and signaled I was ready. She stepped out, looked both ways like we were crossing the street, then gestured for me to follow. The image was confusing to say the least, as I simultaneously saw not only the twenty-something she presented but who she really was beneath it all. It felt childish putting my things in her bag and letting her decide when we crossed the street. Yet, there I was, stepping out and looking both ways too.

I filed that into "future therapy sessions" seeing as "unpleasant implications" was getting full.

As we passed through the Undercity, she offered me a hat and a pair of sunglasses. Given my years in the ACTF, it was probable the cameras would recognize me more with the sunglasses on, but the cap was nice. When we emerged from the underground, walking out into a wide-open space, it appeared the two of us had successfully slipped our pursuers. There were no cameras, no flashing lights, no sight of agents, and no sound of sirens on the way. In fact, it was amazingly peaceful outside with only the sounds of passing traffic, the rustle of leaves from a faint breeze, and what sounded like the distant laughter of children. Checking the gPhone's DAO app, though, I realized how worthless the thing was as I saw the most recent updates were way behind and that the conflict with Stevens was just now hitting their system.

"This app's a piece of crap," I muttered, swiping through to see if maybe there was a way to manually update, "we need a legit module."

Starting her way casually down the block, Marionette shrugged. "Unless you know someone who has a physical DAO, I think we're doing this the old-fashioned way."

I scoffed, "There's an 'old-fashioned way' of ducking an Oracle and modern surveillance equipment?"

Glancing back over her shoulder with a mischievous smirk, she didn't really need to answer that question.

Still, I knew from tracking her down that it wasn't completely impossible to pin down a Witch, even one as crafty as her. We needed to know more about what they knew. Needed an idea of what the system was up to. And, though I couldn't tell how important it actually was at the moment, I needed to figure out just what happened with the Oracle as we escaped holding. Fortunately, as I tucked the phone back into my pocket, I realized I did actually know someone with a physical DAO.

At least, I did if the prick was still in town.

There was a bus stop just up the block and across the street. It'd been ages since I had to actually take one but I was pretty sure the routes were still the same. Picking up the pace, I tapped her shoulder and cut across the street. She followed me, slightly more cautious of the traffic as we jaywalked, and hurried to catch up to me as the bus was just starting to come in. Demonstrating more of that keen awareness, she produced two transit cards and handed one over to me.

"You've done this a lot, haven't you?"

Just as casually as anything else she'd done, she just shrugged and climbed onto the bus. "Cars are expensive."

There wasn't time to call her on the dodge. Once we were on the bus, Marionette peeled off and weaved through the crowd. I followed to a point, but the pace she took and the way the people were starting to crowd on made me realize it was best to stop. Despite all the modern developments of public transport, taking a city bus was still basically volunteering to become a sardine.

The difference now was that every stop meant the bus got to take a moment to charge while waiting for the people to finish jostling around. Aurorastin panels along the roof of the bus stop made it so the city never really had to worry about gas for their fleets – finally allowing them to turn a profit for once. Though, from the slight hum I heard as it charged, I wondered if their charging port needed maintenance or if that was just normal for the civilian ports. I slept with an Aurorastin cell charger pretty close to my head, so I usually had an idea of when the thing needed some work. Still, it was a tough call, considering the city was too cheap to just solar paint the bus in the first place.

The passengers were all human or at least mainstream passing. I knew at least Marionette was an Alter, so I couldn't discount the idea anyone else might have been. It was surreal being surrounded by so many in the last day. I'd been so embedded in the night life that I forgot the Alter demographics were still a fraction of the city population. At least these people weren't as likely to recognize the Vesperadin weave in my pants or the dark plates along my shoes. Though, I couldn't help but notice *their* little quirks as the bus pulled away.

The stitching at her seams told me the woman sitting to my right was wearing Arachne silk, legal but expensive for someone riding transit. On top of that, I noted she was wearing a high collared blouse made of a breezy fabric only barely covering a notably aggressive hickey. She completely lacked jewelry, which again contrasted with the high dollar fabric but started to paint a picture. After all, if you're a conner you spend most of your money on the clubs and couldn't risk any silver or nickel that could ruin the vibe or leave a mark.

To her left was another woman looking completely buttoned up and downright bored. Either she was headed into work or out on her break as she still sat with the posture of someone who had energy to spare but was really just waiting to get this over with. She seemed to notice the hickey too, given a few quick glimpses at her neighbor followed by feigned attempts to look like she was just checking what the next stop was. I smirked when her eyes drifted up for a second and she realized I saw exactly what she'd been doing.

But the really interesting guy was standing behind me. Hair and beard perfectly trimmed, he'd probably spent a pretty good chunk of his morning making sure everything was expertly coifed. Though he wore a vest despite the heat, his sleeves were rolled up to expose a series of expensive, time consuming tattoos of mythical creatures and heraldric symbols. Given the uncomfortable outfit and the impeccable grooming I had to figure he was definitely just starting his day. My guess was he was maybe a bartender at an upscale club given how high the sun was in the sky and how fresh he seemed. But the thing that really caught my eye was the cross mingled into his ink.

A cross on its own was never a big deal, despite the supposed lore about holy ground. But this particular cross was a different story. At first glance, you could almost mistake it for the Cross of Saint James, a sword-like cross used by military orders in the Iberian Peninsula for centuries. But on closer examination, the cross was set against a golden circle, the "blade" was shaped like an arming sword, and the arms had a set of vicious looking prongs that turned the more flowery fleurs of a traditional cross into a more aggressive form. This was a Cross of the Sunset Blade. Our boy fancied himself a Vampire hunter. Though, given the look of him, the girl with the hickey probably stood a better chance at surviving.

Sadly, as I monitored the guy, I realized there was nothing I could really do about him. He wasn't breaking any sort of laws at the moment and, even if he were, I wasn't exactly in the position to do anything about that anymore. I wondered if he was even aware of what the hell that cross even meant. He didn't exactly seem built for fighting a super soldier. Unfortunately, that usually didn't stop someone stupid enough to get the mark in the first place. If I had my link, I would have run his profile. Instead, I just got to stare at the guy behind my new sunglasses and do my best to not think agent-y thoughts.

The good news is my staring seemed to make the guy uncomfortable. Maybe he recognized the scraps of gear I still had on me. Maybe he knew I could understand the heraldry on his arms. Then again, maybe I was just being creepy. Any way you cut it, he booked it off the bus at the next stop along with just enough people for me to migrate closer to Marionette's seat.

As I approached, there was a look on her face I couldn't quite place. She seemed somewhat lost in thought, distant, but still locked onto me. Was she watching me the way I was watching the others? What was going through her head? When I reached her, we were reflected in each other's sunglasses almost perfectly. She was definitely watching me. And then, like she suddenly saw the same thing, she looked ahead at the front of the bus and took a stab at small talk.

"You know, when you were a kid, these had drivers."

Glancing to the front of the bus, I did remember a time when someone used to sit up front. It really wasn't all that long ago, a time when every vehicle was manually driven, but it still felt like a lifetime. I couldn't even remember when they got confident enough in the self-driving models to cut that particular part of the budget.

Doing my best to reciprocate, I replied, "I kind of remember that."

She fell quiet, her voice barely audible over the electric hum and bustle of the passengers. "Some of them used to run on steam."

There was that distant tone of remembrance as she said it, like maybe she'd actually seen one of these things. Was she getting nostalgic all of a sudden? I started trying to remember the date of birth on her profile.

"Sometimes things change so fast," she continued, "keeping track of it all gets overwhelming."

The realization swept over me like a cool breeze. I shrugged. "It helps if you're paying attention."

The words escaped me before I fully processed what I was saying, filling the space between us with a whole new unease. It made us both uncomfortable and I could see her wince in unison with the cringe I did my best to suppress. I couldn't exactly say I was sorry, but I still didn't mean to do it. It wasn't the time or place for that sort of confrontation.

Looking away, I caught sight of the next stop and thanked whoever the god of buses might have been. We were thankfully close to our destination, a series of apartment buildings on the block awaiting us. Silently, I waved to get Marionette's attention again and gestured to the stop, beginning to drift my way to the door as I did. She gathered herself and let me get a good lead before she followed me off.

The two of us walked in utter silence the rest of the way. She maintained her distance, forcing me to check back to make sure I hadn't lost her more than once. Still, even if she was avoiding me, she never drifted off the path.

The space between us remained consistent all the way into the building and through the lobby. There were no doormen or security measures down there, even the mailboxes in a state of disarray as their locking mechanisms seemed to have been either busted or hacked. I wasn't particularly surprised, given the fact I'd been there a couple times before and was currently there for what amounted to an advanced police scanner. But it always did seem out of place with what I knew of the neighborhood's rent.

There were nice places in the area, I'd failed the credit check for a couple of them back when I was fighting, but this was the building of mild neglect you'd find with a landlord who stopped giving a shit. The paint was chipped, doors squeaked in the distance and echoed down quiet halls, and the light fixtures buzzed in a way that said they were at least as old as I was.

As I reached the elevator and hit the button, Marionette joined me and the two of us stood under one of those buzzing lights. I almost felt like apologizing but didn't know how to even start without lying. Part of me was kind of glad I shut her down. Another part wished I'd have let her finish. Watching her, I saw signs of the same back and forth in her. I could feel both of us getting ready to say something, but neither of us did before the doors opened and we mechanically assumed our positions.

Awkwardly standing shoulder to shoulder, we rose through the apartment building on a busted-up elevator in a silence so deafening I was actually wishing for the cold embrace of muzak. Besides the harsh words, the weight of the day's events continued to settle over me like an oppressive fog. I'd been disobedient before, damned obstinate more than once, but this was a whole class of its own. And it was all for someone I barely knew or liked a couple days ago and currently resented in ways I was just starting to process. On top of it all, I hadn't slept in so long that I was now probably on what could best be described as a fourth wind – held upright by adrenaline, witchcraft, and what I assumed was the blessing of Juan Valdez.

I've had elevator rides that felt shorter in Acheron.

Finally cutting through that silence, Marionette blurt out, "I know this has been hard on you, but you didn't have to resort to the ward."

"The what?"

"The oils," she continued, moving to shield her nose and taking the widest step away she could in this tiny box, "it's getting hard to ignore."

Was it the Werewolf mace? I hadn't smelled it at all since ditching the coat and assumed it was gone. Giving myself a sniff, all I could pick up were the scents of Dulaf's mysterious soap on a rope still lingering like a strange deodorant. I'd long grown used to it and what little was left of it was even pleasant compared to what I'd had to bail out of. No doubt there were some traces of the mace somewhere, but nothing powerful enough to draw that reaction.

Eying her suspiciously, I shook my head. "I tried to get rid of it."

"Really," she balked, "you mean you didn't slather yourself in baby's breath and lilac on purpose?"

"Baby's breath and lilac?" I echoed. "I don't even know what you're talking about."

Giving me a look similar to the one I'd given her seconds before, she relented. "You really don't, do you?"

I shook my head, crossed my arms, and returned to glaring at the door.

Staring at the door alongside me, she commented idly, "It's a Faelish blend to draw in good spirits and protect against malevolent ones. It's been making my eyes water since holding. It got overwhelming at the G-Mart."

I gave her a sideways glance and tried to peek at her eyes behind the shades. I'd assumed whatever irritation we had was from our short fun romp with the Helsing. Was the soap really so much worse? Then again, how'd it manage to linger past all of that? Even for an expert chemist, it probably took some effort to make a fragrance that could survive Werewolf mace.

Just like that, I knew exactly who to call.

When the doors opened, I stepped out and led the way down the quiet, unassuming hallway above. It wasn't in quite as much disrepair as the lobby below, in part because fewer people likely walked the same space on your average day and in part because the tenants on that floor had made special arrangements. Though the old fixtures still gave off a bit of a hum, the quality of light was wholly different up there. They were a different shade, meant for people with light sensitivity, and didn't give off very much UV.

Down the hall were a set of high-quality blinders with a shutter system I'd seen in a couple buildings before. In the middle of the night, they would open automatically, looking out over the city street, but at the earliest hint of daylight touching the building they would slam shut and not open until the sun set again. Lucian actually had a more elegant ivory set at his own house. They weren't particularly expensive, but you did need to maintain the sensor and the mechanisms, so few buildings did it unless they had to. In this case, it was a bit of a requirement with half a dozen Vampires living in the building that had all filed a specific complaint to get it done. One of those was my guy.

Stopping at his door, I waved for Marionette to bring the bag over and swapped my gloves for the cap. I didn't really need them but I found certain people, woken midday, tended to cooperate more when they got that specific nanoplated thump at their door. After a moment of considering whether to turn them on, I resisted the urge and gave a firm, authoritative knock. The apartment remained silent for a minute, prompting me to knock again. I knew from the mailboxes that my guy was still a tenant, and I knew for a fact he had to be inside at the time. Waiting for a moment again, I knocked a little harder this time, finally hearing someone grumble and stumble behind the door.

After what felt like forever, the door cracked open and a pale, wiry figure appeared briefly in the pitch-black apartment beyond. Cat-like eyes, shining under the hallway lights, shot open with shock as he slammed the door shut again.

Unfortunately for him, I wasn't in much of a mood as I shoved the door right back open into his sleep deprived face. He grunted and staggered through the dark and nearly tripped over a chair before looking up at the two of us entering.

"Yo, Nate," he stammered, "what're you doing here, man? I didn't…"

His voice trailed off suddenly as he looked beyond me, still shining eyes fixed on Marionette at my back. "Shit," he gasped, "Marion."

Almost annoyed, Marionette stepped up next to me, studying the darkened apartment for a moment before replying starkly.

"Hello, Emil."

Chapter 23
Groggy & Yielding

Despite how often I'd come to his door, this was the first time I actually stood inside Emil's apartment. Generally, when I came to haunt him, it was out in the hallway and we soon left the building. Honestly, it was about what I expected. The corner of his living room was like a small warehouse with a wide array of items that I was sure fell off the back of a truck somewhere. None of his furniture matched and had that "lightly used" feeling like it was something he just picked up off a curb. It was all amazingly clean, though, with every piece showing signs of recent steam cleaning and wood polish buffed to an impressive shine. He was sketchy, but he still had a Vampire's OCD.

Emil himself was wired, more than usual, and scurried about to get the lights on and drape sheets over the pile of goods. He was paler than usual and a little more disheveled. It made some sense, seeing as it was somewhere in the midday and he wasn't really used to being awake. But his eyes, shining like a cat's before he got the lights on, were fixed on Marionette instead of me.

"Hey Marion," he said in a sing-song voice, presenting a broad, fanged smile to try to hide the sheer panic in his eyes. "How's life been treating ya?"

Marionette strolled through the room with an air of discontent that I could feel through me. Emil was an old "friend" of my father's, an informant turned pusher. As far as I knew, Marionette was gone long before my dad ever met him. Yet there she was, stalking the perimeter of the room like a predator in a cage, glaring at Emil through the proverbial bars.

Stepping between them, I nodded and pulled the gPhone from my pocket. "We don't have time for small talk, Emil, I need to yank the transceiver from your DAO."

Those panicked eyes shot between us as he ran his fingers through matted hair. "I don't know what you're talking about," he stammered, "you took my last DAO."

"Cough it up, asshole," Marionette snapped, crossing her arms, barely containing her rage. "I'm not in a good mood."

Emil's eyes stopped shifting and settled on her as he started to circle to the other side of the room, keeping me between them. Shuffling along towards a door, he said, "If I had one, I'd give it up."

Marionette stepped up and for a brief moment I could have sworn the lights darkened. "I can tell when you're lying."

Recognizing the dynamic, I slipped into the only role available: good cop. "Look, Emil, we're not here to bust you for anything," I assured, "we're in a rough spot and you'd be doing us a favor. And it seems like this relationship could use an olive branch."

Marionette glowered. "A couple cloves of garlic down his throat should do."

Emil looked between us again, now settled into a space right next to that door. I could feel the loathing radiate off of Marionette and, I have to admit, it was the first thing I really shared with her. I actually felt like sitting down with her over a cup of coffee and chatting about our mutual hatred of the guy. But, for now, I really needed that DAO.

"Look, man," I interjected, "you can see I'm missing most of my equipment. If you keep pissing her off, there's not much I can do about it."

Rubbing his face, Emil muttered, "It's my last one, you don't know how hard it is to get those things anymore."

"I'll bring it back after this is settled," I promised.

Releasing the tension in his shoulders and slipping into his usual slouch, Emil wandered across the room to the pile and started to rummage through it. “What do you need a DAO for anyway?”

Hesitantly, I answered, “We’re trying to avoid the ACTF.”

He perked right up at that, turning to look back at us with the shittiest grin on his face. “No shit?!”

Marionette lunged forward again and stopped just behind me, Emil flinching from all the way across the room. I glanced at her, seeing the deepest of scowls on her face and wondered if we’d get the chance to get that coffee soon.

Finally pulling it from his pile of crap, Emil edged closer and presented me with the DAO. It was somewhat bulkier than the phone, designed to be mounted to just about any dash imaginable using a stand with a strangely grippy surface I’d learned indicated setae. The rest of it, meanwhile, seemed to be designed to go through one hell of a beating with heavier materials and a reinforced frame. Even the touchscreen seemed like something meant to withstand a car crash as the glass looked considerably thicker than average. It really seemed to be higher quality than you’d expect from a device generally supplied only in the underworld.

I kind of enjoyed tearing it apart.

Shockingly, the interior components were just as high quality. I’d seen the insides of a couple Argyre devices in the past and could see the tell-tale signs of Dwarf-Elf cooperation. There’s an old saying in Argyre from before the place was even founded: “Elves sculpt art, Dwarves forge hammers.” The two styles worked well together in a strange compromise as delicate circuits crossed a board connected to heat sinks that could probably stop a bullet. But, most importantly, the modular design of components meant I could just pluck out the transceiver and plug it into my phone.

Snapping it back together, I checked the gPhone’s settings and activated the function. Suddenly, that shitty little app came to life and populated the screen with the kind of information I’d long grown accustomed to. The search parties were still deep in the underground from the way they were grouped, every training lancer on the move with a couple doubled up. The guys I'd roughed up down by the Emerald Den were thankfully okay, getting checked out by the doctors in the medbay but showing no lasting harm. Breathing freely for the first time in a bit, feeling the tension lift, I nodded to Marionette as she continued to prowl the room. Taking the cue, she quickly turned for the door and marched halfway there before abruptly stopping, spinning on a heel, and shooting a look at Emil.

"Bastard's going to turn us in the first chance he gets," she muttered darkly.

Even without the visor, I knew she was right; it was just the way Emil was. It wasn't a matter of duty, morality, or even petty revenge either. If anything, he was going to turn us in hoping for a reward.

Shrugging, I replied matter-of-factly, "Probably true."

Emil shifted into the slimy tone he always had when he'd been caught red-handed. "What do you mean? I would never do something like that. We're old friends."

Dryly, I interjected, "There's no reward."

He looked me over from head to toe, then slowly turned his gaze to Marionette. I knew he was trying to figure if we were lying but I also knew he was lousy at reading people. I wasn't lying, exactly, but I couldn't tell him why. As a rogue agent, I was a PR disaster, and there was possibly room for him to leverage that another way. Still, for now it meant there was no direct compensation to be had from my fall. Unfortunately, that wasn't really enough.

Marionette's scowl deepened as she started towards Emil and reached into her bag. "Let's restrain him."

Looking around the room, I rubbed the back of my neck and mulled over the ramifications. Emil lived alone. If we secured him, there was a chance Emil never got free, which wasn't something I was particularly good with. Sure, he was slime, but he was still technically a person. We couldn't leave him like that. Though, seeing the shutters, I realized an alternative we had.

"Wait a second," I said, catching Marionette by the arm. "We can't just lock him up and leave him. I have a way to keep him secured for a couple hours."

Producing a pair of cuffs from her bag, Marionette clenched her fist around them before begrudgingly relenting and stepping back. "Fine, but it better be good."

Marching through the apartment, I started opening every door I could find. His bedroom was incredibly dark, the windows permanently shuttered and reminding me of the mausoleum styled buildings back by the Forum. His bathroom was surprisingly cluttered, indications he'd been mixing something in his tub but lacking the acrid smells I was used to from a drug lab. Shooting him a questioning look, Emil shrugged and grinned sheepishly. Still, with similarly shuttered windows and some space for him to get comfortable, it would have to do.

"Get in," I ordered, pointing.

The sheepish grin faded and Emil stammered, "What are you going to do?"

"Is anything in there dangerous?" I pressed.

"Well," he hesitated more, starting to edge away, "no, not really. I wasn't mixing anything illegal there."

Reaching out and grabbing his sleeve, I pulled Emil over. "If there's nothing dangerous," I remarked, "you have nothing to worry about in there."

He resisted for a moment, eyes darting between Marionette and the door like I wasn't even a concern. That settled fast once I swept the flannel back and rested my hand on the Helsing's grip. With his eyes locked to the gun, Emil stepped over the threshold and smiled broadly.

"Well, hey," he said amenably, "it's not the first time I've slept in a tub."

Staring for a moment, not wanting to think about that image or how it came to pass, I gestured at the wall. "Assume the position."

Without a word or a hint of hesitation, Emil turned and took a wide stance with his palms planted firmly against the wall. The man had been frisked so many times it was probably muscle memory by this point. Though he didn't really have time to hide anything on him as we approached, I knew better than to assume Emil couldn't be carrying all sorts of shit under his robe. So, I made sure my gloves were secure and patted him down like I was running security for the President.

Finding nothing, I exited the bathroom and closed it behind me, calling back through the door, "Okay Emil, we're opening all the shutters out here, so you stay in there until the sun's gone."

Muffled, he yelled back, "Toss a pillow in here before you go!"

Much as I hated the guy, I had to admit he rolled well with the punches.

As I reached Marionette, she was already well on her way to opening every shutter in the apartment and making it one of the brightest places on the floor. The sun was still high in the sky so it wasn't coming directly through the window, but the reflections off the neighboring windows alone were enough to make me glad for my sunglasses. I left her to it and went to fetch the pillow Emil asked for.

"You made sure he doesn't have any sunscreen, right?" She asked as I passed.

Admittedly, I hadn't considered that angle but it was quickly remedied. Stepping into the bathroom, I chucked the pillow to the tub and watched the spindly hand snatch it out of the air. He'd fully curled up in the thing already, prepped for a day of napping in the cool porcelain tomb, and didn't even bother to lift his head out of it to look my way. Taking advantage of the moment, I checked his medicine cabinet and drawers.

Once again cleared, I stepped out and called back from the door, "Sleep well, Emil."

"See you next time," he said with a yawn, "don't forget to bring back the chip."

Closing the door, I went out to rejoin Marionette, finding her setting a Halo strip at the entrance to the hallway.

"A little overkill, don't you think?" I scolded.

Undeterred, she rolled it out and ignited it. Standing again, she frowned at me through the thin sheet of light and mist. "Never turn your back on Emil."

Sighing, I stepped over it and started for the door. "You know that was meant for something more important," I said. "What happens when we need one of those later and we don't have it because you *really* needed to put Emil in a time out?"

Ignoring my question, she pushed past me and exited the apartment with an assertive pace. I jogged to follow her out, closing the door behind us and hurrying to catch up. She didn't slow, waver, or even bother to look back the whole way and only stopped because the elevator was still faster than the nearby stairwell.

"So," I said as casually as possible, slowing to a stop and crossing my arms, "how do you know Emil?"

She glared my way, brow visibly furrowing behind the sunglasses, hands wringing the strap of her bag with white knuckles. "The same way you do."

Words escaped me. I'd started to remember seeing her over the years after breaking through whatever block she had on me, and I remembered seeing her in the distance at the funeral. Despite that, I'd never considered that she was close enough to know what had happened. Then again, it was a long time ago, and I didn't really understand much about the world back then.

"You mean," I started only to be cut off by the elevator suddenly opening ahead of us. She maintained eye contact with me for a second and then stepped on without a word. Following her, I wasn't even sure how to continue.

"I didn't think," I said quietly, "I didn't know you were still around."

"I never left," she murmured. "I've always been in the city."

Thinking back on all those times I spotted the strangely familiar face in the crowd, more of them coming back all the time, I knew at least that much was true. Though, I had to admit, it irritated me more that I didn't recognize her back then than now. Hell, for everything that happened to dad, at least he never left me behind.

Idly adjusting my gloves, securing them again despite already doing it at Emil's bathroom door, I murmured back, "You never let me know."

White knuckles finally relaxed and shoulders slumped as she started to turn my way. I could feel her wanting, needing, to say something, but I couldn't look directly at her. I wasn't sure I wanted to risk it.

"Nate, I," she started, trailing off. I could feel her look me over and study my posture, eyes settling on my hands as I kept mechanically fidgeting with the gloves. As the elevator chimed, I stripped them off and tucked them back into my pocket.

This time, *I* got to escape through the door.

Marching through the lobby with purpose, I checked the DAO on the phone and made sure Emil hadn't found some way to a phone. The signatures were still clustered in the Undercity, patrol units moving methodically block by block for a sweep. They were still well south of us, probably assuming we were still down below. Somehow, the Oracle either hadn't spotted us or hadn't reported it. Pocketing the phone again, I took a cleansing breath and watched people walk by from the stoop.

Even if she was shielding us, there was only so much the Oracle could really do. She could make choices but couldn't override the system as far as I knew. If we could jump across the rooftops, we could probably stay ahead of her longer. At least, that's how it worked for a certain behemoth that'd been eluding everyone for quite some time. But on the ground, in the heart of the city, was a whole different story.

People slip through the cracks all the time because the Oracle's attention is spread across most of the district. We didn't have that luxury right now. We were high priority, surrounded by thousands of poorly secured and networked cameras, and had our location confirmed by agents on the ground. How long could it last?

Sounding incredibly reluctant, Marionette spoke up, "I think we need to go to Glinda."

I took a deep, cleansing breath and looked northward. "We can't just hide there. They're still working under the assumption we're in the Undercity, but once that's done they're going to check contacts and backtrack our movements."

Sighing, she snapped, "I'm not planning on setting up camp! There's something I need to do."

Still not feeling it, I added, "It'd be an hour on public transport, that's a lot of witnesses."

She shook her head, then reached out. "If you let me see the gPhone, I can have her come to us."

I winced and groaned. "I might have tagged her car."

She sighed, then extended the hand again. "Then I know a service that still takes cash."

Dubiously, I handed her the phone. I didn't particularly want to go back to one of her dear friends and I didn't leave Glinda on the best of terms. Worse, with the warrant and the tag on her car she was going to get visited eventually. The Oracle wasn't quite providing them the best support, but it was only a matter of time before they extended their search. To that end, at least Glinda lived out in a residential area and with luck her neighbors would think I was there to follow up rather than hide. Either way, Marionette soon tugged me along as a black hatchback pulled up to Emil's building.

It had been customized with flame decals all along the sides, chrome rims, and a horse head ornament on its hood. The interior was similarly customized with leather seats and fine detailing. Great care had been taken to polish various metal trims to a high shine and to keep the leather in an immaculate condition. A woodsy scent filled the space like we'd suddenly wandered into a peaceful meadow. The driver sat silently and motionless, a firm grip on the wheel, clad in black with a matching racing helmet. On the passenger side was what appeared to be a human skull, carefully secured to a booster seat.

I stared at the skull for a moment then at the driver's helmet, murmuring, "A licensed Dullahan?"

The driver reached up to the sun visor and flipped it down, displaying multiple licenses for a "Liam" with the faces obscured on all. Dullahan had a cultural taboo of revealing their faces, going so far as to pretend they didn't have heads at all for most of history. At first it started as just a simple myth from the fact no one had seen them without the hoods or helmets, then they'd encouraged that myth with spare heads they'd carry on the bench or under an arm. This was tricky for licensing, but a deal was arranged to let them be photographed and have a special filter applied to their cards. But, all things considered, that wasn't the reason why it stood out to me.

Besides the well-known myth of being headless, there was another aspect of their culture that was shrouded by myth and legend. Tales stretch back for centuries of these creatures riding on carriages made of bone that would leave flames in their wake, pulled by terrifying horses. Studying the car more closely, I soon realized the most bizarre feature was a manual gear shift on what was clearly an electric car. I'd heard of that kind of custom job being done in the past, but never on a hatchback. But a feature like that totally fit with the other thing I knew Dullahan most for: they tend to have a lead foot.

Aggressively shifting into gear, our masked driver pulled into traffic with an air of invincibility and reckless abandon. Tires squealed, horns honked, and I cursed a little. Our boy Liam, while pulling out like a bat out of hell and making the very act of merging feel like a jousting match, managed to go right up to the very edge of speeding without doing so. In fact, as he started to enter the zone, things continued at a hectic pace but entered a strange state of calm. The silent driver weaved his car through traffic like a monk carefully stepping around various creatures that happened to be in his path, a Zen-like state masked by the thumping Eurobeat he started blasting over the stereo at the first stoplight.

Turning to Marionette, I yelled over the music, "You take Dullahans often?"

She leaned over. "They're the only carriages that don't get robbed."

She had a point.

Once the initial shock of his aggressive style passed, I had to admit the guy was efficient. He took shortcuts even I wasn't fully aware of and managed to avoid jams that even the GPS barely registered. It was like watching someone become one with the flow of traffic while simultaneously driving like he wanted to murder it. He also seemed to be aware of where traffic had stopped, moving to avoid every red light and stop sign he could. Like the perfect getaway driver, he danced through urban gridlock with a natural grace and flow while carving through the city towards Glinda's neighborhood.

Nearing our destination, the aggression faded and that stream of flow slowed down. Suddenly, our masked driver stopped at the lights and treated other drivers with the upmost of respect. Silently, sitting at one of those lights, Liam reached to a screen and typed out a simple message:

"How close do you need to be?"

Turning her attention to the neighborhood, Marionette made a dismissive gesture and replied, "Another block should do."

Liam remained silent, raising a gloved hand to give us a thumbs up, then continued towards our destination for exactly one block. He pulled over after that, much more carefully and cautiously than he'd pulled out, and tapped his screen again to bring up our total. Marionette paid the man, exchanged a few silent gestures, climbed out and waved for me to follow.

We were still a lengthy walk from Glinda's as we existed the car. Frankly, I couldn't understand why we'd stop so far out. Just being a residential district didn't necessarily put us outside of the Oracle's field of view. Security cameras were a lot harder to spot anymore and I was fairly confident the only excuse for certain creepy lawn ornaments was to conceal their location. Even at that very moment I'd made eye contact with a garden gnome that could have been sporting a camera behind its cold, lifeless eyes.

Though I suppose we were all lucky the cameras were common before actual Gnomes could be hired to stand guard in those getups.

Liam pulled out just as cautiously as he'd parked and drove away well under the speed limit, turning away from our destination the very first chance he got. Marionette turned the opposite direction and casually strolled like she didn't have any reason to hurry. Frankly, the sudden shift in energy left me confused as I watched them leave for a moment before jogging to catch up to Marionette.

Settling on which of many questions to go with first, I asked, "Is there a reason we're cutting the ride short?"

She maintained a steady pace and a laser focus on her destination while replying off-handedly, "This neighborhood is covered in various wards. The flowers in the gardens, the metals in the fixtures, the kinds of trees – all of it scares off something."

Looking back at the now empty road where Liam once was, I wondered aloud, "What exactly are the locals afraid of?"

She scoffed. "Just because they started a country doesn't mean Alters are all on the same side."

With that we walked silently side by side through the rest of the neighborhood. That familiar feeling crept back even stronger than before as I started to see old cracks in the sidewalk filled with weeds and tuft of grass, rose bushes pressed against wrought iron fences, and old mail boxes in the shape of little houses. Images of reaching out to touch some of the things with tiny hands came to mind and, admittedly, I might have let my fingers graze across at least a couple mail boxes as I passed. Distant memories of a small giggle echoed back to me, met with the more unnerving sound of a few giggles in our wake. Glancing back, distant trees rustled far down the block, just beyond the first lawn with a wrought iron fence on the street.

We continued up to Glinda's home, Marionette a little more confidently while I lingered a few steps behind. She knocked at the door while I stood a couple feet back and glanced over her shoulder at me while she waited. It probably looked strange to have me almost cower from the place. Still, as the door opened and Glinda invited us in, I couldn't help but feel like I didn't belong there. Yet, with everything that happened, I couldn't turn down the safe haven.

After all, I'd burned all my other bridges.

Chapter 24
Innate Tensions

Glinda's couch had my name on it. It was only a matter of time before I sat down or closed my eyes long enough to collapse and, despite my reservations, it happened there. I'm sure most people would be uneasy going unconscious with a loose weapon and a pair of Witches with a criminal history buzzing around the house, but honestly it was the best nap I'd had in months. The couch was either amazingly comfortable or I'd hit a point where I just didn't care anymore. Not to mention the fact the air was probably laced with something I wouldn't ingest willingly. Regardless, after ninety minutes I was awake and remarkably fresh. Though, mind, anything above undead was "fresh" at the time.

I didn't sit up right away, playing dead for a bit so I could process in silence. Marionette and Glinda buzzed around in what I recalled was probably Glinda's kitchen, chatting in low, rapid whispers that bordered on white noise. Stray words stood out like "border" and "Salem" but full sentences were few and far between. The few I could hear were well without context and meant nearly nothing to me. Though, that wasn't true for all of them.

Echoing into the room, Glinda murmured, "He looks so much like Michael, it had me flustered."

"It's the eyes and the jawline," Marionette agreed.

Slightly louder, stressed, Glinda remarked, "I can't believe you let him join the ACTF."

I opened my eyes finally, hearing the deafening silence from Marionette as Glinda's old clock began to fill the void. She didn't really have a choice in the matter: she would have had to show herself to get a say. Part of me was even a little insulted the woman who helped her bail couldn't do the math. Then, quietly, Marionette replied in a tone so hushed it couldn't get past the tick of an old pendulum and a few gears as anything more than an indecipherable murmur.

Sitting up, I grabbed the gun belt and my boots and started putting them back on. Tightening the boots, I stared at the gPhone on the nearby coffee table. It was practically challenging me to think of what to say to Dulaf. I knew she was more than capable of dealing with the situation if I gave her the heads up but I wasn't exactly sure what *my* next steps would be. Would I just leave it to her and keep my head down or would I have a plan? What if she needed me to turn Marionette over? Standing and fetching the phone from the table, I tucked it away for the time being and followed the voices back to their source.

The two of them were casually chatting over coffee in the kitchen, the rustic aroma hinting of one of those herbal blends I'd learned could keep someone running well past their expiration. I slowed my approach as I caught sight of them, considering putting the sunglasses on out of force of habit. The only thing staying my hand was the knowledge that the gesture would tell them much more than direct eye contact. Resisting the urge, I stepped into the kitchen and made them aware of me.

Glinda looked up with a warm smile and stood from her seat. "Oh look, he's awake. I should hurry up then. I don't want to slow you two down."

The Witches shared a light hug and Glinda hustled out of the kitchen. I stepped aside to let her pass. Even though the path was clear, she slowed to a stop and looked up at me. Reaching out, she gently rested a hand on my shoulder and rubbed it.

"You're looking better, Nate."

Better was subjective and I wasn't about to question it. The last time I stepped into the house, I was scraggly and beyond stressed and this time I ended up on her doorstep with somehow even less rest. I couldn't help but nod in agreement. Smiling softly, she returned the gesture, patted the back of my arm, and continued on her way.

Quietly, Marionette asked, “Are you sure you don’t want to get a couple more hours?”

Scanning the room for a coffee pot, I migrated across the kitchen. “A ninety-minute block completes a full sleep cycle,” I mused aloud, “restores function without risking a sleep hangover.”

Fishing through the cupboards, I found older mugs with hints of someone carefully preserving them over the years. It wasn’t likely Glinda used them all, no one could have used the couple dozen mugs all on her own, but not a one had dust on them. Each of the mugs were uniquely designed, hand painted with old pagan symbols for good luck and positive energies. Some of them were even molded to have their designs embossed across their surface with careful texturing and ergonomic contours. One particular row of them, labeled with a series of vaguely familiar names, stood with two missing – the two on the table behind me. But one on the far right caught my eye more than the rest.

With green designs over a blue background, the mug on the right had a woodsy feel to it. Pine trees stood against a sky-blue field, painstakingly molded and painted like a genuine landscape preserved in ceramic. The handle was a bit larger than the rest of the collection, though not so much as to be completely out of place. Plucking it from the shelf, I found it nearly perfectly fit my hand. Turning it over, I stared at green letters spelling “Mike” over a broader blue field.

He’d been here too.

“Forgot that one was there,” Marionette said. “I’d say it’s yours now.”

My grip tightened before I reminded myself the mug was probably older than I was. Easing up and making sure I didn’t crack anything, I filled it with whatever brew they’d been drinking. It was a rich, complicated blend and I could tell immediately my nose was right about the stimulants. I was still afraid to ask Babs what went into something like this. But another question took priority here.

“So, he knew Glinda too?”

After a moment, Marionette relented. "I didn't hide what I was from him. At first he was under the impression I just meant I was a Wiccan, but…"

As she trailed off, my eyes drifted back to the mug and the dark reflections inside. The most obvious unspoken question started to weigh on me again. It was the same question that had been haunting me since I read her profile.

"Then why did you leave?"

Marionette shrank in her seat and stared into her own mug as the question hung in the air. It felt like forever, but I could hear by the distant ticks of that old clock that it was only a few seconds at most. Still, even the space between those seconds seemed to slow down.

Finally, she said, "I was afraid I was going to put you in danger."

The irony was too thick to hold back my snort. "What, with your mob ties and cleanup work?"

"They were cataloguing us, putting us all on lists!" she exclaimed. "Anyone could have looked us up and realized where I was, who we were!"

Frowning, I muttered, "It was a census."

"It was a mistake!" she snapped, nearly leaping from her chair.

The tone, the posture, reminded me of a faraway living room under the shade of pine trees and the glow of a television. The blurry memory of my dad trying to reassure her as the news of "monsters" hit the air was suddenly colored in a new light.

"You didn't want to go public," I said, shocked, putting the mug aside before I continued. "This whole time it was so you could hide? You hid from us so you could hide from Argyre?!"

Stepping out from behind the table, she shouted, "I did it to hide ***you*** and then you ***joined them***!"

"What choice did I have?!" I yelled, glaring down at her. "They took me in when I had no one left!"

She scowled and hissed, "You mean Lucian."

"Damn right," I snapped, "wasn't that the plan?"

Her glare disappeared in a bolt of shock and confusion as she backed up a step. "What do you mean by that?"

I closed the distance, almost growling, "Rufus said Lucian sent you to meet dad as some plan to get an Empyreal!"

"That wasn't what happened," she stammered, "Lucian didn't have anything to do with our relationship."

"Stop lying to me!" I roared, feeling a surge of adrenaline as I finally let go. For a brief flash, I felt my fists and jaw clench. A few years ago, before Lucian and Dulaf took me in, I'm not sure I could have reigned that anger in. There, in that kitchen, watching Marionette's face and seeing her fear, I felt them pull me back. My fists relaxed and my jaw unclenched as the cold realization of what I was just feeling came over me.

Barely keeping it together, I pointed at her and repeated as calmly as I could, "Stop lying to me."

Fear turned to pure grief as I could see her let go too, tears streaming down her face. "Lucian told me to make sure the Leones were okay, he never told me what to do from there," she sobbed. "I never wanted you or your father to be part of this world."

Thinking about Emil and how she reacted to him, I finally felt sympathy for her. The world of Alters had managed to ruin dad. But as for me? It was't always easy, and I lost my way a couple times, but...

"They saved me."

Though the tears still flowed, her expression softened. "I was there to make sure the family was okay, and I wanted to keep him, you, out of all of it."

Returning to her seat, she sank into it and practically melted. Her head and shoulders slumped dramatically, to the point it almost looked like the elbows rested on the table were the only thing keeping her up at all. Fingers twitched lightly as I could see her picking at the edge of a fingernail absently. She was trying to conceal her ticks, the same way I had most of the day. Taking a deep breath, she gathered herself enough to stop the quivering in her voice.

"I don't know if you've noticed," she said sadly, "but our people aren't exactly a united front."

I shrugged. "No one ever is."

She shook her head. "We weren't ready to come out to the rest of the world. When they started the census, before coming out, I tried to avoid it for as long as I could. When they went public, I knew they'd find me eventually."

Picking up dad's old mug, I wandered over and sat across from her. "So, you went into hiding, even from me?"

"No, I," she paused and laced her fingers together, squeezing them to stop fidgeting, "I registered as soon as the divorce cleared."

"So, you just," I started, trailing off as I felt that energy from before slip away, "hid from us."

"Billions of *latent* Alters wander the Earth unregistered," she said.

Understanding where it was going, I finished her thought. "But the family of active Alters get registered too."

For years, I'd seen and forgotten that face in the crowd. She'd been tracking me every step of the way and never interacting. What was everyone else thinking during those moments? Did my grandmother know Marionette's motives or did she just think the act alone meant I was better off? Did I screw up Marionette's plan by walking straight into the system she was trying to keep me out of?

Shaking my head, I muttered, "You couldn't give them a latent Empyreal."

Sitting up a bit straighter, starting to regain her composure, Marionette got up and went to an out of the way cabinet to pluck out a bottle of whiskey. It was effortless, practiced, like she lived there and knew where everything was. Returning with it, she poured some into her coffee and sat down again. After stirring for a moment, she glanced at the bottle, then me, and tilted the bottle my way. Tempting as it was, I waved it away.

"I try not to."

Looking at it for a moment, she nodded faintly before putting the bottle back down. Sitting back, she took a deep, cleansing breath before a long sip of her coffee. As she watched her cup, practically meditating on the dark liquid, I was amused by the idea I might have looked the same on more than a few occasions.

"It's bullshit, you know," she finally said, looking up. "Lucian doesn't want an Empyreal."

"Then why would he send you to check on the family?"

She shook her head and rolled her eyes. "It's not about what you are, it's about who you are. The Leones have given a lot to the cause and they keep coming back for some damn reason."

"There's a man in a box who thinks that isn't an accident," I muttered.

She snorted. "Rufus is full of shit. There were stories that Leo might have been an Empyreal, but if you go far enough back every holy man and war hero gets labeled one eventually."

"What, an angel?"

"A lot of things," she corrected. "You go almost anywhere in the world and you'll find shining figures with halos of light. Who knows what they really are, but I've never seen someone turn into a wheel covered in eyes or literally sprout wings."

Shrugging, I remarked, "Unless you count the Nosferatu or pixies."

"Okay," she acknowledged, "but that's still a far stretch from flaming wheel with eyes."

Watching her, I felt the weight lifted from us both. But there was still part she wouldn't address, something I couldn't ignore. Those few times we talked in the club were always hushed, expedient. I distrusted her, she clearly pushed me, and then we were supposed to just part ways.

"Why did you keep hiding after I joined?"

She didn't cower away or get defensive this time and answered quietly, "Shame, I guess. There were times I wanted to go back and help you. Then before long you were an adult and we were standing on very different sides of the line."

She reached across the table and rested her hand on my arm. "I didn't want you to know who I was if you had to arrest me."

I chuckled. "Guess that didn't work out."

Wryly smirking, she huffed, "Not at all."

Remembering why we were sitting in that kitchen at all, I took it on myself to address the elephant in the room. "So, if you don't know why they want you dead or remember what this 'Salem' thing was about, what can you remember?"

Her brow furrowed into deep concentration. Assuming she was telling the truth about this "Salem" thing, she was likely trying to dig out what scraps of memory remained. I knew that she was telling the truth about the hit, given what happened with Alston, but I wasn't quite sure how to prove she wasn't still playing me over the rest. All I could do was hope that following the breadcrumbs would prove her claims.

"There was something in the Undercity," she said, stressed, "something they wanted completely scrubbed, even from the coven."

"Is that why you were down there?"

She nodded, still looking a touch uncertain. "I was trying to find it. I had a key and hoped that whatever it was," she hesitated, searching carefully for the right words, "might give me some leverage."

It was an honest admission, I figured, though I had to wonder why people like Kate and Angelique didn't do the same.

"Why are you the only one that remembers anything?"

She grimaced and lightly shrugged. "When you do this long enough, you start to expect it to come back your way. I took safeguards against being burned a long time ago."

"Then why did you need to go to Orin?" I asked.

She pursed her lips and fidgeted for a moment before saying, almost embarrassed, "My safeguards prevented a clean wipe, but it wasn't thorough enough to prevent it all. It's the difference between being brainwashed and being drugged. Orin's skilled at lifting those effects."

Leaning across the table, I took my agent tone with her as I pressed, "But you were already in the Undercity where you were supposed to find that leverage. Why would you go to her and then try to skip over the border?"

"Well, *someone* intercepted me and flooded the area with agents," she said sardonically.

Wincing, I asked, "Wouldn't happen to keep that key, would you?"

"I hid it before I switched to Victoria," she said. "I had a feeling that I couldn't keep it safe while on the run and I needed time to let my memory come back."

Hopeful, I chimed in, "And your memory is coming back?"

She shook her head and drank deep of her Irished coffee.

"So, we'll just take the key and find out what they hid," I said, "and hopefully figure out who started having people killed."

"It was a group in my coven," she hissed, "though I don't remember who the hell they were."

I had a list of coven members before, shining across my windshield and scrolling through my hand-link – both of which were now sitting either where I left them miles away or in the ACTF's impound lot. The DAO in my pocket could tell me what the Oracle was doing, but trying to dig up information was another matter. The only way to track them down now was through old-fashioned means. Unfortunately, one of those was to ask their associates and the only one I had available had amnesia like the protagonist of a JRPG.

It would have been funny if it was happening to someone else.

Fishing the gPhone out of my pocket again, I considered if Dulaf could have fed me the information we needed. She was day shift and probably at an Oracle terminal as we spoke. The question was if she was free to talk with half the force on the streets trying to find a rogue agent and his apparent puppet master. Maybe it was better to just leave her a message – one that the Oracle would overlook. Checking the time, I dialed one of the only numbers I knew off the top of my head.

After a moment, a pre-recorded, mechanical voice rang through: "You have reached the phone of Amelia Wright, please leave a message at the tone."

Unfortunately, Dulaf had taught the kid never to pick up for strangers. Though she was the pinnacle of irresponsible behavior in her personal life, Dulaf was actually a fairly responsible parent. However, I'd already planned for this.

"Hey Amelia, it's Nate," I said cheerfully, "sorry about the number, new phone. I just need you to remind Dulaf that Commissioner Alston is ***65*** today. I can't get her on the phone right now, so it'd really help me out if you could remind her for me. So yeah, just let her know Alston's ***65*** and tell her I'll see her at the party! Thanks kiddo."

Hanging up, I looked up to meet Marionette's deadpan stare.

"What the hell was that?" she asked. "Your one phone call and you're babbling about birthdays?"

Downing what was left of my coffee, I got up to refill, shaking my head all the way across the room. "We don't use the standard numerical codes – the Oracle handles all of that," I said. "We have different numbers tied to specific code words for when something fundamentally compromises the system: Ghost translates to 69, 85 means Shifter, Exodus adds up to 88…"

"And 65?" She asked.

Nodding sagely over my fresh cup, I replied, "Siren – for when someone's been brainwashed."

I could practically see the dots connect behind her eyes as she remarked, "That's why you kept yelling that number at them!"

Ruminating over that failure, I nursed my coffee and tried to ignore the faint pangs of regret. "New guys need a refresher on their codes."

Still processing, Marionette's voice rose. "If the Oracle is always watching, why the hell hasn't she told anyone about this?"

“Well,” I hesitated, rubbing my neck, “there’s two components to the system. The girl inside is basically sleeping while the computers relay information in and out of her tank.”

“You mean she physically can’t?”

Reluctantly, I nodded, deciding it was best not to go into detail about the several overrides put in there to keep the Oracle from acting on her own.

Regardless, Marionette connected the dots anyway. “So, she’s basically a prisoner in there!”

“Hey, no,” I protested, “the Oracles who join up are all there voluntary and they get shift rotations just like the rest of us. It’s less like she’s trapped and more like she’s…” I trailed off, trying to search for the least damning words possible before settling on, “stuck behind red tape.”

Snorting, Marionette stood up, put her mug in the sink, and started to pace the room a bit. “Well usually if someone disagrees with the policy they’re allowed to quit.”

“She is,” I interjected, “but I think she’s staying where she is so she can help.”

“Help?” Marionette snapped, “What exactly is she doing to help right now?”

“Well, we did get out of holding without that elevator stopping us.”

Halted in her tracks, Marionette’s eyes darted about for a moment as she chewed on that thought. Looking back up at me, her expression softened considerably. “She let us go.”

Nodding, I went back to the necromantic brew in my cup and let it run through me. Thanks to my nap, I had enough grey matter to make the stuff useful again. I still couldn’t quite grasp what all was happening on the Oracle’s end of things, but it was unmistakable that she helped us get clear. The commissioner probably had his own version of the silver line command to keep the fact he was compromised quiet – likely activated before he even went into the interrogation room. But, with the message hopefully on its way to Dulaf, I just needed to identify who exactly did the compromising.

"So," I said brightly, "where's that key?"

Chapter 25
Liberal Support

Fortunately, the key wasn't very far away. Marionette knew she was fleeing the country as soon as she reached Glinda's. Like she said, she didn't want to risk losing it on the run. So, as Glinda returned with a batch of herbs, a few metal charms, and a stick of Witch-friendly deodorant for me, I got sent out with a gardening trowel and told to dig up a specific spot in the back yard. There, beneath decorative rocks that encircled her garden, I found what we needed in a plastic baggy.

The "key" wasn't quite what I expected though. Inside the baggy was an envelope containing three seemingly unrelated items. The first was a piece of paper with a six-digit code written on it in broad, shaky handwriting that didn't quite seem Marionette's style. The letters were blocky and slightly smudged in a way that suggested something dragged across the ink. I was taking a blind swing, but my gut said whoever wrote it was using a meaty left hand to do it.

The second item was a key card with a kind of holographic strip I'd seen on high end security systems in Argyre. It looked simple, shimmering as the light ran across it, but that thin, translucent strip held densely packed information that made it damn hard to duplicate without access to the original machine. My guess was it probably belonged to the man who wrote down the number. But as strange as the first two items were, the third item was the least key-like of them all.

Fishing through the envelope, I pulled out a small audio recorder the size of a tiny thumb drive. Pressing the button, a slow, deep voice bellowed out of it. With a weighty baritone, it sounded like a guy who would've struggled with holding a delicate item like a pencil or pen. With all that weight to his voice, I was kind of surprised what came out of that recorder.

"Carnation, iris, daffodil," the recorder played in crystal clarity as if the fingers that struggled with a pen managed to hold the tiny stick up to his lips. Yet, strange as that mental image was, he continued, "daisy, rose, lily…"

Shutting it off, I tucked all of the items into the envelope and stuffed it back into the baggy. Lurch's gardening monologue was confusing but, considering it was all supposed to be for a key, I imagined I would understand once we encountered the lock. Regardless, I had what we needed and carried it back to the Witches.

As I approached the door and heard faint giggles, a small part of me considered not wiping my feet on the mat before walking inside. Realizing I was being petty, I begrudgingly cleaned the dirt off my boots with some fairly petulant stomps.

I strolled through as Glinda and Marionette continued to chat away. Showing Marionette the baggy without a word, I put it on the counter quietly. She briefly glanced up, mouthing the words "thank you" so she wouldn't interrupt Glinda's updates on the neighborhood. Digging out the gPhone on my way out, I silently indicated I was going to arrange for a ride so I wouldn't interrupt. Marionette nodded and gave a light smile before returning to Glinda's commentary of the local marijuana dispensary.

I slipped out of the kitchen and down the hall as the giggles returned, Marionette laughing hardily at the description of some well-baked guy around my age wearing an ill-fitting green shirt and bellbottoms he apparently bought from a vintage store. I wasn't sure why it was funny, but the two of them burst into raucous laughter as Glinda explained his best friend and coworker was an equally baked Werewolf. Escaping to the relative quiet of Glinda's living room and flopping onto the couch, I made a call to one of the few lifelines I had left at a time like this.

Deeply in warded territory with nothing but some cash reserves and a gPhone, our options for getting around were fairly limited. The Dullahan wouldn't approach the house, most services weren't keen on cash anymore, and good luck trying to rent a car on a cash only transaction and no background checks. Marionette initially considered Glinda, but if the car stopped getting tracked it would have been a big red flag and we couldn't afford to be in a marked vehicle. No, we needed someone who knew the city, knew the covens, had no reason to be tracked, and was willing to drive half way across town for a song and promises of favors. Fortunately, a name came to mind rather quickly as I sat in a house full of witchcraft and knickknacks.

After a relatively brief wait, I caught the shadow of the car pull up and gestured for Marionette that it was time to go. She lingered for a bit as I marched out of the house, exchanging a few parting words with her friend and sharing a hug. I stopped near the door, hand on the knob, waiting for her to catch up so we weren't exposed to the outside world any longer than we needed to be. Once again, the quiet ticking of clockwork filled the house and emphasized every sentence. Funny enough, it reminded me of when she'd run into people at grocery stores.

When she finally emerged from the back and came to join me, I opened the door and walked out to see Babs in her old clunker of a car. An electric car from back around 2012, Babs' car wasn't exactly the most reliable thing anymore. Fortunately, I had convinced her to let me pay for some upgrades after she did me a solid a while back. The windows were now tinted to filter out infrared, the batteries were updated, and the paint job was now a psychedelic white, blue, and pink affair made of a shimmering coat of solar paints. It still wasn't going to win any races and the motors could barely get up some hills, but at least we wouldn't cook without an AC and it wasn't going to die on the side of the road.

I still couldn't talk her out of the flower decals on the hubcaps, though.

Half way to the car, Marionette grabbed my arm and spun me around. "You never said your contact was Barbara Zdunk!"

The look on her face was one of utter shock. Brow furrowed, a bit pale, eyes wide – she was on the verge of panic. It didn't quite have that look of fight or flight about it, though. Her posture wasn't that tense and she didn't look particularly terrified. Rather, it was the kind of look you saw on someone's face when they were stuck in a sudden, unexpected problem. It reminded me a little of the look the lab techs got when Dulaf yelled from across the room.

"What's the big deal?" I asked.

"The big deal," she hissed out a whisper, "is that she's Barbara *fucking* Zdunk, one of the oldest Witches in the world!"

She seemed genuinely anxious for some reason. Looking at Babs, all I saw was tie-dye, flower decals, and a Tupperware on the dash board that I suspected to be full of baked goods.

"I'm not following, here."

Frustrated, Marionette pinched the bridge of her nose and let out a heavy sigh. "They burned her at the stake in 1811 and *she didn't die*," she exclaimed. "What if she's in with them? I can't stop her!"

Oddly enough, up to that point, it hadn't fully occurred to me that Witches had a hierarchy. Ironically, the fact that Marionette was nervous made me feel better about calling Babs. On the one hand, Marionette couldn't stop Babs if she wanted to take a go at us, apparently. On the other hand, this meant Babs probably wasn't being pushed or under threat by the people we were dealing with.

"Perfect," I said, grinning.

Marionette pursed her lips and bit back something, then muttered, "Fine, you sit behind her then so you can restrain her."

"What?" I objected. "I always ride up front."

"We just rode in the back of the Dullahan car," she corrected.

I shook my head. "That's different."

"How?" she balked.

"He had a skull in the passenger seat!"

Darting past me and bounding to the car, she called out, "Shotgun!"

Before I could even try to stop her, she was already in and buckling up. I'm not sure why it bothered me but for some reason it felt like getting demoted to the kid's table. Granted, since both of them were older than me by centuries, I was never going to be able to argue that I didn't belong at that table. Still, a small, immature part of me resented getting in that seat and watching the two of them up front.

"Oh dear," Babs said with a mixture of amusement and nostalgia, "I remember when there was an actual shotgun involved."

Marionette chuckled. "Never let us do it though."

Sharing a glance and knowing grins, they rolled their eyes and scoffed in harmony, "Men!"

The ice broke fairly quickly after that. As gun-shy as Marionette was about meeting with Babs, it turned out they had a lot in common. Both of them were originally from Europe, Babs from Poland and Marionette from France, and had similar lifestyles for much of their past. There was an ease between them as they waxed nostalgic over small-town life in the era of horses and steam engines. But their conversations soon turned to subterfuge, secrets, and double lives. Both had also immigrated into the United States after faking their deaths, had gone by multiple aliases, and had joined quite a few covens and secret societies over the years before inevitably leaving when the mainstream public got too interested. As it continued, I started to feel uncomfortable about listening in – partially because of the personal nature of it all, partially because it explained some of Marionette's instincts.

The trip through the city itself was relatively uneventful. The DAO was telling us that the search parties had left the Undercity and relocated to the surface where they'd taken to trying to track down our most likely routes out of the city. They hadn't quite escalated to checkpoints, probably because that would require cooperating with the SPD and Mayor Hale was shy of looking too authoritarian. But, if they hadn't found us by nightfall, it was only a matter of time.

Navigating around the patrols with relative ease, we made our way to the entrance closest to where Marionette unleashed the pixies. The area was still quite a mess, with bins full of feathers, broken glass, and smashed fixtures gathered around a couple dumpsters. A couple employees emerged with trash bags near ready to burst and carried them out to the still growing pile. Walking with the same energy and posture of a couple Zombies I'd seen, they'd clearly been working overtime to clean up our mess.

Peering around and leaning to peek up through her windshield, Babs watched the sky and murmured, "Something to deal with later."

Curiously, I put my face against the window to see for myself and felt a subtle anxiety creep over me. Dozens of tiny shadows streaked by the side of a building, accompanied by flashes of color reflected in the windows. The figures dancing across the glass were moving too fast to make out clearly, but their vibrant colors reflected shades you wouldn't normally see in the Pacific Northwest. Even as I watched them through the car windows and past the noise of the traffic, I could swear I heard a faint giggle on the wind.

Parking in front of the entrance, Babs looked back at me and smiled warmly. "I won't even begin to ask if I should come along, an old thing like me would just slow you down," she said, "but should I wait for you?"

Briefly scanning the area for signs of a stakeout, I remarked, "It's probably best if you aren't here for long, the car stands out."

Nodding, Babs asked, "Would you like me to meet you somewhere, then? Or come back to pick you up?"

Marionette interjected, "No, if my coven was involved in this, then it could be a bad-"

"Nonsense," Babs interrupted. "If it's a coven then I think you'll be needing all the help you can get. Which coven are we dealing with?"

Marionette's brow furrowed as she chewed her lip for a moment before shaking her head in defeat. "I still can't quite remember," she said, "I'm starting to remember faces but not names."

Babs frowned and reached over to take Marionette's chin in her hand. "Oh you poor thing," she said sadly, "I just thought you were shunned."

"Salem'd," Marionette corrected, "along with quite a few others."

Babs' frown deepened. "I'm not very fond of that term, or the practice."

Shrugging lightly, eyebrows quirked, shitty grin on her face, Marionette replied, "How do you think *I* feel about them?"

Disapprovingly, Babs gave Marionette a pointed look before sighing and saying thoughtfully, "I suppose while you two dig around below, I'll see what I can do about finding your coven."

Leaning forward, I grabbed at the back of her seat and protested, "I can't ask you to do anything like that."

But, despite my worries, she laughed and waved me off. "Dear, I know you wouldn't be out here if there wasn't a good reason. Someone's put you in a bad position, so I intend to help you."

Truthfully, even before I knew she was officially a Witch, I knew that Babs was fairly well connected in the area. Even in the Seattle real estate market she somehow privately owned an apartment building and had done so fairly quickly. For all her hippy trappings, she was clearly sitting on some resources. Plus, given Marionette's reaction, I suddenly realized the flower decals were clever camouflage for what might very well be an apex predator – like neon tiger stripes.

"Besides," she said warmly, turning to smile back at me, "I'm not giving you a choice."

I accepted my defeat and patted her shoulder. "Thanks for everything, Babs."

She placed her hand over mine and nodded along. "Of course, dear," she said sweetly, "you still haven't paid off all the damages, after all."

I started to stammer out my assurances that I was going to cover it before getting cut short by a mischievous grin crossing her face. Stopping and realizing she was poking fun at me, I returned the grin, shook my head, and exited the car. At first, I avoided eye contact with everyone outside, expecting some angry glares, before realizing that I probably looked different now without the coat or the shades. Exchanging a few polite smiles and nods, I determined I was sufficiently forgettable.

Probably worrying about the same, Marionette sidled up next to me and whispered, "What damages was she talking about?"

"Angry dude followed me home once," I said casually while hurrying down the stairs, "figured you would have heard about that one."

She shook her head and resigned herself to not knowing for now before following me down.

The Undercity was cleaner than I expected after the mountain of trash above. The lights were still somewhat dim, what with several fixtures smashed out and a great deal of the wiring fried by my Wisp. Several shops were closed for repairs, obviously, but there was a distinctive lack of debris. All of the glass and feathers had been swept up, the remains of once hanging lights now sat in a neat pile covered in what looked to be tiny bite marks and scratches. It was far from fully restored and was going to be a boon for the local glaziers and electricians, but I had to give it to them that they managed to sort the place out. Unfortunately, the thought of cleanup crews made me aware of one very key problem ahead of us.

"That shop's probably swarming with animal control."

Nodding along, Marionette tugged at my shirt and turned away from the club's entrance, pulling me down an adjacent passage. "Now that my memory's clearing, I know a couple other routes."

Passing through an increasingly narrow set of passages, Marionette led me through the Undercity into what could best be described as the "back roads" of the underground. Wedging between more developed locations like Goblin paths someone forgot to seal off, we snaked our way through a labyrinth of brick, mortar, and old rusted pipes. They weren't quite as narrow, a small mercy, but they were certainly more claustrophobic than your average tunnel in the Undercity. Worse, away from the bustle of the more active locations, I could hear the scurrying of small rodents moving in the deep shadows of harsh lighting. Eventually, as we only had enough room to walk single file, I felt it was time to speak up.

"What are we looking for down here?"

Looking over her shoulder, effortlessly navigating over debris and what appeared to be a couple moving shadows that she paid no mind, Marionette replied, "There's a door down here that I made a point to remember. I just can't remember what's behind it."

Watching one of the shadows dart around between her feet, I murmured, "How much further?"

Shrugging and nodding ahead, she gestured to a brick wall blocking our path. "Somewhere past that wall."

Seeing the wall, I was torn. On the one hand, I had to figure that she wouldn't have come this deep into the back tunnels if she didn't know where she was going. On the other hand, I didn't know quite how much the "Salem" left intact. Worse, knowing she was ancient despite appearances, there was some brief consideration that she could have Alzheimer's while looking like her mid-20s.

"I'm going to give you the benefit of a doubt and assume this is a concealed door."

Eyes rolling into the back of her head, she marched ahead and fished out the "keys" that I'd dug out of Glinda's garden. Feeling the wall, she slipped her fingers into a groove and pulled open a panel with a brick façade covering it, exposing a fairly impressive looking locking mechanism with a deceptively simple control pad. A touch screen sat where a keypad or card reader would have normally been, an animated logo for a company called Uriel cycling across its surface as wings unfurled before being consumed by flames. As I stared at the constant cycle of creation and destruction in the strange logo, Marionette fished out the three items from the baggy and went to work.

She slipped the card into a nearly invisible slot along the edge of the screen, the logo changing instantly into a dazzling display of colors and lights that soon settled into a numpad. It wasn't a conventional numpad either, the numbers in seemingly random locations, possibly to keep people from tracking the fingerprints or smears on a screen. She looked at the number on the paper and tapped out the code, then reached for the audio recorder and quietly played it at her ear. Standing there for a few seconds as the heavy voice doled out flower names, she eventually stopped and rewound it a second before turning it back up. Reaching to the lock, Marionette played the deep, rumbling voice as it grunted out "rose".

The screen showed what seemed like an audio analysis for a moment, a knot of waveforms wrapped up into a ball, then froze and turned green. The wall suddenly shifted, pulling away from us just a crack before sliding out of the way and tucking into a groove in the actual wall. Looking back at me, Marionette smirked, wiggled the recorder, and carried on into the new passage beyond. Narrower than the one we were standing in, the sound from the recorder echoed off the walls of the new passage as it continued to march through the botanical list that I now realized was a set of rotating code words. At first, I wasn't quite sure how she knew to stop on "rose" or how it was she got the guy to go over so many of them. Then, as the list wound down, a younger, sing-song voice broke through.

"Need anything else?" a young woman asked on the recording just as Marionette finally turned it off.

I felt my face sink as I registered who it was. "Got a Siren to mimic someone's voice?"

Staring at the recorder for a second and running her thumb along the surface of it, she looked back and nodded. "I think I did, yeah."

Angelique's death came a little clearer, even though it put Marionette's story into question again. Why would the coven push Marionette to kill someone she used for her own key? How did they even know about her? How could I be sure that part was actually a push? The specter of my missing visor loomed large as the door closed behind us, casting a shadow across us as a dull metal click sounded from the lock.

"So that was the door we were looking for?" I asked, hoping to get my mind off of the other questions.

Shaking her head, she led me through a labyrinth of even narrower passages and opened up another panel to reveal yet another console like the one she just cleared. The same screen and the same routine opened another hidden door to yet another dimly lit tunnel.

Tucking them away again, she said sheepishly, "I think we're in for a few of these."

Grunting, I swallowed my reservations and stepped through the next door. Whatever questions I might have had, I had a better chance of answering them somewhere beyond that maze. At the very least, I would know some level of her motivations. I could only hope, somewhere down there, a door would open to something more promising than a claustrophobic set of brick walls and leaky pipes.

Holding onto that hope, I followed her as we pressed on into the dark.

Chapter 26
Equivalent Order

After the series of narrow passages, concealed doors, and more locks than I cared to count, the actual entrance we were looking for was exceptionally boring. Standing at the end of a long hallway that was clearly meant to go somewhere else before the Goblins got to it, a simple blue door stood in our path. It didn't have any visible security measures, locks, or even a camera to watch our approach. It was a simple push and pull door set to swing out towards us. Yet, because it was so simplistic, every fiber of me felt like something was off.

Marionette didn't share my bad vibes, her audible gasp of excitement telling me that all she could see was the blue door to her freedom. Scampering over to it with all the excitement of a kid arriving to a candy store, she reached for the handle and pulled the door open with not a hint of hesitation. Part of me expected it to explode right then and there. But, as she swung it open and revealed a dark room beyond, nothing else seemed to happen. And, because it seemed clear, I watched the otherwise cunning Marionette about to make a really dumb mistake and walk straight on in.

"Wait!" I yelled from down the hall, jogging to catch up.

She stopped cold and stepped back, looking my way with a surprising level of deference as I caught up. Gently ushering her away from the door, I took a brief look at the frame for any signs of electronics and then leaned slightly into the door to see what the room beyond looked like. Round columns and desk-like silhouettes filled the room, backlit by the ambient light of what equipment was active. I couldn't get a good look at what exactly was creating that light, but I had a hunch at least one workstation was still active to monitor whatever was in the room beyond.

Peering in with me, Marionette murmured, "Trap?"

I didn't think it was a trap, exactly. I just figured there had to be security measures we weren't seeing. Even with that labyrinth of Goblin tunnels cutting it off from the rest of the Undercity, something in Marionette's Swiss cheese memory was telling her this place was worth killing over. There was no way this space wasn't somehow monitored. Searching for a light switch to no avail, I turned on the gPhone's light and revealed an uncomfortably familiar sight. They weren't columns – they were storage tanks like the ones found in the "orchards" or that lab in the lowest levels of Sindri.

Studying them quickly while backing away from the door, I took note of the fact that most of them were covered up while the ones that weren't seemed empty. I wasn't sure what exactly that meant, but it was comforting not to see hulking shadows inside. I also noted the bases of the tanks were configured a lot like the ones in Sindri's hidden levels, and that told me a lot more about why that door opened so easily. Kneeling to get a better look, I switched the gPhone's light off and set its camera to stop filtering out the infrared, revealing an ominous series of sweeping lights in the dark.

"Shit," I muttered, "we can't go in."

"What?" Marionette snapped, "But this is literally the only chance we have!"

"Take a look," I said, waving for her to kneel with me and waiting while she crouched. "See that sweeping light? That's a kind of motion detector designed for these places."

"Shit," Marionette hissed, "have they seen us already?"

Studying the room, I remembered the strange configuration from Sindri a while back. I didn't know why they used such a strange design at the time, but Dulaf and Lucian seemed to. Now, after filling in the gaps myself, I had some clue about what this setup meant. At least, I knew enough to be confident we were still outside the grid.

"No, these are based on proximity sensors and we aren't close enough yet," I assured. "There's too many blind spots for conventional infrared and whatever they put in those tanks would disagree with sonar. So, these things sweep light and look for out of place reflections within a certain distance."

Frustrated, Marionette urged, "There has to be a way to get past some stupid proximity sensors."

"There's always backups of some sort," I mused absently while studying what else I could see from the door. "That's how we fucked up last time."

Standing and backing away from me, I could feel Marionette's gears starting to turn. "What about the door?" she asked.

Using the phone as the closest thing to a visor I could, I scanned the frame for any signs of that door being secured. No extra infrared lights, no signs of any contacts, and the standard push plate on the inside like it was rigged for a Vampire. Hell, if it weren't for that mess behind us, it would basically be wide open.

In fact…

"Of course," I said, standing and pocketing the phone. "We just came through their emergency exit."

Turning to face the door we just came out of, she exclaimed, "Oh my god, you're right!"

"It swings out and there's no light switch by this door," I continued.

"And they didn't wire it so if they lost the front end," she added, "the alarm wouldn't tip off the security room."

Nodding along, I pointed at the locked door at the far end. "Then we would have to chase them through that quagmire of narrow tunnels and self-locking doors."

A contemplative look crossed her face as she quietly said, "So they don't have a way to lock those doors remotely."

I didn't quite follow why that would matter. In fact, I was a lot more concerned with the potential of a gunfight carrying an antique. But, as she finished saying it, she stepped up to me, grabbed my hand, and then very confidently stepped through the door, pulling me along. I couldn't even protest before she'd stepped into the path of the closest sensor. Relenting, I stepped next to her and reached for the Helsing while the door swung closed behind us.

Quietly, she commanded, "Calm down, breathe deep, and hold my hand."

Even without the phone ready, I knew every alarm in the place was going off. We were knee deep in infrared light even if we couldn't see it. Beyond the cold electric hum of unseen equipment, I could even hear the hurried beat of seemingly large men running our way. Every step echoing louder than the last made my hand clench tighter on the pistol's grip as I readied myself to draw. As two slabs of meat in cheap suits burst through the door, I jerked the gun free of its holster.

Marionette's free hand reached over and grabbed at my wrist, stopping me before I could level the Helsing their way. I gave her a look as she very subtly and quietly shook her head, then returned my gaze to the door. A Troll and a Cyclops stood at a door they narrowly fit through before splitting up and drifting between the tanks, searching every corner and shadow as though we weren't even standing there. We were invisible to them, like the cast and crew of the theater and everyone in the club.

I'd seen her do it before, but Marionette's talent at hiding in plain sight was never more impressive. The pair of guards were a perfect choice in a place like this, having talents comparable to an electronic device. Cyclopean eyes were big, with retinas packed with a wider variety of cones that could pick up light frequencies invisible to most of nature. Troll noses were so sensitive that people used to think they could sniff what religion you were, and some documents showed it was actually kind of true thanks to rituals. Together, they were effectively a barrel-chested organic security system. Yet, despite their talents, they didn't have a clue where we were.

Scanning everything thoroughly, they seemed to be none the wiser that two people stood there with them the entire time. The Cyclops even made eye contact with me before turning away to look under a desk. Meanwhile the Troll sniffed like a hound on the trail of a suspect, slowly working his way towards us. Part of me was worried that her talents didn't work on smell. As he got within a few feet of us, I made a few quiet attempts to pull my wrist free of Marionette's grasp. But as he stood ahead of us, sniffing vigorously and getting dangerously close to making contact with his impressive nose, he stopped and turned away all the same.

Glancing at Marionette in utter disbelief, she held a finger to her lips, nodded slowly, and then started to pull me through the room. No matter how soft our steps were, I kept picturing the two lumbering guards coming up behind us and checked over my shoulder repeatedly as we made our escape. Neither looked our way again once we were in the spaces they considered "searched". They even checked the emergency exit as Marionette and I crossed the threshold and entered a sterile, spartan hallway consisting of polished metal walls and recessed light strips.

"I still don't understand," I whispered, halting as I realized how much my voice was carrying, lowering it even more to continue, "I don't understand how you do that."

She looked at me thoughtfully. "You're always able to see your nose but your brain just ignores it," she said softly, "Imagine what else it could be convinced to ignore."

Becoming suddenly aware of my nose, I did my best to try to stop looking at it again before catching a smile on her face. I think, in focusing on it, I probably went cross-eyed at the idea.

"Bakes the noodle, doesn't it?" She asked with a grin, carrying on down the hall with me in tow.

Though the hallway was relatively short, it contained multiple unmarked doors. Strangely, all of the doors along the back wall were the kind of swing doors you'd find in a hospital, like they were expecting to cart things in and out on the regular, while the ones across the way seemed more secured. The electronic locks back in the maze were Vampire friendly, opening the door automatically, as were the swing doors, but the ones along the wall to my left featured inconvenient little details like knobs that suggested it wasn't constructed by a group like the Locusta at all.

Turning the corner at the end, we came to see a large reinforced blast door like something out of one of my old sci-fi movies. Built like a shutter, it seemed to drop out of the ceiling to a groove in the floor. Like the doors with the knobs, it wasn't particularly Alter friendly. On closer inspection, I couldn't even figure out how to open it. However, two smaller doors sat on either side of it, each of them having a console like the ones back in the maze and soon Marionette was making a beeline for the one closest to us.

"Keep an eye out," she said quietly, finally letting go of my hand so she could operate the card and recorder at the same time.

I stood watch over her, listening for the sounds of footsteps down the metal corridors. Every little beep and hum from the lock echoed back to us, the sound of Angelique's impression of the lumbering man particularly hitting the walls with some weight and coming back at us like the disembodied ghost it was. Hearing it again and thinking on the guys we just slipped by, I wondered if she was mimicking one of them. The Troll, I figured, probably had a nasally tone.

Taking me by the wrist, Marionette dragged me out of the train of thought and into another room. We stumbled into the ambient glow of consoles, monitors, and the slightly refracted light from a nearby window. The place was packed with monitoring equipment and terminals going over security feeds of the complex and a bunch of other information that I couldn't quite parse out at first glance.

Through the window I could see the shielded room with the blast door, some sort of surgical bay with a table large enough to be a small car lift. The image was somewhat distorted, the window was a single pane so large and thick I had to wonder how they even got it down here. But it was just translucent enough to make out your usual medical monitors, surgical equipment, and a small station for the crew to clean up. On top of that, though they looked like little more than blurry shadows, you could see that there were two more windows on the walls that didn't have a giant shutter in the way. A door opposite the one we just came through even suggested we could completely circle the operating room if we wanted.

"What the hell is all of this?" I muttered, walking up to the window and lightly rapping a knuckle against it.

The tone I got off of it as I knocked was familiar but distinct. It wasn't glass, at least not pure. No, the sound was the kind of reverberation I'd heard often off of Rufus' Vesperadin cell. That was a bit disconcerting since it suggested that door, thick as it was, was supposed to stop the things that would be in that room. It also suggested this space, like his cell, might have once been a vault.

Marionette let go of me again as the door closed behind us and walked on for the next, passing through to the room positioned behind the armor-plated operating theater. I lingered for a second, trying to figure what they strapped to that monster of a table. But, shortly into that train of thought, I heard Marionette yelp from the next room over. Jogging to catch up, I nearly stumbled at the sight beyond that door.

Floating in a vat, backlit by the eerie green glow of several monitors, a familiar fleshy form greeted us in the next room. Under the lights it could have been mistaken for some incomplete experiment, but I could see the wrinkles along the grey mass.

"Is that," Marionette stammered, "is that a brain in a jar?"

It was a little larger, smoother, and had a more primitive life support system, but it was very much like a similar creature I'd seen in a room hidden beneath a pier. After all, how different can a brain in a jar ever really be?

Recognizing the setup, the DAO was suddenly burning a proverbial hole in my pocket. This was an Oracle support node, controlled and operated by someone other than the ACTF, buried in the heart of the Undercity. As I circled around the morbid column in the center of the room, I could even see the DAO interface running across one of the monitors. We'd always known they were listening in on our system somehow, but the true extent was only now becoming apparent. They'd built their own funhouse mirror version – with all the implications that could have.

Looking at Marionette, I remarked, "I think you helped build the DAO."

Horrified, Marionette pointed at the tank and cried out, "That's an Oracle?!"

"Kind of," I corrected, starting to take pictures of the room with the gPhone. "It's part of the system that feeds her information, a buffer so she doesn't get overwhelmed by a whole city."

She slowly approached the tank, mouth agape, asking in hushed tones, "So there are others out there?"

I nodded solemnly, remembering my own disgust at the first one I saw. "But, weird enough, this one's uglier. I don't think our guys made it."

Studying the terminals, the computers seemed different than what you'd have from an ACTF operation. The operating system on the screens wasn't quite right, looking more like something I could get on a laptop than an Argyre facility. The interfaces were also a little more tactile. If I had to guess the computers were either consumer grade, here long before the brain, or came from somewhere that wouldn't miss them.

Circling the tank and studying the setup, Marionette said idly, "Alter Affairs Division."

A chill ran up my spine as I snapped to attention and looked back at her. Eyes distant like something was coming back to her, she ran her fingers along a piece of equipment attached to the tank. Text under her fingertips, barely visible under the ambient light, showed a serial number beginning in SNR ending with AAD.

"You know about the division?" I asked, walking over to get a better look at the number and take a picture of it.

Glancing my way, concern etched into her face, she answered in a faltering voice, "I think I have for a while."

The serial number wasn't quite a smoking gun. If it were, they would have scrubbed it off a long time ago. But the fact the name popped into her head like that didn't leave me a lot hope. Worse, given the history of equipment like this, I suspected SNR was "Sindri". If she was right, that suggested that equipment, maybe even the whole facility, belonged to the AAD, was supplied by one of the biggest industrial firms out of Argyre – one that literally made monsters – and sat in the heart of territory the Locusta bought up a few years ago. But the really troubling thought was a simple but disturbing question: which was here first?

"I don't understand, Nate," Marionette uttered quietly, "what's the Alter Affairs Division?"

I watched as a faint tremor rolled through her, like her skin was crawling. It was a strong reaction for something she apparently didn't fully remember. Hell, I remembered them and my skin wasn't crawling. Some part of her knew some shit she wasn't supposed to. That was the kind of thing that could get someone Salem'd, I figured, considering the AAD was already an American agency with questionable legal standing.

"Conversation for when we get out of here," I said, taking a few more shots and reaching into her bag to fish out the Will-O-Wisp. "After we're clear of all this."

Holding the rod in hand, I paused to consider what I was about to do. This thing was clearly part of the DAO network. For all I knew it was the heart of it and every piece of data had to go through this eldritch horror. But recognizing what it was, knowing what it meant about how the DAO worked, could I really leave it here? Could I let the Locusta control something like this?

Staring a moment longer, the answer was too clear even if it meant blinding ourselves again. I lifted the rod and started setting it for a delayed EMP. Within a second of my decision though, every monitor in the room changed. Red alerts appeared across the board as the room seemed to be stained with blood. Watching the brain past the rod, I could almost feel it staring back at me despite a lack of eyes. It knew what I was doing and what I was planning, and it just called for help.

Setting the Wisp and planting it at the base of the tank, I took Marionette's hand again. "We need to go ***now***."

Startling at the touch, Marionette took a moment to compose herself and took a couple cleansing breaths before nodding and pulling me along again. As we made our way to the exit, we were greeted with the two walking sides of beef again as they opened the door right ahead of us. Marionette pulled me aside, swaying just out of their path and making sure I did the same, and allowed them to carry on to the DAO room just as the rod started to pulse.

The two walked right into an intense burst of light. The Cyclops took the brunt of the visible spectrum, blinded by the flash, while the Troll took the stronger hit from the UV under it all. Recoiling, the two of them stumbled back out of the room and took cover for a moment, the Cyclops waiting for his eye to stop burning as the Troll's skin started forming dry white patches. The UV from a Wisp wasn't a fatal dose for anyone, otherwise it would have effectively been a live grenade, but it was enough to cause surface level harm and deter even the sturdiest creatures. Exiting out the other door, I watched them bicker over who should try to grab the thing as we made our quick retreat back to the emergency exit.

"How much longer do we have?" Marionette asked, sounding strangely winded.

Looking back as we passed through the door and went for the rear exit, I watched as all the lights behind us abruptly died and the ones above flickered briefly. "Pretty sure it just went off."

Nodding, she released my hand and fished out the recorder, hitting the button to ensure it still worked before rewinding it back to the right flower. Watching, I couldn't help but notice how unsteady her hands were and the fact her already alabaster skin was taking on a different look as dark circles were starting to form under her eyes. She took a slight sway as she walked and her eyes started to glaze over. I'd noticed a shift while she was touching the serial number, but this was looking more like something was physically wrong now.

"Are you okay?" I asked quietly as we reached the door, grabbing at her arm lightly to steady her.

Nodding along, she started unlocking the door while mumbling out a response. "Always a little strain doing that," she said, "especially alone."

Guiding her through the door as it opened, I looked back to make sure we weren't followed and stepped through behind her. When the door closed, she braced against the wall and used it for support as she pushed on through the maze.

"You seemed fine leaving the theater and going through the club," I remarked, picking up my pace so I could catch her if she suddenly keeled over.

"Well, you know how rough the next day is after a night on the town," she quipped, stopping for a moment to catch her breath and stand straighter. "Maybe after this, we hole up somewhere for a day and rest."

Resting a hand on her back, I nodded and gave my best reassuring smile. "We'll get a hotel and order room service."

She smiled weakly and started shuffling along again, each step a little steadier than the last but still feeling just a touch off. Seeing her actually weakened, recognizing there was strain after all, some of her cloak and dagger made a little more sense. If your strongest techniques were physically taxing, you'd do what you could not to use them all that often.

"How much did it take out of you to do that thing with the lamp?" I asked.

She glanced back with a raised eyebrow. "You set off my poltergeist? That was a group effort!"

"If it makes you feel any better, it did throw me out of the apartment," I assured, smirking.

Despite her fatigue, we made it through the maze of narrow crawlspaces faster than we had the first time. The doors were simple enough once you knew the routine and had all the pieces, and I took it upon myself to open a few of them as she took time to lean against the wall. For the first few doors I felt like someone may have followed us, but by the third I realized that any attempt to open and close one of those doors would have carried quite a bit of sound to us – likely by design. In the chaos, confusion, and crusty sunburns, they didn't seem to have much of a lead on where to find us and I wasn't quite sure if the DAO system would help them after losing that node.

Considering the phone in my pocket before the last door, I reached out and rested a hand on Marionette's shoulder to stop her from opening it. Maybe they knew we'd taken the emergency exit and had some way of getting to the other side faster. It would have rendered the exit nearly moot, but it wasn't a possibility I could ignore. So, fishing the phone out and hoping for some functionality to remain, I checked the DAO to find that it was still perfectly functional and showed nothing of interest aside from a couple agents wandering near the club.

"Door's clear," I murmured, "but the way out of the Undercity's blocked by agents."

Marionette nodded and started opening the door. "We'll just have to take a longer route to the next exit."

The words flowed easy but her posture didn't exactly inspire confidence. She was steadier than before, no doubt, or I would have had to carry her by then, but what little color she had in her face hadn't returned.

I'd known that Witches underwent some extreme physiological processes while using their powers – it was the reason why she looked my age despite being older than the city – but not the toll it took. It made sense, given how much had to happen, that it could hit someone like running a marathon. And, now that I'd had time to process, I realized she was running on her fourth wind herself.

Putting an arm around her as we exited the last door, I propped her up and helped her off into the right direction. I wasn't quite as familiar with the area as she was, for increasingly obvious reasons, but I had patrolled the area before. There was a market in the direction we were now headed with some fresh produce and a convenience store. At the very least we could use turning tail and running from the agents as an excuse for picking up some electrolytes along the way.

"I'm okay," she insisted. However, despite her protests, I could feel her lean into me as we went. She was stubborn but not stupid and I could respect that.

Restraining my subtle desire to gloat, I guided her away from those cramped tunnels and towards the more useful passages below. Before long, we heard the bustling of a crowd and started following the sound like lost hikers headed for the freeway. As we came in view of a few people strolling by, the knowledge we were close to the home stretch put a little bit of spring in my step. We were going to get out of there, get some rest, and figure out the next step. And, hey, Dulaf might've gotten the situation under control while we were holed up.

Watching her for a moment as we turned a corner, I smiled and gave my most reassuring tone. "We'll stop to grab a couple things down here, then we'll take some time to recover."

She smiled faintly. "Thank you, Nate," she said softly, "I'm sorry for—oh my god!"

Her eyes went wide and I turned just in time to see what felt like a tree branch swing for our heads. Instinctively, I ducked and pulled Marionette with me, scampering back a couple steps as the wind blew through our hair with an audible whoosh that made the hairs on my neck stand on end. In a frantic series of grabs and lunges, the Garuda tried repeatedly to get his hands on us. I weaved back several steps while doing my best to keep Marionette upright with me. But it was futile, he was too fast and she was struggling to stay upright at all. After narrowly dodging the third swing, I let her go and hoped she wouldn't crack her head open on the way down.

She hit the floor with a yelp but I was in no place to check on her. In the split second it took her to fall, the Garuda caught my arm and enveloped my entire left forearm in his palm. Squeezing and yanking me towards him, the big man nearly dislocated my shoulder as he whipped me into the wall with ease. I grabbed for the Helsing and fired into his face, macing him with a concoction I couldn't be sure would do anything, and thrust a foot hard into his instep in an effort to get him off balance.

To my relief and surprise, while I knew it wasn't going to actually hurt him, the Garuda was not happy with chemicals directly in its face and recoiled from the Helsing. I darted out from between him and the wall and circled around to Marionette as she was starting to get back to her feet. Leveling the gun his way, I positioned myself between the two of them. Looking past the Helsing's sights, I stared straight into furious, bloodshot eyes with irises like pinholes.

If it were a Helios, I might've hesitated since the guy was being controlled, but with a Helsing there was only one clear answer: unload. Pulling the trigger as fast as I could, I pelted him with everything I had, grouping every shot into his chest just under his chin. Without the visor to guide it, I had to aim center mass, but thanks to the fact it was a mace ball I was basically hitting him in the face anyway. Unfortunately, he marched through the onslaught nearly unfazed, eyes narrowing more with every step and glare deepening.

After at least a dozen shots to his torso, the Helsing let out a distinct electric hum and several hollow clicks as the gun ran empty. Still more angry than hurt, he closed the distance between us and balled up a fist the size of a bowling ball. Backing up into Marionette, I watched the giant fist raise and scrambled for an idea of what to do from there. Marionette grabbed my shoulders, holding firmly onto me as the enraged birdman prepared to turn us into paste. Then, as he was in position to finally bring it down, I heard her say only one word: "sleep".

Everything went black in an instant.

Chapter 27
Noteworthy Encounters

A gentle breeze rustled a tree outside an old multi-pane window, light shining between the leaves and casting dancing shadows across a room littered with colorful, almost cartoonish objects with rounded forms and nary a sharp edge in sight. Something giggled out of view, in rhythm with one shadow, making me almost think it was the tree itself for a moment. As my view of the room cleared, I laid my eyes on a tablet with a bright blue case and sturdy screen protector as it blasted some sort of giggling cartoons out of small built-in speakers. It'd been toppled over despite a stand coming out of the back of that amazingly blue frame, lying next to an old juice-box that had leaked all across a wood floor just beyond the edge of a plush carpet.

Staggering to my feet, I found myself standing in a room built for giants. Every piece of furniture just a hair too large, every ledge just out of reach, and counters that I couldn't see over. Memories of the giant bird man clawed at the edges of my mind as I blearily examined the room for some clue as to where the hell I was. There weren't any registered Giants living in Seattle proper at the time – the closest was a former fighter living out in Bellevue I'd kept tabs on for the last couple years. He'd opened a gym and sworn off of fighting after the last guy he fought died trying to squash some dipshit during a bust. But Bellevue was at least ten miles from where I dropped and I couldn't help feeling like I'd been here before.

Rising over the sound of the cartoons on the tablet, a pair of female voices echoed from down a hallway. Agitated, nearly screaming but trying to stay restrained, they took a rapid, aggressive tone without raising their voices to full volume. An argument they didn't want the neighbors to hear?

I started to follow the voices, finding walking a little more unsteady than I would have liked. I was light, almost floating, but every step just felt a little bit out of sync. Something about it annoyed me, that clawing at my mind coming back as I remembered a voice whispering in my ear. But then that same voice became one of the two down the hall. My mom was arguing with someone, not only sounding agitated but on the verge of tears.

As I entered an incredibly long hallway, I watched two blurry but absolutely towering shadows move through a room at the end. Rubbing at my eyes to try to clear them, I looked up again to see the figures gone but could hear those voices continue to flutter about. Try as I might, I was too drowsy and confused to make out what they were saying, but all went silent as a door slammed. Startled by the bang, practically feeling it in my bones, I hurried to the far end and peered around the corner from where it came.

The room beyond was now empty besides the giant forms of old, comfortable furniture. The only door there, the only one that could have been slammed, stood as a strangely imposing form. I could feel this foreboding from it, like I wasn't supposed to even touch it. Something beyond it was intimidating, almost terrifying, yet seemed to call me towards it. Did mom go through it? Why?

An oppressive silence filled the house. The light outside the windows faded like a cloud had just covered the sun. I stood alone in that room, the notion that no one else was there somehow becoming overwhelming. Was it always so quiet?

Where did everyone go?

Suddenly reaching from the void, a pair of hands gripped at my shoulders and a distant voice yelled out, "Nate!"

I startled awake, the old brick archways of the Undercity stretching over us as Ramirez knelt over me, trying to prop me up against the wall, the distinct hum of our wakeup device ringing in my ears. Staring at him for a moment, the memories clawing at my mind before now flooded forward and I remembered Marionette putting me on my ass.

"That bitch," I slurred out, trying to push off the wall to get back to my feet and failing at every level.

Holy shit, she dropped me hard.

Ramirez helped so I wouldn't bang my head on the concrete a second time. Together, we got me to something resembling standing against the wall. I would have tried to stand on my own power, but the dull ache of my head bouncing like a basketball discouraged me from any attempted power moves.

"Man, Nate," Ramirez said hesitantly, "you look like you got mugged."

Lifting my chin enough to make eye contact with him, I tried to think of snarky comments but found the reserves empty. He was looking genuinely concerned, anyway, and was keeping hands ready to grab me if I fell over again. This seemed normal at first, until my brain's lag caught up and I remembered the uniform he was wearing meant he needed to arrest me. Except, as I looked closer, I noticed something important missing.

"Where's the badge?" I murmured, resting my head against the relatively cool wall and waiting for my legs to stop feeling like warm jello.

He glanced down quickly, then shot me a wry smile, "Nguyen told me to clock out and hand her the badge before I found you."

"And you just stumbled on me after that?" I asked cautiously.

He chuckled softly. "Well, she did point out where she wanted me to go before taking the badge."

Trying to piece together the situation, only one possibility presented itself to me. "Dulaf?"

His brow furrowed for a moment before he shook his head and answered, "We haven't talked to her today, why?"

I snorted and pushed off the wall to stand straighter. "I sent a message to her about a code 65."

"Shit, man," he retorted, "everyone thinks that's what happened to you after Stevens."

Frustratingly, the fight with Stevens' lancer of rookies came back to haunt me. I knew I should've stopped to try to convince him, but Marionette's argument made too much sense at the time. Shit, maybe that was a sign I was compromised.

"She took me down and ran off with her Garuda," I muttered.

He shook his head and rested a hand on my shoulder, "Reason Nguyen sent me ahead was we got here in time to hear witnesses say she fought that thing tooth and nail while it carried her off."

Looking around, the signs of a struggle were clear even beyond the ones I could take credit for myself. Marionette's bag was on the ground, strap torn, seams burst, our rough assortment of supplies scattered some distance. A Manticore rod that had been armed but not fired was lying between a set of scuffling footprints. The prints, left in dust and a layer of Werewolf mace residue, told a story that fit the description. Marionette continued fighting him even after I went down before eventually being scooped up into the air.

But then why did she put me down first?

"So, why'd Nguyen log you out?" I asked, wandering the scene. "Even if Marionette was dragged out, that doesn't clear me."

Ramirez circled the area opposite of me, shrugging as he replied, "Either you were being controlled or something happened, and after the shit we've seen, we figured we could use you on the ground still."

Looking back at him, I was relieved that someone was going to give me the benefit of a doubt after what I did to those rookies. Though, given Nguyen and Ramirez were once both police, I had to wonder if this was a little bit of that thin blue line mentality bleeding over. Either way, it gave me a chance to figure out just what the hell happened. Maybe, now that they were helping, I could even set everything right.

“Where’s Nguyen now?”

Ramirez nodded down the passage. “She went on towards the next surface exit, following the tips from the crowd. With luck she caught up to them.”

Looking at the goliath footprint of the Garuda, I wasn’t so sure that was the lucky outcome. Shaking my head, I gathered up some of what I could off the ground, including the armed Manticore , a Banshee, and the now empty Helsing, and hurried after Nguyen’s trail.

“Let’s hope we catch her before she catches them,” I remarked, waving for him to follow.

Nguyen was a good lancer, training a lot of good agents over the years, including at least one guy on the SOL teams. If anyone had a fighting chance against a Garuda it would probably be her. But the fact was, like me, she was boringly mortal and would be fighting out of her weight class. Even if she could take the guy, it was better to make it a three on one than to just hope she could come out ahead.

The path to the exit was mostly clear, a few stunned onlookers still murmuring among themselves as we passed. The small farmer’s market running just inside the Undercity’s Persephone district was in shambles as we turned the corner, but few were ready to come out of cover just yet. Produce littered the ground in the Garuda’s wake as he seemed to crash through a couple stands seemingly at random along the way as through something threw him off balance. Either he was drunk or Marionette was still putting up a fight on the way out.

Sprinting up the stairs, taking the steps two at a time and adjusting the settings on the Manticore, I emerged on the surface to find Nguyen standing over a set of skid-marks, scattered fragments of broken glass, and spots of blood and paint. Despite the seeming carnage at her feet, the area itself felt more peaceful than it had any right to be. There was no foot traffic above, no cautious witnesses in hiding, and no cars driving by. The bustle of the city was a distant echo, nearly overwhelmed by the sound of the breeze and a strange giggling noise straight out of my dreams. Unnerving detail aside, it had the hallmarks of a pissed off giant storming out of the underworld into a space where people actually had room to flee.

Nguyen was diligently documenting all of it, visor on and hand-link out. I slowed at the sight of them and started to circle around at a distance. As I moved, she turned away, always keeping her back to me while recording every detail she could. It was subtle, maybe even subtle enough the Oracle wouldn't pick up on it, though I probably only had a couple minutes before the CSIs arrived.

"Ramirez," she said authoritatively, "I thought I told you to go the other way."

"We," Ramirez started to answer before the words caught in his throat and he recognized what was happening. "We shouldn't have split up like that, I know you were trying to protect me but the witnesses weren't describing anything good."

Nguyen nodded lightly and spoke in an obvious stage whisper, "Well by the time I arrived they were already gone, but I've found evidence they continued to struggle out here by a vehicle parked near the entrance. Given the spread of the glass and where the blood landed, it seems like someone broke through the window and cut themselves in the process. The woman seemed to step on the blood at one point based on one of the smudges, but it's too early to know if it was her blood or not."

Ramirez nodded along and started looking over the area by eye, avoiding pulling out his hand-link or visor to limit the number of ways they could spot me. "So do you think she might have escaped in the vehicle?"

Nguyen put her hand-link away and took off her visor before glancing over her shoulder, replying firmly, "I don't know if she had a car on standby, but it's possible she was in it when it left."

I eavesdropped, trying my best to ignore the ominous giggling, and knelt by one of the treads. It was too beefy for Babs' little creampuff car, peeling out solidly and leaving genuine burnt rubber in its wake. There wasn't any scent of biodiesel or ethanol, leaving out an older muscle car upgraded for greener fuels. Yet, given how much traction it got and the nature of the marks, the thing had to be heavier and more powerful than a standard electric. I wasn't even sure one of our units could have left it. If it wasn't carrying an old internal combustion engine, it had to have a heavy power supply inside.

A uniquely dense one...

"Marathon," I muttered quietly before getting up to retreat back into the Undercity, stealing glances of tiny silhouettes darting overhead.

Ramirez watched me for a few steps before turning his attention to Nguyen and waiting for a signal from her. She nodded very lightly while continuing to face away from me and stared off at the crime scene, folding arms over her badge. He patted her shoulder and jogged to catch up to me, following me back into the depths.

"Okay, I guess I can count on you and Nguyen right now," I said once we were out of range.

"Yeah," Ramirez echoed, "Alicia's solid. Too bad she had to call this in, we could probably use her for whatever's next."

Catching up to me at the foot of the stairs, he rested his hand on my shoulder and asked, "What is next, anyway?"

Pieces were falling into place with every step down those stairs. Mark Robinson, supposedly mainstream human, was the last person to see Kate before she blacked out, was in the headquarters before Alston tried to juice me, and owned a car with one hell of a heavy power supply. It sure as hell wasn't a smoking gun, but it definitely warranted a second look. The problem was that if he was unregistered then he definitely wasn't someone you'd catch easy. Even Marionette, slippery as she was, didn't evade the census. It was a feat generally reserved for Shapeshifters, people living in the middle of nowhere, and a rare race of giants in Croatia called the Vedi. So, what the hell had Mark done to avoid it?

Regardless, taking Marionette captive meant they needed her for something. They tried to "Salem" her first, then kill her, now they suddenly wanted her alive. Something had given them an idea of what we were doing and was resulting in them getting spooked. That meant, if I could find her in time, they would probably still have her alive and well in whatever hole their coven congregated in. I was going to need supplies and a plan.

Looking at the Helsing at my hip, the first step was clear.

"Flower shop," I declared, marching through the market and fishing out the gPhone.

"Flower shop?" Ramirez echoed, bewildered. "Bribing an ex?"

I shook my head and held up a finger to let him know I needed a moment while placing my first call to Babs.

"Hello dear," the sweet old voice answered, "are we ready to go somewhere else?"

"Actually Babs, we've run into some trouble" I replied.

"Oh dear," she gasped, "what happened?"

"We were attacked and I lost track of Marionette," I said tightly, trying to suppress my frustration, "I was wondering if you could find out if there's a Warlock in the area going by the name Mark Robinson."

She made a troubled little grunt before commenting, "The name does actually sound familiar, for some reason."

"Whoever he is, he has her," I said in a slightly more hushed tone, feeling Ramirez at my side again and remembering he was there, "he has my--"

The word caught in my throat and I fell silent for a few agonizingly long seconds before continuing, "We have to find him."

Thoughtfully, Babs replied, "I understand, hon. I'll see what I can do."

Hanging up, I realized I was going to need more than a devotee, a Witch who hadn't used her powers substantially in decades, and whatever gear I could scrape together. This was a coven, one that was somehow tracking our progress and had control over a Garuda of all things. I could potentially call the ACTF down on the coven's location, but I couldn't just sit back and unleash a raid. If I was sending them after the wrong people, I could be getting a bunch of innocents arrested based on my shitty intel. I had to be sure before I called in the cavalry.

So, if I couldn't bring the ACTF with me, who was left?

Staring at the phone, thinking of who I could dial next, a name popped into my head. I needed someone who could handle a Garuda and was okay with the idea of keeping a low profile. And, through a sheer stroke of luck, as I fished through my pockets I found that I miraculously hadn't lost my lifeline while ditching everything else I had. Pulling out the small business card, feeling a tremendous yet surreal relief, I flipped it over and started dialing the number. After a few rings, a surprisingly welcoming voice answered with a cheerful "hello" that I wasn't expecting on the line I just called. Wading into uncharted waters, I tried to keep it brief.

"Yeah, hi, this is Agent Leone," I said. "I think I have a lead on your friend, Akemi."

Chapter 28
Preparing Invasion

Confused as he was, Ramirez didn't complain much as I detoured from the mission and dragged him through the nearest florist. Despite everything that happened, he trusted Nguyen's instincts that I was, at the very least, sane. I probably tested that trust as I negotiated with the florist for all the baby's breath and lilacs they might have had. We even had to pay a premium since it would prevent them from being able to do some of their standard bouquets for a couple days. Yet, for a good chunk of what was left in Marionette's fallen bag, we marched out with bags bursting full of flowers.

With those bags in tow, we weaved through the marketplace to do a little last-minute shopping. With some Dryads working as herbalists and independent farmers, it was pretty easy to find a few of the items I was looking for. But others, like a few cloves of garlic, basically turned into conversations eerily similar to a drug deal – right down to the officer in full uniform hovering behind me the whole time. There was nothing illegal about it, mind, but it wasn't exactly something you wanted to be openly selling in the Locusta controlled underground.

The daylight hours were burning away as we emerged and waited for Babs' return. As the bubbly little car came up the block, Ramirez helped me load Babs' trunk with the flowers before hurrying off to relay some messages to Nguyen. We needed her to check where Mark might have been and confirm he wasn't sitting around his apartment. So far all we really had on him was circumstantial, after all. But the timing of his visit to headquarters felt too perfect to ignore at this point.

"Any luck on that Mark guy?" I asked Babs as I stuffed the bags into her trunk.

"Not yet, unfortunately," she sighed. "The name bothers me, so I'm sure there's something, but I'm waiting for a few of my friends to call back."

Slightly disappointed, but not wanting to show it, I glanced back to put on my best fake smile. Babs, however, had that same disgusted look on her face that Marionette had over Dulaf's soap – an unfortunate confirmation I was on the right track with the flowers.

I double checked on the gPhone and confirmed that more than a few flowers were used by Wiccans to lure good spirits while pushing away the bad. This was ironic because, effectively, it meant human witches had been offending the senses of Alter Witches for decades if not centuries. The stuff in the soap, specifically, presented an opportunity even if it was causing a little friendly fire. Considering my present situation, I figured it a necessary evil and did my best to get it put away before it cost me my ride. Though, as I closed the trunk and the shadows started to giggle, an uncomfortable question rattled through my head.

"Is there anything else that offends Witches?" I asked reluctantly.

Gesturing for me to get in the car again, she replied ever so casually, "A lot of things offend us, dear."

I followed her lead and got in the car, waiting for her to settle in before I pressed. "I mean, something that wouldn't be generally known, something that doesn't overlap. I know the right kind of metals can disorient, like a fairy, and aromatics, but--"

"You mean to become a Witch hunter, do you?" She asked quietly, hints of a long buried Polish accent lurking along the edges of her voice.

"No, Babs, of course not!" I protested quickly. "It's just the tactics I know for a coven would put others at risk. I need to rescue one from a whole group. I need to go in as smart as I can."

Her expression softened and the almost motherly Pacific Northwest voice returned. "I'm sorry to say, Nate," she started sympathetically, "aside from what they've already told you, we're not much different than human. We don't have any particularly exotic allergies, we're just more sensitive to our environment."

Mulling it over, everything she was saying tracked. The ACTF's tactics were more about disorienting Witches and their covens than anything, a reason why we couldn't just bring Marionette down while she was surrounded by civilians. In hindsight, the fact she lived in a building full of old iron supports and brick was probably to keep other Witches from knowing her exact location.

"A bit of a double-edged sword, really," Babs continued. "It's easier to manipulate your surroundings when you're more in tune with it. But sometimes it's all a little overwhelming."

Looking over to me with the beginnings of a wry grin, she mused, "Though it helped us find the best drugs before anyone else, even if they hit us harder than we would have liked."

"Come to think of it," I mused, recalling all the chemicals I'd been exposed to, "I thought Witches were supposed to be more sensitive to mind altering drugs than baseline."

A hoot-like laugh bubbled out of her as she replied warmly, "Do you think dancing naked around a bonfire is something you do sober? There's a reason our parties would become legendary."

"Then why is it the stuff you do doesn't impact yourself?"

Shaking her head, she said with a subtle hint of nostalgia, "There's a difference between forcing control and losing it."

Watching the kindly old lady in her tie-dye clothes, sitting in her old car with the psychedelic paintjob, a thought occurred. "Did you ever take LSD?"

Fondly, she replied, "Not in your lifetime."

My plan was going to have to rely on something a little more devious than a simple plug and play weakness. There were some things I knew could hit Witches hard like the right kind of EMF and certain plant extracts, but with a possible Kitsune and her

Jiangshi entourage I had to be careful how I used it. I was going to keep things precise, rely on my ability to keep my wits about me, and hope they didn't have any spare lamps lying around. Though, even if that all worked out, I still wasn't sure what I was going to do about the Garuda.

Garuda are practically invincible to chemical deterrents. They evolved to put up with venomous attacks nastier than anything a human might have encountered. Word has it, if you were lucky enough to match, a liver transplant from a Garuda would make you impossible to poison. The black market had been trying for a while to make good on that promise while failing to obtain willing matches. As for the unwilling, few came back to tell the tale of those attempts.

That encounter wasn't going to be fun.

Looking out the window, regretting some of my life decisions again, I caught sight of Ramirez returning with a duffle bag. Rolling down the window, I called out to him. "What's in the bag?"

He lifted it and tipped his head towards the trunk. "A few extra supplies for the trip!"

Babs opened the trunk for him and he stuffed the duffle bag in with the rest before getting into the back seat. I nodded between them.

"Barbara Zdunk, Devotee Ramirez," I introduced them.

Ramirez took his glove off and reached his hand out to Babs with a broad smile and a warm chuckle. "Please, Carlos, I get called Ramirez enough at work."

Babs shook his hand and replied, "Everyone calls me Babs. I try to keep it light around the building."

"She's my landlady," I interjected.

"Oh yeah, the one he owes for the doors," Ramirez chuckled.

"The new ones are so much nicer," Babs said excitedly, "I'll show you when we get there!"

I waved and interrupted, "We can't go back there, they'll be watching for me."

"Then where?" she asked.

After a quick debate and a relatively short drive, we appeared on Glinda's doorstep with arms full of flowers, herbs, chemicals, and whatever Ramirez had in the bag. With us being spotted in the Undercity once again, and Nguyen apparently running interference, I figured we had reset the clock on how long it would be before they started crawling her place. Unless they figured Glinda had a Garuda, they had to know Marionette wasn't there at the very least. Though, I may as well have showed up with a Garuda since she seemed disturbed to have another uniform on her doorstep, eyes locked on Ramirez warily even without the badge, but then her expression shifted from unsettled to downright shocked.

"Where's Marion?!" she exclaimed, stepping outside to get a better look of the area. "Why isn't she with you?"

I could feel Babs and Ramirez retreat slightly as I stood in front of Glinda. "We lost her," I said, resigned, "and we need to figure out where they took her."

"They?" Glinda echoed, taking another look around the neighborhood before stepping back and holding the door for us.

I waved Babs and Ramirez through, watching Glinda and suddenly wondering how much she might have known. "A coven," I answered hesitantly, "Marionette's coven."

Babs smiled sweetly. "Wouldn't happen to know their covenstead, would you, dear?"

Studying us with a knowing expression, Glinda replied reluctantly, "Not exactly, she technically never left our coven."

"And where would yours happen to be?" I asked.

She rolled her eyes and retorted, "They left for Vancouver years ago and I stayed behind for any stragglers like Marion. I thought that's where 'Victoria' was going."

Looking to Babs, I asked a question I'd had for a couple days, "Can someone be in more than one coven at once?"

"It's possible, but generally discouraged," she said with an air of caution. "Then again, your mother seems to be adept at weaving in and out of groups."

"Do you happen to know a Mark Robinson?" I asked. "He wasn't listed in the coven the ACTF knew about."

Like the answer was on the tip of her tongue, Glinda lowered her eyes, brow furrowing, as she muttered distantly, "No, but it feels like I should."

"It does, doesn't it?" Babs asked. "Would you happen to have a computer, dear?"

Glinda, seemingly dazed by the question of Mark's existence, snapped out of it long enough to stammer out, "Yes, yes, of course, this way."

The two disappeared down the hallway, suddenly oblivious to Ramirez and I even being there. They both had the same reaction to Mark's name, a fact I probably should have been nervous about. In the years of dealing with the world of Alters, hushed tones were rarely a good sign. Worse was knowing that these were people who dealt in secret societies and rites. Whatever hushed them was something buried unnaturally deep.

"Okay then," Ramirez chimed in, lifting the bags, "where do we go?"

I lingered on the thoughts for a moment before shaking it off and waving off-handedly. "We're turning this shit into ammunition."

Snorting, Ramirez grinned. "I knew it!"

I led the way through the house and into the kitchen, setting bags on the same table I'd had coffee only a few hours ago. Ramirez set aside his duffle bag in a corner and the two of us took our seats and got to work. In our quick shopping trip, we'd gathered what we needed for three kinds of ammunition – starting with a little something for the coven itself.

Modern neo-paganism obscured some details of witchcraft behind a more benign design. Spells using plants or charms in most traditions became a positive application of aromatherapy, herbal medicines and good intentions. But if you dug deep enough, especially in old European lore, or an ACTF course on Alter deterrents, you'd find that some plants Wiccans love are not so liked by their Alter cousins.

More aromatic flowers could be overwhelming, even disorienting in the right amounts, which was why Babs and Marionette were both upset by the lilacs. Garlic and other allium extracts, like for Vampires, was particularly irritating and people used the smell as a deterrent for centuries. Mugwort, used by human witches for quite a bit, was often said by Wiccans to have protective qualities. What they didn't know was that one of the things it protected them from was the Alters who cooked up the original recipes. My guess was a sort of witchcraft infighting bled into the literature. Ground up into a fine powder, we mixed these in with some iron shavings from an arts and crafts store to get ourselves a Witch-mace.

The Garuda was going to get something a little more mundane. His kind were incredibly resistant to chemicals, possessed tremendous strength, and could probably shrug off anything I had direct access to. But one thing that he didn't have was a lot of stamina. Garuda were damn near unstoppable in history and mythology, but the one story where they were defeated involved wearing them out to the point they died of exhaustion. Big muscles require big oxygen, so I was hoping simple smoke bombs would make it hard to catch his breath.

As for the baby's breath? I wasn't sure if my theory on those would pan out so I kept that one close to the chest as I effectively crafted potpourri grenades.

As Ramirez took a batch of floral IEDs out to the car, Babs screwed up the courage to wander into the kitchen and started to rummage through the cabinets. She never quite approached the table, the smell of garlic and lilac probably more intense than she would have liked. Instead, she stalked the edges, on the prowl for what I soon figured to be mugs, while I quietly loaded iron laced pellets into a strange gun clip.

"Any luck with the coven?" I asked quietly.

"Unfortunately," she started, pausing as she discovered the treasure trove of old mugs, "there are quite a few of them and that Robinson man doesn't seem to be listed by that name."

I sighed. "A dead end, then?"

"Oh, not at all," she crowed, smiling warmly. "It just means we dig a little deeper. A good coven keeps track of its members. Too big and it becomes unwieldly, too small and it lacks the proper kick."

Setting my tedious project aside, I turned towards her. "What exactly counts as too small?"

"Well, technically anything more than two could count," she said, going about preparing tea. "Two is a working couple, able to do a few tasks, but for larger effects you need at least three, and many orders get uncomfortable with more than thirteen."

"A working couple, huh?" I found myself thinking about the strange relationship Marionette had with Lucian. "Could you form one with a Vampire?"

"Oh no, it wouldn't work I'm afraid," she remarked, "though I have heard of Witches taking up a role as a Vampire's familiar from time to time."

A familiar, a relationship I hadn't even considered. There were often things that an Alter couldn't do for themselves that they'd get a personal attendant to do for them. I even knew a few agencies who provided them like office temps today. But normally they were conners trying to get bit or find favor with an immortal. I hadn't considered a Witch might do it. Not that I ever had a lot to go on with Marionette.

Frustrated, I grumbled, "I wish I knew enough about her to help the search."

"Nate, dear," she said warmly, coming as close to me and the table as she could, "I can't speak for her, but I recognize someone on the run."

"And that justifies leaving me?" I snapped.

"No, of course not," she continued, moving even closer as I could see the red in her eyes. "But I remember running from the hunts, a lot of us do. Some never quite leave that behind."

"That's what Argyre was for," I muttered, looking at where my badge used to be. "That's what the ACTF was for."

Clutching the mug tightly in her hands, she moved to sit across from me, struggling to suppress that disgusted look as it made every little wrinkle just slightly more severe. "Of all the Alters, the Witches have had the hardest road behind us. The trials and the hunters were so terrified of us they persecuted everyone that could have even been hinted to be a Witch."

"They would have had to go through me," I interjected.

She nodded and reached across the table, resting a hand on my forearm. "I'm sure they would, but maybe she didn't want that."

"I'm her son," I bemoaned, "there's records out there that a government could easily use."

Squeezing my forearm gently, Babs replied, "But the government isn't the only group to worry about."

It wasn't the first time I'd heard mention of other threats, they'd been slipping in and out of conversation for a while. But with Babs, there was a hope that she might tell me what others would only imply. Lingering on the silence, I waited on bated breath for her to add the missing piece.

Averting her eyes, she continued regretfully, "Most successful trials were conducted by other Witches. Our people were so divided by the constant pressure from the outside that some would turn on each other."

"I heard about that," I said quietly, "but I thought that was done with."

She shook her head and sighed. "Scars don't fade so quickly. The people who did it in the past are still out there – still trying to navigate safety for themselves at the cost of others. Some of the most infamous hunters were Witches or Warlocks working for a government body."

As the words left her, her bloodshot eyes suddenly lit up like an idea had struck like lightning. She stood from her chair, lifting her glasses to wipe away some tears, before turning and walking away in a hurry.

"Glinda, dear!" she called out from the kitchen, hurrying back to where they'd been working, "Look for any splinters of Fireside!"

Lured by the sudden spike in energy, I hopped up and followed her as she quickly shuffled down the hall mumbling to herself.

Glinda called back from her office, “Fireside? Why would we look for Fireside?”

Entering the office, a tension in her voice, Babs uttered pensively, “Hopkins!”

Confused and peering over her shoulder, I asked, “Why would you look for someone named Hopkins?”

Glinda, similarly confused at first, suddenly got the same look of epiphany on her face. “Son of Hob!”

Babs half turned to me and declared urgently, “One of the most notorious hunters was a man name Matthew Hopkins. The humans recorded him as just a zealot, but the fact is he was from a family of Witches and Warlocks himself. He entered deals with government officials to weed out Witches and threw in some mainstream humans for various trumped-up charges.”

Nodding along, still not getting it, I asked again, “So you think he’s involved in this?”

Glinda, furiously looking through records, corrected without looking up, “No, no, he died a long time ago. We made sure of that.”

Babs nodded, then continued, “But his family, the Hopkins, them and their coven went to ground to avoid reprisal. The name Hopkins means Son of Hob, Hob is a diminutive of Robert, so--“

That same electric feeling struck me as Babs’ line of thought became clear. “Robinson.”

Nearly falling from her seat, Glinda announced, “Children of Hestia!”

“That wasn’t mentioned anywhere on her file,” I sighed, “could she really be a member of three?”

“Apparently so,” Glinda replied, spinning her chair to face us. “But the Children don’t make their membership publicly known, so there could be several with multiple covens in their midst.”

Grunting, running my fingers through my hair, I asked, "You're sure that would be the one?"

"Hestia had no children," Babs remarked, "but her name was also the Greek word for a hearth or fireside."

Glinda gave a single nod and added tightly, "And I'm starting to remember encountering Robinsons in other Fireside branches."

"Of course," Babs reflected darkly, "they wouldn't just leave the coven the Hobbe-kyn founded."

"So, we know where to find them, then?" I asked.

"Not yet," Glinda answered, "but soon."

Glinda turned back to her computer and started up a browser I hadn't seen before but could immediately recognize its function. Having to reference a small notebook for an address that looked more like a randomized password, she started digging into some corner of the dark web that soon populated her screen with Elvish script, old Norse runes, and what had to be mostly abandoned languages. Though I couldn't read all of it, what little I understood revealed that Witches had a private social network buried in the depths of the internet.

Poking his head in, Ramirez commented, "I got everything loaded up. Any progress in here?"

Murmuring over her computer, Glinda replied, "Think they might be in Windermere."

The rest of us immediately snapped to attention as Ramirez uttered "damn" and Babs whistled softly. Windermere, besides sounding like the setting in a fantasy novel, is one of the most expensive neighborhoods in the entire region. Even when I was a kid, it was known for sprawling, ridiculously priced houses on enough land to house a small village. I'd driven down the street once only to realize even the privacy hedges would require a ladder to see over.

On the one hand, it was the kind of place that matched a guy who owned a Marathon. On the other hand, it was weird that Mark would have an apartment downtown if he had any claim to a place in Windermere. Then again, if you had a place in Windermere, rent wasn't exactly an issue.

"So, basically, if we're right," I reflected, "this guy constructed a whole life, even rented an apartment, to hide who he was?"

Bluntly, Babs responded, "He's erasing memories, sweetie. Renting an apartment is the simple part."

Thinking back on the investigation, an uncomfortable thought arose. "The first one I found, Kate, she said they were on a date."

Glinda, rising from her seat, nodded along. "It's not easy, but you can convince people to remember just about anything once they're in the right place."

That wasn't the troubling idea. The troubling idea was that, if they could do that to Kate, they could have done that to anyone. Somehow, they'd known where to find us and send the Garuda. Who could have been their informant? Would they even remember?

"Would it be possible to know if a memory's true?" I asked.

Quietly, reassuringly, Babs answered, "Eventually."

Ramirez, clapping his hands against the doorframe, pushed away and headed down the hall. "But first, let's see what we find in Windermere!"

I watched the door for a second, thinking about what we might find out there. Looking back at the others, I realized they had a good guess at what was on my mind. The slight worry etched across their faces, the knowing looks in their eyes, left me a bit too exposed for my taste. Starting to back up towards the door, I gave them an easy grin and brushed off their concern.

"Home stretch," I said confidently. "Soon this will all be behind us."

Turning to face the door, I came face to face with Ramirez as he stood with the duffle bag slung over his shoulder. Reaching into the bag, he fished out familiar black fabric with a subtle sheen. Holding it up by the shoulders, he presented to me a spare jacket.

"Can't give you any weapons," he said with a faint smile, "but can't go running into a hail of bullets without some protection, can we?"

Taking it from him, I held the jacket like an old friend. Feeling the weight of armor inserts and thick black fabric was strangely comforting for a warm summer's evening. I watched the light catch on the fibers and shimmer across the thin silver plates along the collar. On one arm, where my aegis patch would have been, sat the crest of the devotees: a silhouette of a knight kneeling with his head down and sword planted in the ground, rays of light shining through the background and over the lone figure. Like the aegis, it was a symbol of protection from a higher power.

Mind you, that higher power was a lancer and they rarely hesitate to remind you.

Chuckling, he patted my shoulder. "Sorry if it feels like a demotion," he said. "I don't exactly have one of the others yet."

Putting it on and closing it up, I said gratefully, "I don't know, I think I could use someone looking out for me right about now."

Devotee's jacket or not, I had to admit it felt good to be wearing one again. After all, he was right: we were probably running into a hail of bullets.

Chapter 29
Ragtag Unit

Marching out of the house shoulder to shoulder, the four of us took the last of the improvised weapons out and loaded them up. We had enough of the potpourri grenades to create one hell of a vapor cloud, half a dozen clips of ammunition for the Helsing, and several rods from Ramirez's bag and what was left of my own. Ramirez's Helios, the only sidearm we had with legit stopping power, was fully charged and loaded up. The ladies, prepping to do some witchcraft, brought along old charms and an assortment of colorful liquids in small vials. We were locked, loaded, and ready to go.

At least, as locked and loaded as you could be in a car with flower decals and a horsepower rating just north of a golfcart.

Ramirez and I climbed into the back seat and watched on as the Witches buzzed about their possible plans. Feeling a bit like the kid's table again, I tried to remind myself that, while we were trained extensively in dealing with situations like this, we were nowhere close to the level of experience in the front seat. Then again, I'd seen a surprising amount of crazy shit in the last few years that would count as unique experience.

Murmuring at a good clip, Glinda said, "Even with your experience, a working couple would struggle against a coven's wards."

Babs, mulling it over, replied, "You're right, we need a third. I haven't had a coven in a long time and yours are a couple hours away."

"Well," Glinda said hesitantly, "we could try to talk to Orin."

Babs raised a hand to her lips and fell silent as she considered. The idea of Orin seemed to trouble her, and I was pretty sure I had an idea of why. Her cloak and dagger were pretty clear when I sat with her. Who was to say she wasn't an active participant in the flow of information?

Shooting me a look, Babs asked, "Akemi is a Kitsune?"

"Yeah."

"That should work," Babs said, returning her attention to Glinda. "It would be different but they're not too far off."

Pursing her lips for a moment, Glinda shrugged and nodded. "At the very least she'll confuse them."

Ferrying us through town as fast as the little car would go, Babs took us to the rendezvous point with Akemi and the Tong. It was surreal meeting with an organization of their reputation with an entourage consisting of two civilians, an off-duty agent, and a certified fugitive, but it had been that sort of day. Akemi didn't want to meet near Windermere, understandably, and had given us instructions to meet with her down in the Madison Park neighborhood on the waterfront. Given the location of the Fireside stronghold, I had a hunch we were there for a boat.

Pulling up to a set of waterfront condos an hour after sunset, Babs parked her car into a space too small for any real car and the four of us exited to meet with the Tong. The area was surprisingly well lit for such a clandestine meeting, though quiet at this hour of the night and starkly less busy than any location in Fangtown or the International District would have been. Despite this, Ramirez and I took point, keeping the civilians behind us as we walked towards the water.

With the great bulk of city lights at our back and a far more modest skyline across from us, the lake was a great dark mirror for the sky above and the light of the rising moon to the west. From the water we were greeted by the sound of waves lapping across the shore and the creaking of wood as boats strained against an unseen dock. Still, as I listened closer, I looked for another sound and barely made it out in the breeze. Between those rhythmic splashes and groans were the quick, quiet beat of small wings and hushed, whispering chatter from the eaves of the building above. Even out there, far from the heart of the city, we were being watched.

Emerging from around the corner, Akemi stepped into the light, disguise fully dropped so her fox-like traits were in full view. Her tail was actually more impressive than I realized, gently swaying behind her as she approached us, the fiery red coat catching the moonlight with an unreal sparkle. Noticeably sticking out now were a pair of short fox-like ears, set like an Elf's but with short fuzz along them that blended with her hair. The human ears I'd seen before were apparently part of the illusion, telling me that she was somehow better than Marionette at making me ignore things right in front of my face.

Examining these traits, Babs exclaimed, "Oh you're from a strong bloodline, aren't you?"

Taken aback, Akemi hesitantly nodded and replied, "I suppose I am, yes."

The Witches descended on the fox girl and presented their kit of strange liquids to her with an explanation I couldn't make out through their hushed tones. Akemi, leaning back from them initially, soon eased and started to nod along, her ears very subtly moving like an Elf. Meanwhile, her entourage emerged from the shadows near Ramirez and I and silently guided us to a boat resting by a small dock.

Despite her position, Akemi didn't bring a lot of muscle along. We were being joined by two Jiangshi from the looks of them, paler Asian men in relatively high-priced clothes. The one on the left was stiffer than the right with an obvious hitch to his gait, every step being clearly thought out. As we started to go downhill, there was suddenly a slight spring in his step that would be seen as peppy out of anyone else. For a Jiangshi, though, it was a sign he was doing his best not to bounce down the slope like a rabbit. I had to figure he wasn't too much more experienced than I was. The guy on the right, however, had all the signs of being a ringer.

Wearing a nice coat and a silk shirt, the guy on the right would have looked like someone a little too high priced to be the muscle. His shoes were well shined, his slacks were creased, and his haircut probably cost a clover in the sort of places a Jiangshi would sit. To the untrained eye, he would have seemed a little too polished to be a threat. But for a Jiangshi, his level of polish spoke volumes. The way he moved with an ease and grace to his steps told me he was much older than he looked and trained to make everything look easy. He wasn't hopping, he had complete control, and any Jiangshi that could do that could unleash what he was holding back.

I found that out the hard way once and had the dental work to prove it.

Climbing into the boat, the four of us sat in an uneasy silence. We had a common enemy for now, and Zhang had told us the organization was turning a new leaf, but there was still history there. For Ramirez and I, the question was just how much these guys had done before that recent change. For the Jiangshi there was a looming question about whether we were going to let them walk away after this was done. We stared each other down, sizing each other up, until the ladies broke the silence with a decidedly friendlier vibe.

"I honestly haven't even tried that," Akemi declared brightly, getting into the boat first and offering to help Babs on.

Babs took her hand and climbed in carefully. "It would be my first time with a Kitsune," she said, steadying herself as the boat swayed.

Akemi looked at the available seats and gave the Jiangshi a stern look. The older of the two stood and offered his seat to Babs with a subtle bow, then moved to help Glinda aboard. Following his lead, Ramirez and I moved to clear space for Akemi and Glinda, sticking close to each other as we did and instinctively keeping our sidearms turned away from potentially grabby hands.

The elder Jiangshi continued to gracefully move across the swaying deck to take the helm as his protégé freed us from the dock without a word exchanged. As soon as the ladies were seated, we left the dock and took off across the lake, headed towards the shore of Windermere to the north. I'd had a feeling this was the way we would approach. The street would have been secured and there was likely an iron fence across the front, but the back of the house faced the water, with a private dock, and it was a lot harder to ward the shore.

As we traveled along, the ladies went to work blending what could only be described as potions and taking part in a ritual I could hardly understand. From the kit that they brought with them they had an assortment of dried herbs and flowers that they set alight in a dish, creating a strong aroma as the three began to recite old Faelish phrases in unison. As they recited, they would drink between lines and breathe deep of the unusual smoke. I could feel something in the air, like I could when Witches had been trying to push me, and felt it grow stronger with every new sip.

At first, their voices grow more disparate. Accents long practiced to blend in started to fade away, putting a new spin on an already rare language. Before long, the accents of their previous lives took hold: Babs Polish, Akemi Japanese, and Glinda French. With each passing phrase they were more and more in sync, finding a growing harmony until they were suddenly chanting in perfect unison. Their accents, as far apart as they could be, slowly began to blend into a single sound. I don't know if the others could feel it, but there was a presence over us.

I think they formed a new coven on that lake under the light of the moon.

From the water, the part of Windermere we were approaching looked like it had a small forest growing over it. The dark treetops were shrouding obviously impressive houses as dozens of windows were lit on large lots of land. The house we were aiming for was particularly noteworthy as a hedge maze took up its back lawn while strange lights seemed to dart through the leaves like fireflies.

As we approached, the new coven joined hands and entered a deep state of concentration. Something lifted in that moment as the air seemed fresher and a sweet scent drifted over us. The older Jiangshi cut the engine and let us drift in towards the dock. His friend took the opportunity to put those Jiangshi legs to good use and leapt from the boat all the way to the dock with an ease I'd only ever seen from Lucian. He landed with a rope in hand and started to reel us in like an exceptionally large fish.

Loading the Helsing with my first clip of improvised ammunition, I stood again and grabbed a backpack I'd borrowed off of Glinda stuffed full of our potpourri grenades. Ramirez opened up his bag again and started to double up on the rods he was carrying before taking out a pair of sunglass cases. Looking my way, he offered one to me. Taking it, I cracked it open to find my reflection staring back at me across the iridescent surface of a new pair of shades.

"Doesn't matter what she sees now, does it?" He asked, putting on a pair himself.

Taking a second to consider it, I shrugged and put them on. "If anything," I said, "she might send help."

Slinging the backpack of explosive air-fresheners onto my back, I climbed onto the dock and studied the area ahead of us. If the house looked imposing before, it was a whole other story once I had a visor. They cut through the darkness and highlighted a small compound cloaked in chemical traces that looked like a wall of light shielding it from the world. The lights that danced through the air swept through these strange clouds of vapor with barely a visible trail, suggesting they weren't fireflies at all but wisps manifesting from whatever the coven had done.

"Alright," I said, glancing back at the boat, "Ramirez and I are going to take point and cut through that hedge maze ourselves."

Puzzled and worried, Babs asked, "Are you sure, dear? That's a dangerous house."

I nodded to Ramirez' gear and jostled a bit to rattle the grenades in my bag. "We're going to confirm we're in the right place first," I said, "then we're going to make some noise."

Glinda reminded sharply, "Remember, your mother's still in there, so you can't set things off indiscriminately."

I almost snapped back, but I could understand where she was coming from. Instead, I reassured, "I'm getting her out of there in one piece."

Giving the group a once over, I waved for Ramirez to follow and started down the dock, drawing the Helsing and keeping it ready in case of an ambush. We weren't going to have a lot of time to debate things, the dock probably had cameras on it and that hedge maze was probably warded and wired. But of the people in the boat, only two of us were equipped to take a beating and respond with some shock and awe.

As we entered that hedge maze, the visors caught an array of sophisticated, interweaving colors. The plants in the hedges were part of some elaborate mask for chemical trails and almost immediately that same surreal, disorienting feeling from Marionette's apartment came over me. The lights dancing through the vapor were suddenly much brighter and yet more obscured as they ducked behind hedges that now seemed to tower over us. The area was somehow darker as the path seemed to narrow and the leaves looked like daggers threatening us from the shadows.

If I was resistant, like recent events had suggested, Ramirez had to be *really* tripping out.

Confirming the feeling, I heard the uneasy breathing of someone trying his hardest not to hurl. Glancing back, I watched as he slowly started to assume a 30-degree angle like the ground had sloped, his lips pursed and brow furrowed in deep concentration. He returned my gaze, mirrored visors reflecting infinitely and making the contact high all the worse. Reaching out, I grabbed at his coat and steadied him.

"Hold onto me," I ordered, "and don't let go until I say so."

Hesistantly, he holstered his Helios and grabbed onto my backpack. I wasn't entirely confident on being resistant, but I was still being hit less than he was. The path ahead was starting to warp for me too, but as far as I could tell I was still standing upright. My stomach was settled, the ground wasn't moving, and

I was pretty confident the hedges wouldn't try to grab me. Pushing ahead, I just hoped my judgment was still intact.

It was a pretty well-crafted maze, especially with the high. Every turn came with a feeling of uncertainty and a disorienting rush of adrenaline that I figured was part of the trap. The wisps buzzed about our heads, pestering us like flies on a humid summer night before darting away into the shadows.

Ramirez groaned, clutching tighter at the backpack, his weight shifting like he was about to fall way, "We've got to get out of here, man."

Glancing back his way, seeing the color wash out of his face and his aura turn shades of yellow reserved for those under heavy influence, I could see he was right. I needed a quick way out and started looking desperately for any signs. But the only signs to be found were those damned wisps harrying us. Frustrated as one zipped away, I gave chase, hoping it would go somewhere different. Unfortunately, all it did was lead us into the darkest space yet, hedges towering over us and blotting out the sky, an unnerving breathing sound building behind me like a beast had cornered us.

Slowly turning back, tightening my grip on the Helsing, I saw a dark figure reaching a hand out to me. Its ragged breathing sped up as it lurched closer, its aura outlining it against the black backdrop that had surrounded us. For a split second, my shoulders tensed as I momentarily considered fighting it. Thankfully, in the next breath, I realized I was looking at Ramirez – who was now on the verge of hyperventilating.

It was strange to think, but the maze itself was clearly trying to make us panic. I'd nearly lost it for a second and it was definitely getting under Ramirez's skin. Calming myself, setting my shoulders and turning us back around, I led Ramirez out of the dead end and back through the maze. Though I did my best to trace our steps to where we took the wrong turn, everything looked different now. After a dozen more turns, I wasn't entirely sure where we were headed anymore. Worse, the wisps continued to pester us, almost like they were trying to provoke me to do it again.

Then it clicked: that was exactly what was happening.

The maze was trying to make us panic, make us sloppy, and then turn us around. It was trying to keep us out. But, more importantly, it was only trying to keep ***us*** out. If they wanted to keep everyone out, they would have erected a wall. Like the black-market signs, like the Alter music, there had to be something hidden in there for the people who could feel it. Thinking back on someone who tried to teach me to look past the surface and feel the music underneath, I realized I was playing into the coven's hands.

Closing my eyes, breathing deep despite whatever bullshit was in the air around us, I tried to feel out the parts that were hiding from me. I wasn't part of the coven, the road signs weren't meant for me, but someone in my family was. Letting go for a moment, letting the maze's influences in, I felt something through it that wasn't hostile. The wisps were turning the wrong ways on purpose, the maze riling us up so we'd give chase, then punishing us with a dose of whatever was coming off the hedges when we took a dead end. Opening my eyes again, watching the wisps follow their paths, everything was now amazingly clear.

Cutting through it like the whole thing had been mapped out for me ahead of time, I dragged Ramirez through the hedges like I'd been there a hundred times before. Thankfully, with each correct turn, the effects got a little less severe. The place stopped looking so intimidating, the wisps stopped seeming so aggressive, and even Ramirez seemed to sober up as the lights of the house loomed over our hedged horizon. Before we knew it, I'd somehow felt my way out of a maze and came within view of the light at the end of our leafy tunnel.

Ramirez, still dazed, gasped. "Dude, how the hell did you do that?"

Peering back, I whispered, "I think it's in the blood."

Emerging from the maze, we walked out into a well-lit and completely exposed region at the foot of an impressive patio deck. The house, three stories tall and covered in windows that had direct line of sight on us, was abuzz with activity as figures rapidly darted about well-lit windows. I wondered for a second if they detected us in the maze.

The rifle suddenly peeking out of a cracked window answered the question pretty well.

Scrambling for the deck in a mad dash, Ramirez and I narrowly avoided several rounds going off just over our heads and tearing through the hedges behind us. Ramirez, still moving like a drunk, fell to the ground but continued to roll towards the relative cover of the solidly built deck as I slid for it like home plate. The deck, solid but still not bullet proof, soon had new holes bored through it as bullets ricocheted around us and thankfully hit our jackets. Leaning against one of the deck's supports for additional cover, I looked over to see Ramirez doing the same with the expression of a man who just snapped out of a stupor on pure adrenaline.

"I think we found the right place!" He joked through gritted teeth.

"Let's formally introduce ourselves!" I yelled over the gunfire.

Holstering the Helsing and pulling my Banshee, I hurriedly set it to the most damaging mode possible. Pulling his and a spare he loaded before we left the boat, Ramirez nodded along and did the same. Without so much as a word, the two of us fell into sync as we triggered the rods and lobbed them up and over the deck towards the back of the house. Guns fell silent as people frantically scrambled away from the windows.

A single Banshee is enough to break windows, blow open a closed space, or clear a room. Three Banshees, on the other hand, rocked the deck, shattered every window on the house, and set off a car alarm half a block away. Ramirez and I, stuck at the foot of the deck, felt the bass in our bones and the rumble of wood and nails trying not to collapse. Even as the sound passed, the wood continued to settle like an earthquake just hit.

Listening to make sure the gunfire hadn't restarted, I quickly pulled the backpack off and nodded to Ramirez. "Cover me!"

He nodded, pulled his Helios and peeked just over the edge of the deck, opening fire on light fixtures to try to even our odds and spook the occupants. I scurried towards the stairs to get a better angle as a shooter inside started to return fire. Squatting just at the corner of the stairs, I opened the bag and pulled out our arsenal of fragrant roman candles.

The occupants continued to regroup as gunfire opened up on Ramirez's location from multiple directions. Taking my chance, I popped the makeshift pins on two of the grenades. Plumes of aggressively scented smoke coiled around me as the contents rapidly burned. Taking a quick assessment of the position of the guns, I lobbed one up the stairs towards the closest window, then stepped out of cover just enough to flick the second at the next. The smoke rapidly obscured their view and soon they were firing blindly at both of us. Ramirez, noticing the shift of targets, returned to harassing the one that had focused my way.

After lobbing a few more onto the deck and making it harder for them to see where we were, I took multiple grenades out and eyed the first window I'd blocked. Though the smoke was now making it hard to see the frame itself, the light still shone through and gave me a big rectangular target floating in thin air. I pulled the pin, took a couple steps back to get a better angle, and lobbed one straight through the frame. Repeating the motion, I managed to do the same to the next couple of windows, startling at least one of the shooters into stopping as the smoke bomb whizzed past them.

Scrambling back to cover just before they blindly fired in my direction, I found my supply exhausted and looked up to see if the plan was working. Watching the hedges and the trees in our wake, I saw movement in the leaves as the chaos ensued. Those leaves rustled randomly as small shadows darted about. And, though I couldn't hear it, I had a hunch there was a particular sound covered by the bang of gunpowder and the buzz of the Helios splitting the air.

Taking my cue to do the final step, I pulled out the gPhone and started up an app I'd downloaded before we left. The screen populated with a series of waveform graphs and continued to add new ones as the app sprang into action. I reached into the bag and pulled out the flannel shirt Marionette got me, wrapping up the phone as quickly as possible before stuffing it back in. Closing the backpack and grabbing the strap, I scrambled out of cover again, took aim, and whipped the whole thing through one of the windows like I'd done with the grenades.

As I let it go, I caught sight of the rest of our party reaching the exit. They were considerably less rough than Ramirez and I from the looks of it. Babs was confidently taking point and seemed to cut through the aura of the maze like a high-pressure front centered on a little old lady. Looking past them, though, I caught a whole new aura emerging from the darkness.

"Get down!" I called out, waving to them as a swarm exploded onto the scene, emerging from all around and rushing the house. They ducked just as a flurry of colors blew past them. The flock moved like a single force, plowing through the smoke, surging through the windows, and overwhelming the shooters. As the lights of the house started to flicker erratically and the guns fell silent, they were replaced by the sounds of breaking glass and maniacal giggles.

I don't know how Witches would have done it, but with some fire, flowers, and a cellphone practically screaming on every radio frequency known to man I'd done a ritual of my own.

I summoned the goddamned fairies.

Chapter 30
General Mayhem

Into the smoke, the screams, and the giggles, Ramirez and I led the Jiangshi through the doors and went to work clearing that entrance for our tiny coven. Feathers, bullets and glass were flying as we crossed that threshold and the pixies went absolutely batshit on literally everyone in the house. Taking the right as Ramirez went left, I just started homing in on any signature taller than three inches and popped off some Witch balls through the smoke. Their signatures weren't masked at the moment, auras lit up like Christmas, but the scream from the nearby Warlock as the first ball burst across his chest was a strangely satisfying confirmation.

I was punchy – it'd been a long couple of days, they were shooting at me, and it was non-lethal.

Though the pixies weren't keen on my iron dust or Ramirez's ion trails, the Fireside members were stupid enough to keep provoking them. For every instance of one attacking us, they were quickly drawn back on target by some idiot flailing blindly. The combination of the smoke and tiny attackers kept the coven from organizing a better response – not that it prevented me from smashing a lamp along the way. At least one Warlock whipped a fire poker into the air, desperately trying to stave off the little monsters. I almost felt bad as I watched him tumble out one of the broken windows with three giggling terrors latched onto his head.

Practically dancing through the pandemonium, our Jiangshi escorts bounded through the room and closed in on targets that had no chance of reacting. Obscured by the smoke itself, I briefly watched their auras cutting through the air and the voids opening in their wake as they flew through with astonishing ease. The smoke behind them was left streaming and swirling, the air currents even managing to pull tiny figures off course. Though I was sure they had weapons with them, I could see they didn't need them as one struck like lightning into the midsection of a Warlock with a crack that you could still hear even over the gunshots and maniacal laughter. The Warlock's aura turned cold as he was lifted from his feet and flew through a closed door as though it were hardly there.

I'd seen that kind of impact before and was happy not to be on the receiving end for once.

Finding cover behind a bar, I took the opportunity to assess the floor plan and make some guesses at where Marionette might have been. The Witches and Warlocks flooding into the room were coming from all directions and weren't much help, but the distinct lack of Mark suggested he was sitting back. He probably wasn't even on the same floor. Peering through the smoke, the sound of something very heavy moving down a flight of stairs on the east side caught my attention like rolling thunder. Popping the anti-Witch clip out of the Helsing, I swapped for the next and braced for a bird man to come through a nearby archway, only to see a different face instead.

Charging through the archway came an aura too short for the Garuda and with an unmistakable head. Erupting through the smoke, the giant, single eye of the Cyclops from that DAO facility appeared like a big fat bullseye. Not wanting to permanently blind the guy, I aimed lower and hit him square in the chest with a more conventional smoke bomb. Blinded temporarily and not sounding very pleased about it, he stumbled into the room and flailed wildly to sweep the smoke out of his face.

The ruckus drew the attention of the wrong Jiangshi as the older one danced in and kicked the Cyclops in the midsection hard enough that even I felt it. To his credit, he took it in relative stride and backhanded the high-dollar hitman. Weaving through the room, the two exchanged haymakers the likes of which I was happy not to be receiving and forcing the people still standing to get out of the way. Deciding I wanted no part of it, I whistled to the mini-coven outside and waved them in.

Up until that point, no one had a chance to set off something truly phenomenal. The local coven was in disarray with lungs full of irritants and faces covered in scratches. But as I let out the whistle, my visor highlighted what seemed to be a sunrise on the doorstep followed by the rush of colorful flames bursting into the room. As if the place wasn't already in chaos, a flurry of ghostly flames burst through the door and began to harass the occupants just as the wisps had done in the maze. I'd heard of foxfire, flaming wisps driven by Kitsune, but I'd always imagined it to be simple swamp gas. Now, they were providing distraction, setting small fires around the room, and leading the pixies like phantom generals.

Was it actual pyrokinesis? I don't know. I was just happy they weren't coming after me with a lamp.

The trio rushed in shortly after, heads low and looking even blurrier than the rest of the room as they used the smoke to their advantage. As the shadowy figures approached, Akemi stepped up to me first, the soft focus on the others suddenly sharpening like she dropped the filter and revealed Glinda and Babs in formation behind her.

"Stairs this way," I said with a bob of my head, running ahead to lead the way.

The three of them followed me over and went up the stairs as I stood guard at the foot. Though we weren't sure what awaited us, I had a feeling they were safer up there. The gunfire was localized to the ground floor, and even if someone above was armed I had to figure they could stall for time. As Babs took up the rear, I waited a couple seconds and followed them up.

Watching them approach the top, I called out, "Heads low, just in case someone's armed up there!"

Akemi, glancing back, drew a concealed .45 without hesitation, charged up the stairs and did a quick corner check before letting the other two up.

"Oh, right," I muttered to myself, "bodyguard."

As I caught up, I took point again and quickly checked the rooms on the second floor. It was spacious like the ground floor, a couple hallways and multiple bedrooms. Though the sound of gunfire was still overwhelming and the smoke was starting to drift up, it was oddly calm and abandoned. The Cyclops had come down the stairs, so I figured he was positioned as the guard. Unfortunately, that gave me a good idea of what to expect on the third floor. Looking up the next flight of stairs and leveling the Helsing his way, I stared into the eyes of the Garuda as he waited for us above.

"Ramesh!" Akemi cried out, darting between us and raising her hands in the air, "It's Akemi! Whatever you think you're supposed to be doing, this wasn't our mission!"

Warily, Glinda and Babs circled around behind me. I didn't lower the Helsing, just in case Akemi was wrong, but I took a solid step back to give her space in case she was right. His aura didn't flicker a bit, though, as he glared down at us with daggers in his eyes. It was like he couldn't even see her as his aura flowed with a blood red that told me we had seconds before he was going to come down those stairs.

"Please," she continued with a wavering voice, lowering the .45, "I don't want to hurt you."

Hesitantly, I released one hand from my weapon and reached out to rest it on her shoulder, murmuring, "Leave him to me, then."

Akemi looked over her shoulder angrily for a moment as a hint of a quiver crossed her lips. Unguarded in front of a visor for the first time since I met her, the conflict in her aura was clear as day. Unfortunately, as I caught sight of him moving out of the corner of my eye, Ramesh didn't share the conflict. He bounded down the stairs, practically pouncing on us from above.

Shoving Akemi out of the way and jumping back, I nearly bowled over the Witches behind me as I opened fire with smoke bombs into his chest. Thankfully, both saw it coming too and moved away just in time for me to trample through with a pissed off eagle giving chase. I unloaded multiple rounds into his chest, creating one hell of a cloud, before taking a potshot into his forehead to make sure he was nice and pissed off. Judging by the ear-piercing shriek he made, it worked.

"It's Ramesh, right?" I called through the smoke, "How'd it feel getting your ass kicked by pixies?"

Blindly punching for the sound of my voice, Ramesh missed wildly while clearing a considerable amount of the smoke from the landing with one swing of his arm. I ducked the swing, feeling the wind through my hair, then scrambled back as quickly as I could, glancing to each side to make sure I wasn't about to run into one of the women beside me. Babs and Glinda had cleared way and ducked into adjacent rooms to let us pass while Akemi sat on the floor shellshocked and watched me goad her friend into trying to pulp me. Glancing over my shoulder for a quick study of my surroundings, I caught sight of an open room as violet lights flashed outside. Firing another shot into Ramesh's chest, I turned and bolted for the light.

"Find Mark!" I yelled, "I'll catch up!"

I couldn't see if they listened as the outline of a Garuda filled the hallway behind me and obscured everything like storm clouds on the horizon. Regardless, I fired a few more rounds into his torso and lunged into the room at the end of the hall, hoping it would be just sparse enough for me to move freely. Fortunately, it seemed to be some sort of sitting room with a few couches, a small coffee table, and a Ouija board next to a bottle of tequila and a set of shot glasses. Unfortunately, that violet light coming through the window was clearly an ACTF unit and I knew I had a couple minutes before this all got much worse.

Ramesh's shoulders clipped the doorframe as he charged in after me, shaking the walls like they were about ready to break. The hardwood floor rumbled at our feet as he stampeded my way. With another few blind swings, he blew some of the décor off the walls and cut through the smoke I'd been laying down. But for every gap he made, I filled it with a few more shots.

The plan was simple. Garuda only had one weakness in all the stories I was familiar with: stamina. For all their size, strength, and durability they still had to deal with the fact they were giants who needed a lot of oxygen to keep going. With every smoke bomb and missed swing, I was pushing him closer to the red line. Ducking, dodging, and rolling over furniture a couple times to get distance, I pitted our cardio routines against each other. Through all the noise of the gunfire below, the sounds of sirens outside, and the tremors he set off with every step, I could start to hear his strained breathing as he gulped for any fresh air he could get through the smoke. He was getting gassed – all I needed to do was hold a couple minutes longer.

Unfortunately, he was starting to catch up. Every swing forced me to move deeper into the room, every new step cut off an angle I could use. The near misses became nearer and the potential outs grew fewer. One swing that nearly took my head off actually dazed me as it missed, the rush of air feeling almost like a slap across the side of my head. It didn't actually hurt me, but it did catch my attention enough to distract me as he nearly stepped on my foot while lunging in. I stepped clear just in the nick of time and circled around, narrowly missing a grab. Raising the Helsing to fire, I pulled the trigger only to get a hollow click. In that moment, Ramesh got the opportunity he'd been looking for.

My world practically shattered when a punch finally landed square in my chest. As winded as Ramesh had been, it couldn't compare to the sheer agony as that fist knocked every ounce of wind out of me. Thrown across the room by the force and tumbling across the floor, I managed to roll back up to my feet before leaning against the wall that had once been an entire room away. It wasn't my first time being hit that hard, but every punch like that was like having your soul removed.

Not satisfied with his blunt force exorcism, Ramesh closed the gap between us with the grace and speed of a linebacker and took another swing for my head. The fortunate thing about fighting someone that size, even when he could move like that, is you get ample warning when they're coming. Sounding like a freight train and pushing enough air that I could practically see his trajectory in the smoke around us, I used what little clarity I had to move. It didn't matter what direction, or how far, I just couldn't be where that fist was going to land. And, as I went crashing to the floor, I saw that club of a fist crash through the wall exactly where my head would be.

My sheer panic cleared out the cobwebs quite nicely.

Scrambling back to my feet and trying to get away from him, another fist came dangerously close to ending me and punched clear through the wall yet again. Each step I took to try to get around him was countered with another big stride as he repositioned to box me in and try again. The Helsing was out of smoke, I was still too frayed to even slow him down, and I was quickly moving towards a corner I didn't want to be in. If I didn't think of something fast, in that flurry of punches and the growing cloud of drywall dust, I wasn't getting out.

And then, as we came within feet of that corner, two smaller arms erupted from the wall behind me. Clad in black and gold, it was like being embraced by living shadows as they wrapped around me faster than I could react. Beginning to struggle, I found there was little as I could do as the arms pulled me back, the wall tearing like paper as I was ripped through it with tremendous ease and hurled into the next room.

Even in that dazed state, I remembered to tuck my chin before hitting shoulders first to the floor. Tumbling end over end, I came to a stop halfway through a fairly large bedroom and looked back up at the shadow that had plucked me through a wall as easily as fruit from a vine. Tall, lean, with a face so pale it practically glowed, I looked at the statuesque frame of Lucian standing over me with a dour look on his stone-like face.

He did not look happy.

If he was controlled, or if he didn't get the message, I was now facing down not only a Garuda but an ancient Vampire and just the one nearly killed me. As Lucian continued to frown at me and walk my way, the form of a Garuda turned the Nate-sized hole into something much larger behind him. The two of them practically moved in slow motion as adrenaline and possible head trauma worked to turn my world into a blurry mess. Through that blur, however, I could still see Ramesh's tree-limb of an arm swinging through with a trail of plaster dust.

Lucian ducked as Ramesh's arm split the air where his head had once been, turned and jabbed into the Garuda's diaphragm in one fluid motion. Ramesh let out what could only be described as a squeal as the last of the wind was knocked out of him and that massive body recoiled back into the hole it emerged from, grasping for something to break its fall but only managing to rip out more drywall in the process.

Turning to me as Ramesh toppled, Lucian remarked, "Alston's 65, huh?"

Score one for the Elves.

"Thank god," I wheezed out, staggering to my feet and scrambling to reload.

Out of straight smoke, I swapped in the Witch-mace just in time for our substantial friend to blitz into the room again. Giving Lucian no time to counter, he clasped his fists together and swung them down like a hammer. Lucian dove aside, rolling clear while I fired into Ramesh's forehead to blind him. Caught off guard and throwing all of his weight into the motion, Ramesh stumbled ahead and barreled through the room. Hopping aside, I let him pass and took another potshot into the side of his head while I had the chance.

Remembering the mix only after setting off two rounds, I yelled "garlic" to Lucian before he could close in. Lucian nodded, took a deep breath, and darted in to deliver a right cross into Ramesh's face while he was still mostly doubled over. Like the Cyclops below, Ramesh could take a punch and managed to avoid completely falling over but struggled to stay upright. Watching him nearly drop, I hopped in and kicked into the back of his knee while he was off balance. Dropping to a knee so hard I thought he was about to break the floor, Ramesh stopped himself from being fully brought down. Unfortunately for him, he was now down to our level.

Holstering the Helsing now that Lucian was in close range, I threw a knee into Ramesh's back to try to bring him down. He barely wobbled, but leaned into a second knee coming up into his face from Lucian. Thrown back, he pushed off the floor and tried to jolt back to his feet. Punching him in the hip, I put a hitch in his step as Lucian put another punch square into his midsection. Though he still managed to get to his feet, each new blow forced out a new unusual sound as we were lighting him up.

Swinging in blind desperation, Ramesh managed to clip Lucian and sent him through the room as easily as he launched me in the last. Lucian took the hit more gracefully than I, rolling back up to his feet right away, but the towering figure was already on him by the time he looked up. Using the furniture to get a leg up, I leapt onto his back in a futile effort to try to slow him down. Going along for the ride, I held on for dear life while my added weight actually sent us both barreling into another wall as Lucian very smartly just got the hell out of our way.

I instinctively let go as we both received a face-full of plaster, but that wall didn't do much to slow Ramesh at all. Tearing through and hitting another wall on the other side of the hall, the winded goliath stumbled his way back towards the stairwell where we started our little dance. Huffing and puffing like he was ready to collapse, I wasn't sure if he was going to give in or have a heart attack just then. Warily, I followed through the eagle shaped hole and watched him as he lumbered to the edge. Wobbling, his legs gave out and he lurched towards the rail.

"Shit!"

Scrambling after him, I grabbed at his waistband and pulled back for all I was worth. Narrowly stopping the mass of muscle from going completely over the side, I was soon facing the new issue that he bounced off the rail and toppled back towards me. I caught him, barely, and struggled to both stay upright and not drop him on his head. He was within the range of human weight but definitely not on the low end and I'm a relatively average guy. Thankfully, Lucian stepped in to take the load off and help the big man down safely.

Doubled over, I took a moment to catch my breath for the first time in what felt like hours, wheezing out, "I can see why you'd want one as a bodyguard."

Chuckling, Lucian patted my back. "Imagine if he had a weapon."

Looking up, I asked, "How'd you get here so fast?"

Lucian shook his head, knelt and started restraining Ramesh, grinning faintly as he replied, "Ramirez took off his visor and badge but left the hand-link running."

Exasperated and exhausted, I dropped my head and tried my best not to laugh. "Jesus Christ."

Standing once he had Ramesh secured, Lucian peered down the stairwell towards the still ongoing chaos below. Though the gunfire was less extreme, the crashing still rang through the whole house like a series of car accidents. A Witch crawled out of the living room covered in small cuts and scrapes, skin irritated and eyes bloodshot, and made her way towards the stairs. As she reached for the banister, a squad of pixies noticed and was suddenly on her, grabbing and jabbing like a crowd of obsessed fans. Though his visor covered his eyes, Lucian was clearly giving me the side eye as I glanced back at him.

Before I could explain, the sound of a single shot fired on the floor above cut through the building like the sound of a cannon. Jolting, the two of us drew our weapons and assumed positions. Though he didn't know who brought it, I was sure I wasn't the only one who recognized the sound of a .45 being fired in a closed space. We exchanged looks and were already on the move before we even started to speak.

"I'll handle the ground floor," he announced, vaulting over the rail to take the short route down. "Find your mother!"

Running the other direction, I was already halfway up the next flight of stairs, yelling, "Catch up when it's clear!"

The decision didn't require any discussion. Our guys were outnumbered down there, even under the cover of fairies, and we couldn't be sure what the change in the gunfire meant. So, the guy better capable and equipped of handling that crowd would head down and I would charge towards the sound of the only gun we knew was up top. I also knew that the gun in question was probably Akemi's.

Helsing at the ready, I followed the sound of Mark's voice as he screamed over panicked chatter from the women. As that chatter grow more frantic, I picked up the pace, slowing only to make sure none of the adjacent doors had another heavy guard behind it. But by the time I was halfway to the sound and could hear some of the voices clearly, even that consideration stopped mattering and I made a beeline towards the screams.

"Put it down!" Mark cried out. "I **command** you!"

A second shot pierced the air, dominating the entire floor. Several women screamed in shock as I picked up the pace and dashed through the door. Bursting into the master suite, a sprawling bedroom with an impressive view and a fireplace, my eyes were drawn immediately to the shattered window at the far end and Mark clutching his shoulder on the floor in a pool of blood, a second hole from a near miss bored into the floor next to him. Standing between us, with an aura as red as Ramesh's and a gun gripped so firmly I could see her hands shaking, was Marionette.

"Go to hell," she snarled bitterly.

Screwing up enough courage to snap back, Mark yelled, "I don't know what your problem is, Mary!"

Voice wavering, she rebuked, "You know **damn** well what you did."

Easing into the room, I took a quick headcount and made sure all of ours were still standing. From what I could see, they were doing their best to try to calm Marionette while keeping Mark under thumb. Akemi was backed up into the corner, focusing hard as her aura rippled wildly but looking unharmed. Babs was near me, hands in the air like a magician, a steely look on her normally frail face as she kept her aura in sync. Glinda, completing a triangle, stood a few feet to Marionette's right, wavering slightly from the colors of the other two as hints of conflict sparked through her readings.

Whispering to Babs, I asked, "How'd she get the gun?"

Babs, aura not flickering a bit, replied, "She tackled Akemi for it after we broke his hold on her."

"Marion, honey," Glinda pleaded, "we don't need to kill him now."

Shooting a deadly look Glinda's way, Marionette retorted, "You don't know what he's done."

"What *I've* done?" Mark scoffed, wincing as he tried to prop himself back up. "I helped you disappear! I hid your past from everyone short of Argyre!"

Hands tensing, finger getting ready to pull the trigger, Marionette's aura started to lose that blood red and shift into something a bit more dangerous. Hints of purple started to creep in, shades of shame, remorse, and possibly disgust. Voice cracking, she replied, "What was the point if you planned to set me up as the scapegoat?"

Cringing, Mark shifted his weight a bit and started edging back from her along the floor. "You know how Fireside works," he said with a pained rasp, "we make sacrifices for the greater good."

"We were supposed to ***protect*** our people!" she yelled. "What good does the DAO do for them if they're dead or in prison?!"

"The devil of the ninth offered a good deal," he choked out. "He needed the loose ends taken care of."

"When did the people in the coven become 'loose ends'?" she seethed.

"He felt," Mark groaned, "that some of you might be easily compromised."

The words pushed out the violet shades and reignited her rage. Still seething, she asked pointedly, "Why did you send the Garuda after that agent?"

Confused, Mark asked, "Since when do you care what the hell happens to an agent?" Catching sight of me, the bewilderment in his voice grew, "Why would you save him?"

She looked over her shoulder, finally noticing me, and eased her grip as tears started to stream down her face. The exchange might have confused Mark, but it cleared things up for me. Keeping my distance, I started to circle around her slowly. I didn't let go of the Helsing, but I wasn't about to point it at her. Even if I had shot her to protect him, something I wasn't much inclined to do, there was nothing in there that could have stopped her from pulling the trigger. Given what they just said, I had a feeling only one thing could actually save the loathsome man on the floor.

Easing my way into her path, I stood directly between them and said gently, "You can't do this."

Discarding the borrowed visor, I stared into her bloodshot eyes as I started to remove the jacket. The rest of the building had fallen mostly silent, there were no more gunshots or crashes, no more screams. We were left with Mark's ragged breathing, my mother's sobs, and those strange little giggles in the distance, lurking in the rafters. The whole room echoed the dull thud as I dropped that coat so she'd know any shot she took had a chance of killing me. It was a leap of faith, but it wasn't for the guy at my back.

"Don't do it, mom."

Hissing through the pain like the snake he was, Mark nearly snickered. "'Mom', huh? Marionette has a-"

A quick hum and a pop knocked the wind out of him again as one of my last Witch balls exploded across his chest. He gasped and wheezed, rolling along the floor as the concoction burned his eyes and shook his resolve. It was arguably a cheap shot with Babs and the other two still keeping his powers in check, but that wasn't what I was worried about.

"I'd shut up so you don't inhale too much," I growled.

"I have to do this," my mother choked out past the tears. "They'll never leave you alone if I don't."

"Mom, I get it," I said softly, slowly walking her way, "but I'm a Leone. Hiding's never been an option."

Words caught in her throat and the gun lowered ever so slightly with each very cautious step I took. Her finger was still on the trigger, hands shaking very subtly, and I'd discarded the only protection I had. I hate to say it, but I wasn't entirely sure she wouldn't shoot me. I still wasn't completely confident in her motives. But I needed to try to save her from herself. The conspiracy charges were going to put her a couple circles down, but a straight-up murder could bury her under Acheron.

"If you do this," I continued, "we may never get to sort this out."

She fully lowered the gun and relaxed her finger off the trigger once I was in point-blank range. Lip quivering, she pleaded, "We can't let him get away."

Smiling reassuringly, I said, "You already winged him, I just maced him, Babs is baking his noodle, and any second now Lucian is coming through that door to drag him away like a misbehaving child."

She stared up at me, nodded, and dropped the gun. "Do you have to arrest me now?"

Stepping in and hugging her, kicking the gun across the floor, I held back a laugh while reminding her, "I'm a fugitive too, you're a terrible influence."

Catching his breath, Mark said darkly, "What a touching reun-"

Another pop cut him off mid-sentence as I unloaded the Helsing's last round.

"Why would you work with that dick?" I asked quietly, hugging her close.

Finally hugging me back and trying to calm herself, voice full of remorse, she answered, "It's complicated."

"Yeah," I whispered, squeezing her lightly, "I'm starting to understand that."

Chapter 31
Weird Naps

As the coven, the Cyclops, and Ramesh were dragged away by a SOL team and several crews of porters and clerics, I watched Nguyen and Ramirez walk my mom away to their car. Looking my way, she mouthed the words "I'm sorry" and "I love you" before they eased her in. I wasn't really sure what to do with it. It'd been a long time since anyone had said it to me and I'd been bitter for twice as long. But, looking into her eyes, I believed her. I smiled, nodded, and waved lightly. Maybe it was a bit too much like "message received", but it seemed to be enough as she looked at peace before disappearing into the car.

I knew it was my turn as Lucian walked up next to me. I was resigned to the idea I'd be in cuffs next, but I wasn't quite ready for him to rest a hand on my shoulder instead. Honestly, I think I was happy he was there.

Taking a cleansing breath, I said with resolve, "I'm glad you're the one taking me in."

He shook his head and corrected, "I'm not taking you in; I'm offering you a ride so you can turn yourself in."

Looking back out as Nguyen's car started to pull away, I asked, "What did she do as your familiar?"

He squeezed my shoulder reassuringly. "She sorted my life as I slept," he said stoically, looking my way as his voice softened, "and checked in on those Dulaf and I couldn't watch ourselves."

I looked back at him, recognizing Rufus' half-truths and remembering Dulaf once saying she watched over the family for generations.

"Dulaf couldn't do that?"

Shaking his head, he answered, “Dulaf was helping build Argyre.”

“And why weren’t you in Argyre?”

Smirking, he replied with a hint of nostalgia, “I had other matters to attend to.”

Watching him for signs of deception, still wondering if Rufus might have somehow told the truth, I could only see my friend. He had his secrets, I’d known that before, but he’d been by my side one way or another since I joined. Even if there was any truth to what Rufus said, maybe that was the best place for me to be. But then, that left another question lingering in the air.

“Was Leo an angel?”

He turned his attention back to the car as it drove away, a mix of concern and relief crossing his face as he watched it disappear down the block. “I’ve always thought so,” he said distantly, patting my back gently before turning towards his own car, “but, more importantly, he was the lion.”

Following him to his car, ready to take my old seat next to him, I hesitantly asked, “Then what am I?”

He looked across the roof of the car at me and smiled, fangs fully bared. “I don’t know,” he said with surprising warmth, “that was never the point.”

As he climbed into the car, I looked past him and saw Babs and Glinda standing at the gates, a couple of clerics taking their statements. Akemi had made herself scarce a while ago, probably halfway across the lake and doing her best to outrun a few stray fairies. Turning away from the clerics and setting her eyes on me, Babs smiled genuinely and waved my way. Returning the gesture, I mouthed the words “thank you”.

She shook her head and waved it off, then called out across the driveway, “I’ll see you back home!”

Climbing into Lucian’s car, taking my old seat, felt like going home. Nights waiting for him to pick me up before we clocked in came back to me, the pale rider arriving to retrieve his coffee and that free cookie he probably shouldn’t eat. Hell, despite all the time I’d been gone, the seat still felt like mine.

Chuckling, I mused, "Are they ever going to assign you another devotee?"

Starting down the block, following Nguyen's unit in the distance, Lucian shook his head lightly. "They've never assigned my devotees," he said. "I chose you."

Another set of three little words I didn't know what to do with. An uncharitable interpretation would be that he kept tabs on me. But, if he was watching out for the Leones, maybe he was trying to give me a better path to follow.

"Guess I messed that up."

Slowing to a stop behind Nguyen's car at an intersection, the two of us sat in silence and stared at the tinted rear windshield for what felt like an eternity. Wringing the wheel very lightly, Lucian exhaled sharply and looked at me.

"No, I did when I hid the truth from you," he said firmly, "and I'm sorry for that."

Looking ahead again before I could react, he started driving again in silence. I'd never actually heard him apologize before, not for something *he'd* done. He'd expressed sympathy, understanding, even empathy, but never really remorse. I wasn't even aware he *could* admit he was wrong. Realizing the weight of the moment, I chose not to look the gift unicorn in the mouth and sat back instead of pressing him on it.

As we arrived to the HQ parking garage, a pair of Elves sat in wait for us and hurried to the unit as we parked. Amelia darted ahead before getting caught and pulled back by Dulaf. I couldn't see her aura without the visor, but her brow and ears painted a pretty clear picture as she anxiously waited for us to get out. Seeing me climb out without cuffs or serious harm, she visibly released a breath and nudged Amelia along. The kid dashed around the car and latched onto my waist, looking up at me with ears folded back.

"There wasn't a birthday party," she scolded, "and Mr. Alston is 50!"

Glancing at Dulaf, I asked, "You didn't explain the code to her?"

"I did," Dulaf sighed, walking over and hugging me a bit too hard. "The whole place is on Siren protocols."

Letting go and stepping back, she offered me a bag. "Sorry, but you can't wear that in holding."

Taking it from her, I opened the bag to see a black and white striped shirt inside. Raising an eyebrow at her, I protested, "Do I look like an old-timey cartoon to you?"

Grinning, she hugged me a bit more gently and laughed. "Not yet."

Getting processed was a bit surreal. My personal belongings were incredibly off limits. The gloves and boots were technically weapons, the belt had a gun strapped to it, and my remaining clothes were a bit provocative for anyone else that might stroll through. I could have requested one of the inmate uniforms, but I wasn't too thrilled with that concept for what I hoped would only be a day in holding.

The rest of the recently arrested got a damn good laugh as I strolled down the hallway like I just stepped out of a time machine. One of them, damn near in tears, kept calling me the Hamburglar – a reference I still don't understand.

The good news was everyone was pretty sure I was going to be released due to the extenuating circumstances of what went down. The bad news was, since I took the badge and visor off to avoid tracking, they were going to have to clear me the old-fashioned way. The worst news was that the Siren protocols meant every witness had to get checked for literal brainwashing to validate their statements.

For two days I had a cell to myself. The curates checked in on me pretty frequently, usually with warm assurances I wouldn't be there much longer. Dulaf came before and after her shifts, slipping me a book of spells and rituals for turning around bad luck before skipping off to harass her lab techs. Honestly, I was just happy to have something to read. But I did get a good chuckle when I found the section on baby's breath covered in highlighter.

Alston and the Oracle vouched for me once the protocols cleared them. The last thing the commissioner remembered was Mark entering his office uninvited with a small baggy in hand. Turned out to be a potent concentration of chemicals to keep the man compliant. Also turned out that there was a couple dozen of them in the whole building.

Agents I met on the field also confirmed I wasn't trying to kill anyone. The clerics and Stevens even confirmed I tried to warn them before things went down, admitting that the clerics didn't remember what a 65 was and that Stevens openly ignored it thinking I was the one that got hit. Nguyen and Ramirez, for their part, skated by without any problems since they were technically just prioritizing their case over catching me.

Word also had it mom really was negotiating to turn in state's evidence - which was great because the DAO facility had been scrubbed of every piece of equipment by the time agents arrived. The network survived despite losing that node, meaning there were probably others, and I imagined they didn't want anyone finding them. Hell, I knew it based on what they did to hide where it was. There were too many shady groups working together and I had a hunch based on my experiences with Patch that it wasn't the first time. Honestly, the notion put a chill down my spine, but there was little I could do about it.

So we were going to need mom because the rest of Fireside was either in the dark or burned like her. Kate's memory wasn't returning, the last I heard, leaving some question about where she was going to end up. I had a feeling she was going to be spending some time in Acheron if it ever recovered, but for now she was in the psychiatric ward where they could try to help her regain some idea of who she was. To be honest, given that Angelique was eliminated just for helping my mother prepare some contingencies, Kate probably lucked out despite everything. We had our work cut out for us to decipher who was a former member of Fireside and who was just one of their victims.

Meanwhile, Mark was going to get the VIP treatment. He was in the secured medical wing for now, under constant watch to make sure he didn't pull anything again. We knew he was now officially one of the "loose ends" that would need to be tied off. Of anyone involved, he knew the most and was the only one we could confirm was involved that hadn't had their memory tampered with. To say he had a bullseye on his back would be an understatement. He was going to need to be kept in one of the lowest circles just to be sure there'd be enough people to keep watch over him. Even then, no one could be sure it would be enough.

I, on the other hand, was released after a couple days, given back the clothes I'd been wearing before Dulaf's costume, and cleared of any charges due to extraordinary circumstances. The board had determined that I couldn't be certain Marionette wouldn't have been instantly killed if I surrendered her in the Undercity, so I'd acted in good faith. There was still some disciplinary review to consider since I tossed every monitoring device I had, so I couldn't just be put back on the job right away. They placed me on administrative leave and sent my ass home. Despite that, on my way out I was handed back my badge and hand-link.

Stepping out into the sun, I took out that hand-link and stared at the abstract face on the screen, remembering the girl behind it. Mom might have been wrong about her being a prisoner but we certainly took them for granted. I realized that now more than ever. Tapping the screen, I activated the Oracle system long enough to ask a question I figured she hadn't heard that often.

"What's your name?"

After a few seconds, a single word appeared: "Pythia".

"Thanks, Pythia," I said, starting to walk down the block, "I think you saved my ass."

She didn't respond, it wasn't how things were usually done, but I knew she could hear me. Pocketing the link, I walked past my turn and continued deeper into Fangtown than I needed. In all the noise, I knew there was someone who needed to hear about what happened. Given her position as his right-hand woman for a few years, I had a feeling mom was planted to monitor Anubis. It made sense: he was a former member of the Third Avenue Hunt, the Moirae was a major Alter venue, and the Locusta often held casual meetings in the basement. If I were Fireside, or one of their employers, I would want a pair of eyes on him too. He was going to find out eventually and I preferred he got it from me. I figured the family owed him that much.

Anubis sat in a stunned silence at his desk as I recapped the events of the last few days as a half dead lump on his office couch. I was still exhausted, wearing half a uniform smelling like baby's breath and garlic, and covered in tiny cuts from glass, drywall, and pixie claws. There were times I could feel the tension rising as the already towering man had to control some of the Werewolf urges inside, especially when I told him about Danny and how he was part of all of this and the fact that Marionette might have been planted as a handler. As the story closed, he rose from his seat and walked across the room to the liquor cabinet, opening it to reveal what looked like an expensive private reserve even to the uninitiated like me.

Pouring himself a drink, he looked back at me and held up the bottle. "Drink? Sounds like you need one too."

I stared at the bottle for a moment and shook my head solemnly. "I don't really drink, family history."

He chuckled lightly and shook his head, "You've got a lot of that, huh?"

Turning to go back to his desk, he stopped a moment, grabbed a bottle of water and waved it my way with a beckoning nod. Nodding back, I raised a hand to accept his offer. He tossed it to me and headed back for his desk, sitting with a bit of a groan I could sympathize with. Taking a large drink of an amber hued liquid and letting it go down before looking my way, there was a deep, thoughtful look on his face like some questions still weighed heavy on his mind.

"I met Danny in the Hunt," he said nostalgically, "he was a friend of the Hunt's leader, Rhiannon. She always called him 'Danny boy', so the rest of us did too."

"And he came with you when you left?" I asked.

Shaking his head, he corrected, "He helped *us* leave. Set up everything we needed to start the club. I don't know why he would be caught up in this deal, but I have to believe he had his heart in the right place."

"Paved with good intentions," I said, trailing off as I shook my head. "Guess it's like my mom with the covens."

"She was right, you know," he said almost sorrowfully, taking another sip. "Things aren't quite as united as they want everyone to think. That's why groups like the Tong and Hunt even exist."

I looked up to him and saw a hint of pain behind amber eyes that had been there only a few times in a normally stalwart figure.

"When your backs are against the wall, you have to stick together," he continued, studying his glass as he slowly swirled it, "groups get tight so we can take care of each other. Some groups didn't agree about how we were supposed to do that."

I looked to the floor, feeling the weight of what he was saying and everything I went through to hear it. Hell, I picked a side and joined one of those groups without realizing the ramifications. Mom joined three covens trying to navigate it all, and the last one betrayed her to win favor with the devil. Then again, I still couldn't be sure how many deals she'd made herself.

"I never knew how she did it," Anubis said, pulling me back from my thoughts, "but she made problems disappear like magic. She always came out on top of negotiations, made inventory problems disappear, handled unruly customers like some four-hundred-pound bouncer. I knew she was something, eyes like gemstones, but I never dug too deep."

I snorted quietly and shook my head. "It connects a lot of dots, doesn't it?"

He nodded and rose again from his chair. "One thing I always knew though," he said, slowly migrating my way, "was that whether or not I was a mark, Marionette took care of the pack."

I looked up as he loomed large over me and continued, "in my book, that made her family."

Watching him stand over me, hearing the tightness in his voice, I worried what was coming next. It wasn't so much I was afraid of the guy, but I didn't come to make enemies. Plus, while I was ashamed to admit it, if he was ***really*** angry there wasn't a whole lot I could do about it in my current shape.

"But when I think about it," he said, cutting off my chain of thought, "even if you were a bit of a dick, you were the one that found that Shifter that killed Danny. Then when that messed up creature and its master were stalking my girls, you were the one that showed up." After a pause to take another long drink, he shook his head and looked at the wall behind me. "It's a stand-up move coming here to tell me about Marionette and why Danny got hit."

Looking back down, reaching a hand out to me, he declared, "I think that means someday we can count on you too."

Taking that massive hand and standing before shaking it, I was actually surprised by the gesture. It wasn't something I was looking for, but part of me really needed to hear something like that.

Releasing his hand after what might have been way too long, I composed myself enough to reply, "Thanks, that actually means a lot right now."

Patting my shoulder, he said, "I don't know much about who she was before she got here, but if you ever want to know about Marionette..."

"Appreciated," I interjected, "I think I know some people who can fill in the rest."

Slapping me on the back, he turned back to his desk. "The door's always open if you need it."

Nodding, I started for the exit, turning as I opened the door. "I'll take you up on it."

"And hey," he spoke up with a grin, "if they ever bounce you, I could always use some muscle at the entrance."

Chuckling, I waved and took my leave, lighter than I was when I arrived. With the unfortunate news delivered, I was finally free to return home and hopefully find Babs in good spirits. I wasn't sure what all this activity would do to her, what with her having not used her abilities extensively for decades. She held her own, no doubt, but I'd seen how much it took out of mom and knew there was some chemistry involved.

Though, half way home, nursing the water bottle most of the way, I realized I could use another kind of chemistry. Strolling into the Ahab's, I found Trey still behind the counter even in the middle of the day. Chuckling, I called out from the door, "Man, do you ever sleep?"

Grinning broadly, going to get my usual ready, he replied, "Do you?"

Watching him carry a cup across, I raised a hand and cleared my throat. "Hey, do you happen to know what the Witches put in their brew?"

Halting in his tracks, Trey looked over, eyebrow raised. "No one really knows what they put in that."

With a shrug and a half-hearted chuckle, I murmured, "Figures."

He watched me for a moment, still holding my usual size cup, then peered over his shoulder to a door at the back. Gesturing back that way with a quick bob of his head, he remarked, "I got some in the back though, if you want to change your order. Have a deal with a small coven south of the city."

Admittedly a little surprised, I nodded my head lightly. "Two of those, if you don't mind."

He nodded and disappeared into the back, returning with an old clay pot I'd never seen before. Getting two cups ready, he asked off-handedly, "Why the sudden interest in this stuff?"

The question had a couple of answers. It was more potent and I'd gotten a taste for it lately. But, really, the first thing that came to mind, even if it didn't quite make sense, had nothing to do with either of those.

"Just found out my mom's a Witch," I replied. "And I owe another Witch a few favors."

Putting the lids on the cups, keeping his eyes down for a bit as I could see him mulling that over, he looked up and warmly asked, "How's all of that going?"

Considering it for a moment, I gave him the only honest answer I could: "I don't know right now, but I'm better than I was."

Leaving the Ahab's with the two Witch brews and a couple cookies in a bag, I continued on my way home. I wasn't sure if Babs was all that interested in coffee from a shop, but I had to figure she was a little worn down. At the very least, I could return a gesture she'd shown me more than once and present her with a Witch's brew of my own. Though, after all that happened, part of me was a little concerned she wouldn't be in a place to take it.

To my surprise, I found her sitting on the stoop of the building, carefully planting flowers in a box, surrounded in pixies. To my greater surprise, the pixies were calm and patiently waiting while she worked, watching her intently. She looked up and smiled broadly at them, looking at least 10 years younger, and caught sight of me approaching.

"Nate dear!" she called out, dusting pottery soil off before standing with the box. "I hoped you would be home soon. Is everything okay with you?"

"More or less," I said, "just had a few things to get out of the way first."

Smiling warmly, she held the box out to me. "In the meantime, we have fairies to deal with," she said matter-of-factly. "Put this box in your window, leave out some treats from time to time, and don't challenge the alpha."

"There's an *alpha*?" I asked, shocked.

With a quick little motion of her eyes and a tip of her chin she nodded to a light post not far away. I glanced over and set my eyes on a lone pixie perched above everyone, tiny face covered in berry juice like warpaint. She wasn't the biggest of them, and it was clear by her disheveled feathers that she got roughed up in the raid, but those eyes meant business as she watched us like an adorable little hawk.

"I'm thinking of calling her Victoria," Babs declared. "She's tough but I can tell she's a sweetheart under it all."

I knew the name wasn't a coincidence. Nothing Babs did was ever just coincidence. So, I didn't even comment on it, just nodded along with a knowing grin and took the flower box from her, offering the coffee and a cookie in exchange. She took them and gave me a warm smile.

"Is this our life now?" I asked, smirking.

"It won't be like this forever," Babs assured, "they'll migrate south in a few months."

Chuckling, I tucked the box under an arm and started up into the building.

"And if she likes us," she chimed in as I reached the door, "we'll see her again soon."

Facing her, I saw that sly grin on her face and glanced to the pixie watching us. "I guess we'll have to wait and see."

We exchanged a little wave and I went inside, trudging up the stairs with the box in tow. Babs had managed to control the situation pretty well. The building was quiet, not a hint of a giggle anywhere to be found. Not a lightbulb was cracked and everything still seemed to be in working order. Reaching my apartment, I lingered at the door for a moment and felt grateful for the people who gave me somewhere to go back to.

Hanging the flower box from my window, a couple members of the flock perched on it immediately. Finally at rest, I got to see my tiny tormentors without the flurry of claws, feathers, and the ominous little giggles. They were a bit scuffed up from the last week too, childlike faces lightly bruised and a few feathers obviously missing or out of place. The pair at my window were comrades too.

Walking into my kitchen, I raided my fridge for some berries I'd been using for my cereal and brought them out, setting a small basket of them into the box where the pixies could see. Hesitantly, they approached and took the offering, nervously nibbling at them while keeping an unwavering eye on me. Carefully, I closed the window slowly so I wouldn't spook them and stepped away.

Stopping in my room, I stared at my bed and considered just turning in for a while despite just coming back from the coffee shop. It'd been a pretty exhausting week, even if I did get some sleep and three square meals while I was in lockup. But I wasn't really tired so much as worn. I didn't want to sleep, exactly. I just wanted to be unconscious. Looking out at the living room, I saw the old recliner and migrated that way instead.

Getting ready to turn on the television on my wall, I stopped myself and simply sank into the old chair. It creaked and groaned, the cushions letting me sink in a bit too far. The chair was starting to smell like my usual body wash, masking that old odor of pine trees that had been preserved so long. Despite that, I could still feel them there.

My fingers found an old busted seam, stitched together roughly by an inexperienced hand years ago. I remembered my dad tearing the hole accidentally during a Seahawks game, slapping the old arm a little too hard while calling the ref a moron. I remembered him deciding to fix it himself while mom insisted she could do it better. Tracing my fingers across the extra thick thread in the sloppy cross-hatched pattern, I remembered watching him from the floor as she watched on fondly, clearer in my memory than she had been in years. Resting my head back and squeezing the arm, I looked to the ceiling.

After all those years, I'd found her. I just wished he could have been there to see.

About the Author

Lurking in the shadows of many sci-fi and fantasy communities, **Jeremy Varner** started writing stories for his own amusement at a young age and never grew out of it. Exposed to these genres as a kid, he grew up dreaming not only of these amazing worlds but being one of the people to craft them. With his debut novel, **Shards of Glass**, Jeremy started not only the **Agent of Argyre** series but making that dream into a reality.

Continuing his work on the Agent of Argyre series, Jeremy hopes to expand the world of the Alters and draw people into a place where fantastic creatures can exist right next door (for better or worse). A fan of the concept of Clarke's Laws and the idea that any sufficiently advanced or unknown science is indistinguishable from magic, Jeremy wants to bring creatures of legend into a more tangible world – even if that world doesn't always make sense to the characters living in it.

For announcements of future projects, Jeremy's thoughts on various topics, or extra material about the world outside of the Seattle Fangtown, fans of the Agent of Argyre series can find more at Jeremy's website and twitter account. He may, at times, go quiet for a while, but will usually rise from his grave again if someone gives him a nudge. It's cheaper than a necromancer or a new cybernetic body and generally more pleasant.

Website: JeremyVarner.com
Twitter: @JDVarner

www.ingramcontent.com/pod-product-compliance
Lightning Source LLC
LaVergne TN
LVHW050927080826
845145LV00001B/235

* 9 7 8 0 9 8 3 6 2 3 1 9 9 *